I0823332

MISSING SAM

ALSO BY THRITY UMRIGAR

The Museum of Failures

Honor

The Secrets Between Us

Everybody's Son

The Story Hour

The World We Found

The Weight of Heaven

If Today Be Sweet

The Space Between Us

First Darling of the Morning: Selected Memories of an Indian Childhood

Bombay Time

PICTURE BOOKS

Maya's Holi

Sugar in Milk

Binny's Diwali

When I Carried You in My Belly

MISSING SAM

a novel

Thrity Umrigar

ALGONQUIN BOOKS OF CHAPEL HILL
LITTLE, BROWN AND COMPANY

Algonquin Books of Chapel Hill / Little, Brown and Company
Hachette Book Group
1290 Avenue of the Americas, New York, NY 10104
algonquinbooks.com

First Edition: January 2026

Algonquin Books of Chapel Hill is an imprint of Little, Brown and Company, a division of Hachette Book Group, Inc. The Algonquin Books name and logo are trademarks of Hachette Book Group, Inc.

The publisher is not responsible for websites (or their content) that are not owned by the publisher.

The Hachette Speakers Bureau provides a wide range of authors for speaking events. To find out more, go to hachettespeakersbureau.com or email hachettespeakers@hbgusa.com.

Little, Brown and Company books may be purchased in bulk for business, educational, or promotional use. For information, please contact your local bookseller or the Hachette Book Group Special Markets Department at special.markets@hbgusa.com.

Design by Steve Godwin

ISBN 978-1-64375-762-9

LCCN 2025943269

Printing 1, 2025

LSC-C

Printed in the United States of America

For Eust

Without tenderness, we are in hell.

—Adrienne Rich

. . . to the past that never stops happening.

—Don DeLillo

MISSING SAM

PROLOGUE

The Fall

SAM

1

▾ ▸ ▴ ◂ ▾ ▴ ▸ ▴

Monday, July 1, 2019

At the front door, I hesitate.

Ali is still in bed, and for a moment I wonder if I should go back into the house and ask her to join me for my run, as she does every morning. But if she'd wanted to, she could've set her alarm, right?

I'd slept in the guest bedroom last night, too angry to lie next to her. Even now, remembering the way she'd spent a huge portion of the evening sitting on the couch chatting and laughing with Jan at the party, I feel my throat tighten. We'd left early, after I'd feigned a headache and said I needed to get home. She'd known that I was faking it, of course, but maybe she also knew she'd gone too far this time and knew better than to argue in front of our friends. We'd fought the whole way home, my rage growing as she accused me of having a suspicious mind, swearing that she didn't have the slightest interest in Jan and that I'd imagined the knowing looks that had passed between them all evening long.

We were a few streets away from home when she twisted in her seat to face me. "I'm so sick and tired of your jealousy, Samantha," she said. "For fuck's sake. I'm not your father. I'm allowed to talk to a friend at a party without you . . ."

"Enough." My hand hit the steering wheel so hard, my nerves buzzed for a few seconds. "Enough with the gaslighting. This isn't about me or my dad. It's about you embarrassing me time and time again whenever we're around Jan. You did this last time, too. Remember? No, Ali. Face it—you're just a shameless flirt."

I regretted my words almost immediately, but I was tired, and my head was hurting for real by now.

We rode the last two blocks home in silence. The streetlights were still out—two days ago a blown transformer had resulted in a power outage in many areas of Cleveland Heights, and our Cedar Lee neighborhood was still in the dark. Thank heavens Ali had insisted on installing a small generator last year so that at least our phones and the refrigerator were still working. Despite my anger, I was grateful for her foresight. As I turned into our driveway, Ali unlocked the car door before I'd even pulled all the way in, as if she couldn't wait to get away from me. She was almost out of the car when she said, "I'm telling you, Sam, I've just about had it with your jealousy. This is your issue, not mine. So, deal with it."

I stayed in the car until she let herself into the house. Already, I felt incredulous at how out of hand this fight had gotten. I knew Ali would walk over coals for me. No doubt in my mind. I knew I should let go of this tired, absurd argument. But I couldn't. If I had noticed how close Ali had sat to Jan, how they'd giggled at jokes that excluded everyone else, how thirstily Jan's eyes followed Ali across the room, then surely others had noticed also. The thought of our friends gossiping about us, maybe pitying me, made me see red.

I sat in the living room for an hour to keep out of Ali's way, but the lines of the novel I was reading by candlelight kept blurring and I had to read them over and over again. Mostly, I kept tabs on the sounds coming from upstairs, where Ali was getting ready for bed. I listened as the sound of running water ceased and heard the creak of the floorboards outside our bedroom. I waited another fifteen minutes and when I was sure she'd gone to bed, I grabbed a flashlight and went upstairs. I was turning down the sheets of the guest bed when I heard her call my name. "Sam?" she said. "You coming to bed?"

God help me, relief and gratitude sparked in my heart. But then I remembered how she'd hugged Jan goodbye for a fraction longer than necessary when I'd approached them and declared it was time for us to leave, and I stood still, unsure of what to do.

"Sam? Will you come in here? Please?"

I made my way down the hall. "What?" I said, standing in the doorway of our bedroom. She had candles burning on the mantelpiece and I fought against the urge to tell her to extinguish them before she fell asleep.

I heard her fumble for the large flashlight on the bedside table. The sudden light made her dark hair glow. Her beautiful brown face looked small, and her nose was a telltale rust. As I watched, she sat up and leaned against the headboard. "Will you come to bed?" she whispered. She freed her left hand from under the covers and held it out toward me.

I felt myself soften almost immediately. I always did. From the day we'd met in grad school eight years ago, I've never had any defenses against Ali, especially when she beseeched me. But this time I thought, Not so fast. This time, I remembered what my therapist had said to me a few weeks ago—if you give in to her every time, Dr. Yates said, you're simply rewarding her behavior. Ali was an incorrigible flirt, and she knew it hurt me terribly. And though it felt odd, I had to lay down some limits.

"I'm sleeping in the other room," I mumbled, forcing myself to meet her eyes. "I told you, I have a headache."

She made an indecipherable sound at the obvious lie. She was quiet for a moment, then slumped into the bed and switched off the flashlight. I stood in the sudden dark for a second and then made my way out of the room.

"Good night," she called after me, but her tone said, Fuck you.

A strange sort of satisfaction gripped me as I went back to the guest bedroom. I had stood my ground and it felt good.

But my gratification was short-lived. Just as I was about to drift off to sleep, my phone pinged with an accusatory text from Ali. My heart sank at the ugliness of her message, and I responded angrily, too. We exchanged several more of such awful texts. But would you believe me if I told you that even while I was typing inflammatory things, some part of me knew that this was all performative, or rather, that we were merely playing roles that had been decided for us decades earlier? And that no matter what insults we hurled that night, nothing would really get in the way of our love for one another?

Because that's how fucked up we are.

Now, I stand in the driveway wanting to leave behind last night's ugliness, debating whether to go back in and wake her up for our daily morning run. Or, better yet, get into bed with her. We leave at three to pick up Sally and Maureen at the airport and we need to find our way back to one another before company arrives. Having guests over the July Fourth holiday is a shitty time to not be speaking to your spouse.

As I bend and retie my shoelaces, I decide: I don't want to wake up Ali if she's still asleep; she's probably had as disturbed a sleep as I have. And I need to clear my head, rid it of the tangle of last night's angry thoughts. A good, vigorous run, my body trembling with exhaustion and dripping with sweat, will do the trick.

It's a beautiful morning in July, the mild morning sun filtering through the canopy of trees. The sight is so glorious that my immediate thought is, I wish Ali could see this. As if last night's fight hadn't happened. As if the faint sunshine is boring holes into the last of my resentment. This is what eight years of living with someone does to you. It messes with your head.

The birds are awake, sounding as self-important as college graduates on their way to convocation. The sunshine and my feet flying across the pavement are beginning to fill me with a liquid joy. I'll have to do a shorter run today—Sal and Mo will be here for ten days, part of our annual July Fourth tradition, and Ali and I still have to clean the house and go grocery shopping. In the dim morning light, I notice a child's lemonade stand on someone's front porch. It will be hours before they set it up on the sidewalk. In any case, all I have on me is a credit card to pick up a loaf of bread from the Stone Oven bakery on my way back. When Ali drives past a lemonade stand, she will make a U-turn, if neccessary, to give the kids some cash. Selling lemonade in her old neighborhood in Columbus is one of her few pleasant memories of her childhood, back when her mother was still alive and her life had not turned to shit.

But also, that's just who Ali is, kind to all living creatures. I think about the small graves in our backyard for the robins and squirrels and chipmunks she's been unable to nurse back to health. I kid her about how every injured or sick animal finds its way to us, as if news of her kind nature spreads through some underground network shared by all the feathered and furry creatures in our Cleveland Heights neighborhood.

It's one of the first things that drew me to her, actually, that kindness, that generosity. I remember how patient she was with me in the early days. I was attracted to Ali almost from the start, but I'd never been in a gay relationship before. Ali, on the other hand, had been dating women since she was fourteen, first keeping them a secret from her conservative Indian Muslim family and then, being openly defiant. I think those early years of battling her father have left their mark on her. After our first fight she told me flatly that she believed in freedom—total, uncompromising freedom. That she wouldn't tolerate any restrictions on who she would love or be friendly with, not even from me. In the face of our ardor, it was easy to look past such a declaration. But over the years, my own shitty family history has battled with hers. Ali knows damn well that my proud Irish father taught me that keeping up appearances was the most important thing, to never tolerate public humiliation. And humiliation is exactly what I feel watching Ali flirt. I've told her that my earliest memory is of Dad punching a guy at the neighborhood bar because the man had made a joke at Dad's expense.

I was four, but I still remember the rage on his face, his sour, drunken breath as he staggered home with me in his arms, my timid mom cowering in the kitchen after taking one look at him.

I turn the corner and pick up my pace, as if merely thinking of my parents makes me want to run faster, as if I'm still trying to get away from my childhood. Which, I suppose, I am. Which, I suppose, we all are.

Ali, too. But she won't acknowledge it. She has little self-awareness that her childhood has left her as damaged and reactive as mine has. I remember how once, just once, she'd told me that when she was growing up, the only brown kid on her street, the white kids used to tease her and call her ugly. Nobody in their right mind would call Ali ugly now. I've seen how people's eyes light up around her. Still, that might explain her inveterate need to flirt, as if she is still trying to prove those white kids wrong. I try to remind myself of this every time we're together with our friends. Sometimes, I succeed. Sometimes, like last night, I want to slap her silly.

A movement to my left catches my eye and as I turn my head I falter before I regain my balance. I'm running fast enough now that I've already passed the house, but my brain is still trying to make sense of what I had just seen: A naked man sitting cross-legged on a couch on his front porch, his pink flesh gleaming in the early morning light. As I process the surreal image, I realize that he was probably in his boxers or briefs but still, the sight of all that naked flesh is discombobulating. Hell, I won't even go to my driveway in my nightclothes to get the daily paper—it's one of the reasons I switched to the digital subscription last year—and here's some oddball I don't recognize sitting like the Buddha on his porch, with nary a thought about how he appears to others. Must be nice, this male privilege.

I head toward the park. I want to pause for a few minutes on the mulched path that circles Lower Shaker Lake; I want to hear the honks of the wild geese and maybe spot an egret on the placid water. The next ten days with our guests will be a blur—trips to Amish country and

Niagara Falls. A Cleveland Orchestra holiday concert at the Blossom Music Center on July 3. The five of us—my friend Nathan will join us also—lying on our blankets, looking up at the fireworks that will follow the music. Today is my final chance for some solitude, to be alone among the trees and the summer sky coming down upon the water.

The houses get bigger, sitting back from the road. It's even more quiet than usual, people taking off for the holiday week. There's not another soul out, not even a car, and the only sound is that of the gossiping birds. I have run this route so many times in our three years in this neighborhood that some of the older dogs don't even bark as I go past their homes. Ali and I used to run listening to music on our phones, but three months ago we decided to give up that distraction, too. Now, for an hour, we run unencumbered by the dings and whistles that announce the encroachments on our lives.

I see a white SUV coming down the street, the first moving vehicle I've seen this morning. The driver must've spotted me too, because the SUV suddenly swerves, as if avoiding an invisible dog crossing the street. The movement distracts me, and I forget to look for the rickety raised slab of sidewalk that Ali and I usually avoid, remember it only when my toe stubs against it and I feel the sudden, sharp pain that electrifies its way up my shin. And then I am falling, going down

down

down

True Religion

ALI

2

▾ ▸ ▴ ◂ ▾ ▴ ▸ ▴

Monday, July 1

Once I realize that Sam has gone for a run without waking me up, I decide to forgo my own run. With company arriving this afternoon, God knows we have a ton of chores to do. I ask Alexa to play some R.E.M. while I vacuum the house and clean the bathrooms.

It's only when I'm about to start on the half-bath on the first floor that I glance at the clock and realize it's already nine o'clock. Where the hell is Sam? She should have been home a long time ago. Surely she isn't still mad at me? It's not like we haven't had this fight before. In fact, it happens every damn time we're hanging out with friends. Especially if Jan is around.

This is harsh, even for Sam and her famous Irish temper. First, sleeping in the guest room, then going for a run alone this morning? And now, staying out just to punish me, knowing damn well that we have to leave for the airport in a few hours.

I finish my task, then go to the kitchen and pour myself some cereal. I reach for my phone to call her before I remember that her phone is upstairs, on the bedside table in the guest bedroom.

I take two bites of the cereal before I set the spoon down. My head still feels a bit woozy from drinking last night. We'd left before they'd served dinner. I'd had a pretty good buzz going and honestly, I don't remember whether I'd flirted with Jan or not. Maybe I did. The fact is, Sam has become almost unbearably possessive. And the worst thing anyone can do is try and control me. It makes me see red like few other things can. Spend the first seventeen years of your life under the thumb of a controlling Muslim father ("Aliya, that's not ladylike;" "Aliya, no talking to the boys," "Aliya, in our family we don't believe in sleepovers or slumber parties") and you develop an unquenchable thirst for freedom. Sam and I are both doomed to keep acting out our childhood shit until one of us gets tired of it. She thinks I'm clueless about the effect of my childhood on our relationship, but I'm not.

The doorbell rings and my heart leaps. She probably forgot the house key in her haste to leave this morning, before I could wake up and join her. As I make my way to the front door, I resolve to make up with her as soon as she walks in. Sally and Mo are going to be here soon. What're we going to do, pout and give each other the silent treatment in front of our old grad school friends? This time, I'll swallow my pride and resentment. That's the great thing about Sam—no matter how angry she might be, she seldom spurns my overtures to make up. Which is why last night was such a shock.

I fling open the door, my face already breaking into a smile. There's no one there. I look down and there's a small brown Amazon box on the porch. Even as I bend to retrieve it, I feel a crushing sense of disappointment. Fuck. Where is she? I look up and down the street before I shut the door. No sign of Samantha.

The parcel has her name on it, and I leave it on the hallway table. Back in the kitchen, I eye my phone, then pick it up and dial the Stone Oven. "Can I speak to Tatyana?" I say when a man answers.

"Hello?" Tatyana says, a moment later.

"Hey, Tats, it's Ali," I say. "Sorry to disturb you. It sounds like it's crazy busy in there."

"It is," she says. "What's up?"

"Samantha left her phone at home, and I need to reach her. She was going to stop in and buy some bread. She's not there by any chance, is she?"

"Nope. Haven't seen her yet."

I bite my lower lip. A cyclone of competing emotions is gathering in my chest. Anger. Worry. Fear that I've finally driven Sam away forever. "Huh," I say. "And you've been there all morning?"

"Sure have." I hear her talking to someone. "Nope. John hasn't seen her yet either. Want me to take a message for when she comes in?"

"Oh, that's okay," I say hastily, wanting to get off the phone. "I have a feeling she's on her way home."

"Okey-doke. Happy Fourth."

"Happy Fourth."

I eye the bowl of uneaten cereal and pour the soggy mess down the disposal. I rinse the dish by hand. Washing dishes is meditative for me and I'm not the meditative kind. The few times I'd allowed Sam to drag me to yoga—in the early days at the University of Michigan, when I was so head over heels with her that I would've followed her through the gates of hell—I'd promptly fallen asleep during that relaxation thing they do at the end. The memory of this, how Sam would poke me in the ribs to keep me from snoring, how we'd giggle all the way home and tumble into the shower together, brings tears to my eyes. This is what bugs me the most about her insane jealousy—that after eight years of faithfulness, of being devoted to her, she still doesn't trust me.

Eight years of faithfulness.

Almost eight years of faithfulness.

Eight years of almost faithfulness.

Anyway.

I glance at the microwave clock. It's 9:58 a.m. That's it, I'm going to go look for her. Why the hell didn't I do this an hour ago? I race up the stairs to change into my shorts.

Sam's phone rings in the guest bedroom and I rush to get to it, not even stopping to wonder why she'd call her phone and not mine.

"Sam?" I yell.

A short pause. "Um, no. It's me. Nathan."

"Oh, hi." I can hear the cold disappointment in my voice, and I know he'll hear it, too. I feel a flash of regret. Nathan is so damn sensitive.

Like Sam, he is a poet, so I guess it comes with the territory. "Sorry," I say. "What's up, bud?"

"Aha. I was just wondering if you girls need me to pick up anything from Zagara's? I know it's a busy day for you."

"Thanks," I say. He's thoughtful like that, Nathan. I hesitate. "Actually, I'm about to get in my car and go looking for Sam. She went for a run this morning and isn't back yet."

Nathan chuckles. "That sounds like Sam. She's probably at Bremec, buying more plants."

Despite myself, I smile, too. Then, I frown. "But her car's here. So, she couldn't be buying plants. Right?"

"Oh. Right. Want me to go with you?"

"You're not at the library today?"

"It's my day off."

I think quickly. "You know what? I'll take you up on your offer to go grocery shopping. And I'll go look for her."

"Whatever you need," he says, in that quiet, reliable manner of his. "Any other errands you need me to run?"

"Yeah, no, I think we're good. But thanks. So, if you'd pick up some good bread and a bottle of olive oil? Oh and some cereal. I'll text you a picture of the kind we use. I'll leave the cash on the counter for you."

"Ali. Please. I'll just put it on my credit card. Besides, I owe Sam money for the plants she picked up for me last week from Chesterland."

I feel a spurt of envy. I own an interior design business and have no other hobbies. Sam works hard, too, staying up late at night grading her students' poems, writing pages of critiques. But her schedule is so much more flexible than mine and she spends hours working in the garden. She and Nathan are forever discussing plants and pH levels and whether humus is better than mulch. He's over almost every Saturday, and while I'm cooking dinner for the three of us, they work on the vegetable garden and the flower beds, their fair heads bent close together. And not once, not once, have I been jealous of their friendship or accused her of having an affair with him. I catch myself and smile ruefully. I'm leaving out an important detail here. We're close to certain that Nathan's gay. We've never seen him with a girlfriend.

"Hello? Ali?"

"Yeah. I'm here. I'll leave the kitchen door unlocked. If I'm not back by the time you get here, just leave everything on the counter?"

"Of course."

"Bye, honey. You want to come for supper tonight? After Sally and Mo get here?"

"Nah. You get some girl time tonight. I'll see you on the third."

"You're one of the girls, you know," I tease.

I grab the car keys and head out. I drive slowly along our usual running route, remembering the time Gin Blossom had escaped a week after we'd moved to Cleveland Heights three summers ago. But looking for a runaway cat is a little different than searching for my wife. I feel self-conscious as I drive. If the roles were reversed, I know I'd accuse Sam of spying on me, of distrusting me. Thankfully, she doesn't share my hang-ups. If I know her, she'll be thrilled that I went looking for her.

As I drive along Stratford, the houses and front lawns get bigger. Surely Sam would've finished her run a long time ago? Even if she ran into a friend and went for coffee, wouldn't she use their phone to let me know? But she was furious last night. And we had texted some pretty shitty things to one another. Could she have . . . left me? A lump forms in my throat.

Nah. Sam is the kindest person I know. She'd never dump me on the day that two of our closest friends were coming for their annual trip. But then I have a heart-stopping thought—maybe this is exactly what Sam would do. Leave when Sal and Mo would be around to take care of me, nurse me through the first awful days. Panic flutters like a leaf in my chest.

Aliya, I chastise myself. Get a grip. It was just a stupid fight. Sam's not going to leave you over this. Relax. Focus. Who should you call? Where would she have gone?

The ER. The words drop into my head. Oh God. Sam could have been hit by a bike or a car. Probably when she was crossing North Park. People speed there all the time. And if she was preoccupied by last night's fight . . .

I pull over. Breathe, I say to myself. Breathe. She's okay. She's fine. But if she were okay, why wouldn't she have had the nurses call me? She'd know I would be worried. I make a bargain with myself—if she's fine, I won't ever flirt with another woman again. Because Samantha is my everything, and here I am fighting an old, juvenile battle, valuing some tired old belief about absolute freedom over a flesh-and-blood partner. Sam is my family, the only family I truly have. When did I turn her into my father, my loving but bullheaded Abba?

And then, as I do during moments of great distress, I send up an atheist's prayer: *Yah, Allah. Please, Allah. Let her be all right.*

I call the Cleveland Clinic ER first. I'm on hold. Then, someone picks up, but the connection is so bad that I hang up in frustration. I call back. Still, it's several minutes before I get a direct answer: She's not there. Next, University Hospitals. Not there, either. Where else? And then I remember—MetroHealth has opened a small ER at Severance. Of course. That would have been the closest place for an ambulance to rush her to.

She isn't there either. The pounding in my heart slows down. Sam isn't in trouble. She wasn't injured and taken to an emergency room. Then, I have another thought and drive toward Lower Shaker Lake. Maybe she fell on one of the trails and couldn't call for help? Even though I know how implausible this is—the park that circles the lake is always busy, and someone would've found her—I pull into the small lot and take the path that goes from North Park Blvd. to South Park Blvd., our usual route. It is a spectacularly beautiful morning. Usually, we'd pause for a moment, jogging in place while we admired the shimmering water, the dark branches of the trees against the lake. Today, I run the trail as quickly as I can, casting about for any signs of Samantha. There are none. When I get back into the car and touch the steering wheel, my hands are slick with sweat. I turn back. Please let her be at home, I pray. Please.

Gin Blossom is waiting for me by the back door. Nathan has left the French bread and olive oil on the kitchen counter. I sweep through the living room and the sunroom and then go to the bottom of the stairs.

"Babe?" I called. "Sam? You home?"

No reply. A crushing, deflating disappointment makes my eyes sting. I'd so hoped she had come home. Whatever trick she's playing, whatever this punishment, I've had enough. I am ready to cry uncle, to leave last night's mess behind us and step into the full beauty of this brilliant day. Sal and Mo's visit is something we look forward to each year, a tradition we'd started after we'd all finished grad school. I want Sam to come home and for us to make up before we leave for the airport. I want us to bring our friends home, and later grill the steaks I'd bought yesterday—thank God for the generator we'd bought last year—and open the first of the many bottles of wine we'll consume over the next few days. I want to hear about the latest exploits of Sally's husband, Tony, who is an agent in Hollywood, and have Mo, who is a therapist, regale us with stories about some of her crazier clients in Riverside, California. I close my business during this time each year, as we try to recreate the youthful carefreeness of our time together in Ann Arbor.

I glance at my watch. It's 12:30 p.m.

When the fear hits, it's a physical, painful thing. I'd fretted while I'd called the local hospitals, worried that Sam was injured. But this fear is different—it lands heavy, like a physical blow. Something is wrong, I think. Sam is somewhere injured. But why isn't she at any of the local hospitals? Could she be lying somewhere, unseen and unheard by passersby? Could she have taken a shortcut through someone's yard, say?

I shake my head at the ridiculousness of the thought. Why would Sam trespass in someone's yard? It doesn't make any sense.

I lean against the wall as I work out the math. We begin our run between six and six-thirty each morning. Even if she had left late, she has been gone for six hours. Six hours. What the hell was I thinking? How could I have possibly thought this was normal?

I fish out my phone and text both Sal and Mo, who are flying in together, due in at three. *Something's come up,* I write. *Nothing serious, but unable to pick you up. So sorry. Will you take a cab from the airport? See you soon.*

I walk back into the living room and sit on the leather couch we'd bought last Thanksgiving. Sam had picked a less expensive one, but I'd convinced her that the classy, simple design of this piece justified the extra money. As I rub my hand over the soft material, a hole opens up in my heart. I am more scared than I've ever been in my life. Even more so than the morning when I was ten and Abba had gently shaken me awake to tell me that Mummy had died. More so than when I was twelve and our neighbor, Mrs. Harris, had served me pork for dinner, and I hadn't known how to refuse. I'd moved in briefly with Mrs. Harris when Abba had gone to India to marry a woman his older sister had found for him. He'd returned with Yasmin, an unworldly woman, so different than my soft-spoken, cultured mother, it felt as if Abba had gone out of his way to erase her memory. It was Yasmin who, when I was fourteen, had discovered me naked in bed with Betsy Lambert, who also lived in our Upper Arlington neighborhood. I can still hear Yasmin's hysterical shrieks. After she told my father that evening, Abba had said that Allah would never forgive me for this degenerate behavior, that maybe He'd taken Mummy prematurely to spare her this horror. The tears had come to my eyes immediately, but even then, I'd known that he hadn't meant those words, that despite his genuine shock, some of his outrage was simply to appease Yasmin. He'd come to my bedroom the next day and apologized for his words, but not for his belief that what I'd done was a sin. And I was never allowed to have Betsy over again. From that day on, Abba and I were at odds with one another. I'd graduated from high school at seventeen and fled for the safety of Smith College as soon as I could. So, this life that I've built with Sam was never preordained or promised to me.

Now, I look around our comfortable living room as I consider my next move. I detest people who are alarmist; some part of me is still looking for a simple, plausible explanation for Sam's absence, something that will make me want to kiss her and smack her at the exact same moment when she walks in the front door. Like, she ran into a friend and decided to go to the West Side Market to pick up those cream buns that Mo always wants when she visits and completely lost track of time. Sam is truly an absent-minded professor; it's not impossible to imagine such a benign scenario. But the heaviness in my heart doesn't lift.

I google the nonemergency number for the Cleveland Heights police. As the phone rings, I feel relief, a rare sense of having put down my burden into someone else's competent, capable hands.

But then I remember that the police don't consider a person missing until they're a no-show for forty-eight hours. I hang up before anyone answers the phone.

3

▼▶▲◀▼▲▶▲

Monday, July 1

It's after four when the cab pulls up. Mo bounds out first, with Sally following. I hurry to grab their suitcases from them. As always, they've packed far too much.

We stand in the driveway, hugging and grinning at one another. "You look great, Ali," Sally says. "The hair's even shorter than usual, I see."

I run my hand absently over my head. "Just got it cut last week."

Mo looks around. "Where's Sam?"

I blink at her stupidly. "Let's get out of the sun," I say.

Habit makes me hit the light switch in the living room as we walk in. Then, I remember. "Sorry. The power's out. It's been three days already. But we have lanterns and candles and flashlights, and the nights have been cool, thank God."

"No worries," Mo says, looking around.

"Nice couch," Sally says. "Sam had mentioned you guys had been furniture shopping."

"Yeah, we almost killed each other trying to agree on something we both liked," I say. I smile, but suddenly the heaviness is back, coupled with the shame of having to tell them about what all has transpired since that ridiculous fight last night. I feel a spurt of anger at Sam for putting me in this awkward position.

"You said something had come up, why you couldn't pick us up. Not that we mind," Mo says. "We've been telling you guys for years to let us take a cab from the airport."

I'm only half listening, trying to frame exactly how I'll explain Samantha's absence, when I hear myself say, "Sam's gone."

"What time will she be back?" Sally says.

I swallow. "She's . . . left. I don't know where she's gone. We . . . we had a stupid fight last night. And she was really mad. She slept in the guest bedroom." A thought occurs to me. "But I changed the sheets this afternoon. Don't worry."

They are looking at me like I'm crazy and I suppose I am, worrying about dirty linen after what I've just laid on them. "I don't follow," Sally says finally. "Like, she just stormed out or something?"

I sit down heavily, and they take their seats across from me. "No. I think she went for a run this morning. Her running shoes and pedometer are gone. She didn't wake me up. She just left me sleeping." Those words *she just left me* make my eyes fill with tears. Sally and Mo look as shocked as I feel—in our years of friendship, they have never seen me cry.

"Hey, Al, Ali." Sally comes to sit beside me, puts her arm around me. "It's just a lover's tiff, girl. I mean, God, if you knew how many times I've stormed off after a fight with Tony. Sam will be back." She pretends to scowl. "She damn well better. She knows we're here."

But that's just it, I want to say. The fact that Sam has decided to punish me this particular week tells me that this was no ordinary quarrel. She's left you, a mocking voice in my head says. You've acted as if the right to flirt was some goddamn constitutional right and now it's her turn to humiliate you.

I turn to Maureen. She's a therapist and the pragmatic one. "Mo?"

"Let's call the local hospitals," she says. "What if, God forbid, she was in an accident or something?"

"I called every ER in the area. She's not in any of them."

She gets up, paces a bit. "Let's call again," she says. "They may have brought her in later."

I give each of them an ER to call. I speak to the same woman at the Cleveland Clinic. Just as I'm about to hang up, she says, "And you called the Metro ER downtown, honey?"

MetroHealth is the county hospital, at least seven miles away from our leafy suburb. Why would they take Sam there?

"They have a burn unit there," she continues. "You never know."

I shiver as I call Metro. And am thankful when they say there's no patient by that name. For good measure, I call Ahuja's ER, even though it is miles away from us in the opposite direction.

Mo looks rueful when we all reconvene in the kitchen. "Well, that was a waste of time," she says. "Although I guess that's a good thing she's not injured."

We fall silent. Sally says, "We should call the cops?"

"I can just see Sam coming home and being mortified that I'd turned this into a federal case," I say. "Besides, in Ohio a person has to be missing for at least forty-eight hours before the cops will even consider them missing."

"Huh. I didn't know that," Mo says. "It's different from state to state, I guess."

"Toto, you're not in California anymore," I say.

"I keep telling you guys, you need to move closer to us in California. The way everything is going, I want all my ducklings close to me."

Mo is a strange combo of drill sergeant and earth mother. We've been fast friends from the time we took a class together in our first year of grad school. The first day she wore a Pepto-Bismol pink jumper and Birkenstocks and a bead necklace. I am suddenly grateful that Sally and Mo are here.

"Sam and I should've moved out West after grad school," I say. "Now, my business is established, you know? And Sam is on the tenure track at Cleveland State. Makes it difficult to pick up and go."

"I understand," Mo says. "Well, it's past five. What do you want to do?"

I'm sick with worry but my hospitality kicks in. "You guys must be hungry. Would you like some wine and cheese?"

But Mo isn't having it. "What do *you* want to do, Ali?" she asks.

I meet her eyes. What I want to do is to go looking for Sam again. Maybe go door to door, asking if anyone on our street has seen her. But I'm conflicted. Sam will never forgive me if she comes home and knows that I've involved the neighbors in our stupid tiff.

"Ali?" Sally says.

"I don't know. Wait for her, I guess."

"You sure?"

"I think so." Although my stomach is burning with fear and dread.

"You don't want to go looking for her?"

"I don't know where to look any more. I've already driven and checked out our usual path."

As we stare at each other, I come to a decision. Sally and Mo have been traveling most of the day. They've got to be exhausted and hungry. "Why don't you guys go change?" I say. "Take a shower if you want to. You know where the towels are."

"So, we're staying in tonight?"

"Yes."

While they are upstairs, I call Annie Fitzgerald, Sam's colleague who lives in Lakewood. She and Sam are close to one another, and I'm so grateful that she always has Sam's back. "Hi, Annie?" I say when she answers. "It's Ali."

"Hey, girl," she says. "Long time no see. How *are* you?"

"I'm okay. Hey, listen. I was calling to ask if you've heard from Sam by any chance?"

"Yup. She called on Saturday. We were both complaining about our committee assignments for the fall."

I bite my lip. "So, you haven't heard from her today?"

"Today? No. Why? Was I supposed to call her or something? I've been so forgetful recently that . . ."

"No, no. Nothing like that. I . . ." I freeze, not knowing what to say. "I was just waiting for her on dinner and—oh, I just remembered. She was going to stop at another friend's house. My bad. Sorry to bother you."

"No problem. And you're doing fine?"

"I'm great," I say, desperate to get off the phone. "Shit. I have another call coming in."

"No worries. See you."

I call Bremec Garden Center for the hell of it. Sam has not been there all day. I call our friend Lucy, who is in her seventies and takes care of her older brother. She lives a few streets down and Sam mows her yard for her. But Lucy has not seen her since last week. I hear Sally and Mo moving upstairs and know that they'll be down in a few minutes. I go to the kitchen, and arrange a platter of cheese and crackers, trying to control the confusion that I feel. I wash some grapes and put them in a bowl. I take out a bottle of pinot grigio from the fridge.

"Listen, I'm sorry, I bought steaks but I just don't feel like cooking today," I say when they join me in the kitchen. "I was thinking we could order in? Whatever you guys would like. Indian? Thai? Turkish? Chinese?"

Mo's eyes wander past the kitchen to Samantha's vegetable garden in the backyard. "Tell you what," she said. "Your basil looks great. How about we make pesto for dinner tonight?"

Sally nods. "Yum."

"Are you sure?"

"That's settled then," Mo says. "But let's start on the wine first. I want to be sloshed by the time Samantha walks in through that door."

Amen, I think. Amen.

Mo's confidence is infectious. By the time I've finished my first glass of wine, I'm sure that Sam will be home in time for dinner.

With every hour that goes by without Sam coming home, I drink some more.

I don't mean to get drunk, but I do.

It's only after I've gone up to my bedroom that night that it occurs to me: Sam and I share a credit card. I open the Citibank app on my phone and check for any purchases she's made today. I half expect to see a one-way ticket to Ireland or Iowa. But the card has not been used. Sam has taken her other credit card with her, but I don't know her password.

I throw myself in bed and sob into the pillow. If this is my punishment for an hour of flirtatious behavior, Sam has punished me ten times over.

4

▼ ▶ ▲ ◀ ▼ ▲ ▶ ▲

Tuesday, July 2

I wake up before my alarm goes off, a dull throb in my head. Consciousness seeps into my head in strips, like the ribbons of sunlight on the wall—I remember that Sally and Mo are here and that we'd consumed too much wine last night. I nearly smile at the memory, then remember that Sam hadn't come home. The heaviness returns and I feel flattened, pinned to my bed, eyes wide open as I stare at the ceiling.

I roll over to my side and turn on the bedside table lamp. Nothing happens. The damn power is still off. The conviction that something is wrong is growing inside me. Sam wouldn't ever stay out all night long, not even if she were furious at me, not even if she were breaking up with me, and certainly not when our best friends are in town. If Sam is capable of such cruelty, then the last eight years of my life with her have been a sham and I don't know her at all. I know Sam as intimately as I know my own self, and I know that she is not staying away deliberately. If she has not suffered an injury that would've taken her to a nearby hospital, then something else—something terrible—has happened.

The last thought makes me sit up. The amorphous uneasiness I've been feeling since yesterday morning is now replaced by a dreadful conviction that I am right. Why didn't I consider this scenario yesterday? That someone may have hurt Sam? My stomach lurches at the thought.

Habit makes me make the bed. I brush my teeth and make my way downstairs. Sally is already in the kitchen, on her laptop. She looks up as I enter, her brow furrowed.

"Is Sam back?"

I shake my head. "I'm scared. Something is wrong. Really wrong." As I say the words, they become true. Still, I'm hoping Sally will say something—anything—will offer some other plausible explanation that will convince me that I'm overreacting.

"I think you're right," she says.

I turn away, not wanting Sally to see the fear in my eyes. To steady myself, I begin to grind the coffee beans. By the time I pour the first cup Mo walks in. She glances at me and then at Sally. I hand her the cup, pretending to not notice that Sally has silently answered Mo's unasked question.

Mo takes a sip, looks at me over the rim of her cup. "What should we do?"

I control the sick feeling sloshing through me. "I'm going to take a quick shower. And then, even though it's not been forty-eight hours, I need to call the cops."

"Can I ask why you waited until the next day to call us, ma'am?"

"I was told that the police didn't consider someone missing until forty-eight hours after they've gone."

"And who told you this?" asks Patrol Officer Brian Woods. He is a handsome African American man, with close-cropped hair and light brown eyes. I get the distinct feeling that we've gotten off on the wrong foot.

"I . . . I don't remember. It's what I've always heard."

He sighs theatrically. "It's an old myth. You'd be surprised how many people believe that."

"I'm sorry," I say. "Have I botched things by not calling right away? I honestly thought she was, you know, just out for the day."

"And is that something Miss O'Malley does often? Stay out all day and night?"

I feel cornered. How to tell this man, presumably straight, about the ridiculous fight at the party, the reason I believed Sam had stayed away? "No."

"And can't pin the exact time your . . ." he stumbles over the word, "*wife* might've left the house yesterday morning?"

"The exact time? No. I told you. She was sleeping in the guest bedroom."

"May I ask why, ma'am?" His voice is soft, but I sense a trap.

I hesitate. For all my friendliness, I'm a private person. Trusting cops doesn't come naturally to me. "My snoring was keeping her awake."

Woods cracks a thin smile. "I'm sure my wife can relate," he says dryly, and I appreciate the casual equating of his marriage to ours. Like every other resident, we complain about the high property taxes in Cleveland Heights, but this is why we chose to live here. There's probably no town in Ohio more hospitable for a gay female couple than this one.

Mo pokes her head in the living room where I sit with Woods.

"Can I speak to you for a second, Ali?" she says, and I shoot her an incredulous, not-now look. But she looks back at me steadily and I excuse myself.

"You're making things worse," Mo whispers to me as soon as we're out of earshot. "Rule number one is that you don't lie to cops. Just tell them the truth—that the two of you had a fight. Couples fight all the time."

Other than Sam, Mo probably knows me better than anyone in the world. And yet, there are things I can't say to her: That ever since I came out to Abba when I was fourteen, I've tried to portray a positive image of gay relationships to the world. That I don't merely want what Sam and I have to be comparable to a straight relationship—I want it to be better. I mean, I can be honest with close friends about the tensions in our relationship. But I don't want to reveal the details of our lives to a stranger. I stare at Mo, unable to say any of this, but knowing she is right. Of course, she is right.

"Ali," Mo says. "I love you. But you're being an absolute ass. Swallow your pride and walk in there and tell him the truth. For fuck's sake."

I go back in the living room and clear my throat and focus my gaze on my interlocutor. "My friend just pulled me aside to remind me that I'd left out an important detail," I say, my voice stiff with embarrassment. "I . . . Sam and I . . . we'd had a fight the night before. That was the reason she slept in the guest room. And probably why she didn't wake me up for our daily run."

Woods lights up, as if I've thrown a hunk of red meat into his lap. "So that's why you thought she hadn't returned home last evening."

"Yes."

"What were you fighting about?"

I flush, digging my fingernails into my hand. "She . . . she accused me of paying too much attention to someone else at a party."

"Were you?" Woods says. Before I can reply he adds, "Maybe she's staying away because of that. Where would she go? To her parents, maybe?"

"No. She . . . We don't have any contact with them."

Woods pulls on his lip. "She hasn't texted you at all? Since yesterday morning?"

Dread burns in my stomach as I see where this conversation is headed. "She couldn't. She left her phone here. We don't take our phones when we run."

"It's here? Well, let's see it. Maybe she made plans with someone else."

I stare at him, remembering the angry texts we exchanged from one room to the other. The one where I said her jealousy was intolerable, that I was getting sick and tired of it, that something had to change and that I couldn't live like this anymore.

A thousand thoughts flit through my mind. About refusing his request. Asking for a search warrant. Then, I think, You called the cops. He's here to help you, you idiot. Who cares how you come across, so long as they can bring Sam home?

The moments tick by. "Ma'am?" Woods says. "The phone?"

"Yes. Just a minute. I'll get it."

I head up the stairs. In the seconds it takes me to reach the bedroom, something odd occurs—I feel as if I'm guilty, as if I've turned from complainant to accused. I see myself clearly: Brown. Gay. Muslim. The daughter of immigrants. Living in today's America, land of the Muslim ban, of Build That Wall. Who am I, in this world?

Aliya, you're nuts, I say to myself. He's here to help you. To bring Sam back.

But.

Travon Martin. Closer to home, Tamir Rice. You're not a Black male, I remind myself. You're not an inner-city African American boy playing with a toy gun in a park in Cleveland. You live in a middle-class neighborhood. You are a popular interior designer with rich clients in Pepper Pike and Hunting Valley who wait for months until you are available. *Cleveland Magazine* ran a short profile on you in its Forty Under Forty column last year.

But the body knows what the body knows: The upturned noses of the white kids at school when I'd pulled out the batata vada sandwich Mummy had packed for my lunch. Timothy Collins, who bullied me and made my life a living hell until seventh grade, when he suddenly became infatuated with me, which was another kind of bullying. Miss Linner, the third-grade teacher who seemed surprised that I spoke better English than most of my classmates and who referred to me as an immigrant, even though I was born in a hospital less than five miles from my school.

The body knows what the body knows. I unlock Sam's phone—her passcode is my birth date—and before I have time to think, I erase the text messages that flew like missiles between us last night. Then, heart pounding, I come back downstairs.

Woods is gone. Mo says he's gone back to his cruiser, but she doesn't know why. I look out of the front window and sure enough, he's sitting in his vehicle. He appears to be on his walkie-talkie. I know our neighbors must be curious about a cop car parked in our driveway.

Ten minutes later, Woods walks back in, accompanied by another officer. This man is older, with a creased face and kind gray eyes. "Hi, Ms. Mirza," he says. "I'm Detective Mike Herrington. Patrol Officer Woods thought maybe it was better if I was involved."

"Nice to meet you," I say dully.

"It seems as if your partner left her phone behind?" Herrington asks.

"Wife."

"Excuse me?"

"Sam's my wife. Not my partner. And yes, her phone is here." I point to it on the kitchen counter.

"I apologize. Well, would you tell me where your wife would go on her run?"

Herrington has the affect of a kindly country doctor. As I describe the route for our daily run, I find myself relaxing.

I tense again when he motions toward the phone. "Will you unlock it for me?"

I hesitate. Out of the corner of my eye, I see Mo urging me on. Still, I say, "I'm not sure Sam would like strangers going through her stuff."

Woods turns sharply toward the detective, but Herrington's tone is calm. "Ms. Mirza," he says. "You say your wife has gone missing. We are trying to help. We need every possible lead we can follow."

I nod.

"We're at a real disadvantage here," he continues, "thanks to the outage in this area. Otherwise, we could've gotten some footage on someone's security camera along Stratford. Not that every homeowner always cooperates." He pauses. "You're sure that's the only route Ms. O'Malley would take?"

"That's our run in good weather," I say. "Around the lake. But I don't know what she decided to do."

"Al," Mo says. "The phone?"

I hand the unlocked phone to Herrington, who scrolls through some of our more benign exchanges before looking up. "Do you mind if we take this with us? We need to make sure we're not missing something. My hunch is your wife is probably staying with a friend."

I suddenly wish Abba were here with me. Abba, who I haven't

spoken to since his birthday last year even though he's just two hours away in Columbus. Abba would know what to do, how to deal with this situation. The cops have been professional and courteous, but I can't help but feel like we are on opposite sides. I've seen enough TV shows to know the cops have to rule out everything and everybody, but I feel out of my element. This is unusual for me. Most of the time, I'm confident in my own skin. I graduated summa cum laude with a degree in economics from Smith. I have a master's in architecture and urban design from the University of Michigan. My interior design business netted $150,000 last year.

Mo nudges me. "Ali. They're asking if they can look around."

"Oh. Sorry. Yes, of course."

The two officers make their way upstairs. I follow them heavily, with a growing sense of unreality and dread. They take Sam's toothbrush for her DNA. They ask me for a recent photograph of her. They take strands of Sam's hair from her hairbrush. I stand in the doorway and watch, marveling at how delicately but methodically they are going through our things. As they look, they fire question after question at me—did Sam have any tattoos? Any scars or broken bones? What was her credit history? Any financial woes? Any disputes or enemies?

"No disputes unless you count the students to whom she gave a B who thought they deserved an A," I say, when something jogs my memory: Brown leathery skin. Angry eyes. Dark hair. What was his name? Ramos? Ramon? Something like that? My eyes drift toward the bedroom window that overlooks the backyard, where a mound of soil sits. For several days last week, the man had helped Sam dig a huge flower and vegetable bed. Where had she found him? I don't know. But I'd come home on Friday to raised voices. I'd gone into the backyard to find him towering over Samantha, gesticulating wildly, speaking to her in rapid-fire Spanish. And even though I didn't understand a word of what he said, his body language was threatening. "Hey, *hey*," I called as I approached them. "What's going on? What are you doing?"

"Ali," Sam turned toward me, and I caught the relief on her face.

"What's going on?" I said again, positioning myself—all five feet two inches of me—ever so slightly between them.

"She keeps changing her mind," the man said. "I don't want this job."

Sam's face was flushed and sweaty. She'd tied her hair back, but a strand had come loose. Despite the tension, I couldn't help but notice how beautiful she looked. It hit me like that, at the most inopportune of times, her beauty. Something must've softened in my face because I felt her relax, also. It was one of the things I treasured about our life together, those moments of silent communion, this wordless strengthening of one another.

"I decided on a different layout for one of the beds," Samantha said. "He's pissed about that because he's lined up another job for tomorrow. But when he took this one, he told me he works on Saturdays. Now, he says he doesn't know when he can come back. But he wants to be paid in full."

I could see both their points of view, but I knew better than to choose sides. "You can't work for even a few hours tomorrow?" I asked the man. "We're having company on Monday."

He scowled. "She is lying. I tell from the first, I'm not working on Saturday or Sunday. But she was insisting. I'll come back to finish sometime this week. But not tomorrow. No."

I looked at Sam. "How much do you owe him?"

"Five hundred for what he's done so far and two-fifty for the second bed that he's barely started."

I opened my wallet and pulled out five hundred-dollar bills. "Here you go," I said. "But we have your word you'll come and finish up, yes?"

They both turned on me, annoyed and speaking at once:

"What are you doing? If you pay him now, we'll never see him again. I don't want the yard to look like this when Sal and Mo arrive."

Ramon/Ramos spat. "My mistake working for es manflora," he said and even though I didn't know what the slur meant, I could guess by the way the skin whitened around Sam's mouth.

"Get the hell out," she yelled. "And don't bother coming back."

Ramos grinned, as if this was exactly the outcome he was hoping for. But he stood his ground. "Then pay me hundred more for starting the second job," he said, looking directly at me. "Then I go. She can hire someone else."

Sam threw me a warning look, shook her head no. "Don't, Ali," she said.

But I knew Sam wasn't thinking straight, too angry to be fair. And something about the man's grin disarmed me. It reminded me of the Indian immigrants who worked in Abba's restaurants. They were gruff and blatantly dishonest but even when they were ripping you off, there was a twinkle in their eye that let you in on the joke. Besides, all I wanted to do was go in and shower and come downstairs to the glass of wine that Sam would've poured me. I shoved another hundred into Ramos's wizened hand. "Here. Now, get your tools and leave."

He threw his tools in the back of his pickup truck, gave Sam a dirty look, and drove away. "Thanks for undercutting me," Sam muttered as we walked into the house.

I put my arm around her. "Don't be like that," I said. "I just wanted to get rid of him so we could start our evening."

We made love on the back porch that evening. Two nights before the terrible fight. How could we be that volatile and reactive? How could the same couple who held each other so tenderly on a Friday send those awful texts to one another on Sunday?

"And that's the only person you can think of who might have a vendetta against her?" Herrington interrupts my thoughts.

Vendetta? I try to remember how Ramos had looked when he'd left. Was he still angry? Or had the hundred papered over the heated words?

"I mean, people have arguments with workers all the time, right?" I say. "I honestly don't think it was anything much. He did use a homophobic slur. Sam was mad about that."

Herrington perks up. "Tell me."

But there wasn't much to tell. We'd both heard much worse. Hell, my own father had disowned me for being gay.

"Do you know what landscaping company he worked for?"

"He was driving a rusty old truck. I don't remember seeing a logo or name on it. Sam had a habit of doing this, when she needed help in the garden. She'd hire someone she'd just met at Home Depot. Or someone working at a different house in the neighborhood. I have no idea how she found him."

"So, there's nothing more you can tell us about this Ramos?"

"I'm afraid not."

Herrington looks frustrated and I am gratified. He's taking this seriously.

"Hey, Mike," Woods calls from the other room. "Come here for a second."

"Excuse me," Herrington says.

Herrington has a different expression on his face when he returns a few minutes later. He is holding Sam's journal in one hand, his index finger marking one of the pages. He clears his throat. "Ms. Mirza," he says. "Have you ever read your wife's diary?"

"Never," I say. "I don't . . . I would never invade her privacy like that." And it's true—growing up in an Indian family, where the notion of space and privacy didn't exist, has made me a fanatic about respecting boundaries.

"Well, I'm sorry to say, there's some pretty, um, unflattering things about you. Um, it seems like the night before she disappeared, your wife was suspecting that you were having an affair with someone named Jan? And there's something in here about wishing she could disappear and never have to deal with this again."

I close my eyes. This is the reckoning, the moment we've been hurling toward. Sam's irrational jealousy, my defiance, the terrible dynamic between us, have led to this moment. *A house divided cannot stand.* Abba used to say this during my childhood.

"She's wrong," I say, my voice low and tremulous. "I would never cheat on my wife. That's what we were arguing about, on our way home from the party." I fall silent, too overwhelmed with regret, too embarrassed at having to discuss my personal life with strangers.

Sally and Mo are downstairs. I need them here. They will attest for me. They will say: "Yes, officer, Ali is bull-headed and stubborn, but have an affair? Why, she'd sooner stab her own eyeballs than betray Sam."

There is a short silence. Unexpectedly, Woods says, "Well, hell. Couples fight all the time, right?"

"Exactly," Herrington says. He looks at me. "Ms. Mirza? Would you like to sit down?"

"I'm okay."

"Well, I think we're done here."

Both detectives follow me downstairs. Mo takes one look at me and fetches me a glass of water. I sit on the barstool at the kitchen island while she questions Herrington. "So, Detective, what happens now?" she asks. "What's the game plan?"

Herrington pulls on his lower lip. "I'm still hoping there's a simple explanation for Ms. O'Malley's absence. Maybe she's simply taking a break, given the quarrel. But if you're sure that's something totally out of character for her, we can put out an all-alert bulletin," he says. "Go door to door. See if anyone has seen anything suspicious. Check with other jurisdictions."

"Have you dealt with . . . I mean, does this kind of thing happen often?" I ask. "In the Heights?"

"Not really." His eyes flit around the kitchen, taking in the quartz countertop, the expensive appliances. "People don't just disappear in neighborhoods like this, Ms. Mirza. Now, near Noble, it's a different story."

He is referring to the poorer, Black neighborhoods. Even as I am embarrassed for Woods, I feel a sharp sense of relief. Women like Sam don't just go missing. Not in our neighborhood. I suddenly feel better.

I imagine Samantha coming back home, with a strange-but-true story that would explain her absence. The four of us laughing off our anxiety and resuming our plans. The sense of longing that I feel in that moment is so strong, it's like a twist in my organs. Where are you? I whisper. Don't do this to me. No fight is worth this. Come home. Please, come home.

"She's either hiding on purpose, or maybe she's injured somewhere," Herrington continues. "I know you've called the local hospitals. But we'll check all the ERs again. If she wants to be found, we'll find her."

His quiet confidence is inspiring. And despite the contents of the journal, he doesn't appear to be holding me responsible for Sam's disappearance. "How can we help?" I ask. "My friends and I can canvas the entire neighborhood. I'd like to go door to door and—"

"I'd advise against it," Herrington says. "I know it's hard, but I'm going to ask you to let us do our job." He points to the tickets to Blossom on the kitchen counter. "Go ahead and stick to your plans. There's nothing better than an outdoor concert, right? Believe me, sitting at home won't change anything. If there's any news, I'll contact you immediately."

Herrington asks more questions, jots down names and numbers of Sam's friends and colleagues, asks me about her favorite haunts. She often works on her novel in the atrium of the art museum, I say. The Stone Oven is her favorite place for a working lunch. She goes to Holden Arboretum every Thursday during the summer. No, I don't know of any student who bears a grudge against her, and in any case, she's not teaching this summer.

As they get ready to leave twenty minutes later, Herrington nods at me. "Happy Fourth," he says on his way out.

"Happy Fourth," I reply, although the bile rises to my mouth. The Fourth of July had always been my favorite holiday. Even 9/11 and the Muslim-bashing that followed hadn't diluted my pride in my country. But since the last election something's changed, not just in me, but in Sam, too. In all our friends. We will go to Blossom tomorrow night, we will clap along to "The Stars and Stripes Forever," we will watch the fireworks bursting in air, but there will be a crack in the sky. When the national anthem plays, I will get goosebumps as I always do and will feel allegiance to my beloved country. But at some point, I will wonder, as we have all wondered the past two years, whether we still are the land of the free and the home of the brave. At some point, I will wonder if it was all an illusion—American democracy, Sam and me, our marriage. At some point, I will shiver despite the July heat, feel lonely despite being around thousands of people, will feel the oppressive dark while staring at a sky lit up by light and color, and be paralyzed by the knowledge that something sinister and soggy with grief is coming my way and I am unable to prevent it from smashing into me.

5

▼ ▶ ▲ ◀ ▼ ▲ ▶ ▲

Wednesday, July 3

The power finally comes back on, an early Fourth of July present from the electric company. It will make it easier to get home from Blossom with the streetlights working again. I tried begging off from going to the concert, told Mo and Sally that Nathan would drive them, but they wouldn't hear of it. Said they'd stay home, too. So, I agreed to go and now here we are. We carry our blankets and lawn chairs as we look for a spot, while Nathan staggers behind us, hauling the picnic basket and ice cooler, until we settle in under a tree near the back. We feast on salad, roasted chicken, potatoes, and watermelon while the orchestra plays rousing marches and Broadway tunes. The show is titled *A Tribute to America*.

It is a beautiful evening, with a cloudless sky and a mellow, warm breeze. But my chest feels hollow, aware as I am of Samantha's absence. I do my best to smile and laugh at Nathan's terrible puns and jokes—I know he's trying his utmost to cheer me up—but the gusts of laughter and the festive atmosphere around me feel like an insult. I'm glad the music is upbeat and militaristic; I don't think I can handle a sad tune or a minor note right now. Each year, Sam and I look forward to the fireworks that follow the music—she watches the display as she rocks on her haunches, her eyes sparkling, her gleeful face turned up to the night sky, looking for all the world like a little kid; I spend the time gazing at her upturned face, taking in her long red hair, the strong, chiseled profile, feeling something like awe that this beautiful woman is my wife.

But this year, there is no Samantha to watch. I take a long swig from the plastic glass holding my white wine. There is some sinister metronome ticking inside me, marking time, aware of each hour that passes without Sam returning home.

Mo pokes me in the ribs, rolls her eyes at the chatterbox middle-aged woman sitting in front of us, and mimics her. I laugh. Seeing the gratified look in her eyes—I know how hard they are trying to inject some normalcy into my life—I pretend to laugh some more. The next second, a camera flashes, blinding me. I blink, look up to see Candace Brickman, Samantha's graduate student. Before I can react, she drops to the grass and crouches in front of me.

"Hiya," she says breathlessly. "I . . . I didn't expect to see you here. I just heard the news a few hours ago. Is Professor O'Malley okay?"

Candace is older than most of Sam's students, loud and pushy, the proverbial bull in a china shop. She's driven poor Sam, who is directing her thesis, crazy with her demands and delays. I resent her for her endless need for handholding. But she's doing a creative thesis in poetry, and Sam took her on against her own better judgement.

"The news?" I say, stalling for time. "Where'd you hear it?"

"From Dr. Myers," Candace says. "I was on campus today and she said she got a call from the cops asking her a bunch of questions." Candace gives me a hard, knowing stare. "She said she was offended that as the chair of the department, she didn't hear from you giving her a heads-up or whatever. So, what happened?"

As the first rocket bursts in the air, I feel a corresponding spurt of anger. It's none of your business, I want to say. It's none of anyone's business. Sam is not your property, and her disappearance is not for public consumption. "I can't talk right now," I say loudly, to be heard over the fireworks. "This is not the right time or place. If there's any news, I'll let Dr. Myers know."

A bright flash from the fireworks reveals Candace's face: her nostrils flare with anger and her face flushes with insult. It dawns on me that Candace dislikes me as much as I dislike her. She has been to our house several times for the end-of-the-semester parties Sam throws for her grad students, and has always been polite to me. But without Samantha to act as a buffer, her hostility is no longer hidden. "Well, it would be nice to know if I still have an advisor," she says plaintively. "And what, y'know, happened to her."

I flinch at her tactlessness. "Sam's fine," I say. "No worries."

"That's not what the cop said. Allegedly." She pushes back onto her feet.

I stare after her as she weaves through the blankets that dot the lawn and disappears into the clapping, cheering crowd.

"Who the hell was that?" Sally asks.

"Sam's master's student," I say. "And the number one pain in her neck."

Nathan pulls me closer to him. "What a bitch," he murmurs. "Screw her."

It's not until I'm in bed hours later that I remember the camera flash. Why the hell would Candace take my picture?

6

▼ ▶ ▲ ◀ ▼ ▲ ▶ ▲

Thursday, July 4

I get my answer sooner than I'd have liked.

I am grilling burgers when Mo comes out on the patio with her laptop, a funny look on her face. "Have you been on Facebook today?"

"Nope. Why? Did we bomb Iran or something?"

"What? No, no. It's not that. This is . . ." She points to the grill. "Turn that down and come sit. You need to see this." She calls out to Sally, who is watering the coleus in the planter. "Sal, come here for a minute."

Mo flips open her laptop on the outdoor table and there, on Candace's page, is a picture of me, head tilted back, eyes closed, mouth open in a hearty laugh. She has tagged me, which is how Mo saw the public post. I look for all the world like a woman without a care, but it's more than that. There is something wanton about my stance. Next to it is a picture of Sam in the classroom, her hands flung wide, as if she is embracing the world. Her hair is tied back in a ponytail, and she is the epitome of the all-American girl next door. *The brown bitch vs. the white angel. Jezebel vs. the Madonna.* The thoughts emerge from some dark, subterranean place in my subconscious.

"What the actual fuck?" I say.

"Wait. It gets worse."

I read what Candace has written:

> Is this the picture of someone who is mourning the disappearance of their spouse? Yes, my dear professor,

> @SamanthaO'Malley has been missing for over forty-eight hours. And here's her wife, Ali Mirza, owner of @AMDesigns, picnicking, enjoying the fireworks and whooping it up with her friends. I can't imagine being so chill if *my* girlfriend went missing. Hey, if anyone has any information about my missing professor, DM me ASAP. Because *some* of us care very much about finding her.

I turn to Mo, incredulous. "What the fuck does she think she's doing? Who does she think she is?" Then, I stop, astonished. Candace's post, which she has made public, has already been liked by twelve hundred people. It has been shared fifty-one times. There are ninety-eight comments.

"Don't," Mo says, pulling the laptop away from me. "You are not going to read the comments."

"It's my fault," Sally says. "You didn't even want to go to the damn concert. I forced you."

I stare at them, speechless, unable to breathe. It feels as if I'm tied to a railroad track watching a train barreling toward me. "Why would she do such a nasty thing?" I finally say, swallowing the lump in my throat.

Mo shakes her head in disgust. "Doesn't matter. Main thing is, we gotta get her to take down this shitty post. Send her a stern DM."

They read over my shoulder as I type. "Not good enough. Make it stronger," Mo says. "Like, threaten her with legal action or something, I don't care."

"She's an odd duck. She probably means well," I say. "Sam was the only faculty member willing to direct Candace's thesis. I don't doubt that her affection for Sam is real."

"Ali. Stop."

"What?"

"What you always do. Defending the indefensible." Mo's eyes bore into me. "This is not the time to do your usual both-siderism. This is . . . this is serious, Ali."

"Yeah, no, you're right. But . . ."

"Toughen it up. Say you'll sue for defamation or something. I don't know, make it sound stern."

After I hit Send, I go back to the grill. The burgers are now charred but both Sally and Mo say they'll be fine. We spend the next ten minutes bringing out the rest of the food, but we're a subdued bunch, with none of our usual hijinks. This is what Candace doesn't get, I think, as I carry out the potato salad—that we're going through the motions, trying to keep one another's spirits up. That I'm pantomiming last year's rituals, trying to ignore the feeling of fire ants crawling inside my body. My insides and outsides don't match, Candace, I think. But I don't expect you to get that, you obtuse idiot.

Nathan arrives, carrying a bag of chips and a four-pack of wine spritzers, his hair falling on his boyish face. He is wearing a tight floral shirt with khaki shorts and white socks and tennis shoes. If Sam was here, she'd have turned to me and given me that quick, knowing smile. Could he be any more obviously gay if he tried? that look would've telegraphed. We keep waiting for Nathan to come out to us. It's not as if he doesn't trust us—he complains to us about the new library director, the demanding customers, the eccentricities of his coworkers. But not a word about his personal life.

"Hey, girls," Nathan says. "Great weather, huh?" He turns to me. "Any news?"

I shake my head and the smile fades from his face. "I told the folks in our writing group," he says.

"None of them have heard from Sam?"

"No. They all wanted to call you, but I told them you had your hands full. I hope you don't mind that I mentioned it."

"It's fine." At this point, I appreciate not being the one to inform others. Our social circle in Cleveland is mostly made up of academics and writers—in other words, people who gossip and scuttlebutt. Out of the blue I realize that Sam's parents don't know she's missing. Would the cops have contacted them, or is this my job? Hell, what's the protocol for telling your wife's estranged parents that their daughter has disappeared? My neck muscles tense at the thought of getting Joe O'Malley on the phone and dealing with his wrath. There's Good Joe and Bad Joe and there's no way of knowing which Joe will pick up.

"Sweetie, what's wrong?" Nathan says.

"I . . . I just realized. Sam's parents may not know that she's . . . missing. I don't even know if she'd want them to know."

"She would." Sally's voice is quiet but authoritative. She's the mother of five-year-old Rachel. "I don't care what shits they are. They'd want to know."

I nod, miserably. I am not looking forward to this task. "Well, let's eat first," I say. "The burgers are ready."

Halfway through the meal, despite Nathan doing his best to keep up a steady conversation, my stomach roils. I push back my plate and rise abruptly to my feet. "I'm going to go inside and call them. I want to get it out of the way."

It's Good Joe who answers. He doesn't seem surprised to hear from me, which surprises me. The last time we'd visited them to invite them to our wedding, he had shouted at us to get out of his house.

He takes the news surprisingly well. Quiet. Mellow. Then he says, "So when do you expect her back home?"

I open my mouth to say, Soon, I hope. Don't you worry, Mr. O'Malley, I'll let you know as soon as she returns, when I hear a muffled sound and Emily O'Malley says, "Hello? Who's this?"

"It's Ali. Samantha's . . . friend."

"Oh, hi, Ali," she says, so casual, so friendly, that for a second, I wonder if she's getting senile, before I remember that this is just her way, to be nonconfrontational, ostrichlike. These are the attributes that drove Sam crazy, that made her feel she had no ally against her father's explosive temper and abuse.

I break the news to her, and I'm relieved to hear the shock and sympathy in her voice. "My poor baby," she says. "Where on earth can she be?"

"Did the cops not call you?" I ask.

"I don't think so. Unless Joe answered the phone and forgot to tell me." She falls quiet and says finally, "Joe has dementia. He was diagnosed in early 2017. I wanted to let Samantha know. But I didn't want to upset her."

I sigh. The remark is vintage Emily O'Malley. "How are *you*?" I ask. "Do you have help? It must be hard to manage alone." The O'Malleys live out in the country, not too far from the college town of Athens, in southern Ohio.

She lowers her voice. "Actually, it's easier. He is so sweet, so calm these days. Nothing like before. Of course, he lost his job at United Plumbers. Believe it or not, that was a blessing. I mean, that man worked in pain every day of his life. His knees were shot before he'd even turned forty."

We are both quiet. Then she says quietly, "I always hated the way he treated you and my daughter. I'm so sorry."

People have apologized to me before—teachers who had underestimated me, softball coaches who benched me, former girlfriends who wronged me. But I've never had an apology tear at my heart as this one does. I feel an overwhelming sorrow—for my own compulsive behaviors, whose causes I understand but still cannot control; for my harsh exchange with Samantha, which resulted in her running alone or even running away, I don't know; for Mr. O'Malley's bullying and bombast, which drove away his daughter and whittled down his wife into this piteous, mousy woman; for Abba's religious piety, the source of the antigay beliefs that led to our estrangement; for all our family divisions, which seem to dovetail with the rifts and divisions tearing this country apart, the endless battles and wars to which we all contribute. In this moment, I want to lay down my arms, tear off my armor, and step off the battlefield. I am exhausted. I am tired of the incomprehensible pain of being human.

"Mrs. O'Malley," I say. "I'm here for you. If you can think of anything I can do for you, will you please let me know?"

I'm thinking of how to offer money without insulting her when she says, "We are okay. We have Joe's pension and social security. But yes, please come see me—us. But do me a favor. Come after you find Samantha. Only with Samantha."

I close my eyes. I feel lost in the darkness. "I promise," I say. "I'll find Samantha. I promise."

I go back into the yard and notice their tense expressions. "It's fine," I say. "The conversation went well, actually."

"That's good," Nathan says vaguely. Then he says, "Read this."

This is Candace, striking again. The woman has copied and pasted my entire DM onto her post, under the word *UPDATE.* And below my message, the final, devastating sentence: "Is this how you would react if someone was trying to help you locate your missing wife? You think she'd be grateful."

"I'm gonna kill her," Mo growls. "I mean, who does this—publish a private message?"

I don't answer. I'm transfixed by what I'm seeing on the screen. Three hundred and forty comments. Candace's post has been shared by a hundred and eight people; there are more than four hundred emojis. This thing is spreading like wildfire.

Sally turns the laptop toward herself. "It's a public post, right? That means anyone can comment." She types:

> I think your insinuations are troubling at best, and inflammatory, at worst. You owe Ali an apology. She's devastated by Sam's absence and you're feasting on someone else's misery. And btw, I was the one who forced her to go to that concert, hoping to take her mind off her pain. Clearly, we weren't expecting vultures at Blossom.

"Hey, Sal," I say, but it's too late. She's already hit Send.

"Fuck her," Sally says, defiant. "If she wants a public war, she's going to get it."

I don't say what I think: Yeah, but you guys are going home soon. And then I'll be the only one left on the battlefield to deal with the fallout.

7

▼ ▶ ▲ ◀ ▼ ▲ ▶ ▲

Saturday, July 6

"It's a match," Mike Herrington says.

He places a large photograph on the coffee table, and I pick it up. There's a tiny dark patch on the sidewalk, along with a few strands of red hair stuck under the lip of a raised slab. It's hard to believe that anyone walking down that sidewalk could've even spotted this.

"That's blood?" I ask.

"It is. But that test will take a little longer to come back. In the meantime, we can say with about eighty percent accuracy that the hair belongs to Ms. O'Malley."

"But . . . how? I mean, who could've even spotted a few strands of hair while walking on a public street?"

Herrington allows a tight smile. "Good question. I walked the entire route you described with a dog from the K-9 unit. Having one of Ms. O'Malley's old T-shirts was very helpful. She was definitely on Stratford Road that morning."

My heart is racing. "So, what does this mean?"

"Well, by itself, not much. Although we've swept the whole area for other DNA."

"But it's a public street. I mean, there's probably hundreds of people walking there every day."

"That's true. This simply gives us some more information."

"And that little bit of dried blood? Is that all you found? What does it mean?"

Herrington frowns. "That she most likely fell and hit her head. The lack of more blood is a good sign. It rules out assault or—worse."

Mo stirs. "So, Detective, is it possible that she has wandered off or something? That she has, you know, amnesia?"

"We are not ruling out anything. But generally, people with amnesia don't wander off without detection. Someone would've seen her." He clears his throat. "There's a raised sidewalk a few slabs before the one where we think Ms. O'Malley hit her head. Our theory is that's what she tripped on."

And suddenly, I know exactly where on Stratford. That piece of slate sidewalk is not just raised; it rocks from front to back. We've often wondered why the city has not forced the homeowners to fix it. But Sam knows to step onto the tree lawn or adjust her pace when we approach that particular slab. Why hadn't she done so? Something must've distracted her.

"What's the address?" I ask. "Where she fell?"

When he tells me, I write it down.

"It's a large brick house?" I say. "With a blue front door?"

He nods. "Ms. Mirza," he says. "I'd request you to keep this information to yourself. We don't want to tip anyone off yet."

"But have you interviewed the homeowners? All the people who live around there?"

"Yes, we have. No one saw her fall. And several people were out of town because of the holiday." He heaves himself off the couch. "Well. I just wanted to let you know. We're getting closer to solving this."

I fall silent. I know Herrington is pleased with his sleuthing, but he's not told me anything yet that I didn't tell him—that Sam had left the house to go on a run.

"Thanks for keeping me in the loop," I say at the door.

"Of course," he replies.

We eat a salad for lunch. I jiggle my leg compulsively through the meal, unable to control my restlessness. "Hey, girl," Mo says. "Calm down."

I pick up my car keys after lunch.

"I'll be back soon," I say.

"Want me to come with you?" Mo asks, but I shake my head. "It's okay."

I park my car a few feet away from the house with the broken sidewalk. I feel it rock under my feet as I stand on it and then I notice the slight, dark spot two slabs away, where Sam must have hit her head. The distance adds up. I stand under the afternoon sun staring at the tiny bloodstain, feeling as if this might be the last bit of Sam that I'll ever see. I glance at the brick house with the manicured lawn and the slate roof. All that wealth and they couldn't fix a lousy piece of sidewalk.

A dark blue Audi backs out from the driveway. I move to the end of the drive to block its way. The driver hits the brakes and, when I don't move, lowers his window.

"Excuse me?" he yells. "Do you mind?"

I step up to the open window. "Hi," I say. "I wanted to talk to you about . . ."

"Sorry, we have no change," says the woman in the passenger seat and I laugh incredulously.

"Wait, what? I'm not panhandling. "I—we just live a few streets away. That was my partner who tripped and fell on your sidewalk, and I just wanted to ask you a few questions."

The man's eyes narrow. "The girl who's missing?" he asks. He has a German or Swiss accent.

I nod and the woman says, "We already spoke to the cops. We weren't even home. We were skiing in Utah when she allegedly tripped. We had nothing to do with it."

It's the "allegedly" that makes me see red. "Yeah, because you're too damn cheap to fix the damn sidewalk," I say. "We've been running past here for three years and in all that time it's always been in this condition."

"So, choose another route." Even as I gasp, she turns to her husband. "Let's go. This woman is looking to blackmail us or something."

Her husband has the decency to look embarrassed. "Sorry," he mutters. "And we're sorry for your loss." And before I can respond, he guns the car, maneuvering tightly around me, and they disappear.

I stand on the sidewalk, feeling like a fool. What did I hope to achieve by accosting strangers? If I was looking for sympathy or information, I'd failed.

Slowly, I get in my car and drive home.

8

▾ ▸ ▴ ◂ ▾ ▴ ▸ ▴

Tuesday, July 9

"His name is Ramon Garcia," Herrington says as soon as I answer the phone. "The landscaper you mentioned."

My pulse quickens. "And?"

"Nothing much, I'm afraid. He was filling up his truck at a gas station in Painesville at six-thirty the morning of July first. He started a job at seven and was there until three in the afternoon. He was nowhere near Cleveland Heights on that day."

Even though I truly didn't think Ramon had anything to do with Sam's disappearance, I'm disappointed at the lack of progress. "How did you even find him?" I ask.

"Well, that was a bit of luck. I guess our guy was in such a hurry when he left your house that Friday that he almost ran over your neighbor's cat. She yelled at him, and he swore at her. Apparently, this Ramon is a bit of a hothead. She says even after she picked up the cat and started to go up her driveway, he was still berating her. She took down his license plate number."

"But how did you come to know? About this altercation, I mean?"

"When our officers were going door to door asking if anybody had seen Ms. O'Malley, we asked about a Hispanic landscaper in a pickup truck who was in the neighborhood on Friday evening. This woman ID'd him."

I swallow. "I see." It suddenly occurs to me that Ramon Garcia may be in the country illegally. I'd never forgive myself if I got an innocent man in trouble with the law.

"So, he's not in trouble?"

"No, not at all. His alibi checked out. We saw footage of him at the gas station. And the homeowner verified he was at her home most of the day Monday."

I'm quiet for a moment. "There's nothing else?"

"I'm afraid not, Ms. Mirza. But we'll keep looking."

"Thank you."

"I'll be in touch."

9

▼ ▶ ▲ ◀ ▼ ▲ ▶ ▲

Wednesday, July 10

I drop off Sally and Mo at the airport in the afternoon and come home to an eerily empty house. Unable to handle the silence, I pick up Don DeLillo's *Underworld* and go into the backyard. Perhaps a novel about baseball, the Cold War, the atomic bomb, and J. Edgar Hoover will take my mind off my only-too-real predicament, I think grimly. There have been no sightings of Sam at all. It is as if she's vanished into thin air. I feel as if I'm keeping vigil, treading water, waiting for a phone call from the cops telling me whether to celebrate or mourn. I can no longer log on to Facebook or Twitter; Candace's post has taken on a life of its own and the comments have been amazingly racist and vicious—everything from the garden-variety "She's an ISIS sympathizer," to elaborate conspiracy theories about how I "disappeared" Sam in order to silence her from revealing something she'd uncovered about my radical past. There are people commenting all the way from New Zealand! Someone has flown a drone over our home and taken pictures of the huge garden bed that Samantha had dug, saying they were convinced that Sam was buried there. Mo has been monitoring social media for me, but now, with her gone, I don't have the strength to see that strangers are braying for my blood. Apparently, someone from the fateful party that we had attended the night before she disappeared has been spreading a rumor that I'd rushed Sam out of the apartment, not even allowing her to say goodbye to anyone.

I have done my best to ignore whatever has been happening in the wider world. I do know that the president held a huge July Fourth parade and rally at the National Mall, complete with military fighter jets and tanks. The three of us had watched a little bit of it on YouTube yesterday. "I don't recognize this country anymore," Mo said. We have been saying some version of this line since 2015. Still, the relentless assaults on civil liberties, the breaking of political conventions and traditions, are enough to give us whiplash.

The phone rings. I don't usually answer unknown numbers, but now I answer every call, hoping that it will be news of Sam. Most of the time, I hang up before the caller can tell me what they'd like to do to me for killing my wife.

"Hi. Is this Ali Mirza?"

"Speaking."

"I'm Jenny Burns from *The Plain Dealer.* We're, um, doing a story about your, um, partner's disappearance and the fallout on social media. I've interviewed a bunch of her students and colleagues, and I was calling to get a quote from you?"

My brain freezes. To talk or to hang up. If the latter, is that an admission of guilt? But if I talk, what do I say? Defend myself against a faceless mob on social media? I suddenly find myself longing for Abba's counsel. Alone, I am a cork bobbing on a dark ocean. Despite our estrangement, my father would know how to save me.

"Ms. Mirza? Are you still there?"

"I'm here," I say quickly. "What do you want to know?"

"Well, I have the basic facts about the—disappearance—from the police report. I guess I was more interested in the backlash on social media. I mean, some of those comments are quite racist. Are you surprised by them?"

"Not really," I hear myself saying. "Not so much any more."

"You're so right," Jenny says. "People are so crazy these days."

Before I can react, she says, "But also, I spoke to a bunch of folks at CSU? And I'm sorry to say this, Ms. Mirza . . ."

"Please, call me Ali."

"Great. Ali. Sorry to say this, Ali, but many of them appear to be finding fault with you. That is, a couple of them are even, like, suspicious of you?"

The July sun is burning my face and arms, but that's not why I'm sweating. "Suspicious of what? My wife is missing and—

"Yeah, see, that's it exactly. They're wondering why you didn't call the cops on the very first day, why you have been seen out and about with friends at Blossom and at Market Garden Brewery, and why Samantha went missing right after you had a fight with her at the party."

I am so furious, I want to bite off Jenny Burns's sanctimonious head. In this moment I hate everyone—Jenny with her faux concern, Candace for her smug, self-righteous troublemaking, the online mob for wiping their salivating mouths on the sleeve of my misery, and yes, even Sam.

"Nope," I snap. "I'm not playing this game. I don't have to defend my actions to anyone. Not to Sam's students, not to you, not to the holier-than-thou idiots on Twitter and Facebook."

"Ali, please. I'm just trying to set the record straight. Candace Brickman says . . ."

"There's no record to set straight. This is between me and my wife. Candace Brickman is just an attention-seeker. This is nobody else's business."

"That's where you're wrong." Jenny's voice is soft, but I hear the threat curled in her words.

My hands are shaking so bad, I can barely hold my phone. "I appreciate your calling," I say. "But I really must go now."

I hang up. I try to steady one trembling hand with the other. My T-shirt is soaked with sweat. After a while I reopen the DeLillo, but the words swim before my eyes and I give up. Before I can talk myself out of it, I call Abba in Columbus.

He answers on the third ring. "Hello? Aliya? How are you, jaan?" His voice is so warm and loving, tears roll down my cheeks instantly. I've been drifting for days, and Abba makes me feel as if I've reached the shore.

"Abba, I'm in trouble. Please help me."

10

▾ ▸ ▴ ◂ ▾ ▴ ▸ ▴

Thursday, July 11

I walk to the Shell station at 7 a.m. and grab a copy of *The Plain Dealer*, wanting to see the article in print. It's worse than I feared. "CSU Professor Gone Missing; Students Blame Spouse." Front page story; above the fold. The world is burning, the glaciers are melting, and *this* is what my local paper decides to splash across the page.

At home, I read the article with a growing sense of disbelief. Jenny Burns has also interviewed Sam's colleagues and students. The faculty are circumspect, but they express their hurt and astonishment that I hadn't personally reached out to them with the news. Sam's grad students, most of whom I've met, are predictably in shock; Sam is an enormously popular teacher. The undergrads, who I don't know, are brutal. One of them actually mentions the novel, *Gone Girl*, although it's unclear as to whether she's read it, because she appears to be accusing me of having something to do with Sam's disappearance.

To my chagrin, Jenny Burns has also interviewed a few of our neighbors. Carol, the older lady who lives in the brick house across from us, is complimentary. "They are a very nice couple. Always helpful and kind. Sam plants flowers for me each summer. Ali brought me chicken curry when I was sick last year." It was actually Moroccan chicken in gravy, but Americans refer to all Indian food as curry. The other neighbors, most of whom I don't know by name, are less effusive. "I see them walk around the neighborhood in the evenings sometimes," someone named

Bob Jones says. "They seem normal enough. But you never know about people these days."

The story jumps to page eight. There's a quote from Frances Dowd, the department secretary. I like Frances—she's a petite, religious woman, and a hard worker, according to Sam. But what she says stops me in my tracks: "I spoke to Samantha on Friday morning," she says. "She came into the main office for some supplies. And I noticed she looked sad. Sad and tired. As if she had, I don't know, a premonition or something. Or, as if she was afraid of something."

I frown, trying to remember Sam's mood on the way to the party that Sunday evening. She'd seemed her usual self: chatty, funny, holding my hand as she drove. Had Frances seen something I hadn't? Or was this a case of the human brain trying to, in retrospect, ascribe meaning to an otherwise ordinary interaction?

The article ends with news of a vigil organized by Candace, which will be held next Friday in front of the student center. "It would be so great if Ali Mirza shows up to this," she says. "It would show that she supports us in our grief."

I look around my living room, as if I expect someone else to react, raise their eyebrows at Candace's arrogance. *Our grief? You fucking parasitic, limelight-seeking idiot.* I have loved Sam from the minute I saw her walking across the University of Michigan campus eight years ago, her head buried in a book of poems by Adrienne Rich. She almost bumped into me, looked up from the book long enough to apologize, and smiled. And I was a goner. In fact, I was so struck by her that I actually turned around and followed her into Angell Hall, where the English department was housed, got into the elevator with her and introduced myself. She was working on her PhD while I was getting my master's. Two days later, I signed up for the American lit class where she was the teaching assistant. It was a big class, but she had memorized many of our names within the first two weeks, something the professor never did. I went to her office hours, sent her emails asking questions about the texts we were reading, attended the Elizabeth Bishop discussion group that she led every Friday at a nearby watering hole. The day after the final grades were turned in, I asked her out. She said no. Said she was flattered, but that she was straight. We spoke a little longer and she agreed to have dinner with me. We ate at a Thai place near campus that evening, then I cooked for her the following night. We have been inseparable ever since.

But we have paid a price for being together. Neither of our parents supported our union. Sam and I had driven to southern Ohio to hand-deliver our wedding invitation to her folks, which is when Joe kicked us out of his house. Fearful of another rejection, I'd phoned Abba to give him the news, fully expecting a lecture on how Islam considers homosexuality haram, and how I needed to find my way back to Allah—the same sermon I'd received from the time I was fourteen. But his response had been surprisingly modulated. "Aliya," he'd said, "you know I can't attend your nuptials. Yasmin would never tolerate it. I'm sorry. I cannot condone such actions, even if they're now legal. I am not concerned with what the US Supreme Court says. I answer to a higher court. But I pray for both your and Samantha's good health daily. May Allah guide your actions."

We were married in August 2015 at a friend's house along the banks of Lake Michigan. We had invited all our friends from grad school and most everybody came. Mo and Sally gave us away. We both wore Hawaiian shirts and white shorts and after the ceremony, all of us played volleyball on the beach. Later that evening, after we'd showered and changed into white pantsuits for the reception, Sam and I danced our first dance as a married couple to "Happy Together," by the Turtles. She mimed the words to me as it played, vamping it, until I got a cramp in my side from laughing. She was radiant that evening, her red hair set aflame by the evening sun, those blue eyes sparkling like the waters behind us. Sam had always been so serious and responsible throughout her life, placating and managing her moody, drunk father, that when she cut loose, she was like a candle that had been lit from within. She was incandescent that day. We'd gone to Niagara-on-the-Lake for our honeymoon, rented a room at a B and B for four nights. It was all we could afford. We couldn't keep our hands off each other. I honestly hadn't expected anything to change just because we'd exchanged some formal vows, but it did. Our lovemaking was as passionate as ever, but there was a new tenderness there that emptied me out. On the streets, in public, we were careful around each other, but still, I noticed how guys used to turn around to stare at us, knew that we made for an attractive couple: she tall, me short; light and dark; girl-next-door and exotic stranger. In bed, I'd link my fingers through hers and gaze at our intertwined hands, our skin so different in color and yet so alike in how we could make it tingle and burn. And I would think, this is what it's all about, this miracle, this is why people fight wars, this is why they pass laws controlling women's bodies, this thing is too big, too powerful, no wonder they want to tame it, regulate it. "Whatcha thinking?" Sam would say, turning to me and smiling that slow, lazy smile, her face so close that I could count the freckles that dotted her nose and cheeks. And I would answer in the only language I truly believed in, the scripture of the body.

I shake myself out of this reverie, go upstairs to make Abba's bed. He is arriving at noon and it's a measure of how isolated I feel that I'm looking forward to his visit.

11

▼ ▶ ▲ ◀ ▼ ▲ ▶ ▲

Thursday, July 11

Abba has lost weight. It's the first thing I notice when he exits from his black Saab. He is wearing white cotton pajamas and a white kurta, the way he dresses to go to the mosque. We embrace in the driveway, and I'm relieved to see that Yasmin has not accompanied him. I try to take his suitcase, but he won't let me. Instead, he hands me a large tiffin box. "Food from the restaurant," he says. "Goat biryani, chicken tikka. Some vegetable dishes. Made fresh for you this morning by Hussain himself. He's retired but came to the restaurant this morning to cook for you."

Hussain was the chef in Abba's first restaurant. Abba had brought him from Pakistan when I was three years old. Each time I visited Moti Palace, he would give me a gulab jamun before we ate our meal, despite Mummy's protestations. "Sweet for my sweetie," he'd say in his thickly accented English.

"That's so nice of him. How is he?"

"Fine. Old. Like me."

Abba has never visited our home in Cleveland Heights. I see him nod approvingly to himself as he takes in the open floor plan, the way the kitchen leads to the well-appointed living room. I see him run his fingers along the beautiful granite counters, then notice the large Rothko print in the living room. He compliments me on the nineteenth-century tiger maple side tables that flank the modern couch. I have tied different aesthetic elements together to give the living room the airy coolness of an art gallery, along with the warmth of a lived-in home. I feel a rush of pride. This is the home that we have created, Sam and me. This is what we have accomplished, two women on our own, without the help or support of family.

"How is Yasmin?" I ask after we've settled on the couch.

He shrugs. "Good. The same."

I smile to myself. Abba may be thinner and older, but he is as taciturn as ever. Man of Few Words, Mummy used to tease him.

As if he has read my mind he says, "Yesterday was your mother's death anniversary. Did you remember?"

I swallow. "No, Abba, I didn't. I've just been . . . so . . . you know."

"Ah, yes, the Samantha business," he says. It sounds callous, the dismissive way he says it, but his eyes are warm and burdened. They search my face for a long moment, before he sighs and says, "Oh, Aliya. You have traveled so very far away from us."

I surprise myself by shifting to snuggle with him, and he puts his arms around me. I have missed him, despite whatever ugliness has sprouted between us since he married Yasmin or whatever differences we have. "I'm glad you're here, Abba," I say. "I've felt really alone this past week."

"My gudiya," he says, his childhood name for me. *My doll.* That's what he used to call me when I was little, before Mummy died and he sublimated his grief in religion; before he married Yasmin, a devout Muslim woman so different from my secular, liberal mom that it was as if he wanted to erase all memory of Mummy; before I discovered my attraction to girls when I was thirteen. Abba keeps one arm around me as he reaches for the newspaper on the coffee table. His face gets angrier as he reads Jenny Burns's article.

"This is a piece-of-shit story," he says at last. "I thought this was a respectable newspaper. Why didn't she give you a chance to rebut all these charges?"

"She did, Abba," I say. "But I told her it was nobody's business."

He wags his finger before I can finish. "No, no, no, Aliya. That is a big mistake. These goras will want to make you the villain. You must grab the microphone to proclaim your innocence."

It irritates me how Abba reflexively makes everything about race and religion. But he's an immigrant, whereas I'm American by birth and sensibility. And yet, haven't I been hyperaware of my brown skin these past ten days, in ways I never was before? As aghast as I was at the assaults on people of color these last few years, I was able to carve out exceptions to separate me from *them*—my parents had come to this country legally (sorry, Dreamers); I was safely ensconced in America (sorry, citizens of countries facing the Muslim ban); I was educated and had gone to good schools (sorry, Hispanics working at meat processing plants in twelve-hour shifts). I had a white American wife, lived in a city so liberal that it was sometimes called the People's Republic of Cleveland Heights, and ran a thriving business.

"Aliya?" he says, and I bring myself back to the present.

"Why should I, Abba?" I say. "I *am* innocent. It's not like the cops have accused me of anything."

He sighs, shakes his head. "Right now, it's the court of public opinion that matters, beta."

After a minute, he rises and says, "Chalo. Let's warm up some of the food I've brought. No one can think on an empty stomach."

Food. The Indian parents' antidote to all of life's problems.

Herrington calls while Abba is taking a nap after lunch. "Are you home, Ms. Mirza?" he asks. "I'd like to stop by this afternoon."

"Is it . . . bad news?" I ask. "Have you found her?" What I mean is, Have you found her body? My hands turn icy cold.

"No, no, nothing like that. Just a few developments to go over."

After we disconnect, I wake Abba up.

"Let me go change," he says. Ever since I was a girl, Abba has tried to drill this in my head: Clothes command respect. He must've had such a hard time dealing with his tomboy daughter, whose uniform was shorts or jeans and T-shirts.

Herrington arrives a short while later, and I lead him into the living room. "Your company's gone?" he asks, and I nod. My nerves are too fraught to make small talk.

Herrington reports his news: A neighbor on our street had called the cops this morning to say that he'd seen Sam jog past his front porch on that fateful morning. "We already know that she did go running," Herrington says. "But now we have a time. The neighbor said it was just getting light outside. He placed the time around six a.m. or so."

"That sounds about right." My voice is tight with tension. "Which neighbor was this? Why did he wait this long to contact you?"

"He left town that same afternoon and just returned home. He saw the newspaper story and recognized Samantha."

"Can I reach out to him?"

Herrington hesitates. "I can't stop you from talking to a neighbor, of course. But honestly, there's not much more to it. The main thing is, we now have a timeline."

"Well, yes. But with all due respect, Detective, my wife has been missing for over ten days and we're no closer to finding her. If you recall, I'd offered to go door to door. You talked me out of it."

"That's because I didn't want you to interfere with our investigation. And we did knock on doors. Nobody else has come forward to say they've seen her."

"Why can't we put up posters all over the neighborhood? Why can't I offer a reward?"

"Again, I can't stop you. But I will caution you—we're going to be deluged with hoaxes and false tips. And we still can't rule out that she decided to go away somewhere. No law against that. Maybe she had a plan."

"What about the blood on the sidewalk?"

He grimaces. "There's that."

"And she hasn't used her personal credit card even once."

"Maybe she doesn't want to be found."

I shake my head. "Not possible. Sam would never . . ."

"But you guys had had a fight, yes?" Herrington clears his throat, looks at me. "Ms. Mirza. We went through your wife's phone. Seems like the two of you have had quite a tumultuous marriage. There were some older texts we found. They were pretty angry."

I freeze. Abba walks in just then and I've never been happier to see him. He has switched into Western clothes. "Hello, hello," he says heartily, extending his hand. "I'm Irfan Mirza. Aliya's dad. Pleased to meet you."

Herrington rises to shake my father's hand.

"Please," Abba says. "Sit." He is acting as if Herrington is a guest at one of his restaurants. "I heard the last bit of what you said. 'A tumultuous marriage.' I would say that describes eighty percent of all marriages, wouldn't you?"

Herrington looks quickly from me to Abba. "I guess so," he concedes. He turns to face me. "But here's what troubles me, Ms. Mirza. Seven of your text messages were deleted the day you reported your wife's disappearance. In fact, they appear to have been erased during the time we were at your house, taking down the original complaint. We were able to recover them."

Abba is sitting directly across from me, a stricken look on his face. Before I can say anything, he says to me in Hindi, "Don't lie. Tell him the truth."

"What's that?" Herrington says, suspicious.

"I told my daughter to come clean. To tell the truth." Abba speaks clearly, enunciating each word. "Because she has nothing to hide."

"That's good advice, sir." He turns to me. "Ma'am?"

The words come out in a rush. "I was nervous. The day you came to the house. You must understand, I'd never so much as talked to a cop before. I mean, other than during a traffic stop or two. And I was ashamed. Sam and I texted awful things to each other that night, and many other days, but it didn't matter. Deep down, no matter how angry we were at each other, we knew it would pass. But you see, there was no way I could explain this to strangers. I knew how those messages would register to someone else reading them. So, I panicked."

"Which, under the circumstances, is totally understandable, isn't it?" Abba interjects. After all, her beloved"—am I the only one who hears the vibration in his voice when he says the word?—"had gone missing." He pauses. "Also, in our culture, it is unseemly to air one's dirty linen in public. So, there are cultural differences at play here."

I wince inwardly at Abba's playing of the religion card. But it appears to work. "I understand," Herrington says. "But Ms. Mirza. If we are to help, we need full cooperation from you. No more secrets. We're on the same team here."

The last sentence breathes new life into me, and I go from feeling like a suspect to a collaborator in an instant. For the first time since this ordeal has started, I feel like myself again, like I am reentering my own body. And it's all thanks to Abba.

Abba brings up the newspaper article, how biased it appears, but Herrington merely shrugs, says something derogatory about the media. *Fake news*. That damning phrase is everywhere these days.

Abba is in his element now. He offers Herrington some Indian chai and, after the officer demurs, extolls the virtues of Indian cuisine, the best in the world according to Abba, and manages to slip in the fact that he now owns three of the finest Indian restaurants in the Columbus area, with a new one soon opening in Louisville, Kentucky. Next, he brags about my firm, name-drops former clients like Sherwin Williams and American Greetings, among others. Even as I'm digesting the fact that Abba has been following my career from afar, I'm cringing at how blatantly he's trying to impress Herrington. I flinch when I hear him say, "Aliya. Go give this nice man one of your business cards." And before I can react, "The next time you're in Columbus, my friend, you must dine at one of my restaurants. My treat, of course."

Herrington has a bemused expression on his face when he takes our leave. In the driveway, he turns to me and says, "Your father is an interesting man." I open my mouth to apologize, when he says, "You're lucky to have someone who loves you so much. And is so obviously proud of you."

Our eyes meet. I get the distinct feeling that Herrington hasn't been as lucky in his own life.

"So, what's next, Detective?" I ask.

He sighs. "I'm going through our regional intelligence sharing system again. If there's anyone who shows up matching Samantha's description, I'll be on it quicker than a tick on a deer."

As Herrington drives away, I see two of my neighbors from across the street on their front porches staring at me, not even pretending to look away when I half-wave. Eric, Carol's troubled grandson who spends each summer with her, is standing with his dog on the sidewalk in front of my house. He doesn't move until I look at him pointedly. As he walks past me, he mutters, "Fucking dyke."

The Ali that I was two weeks ago would've yelled at him as I did at last year's block party. Instead, I stand rooted in place. I don't want to draw any more attention to myself. My skin tingles as I go back in the house. I'm public property now. My house is a glass cube, my life an open book.

Last month Sam and I had put up a rainbow flag for Pride. Now, I curse myself for not having taken it down. I want to erase every marker of difference: The Pride flag in the front yard; Abba's traditional Indian clothes; the ethnic, ingratiating way in which he spoke to the police officer; the smell of the Indian food that wafts from our kitchen into our neighbors' yards. Last year, at Target, the friendly cashier had asked me where I was from. She looked confused when I said Columbus.

Maybe Abba is right. Maybe, when they look at me, all they see—all they've ever seen—is an alien, someone unlike them; maybe the human eye is unable to look beyond skin color, incapable of penetrating the veil of difference. In which case, my entire life has been, if not a lie, then a misunderstanding. I have misunderstood human nature. I've blinded myself to the ugly truths that are as old as history—that the majority will always pick on the minority, that many will always consider two people of the same gender married to one another to be freaks of nature, that civilization is a gloss covering up the basic truth—we are tribal animals, still swinging from trees.

My age of innocence is over. Sam is gone. And I'm all alone, left to face the music.

12

▼ ▶ ▲ ◀ ▼ ▲ ▶ ▲

Friday, July 12

Abba announced this morning that he has decided to extend his stay. He has spent the morning talking to Yasmin and to his deputy, Vikas, who helps Abba run his restaurants. I feel a new appreciation for how hard Abba still works, how he has built a small empire from nothing. He'd come to the US to study engineering at Ohio State with two hundred dollars in his pocket. He'd graduated at the top of his class and had five job offers before graduation. But three years in the corporate world in Chicago had left him feeling frustrated and restless. Then he met Mummy, and she exposed him to a world of books and art and independent cinema. On their third date, after a mediocre meal at an Indian restaurant, he spoke nostalgically about learning to cook from his grandfather, who had been a private chef to a nawab in Hyderabad. When Abba cooked for her the first time, Mummy said, "This food! Quit your miserable job and open a restaurant." After they wed, they'd moved back to Columbus to open Abba's first eatery because rents were too high in Chicago. Mummy and I used to stop by often on our way home from school, me doing my homework at one of the tables while Mummy pitched in with whatever Abba needed—designing a new menu or finding cheaper vendors from whom to buy the meat. He opened his second, Aliya's Bistro, two months before Mummy's breast cancer diagnosis.

After Abba married Yasmin, I was horrible to him, unable, at age twelve, to recognize that he was a man with needs separate from his devotion to his hellion daughter. Today, as a married woman myself,

I regret my teenage foolishness. "Abba," I blurt out. "Are you happy? With Yasmin, I mean?"

He turns his brown eyes on me and stares for a long time. "You're asking the wrong question," he finally says. "The secret to marriage is to not think of your own happiness. It's to think of your loved one's happiness. And I'm proud to say that Yasmin is happy with me, most of the time, anyway." He smiles wryly.

There's something so intrinsically Indian in this answer—the selflessness, the spirituality, but also the deflection—that it makes me chuckle. "But Abba," I say. "You were so happy with Mummy. I was young, but I remember."

He pulls on his lower lip. "That was different. She was my—everything. But she left me. Left us." A steely look comes into his eyes. "I mourned her death for two long years. But when my older sister, Allah bless her soul, said you needed a mother, she was right. I was busy with the two restaurants. You were growing up too fast and too defiant. And I . . . I was still a young man. I needed a wife."

"But Abba. Why didn't you find someone more like Mummy?"

"Aliya, there's so much you still don't understand. When you go to a restaurant, you don't order two of the same dishes, do you? You try different dishes, isn't it? Every human has their virtues, my child. Your mother opened my eyes to a world of poetry and art and whatnot. Yasmin opened my ears and eyes to a different kind of poetry—religion. To our Sufi saints, our Islamic poets like Rumi and Ghalib, and to the beauty of the Quran."

I think of the women I've dated, how different they were from each other, and I know Abba is right. How tragic that Abba met the love of his life and then lost her. My trajectory has been different—I'd dated some real doozies; how lucky I was to have met Sam after I'd sowed my wild oats, and to be married to her. Then, I remember that Sam isn't here, that she may be dead, and the coldness spreads through my chest.

We sit silently for a few minutes, lost in our thoughts. I look discreetly at the clock on the mantelpiece. I've already delayed going to work this morning, but I do need to go into the office today. My vacation has ended, but with Abba here, I'm reluctant to leave him alone at home. He notices my unease. "Go get ready, child," he says. "But eat something before you go."

There are several emails awaiting me at work. I open the one from Priscilla Hamilton first. She and her husband live in one of the most expensive homes in Pepper Pike. I'd sent her my drawings for her kitchen and bath renovation the day before I began my vacation. Priscilla writes:

> Dear Ali,
>
> Sorry to hear what is going on with your partner. Dick and I are praying for her safe return. But, in the light of all the negative publicity, I think it is best for us to part ways amicably. I'm sure you understand our predicament. We are going to go with a different designer, but as a goodwill gesture, we'd like to compensate you for your time. We would like you to keep the twenty percent that we've already paid. We are happy to return your drawings.
>
> Good luck,
> Priscilla S. Hamilton

I am so furious, my head throbs. What negative publicity, the article in *The Plain Dealer*? I'm to blame for that? And she wants me to settle for 20 percent after I've given her the drawings?

More surprises await. Three other clients write to say they won't be needing my services. I soon notice a pattern—former clients have written to me, expressing their disgust at the *Plain Dealer* article. One mentions Islamophobia; another refers to it as a "lynch mob mentality." But current clients are bailing out, twisting themselves into pretzels as they try to explain their sudden lack of confidence in my work. There's a bitter, chalky taste in my mouth. How easily the veneer of allyship, of liberalism, strips off under the slightest pressure.

There are other, supportive emails. From college friends I haven't seen in years. From two high school buddies I used to smoke weed with. From the wife of the manager of the small independent store where I bagged groceries when I was a teenager. Keep your chin up, writes this white lady, whom I barely remember, Fred always spoke so highly of your work ethic. Don't let the bastards bring you down.

I work the phones the rest of the afternoon, calling back those who've written to cancel projects. Some of them don't pick up. The ones who do are polite and distant. When I remind them about signed contracts, they turn sullen and hostile. "We took a chance on you, already," Bill Giles says. "But to delete your angry messages to your girlfriend? Who does that, if they have nothing to hide?"

I am so stunned, I am speechless.

"Hello? Are you there?" Bill says.

"I . . . what . . . how do you know about the deleted messages?"

He scoffs. "I guess you haven't read today's newspaper then," he says and hangs up.

My hands are trembling as I log on to Cleveland.com. I scroll until I find the story. It quotes an anonymous police source who revealed the erased texts. Herrington has refused to verify or deny the charge, the story says. A call to Aliya Mirza for confirmation has gone unanswered, it says. I strike my forehead in remorse. I had a missed call from Jenny Burns last evening. And I didn't call her back.

Another thought threads through my mind. We took a chance on you already, Bill had said. What fucking chance? I have a stellar professional reputation and an enviable client list. What did he mean? That he'd hired a Muslim? A gay woman? The way he said it, smug and righteous. Aggrieved.

Ali, I say to myself. You have bigger fish to fry here. Abba has been telling you for days—you need to wrestle the microphone out of the hands of "anonymous sources." It's time to seize the initiative. Tell your own story.

I call Herrington, who apologizes for the leak and promises an internal investigation. He once again says they have no leads at this time. "Do you . . . do you think Sam is still alive?" I hate the tremor in my voice.

"Let's hope so, Ms. Mirza." His voice is flat, emotionless.

I hang up and call Jenny Burns.

13

▼ ▶ ▲ ◀ ▼ ▲ ▶ ▲

Tuesday, July 16

I meet with her at my office. With Abba at home, I didn't want to invite her there. Besides, I want her to be impressed by the degrees and awards on my wall.

Jenny is in her early twenties. A rookie. She has straight dark hair, large eyes, freckles on her nose. Her hair is tied up in a ponytail. Against my better judgment, I like her. This is not a malicious person, just a young reporter who's clueless. And ambitious. A deadly combination.

"Ms. Mirza?" she says. She sounds a little breathless, and it occurs to me that she is nervous. This is a big story for her.

"It's Ali," I say with a smile. "Please, come sit. Would you like some coffee? Or a Coke or something?"

She shakes her head no, then changes her mind. "A Coke would be great. It's really humid outside."

"I know, right?" I grab two cans from the mini fridge.

"So, you said you wanted to talk?"

"Yeah. Just . . . you know, set the record straight." I lean forward, look deep into her eyes. Something about the deliberateness of the gesture feels fake to me, but I don't avert my glance.

"Right." Jenny pulls out a pen and notebook from her bag. "Why did you delete the texts to Samantha?"

There's not going to be any small talk. I clear my throat. "Well, as anyone who's been in a relationship knows, sometimes you say things you regret. That you don't even mean while you're saying or texting them."

"Then why say it?"

Jenny's judgmental tone reminds me of myself at that age. Maybe one's twenties are not the time for nuance or complexity. "Because I'm human," I say. My voice is even, measured. "I was mad at Sam that evening. We'd had a nasty fight, and I lashed out."

"What about?"

"Excuse me?"

"What'd you fight about?"

Surely this is not what Abba meant when he said to seize the mic? Right now, the microphone is very much in Jenny Burns's hands. "I'm sorry. I'm not gonna answer that. I mean, there's still a right to privacy in this country, right? My personal life is not for public consumption. It's not just my privacy I'm protecting. It's my wife's, too."

Jenny looks put off but recovers. "Fair enough. Okay, changing subjects, do you regret going to the concert at Blossom so soon after Sam went missing?"

"No, I don't. I had visitors from out of town. Detective Herrington himself advised me to go ahead with our plans." I rub my forehead. "Listen. This is precisely one of the things I want to talk about. There seems to be this presumption that there's a single, acceptable way to behave in my situation and that I'm not doing that. But people grieve differently, you know? It's not like one-size-fits-all."

"So, you're grieving?" Jenny says bluntly. "Why? Do you think Sam's . . . you know, like, gone forever?"

I stare at her open-mouthed. You tactless idiot, I think. Youth really makes people stupid. "My wife has been missing for over two weeks. The police have no clue as to what has happened to her. Of course, I'm grieving. I spend day and night trying to think of what I could've done differently. Why I didn't go on the run with her that morning. I'm consumed with regret and guilt—" I cut myself off, feeling myself choke up.

Jenny's face softens a bit. She shifts in her seat. "I'm sorry. I'm not trying to upset you. I'm just trying to do my job, is all."

"Do you know what your reporting has cost me, Jenny? I have lost five clients since your stories ran. Your first story about Sam's friends at CSU somehow made me come across as guilty. Guilty of what? For not jumping on the phone and announcing to her colleagues that she had disappeared? I understand that there are many people who care about Sam. But to compare their pain to mine? Would you have dared do this if we were a white, heterosexual couple?"

Jenny turns pale. "Are you accusing me of being a racist?" Her voice rises on the last word.

I rub my face wearily. "Look, I don't know you. But that's the point. You don't know me either. All I can tell you is that your initial story has given people permission to act out. Last evening, I went to get takeout from a nearby restaurant and a perfect stranger came up to me and said, 'I don't know why you're not out looking for your partner instead of stuffing your mouth.' Like, am I supposed to put up posters of Sam, like you do for a missing dog?"

"That's crazy," Jenny says, in her flat way.

"What I'm trying to say is, I don't understand why I'm even in the news. I am . . ." I wince at what I'm about to say, "I'm the victim here. I'm the grieving spouse. Not Candace, not anyone else. *Me.* And yet, I'm made to feel like the enemy."

"I'm sorry that you feel that way," Jenny says. Her tone turns righteous. "But you *did* erase those messages. Before giving Sam's phone to the cops."

I am about to defend myself again, when she cuts me off. "About the vigil. You're going to attend, right?"

I had indeed planned to go after Abba had convinced me that I needed to. But something about that "right?," the presumption of it, rubs me the wrong way.

"No," I say shortly. "I'm going to be washing my hair that night."

I regret the flippant words as soon as I register the expression on

Jenny's face. "Wow," she says. "Those folks are just trying to help, you know."

This was a bad idea. I'm not Abba, my charming, unflappable father. I am stuck with my own personality—impetuous, blunt, trigger-tempered. "I know. But the only thing that can help is for Sam to be home when I get there."

"Okay, well. Do you want to add anything?" Jenny asks.

"Listen, that last thing I said? About washing my hair? That was obviously a joke. Do you mind deleting that?"

Jenny shuts her notebook. "This whole interview was on the record," she says.

I stare at her helplessly, knowing I need to make amends. Quickly. "I want to announce a reward," I say. "For any tip that will lead to Samantha."

Jenny perks up, reopens her book. "Great," she says. "What's the reward?"

I close my eyes. I have no idea where I will get the money from. And I should have run this by Herrington first. But here I am. "Twenty-five thousand," I say.

"And I have an exclusive?" Jenny says. She tries, but she can't keep the excitement out of her voice.

"Sure," I say. "When will this run?"

"I'll try and convince my editors to run it tomorrow," she says. "Which, I'm confident they will."

I am already nervous about this step, remembering Herrington's warning about crank calls and fake tips. But it's too late. Besides, maybe it will feel good to be doing something rather than moping around the house praying for Samantha to show up. To hell with Herrington and everyone else. Maybe this step will flush Samantha out from wherever she is.

We talk for another few minutes and then I walk Jenny Burns out of my office. It's only when I return that I notice that my hands are shaking.

14

▼ ▶ ▲ ◀ ▼ ▲ ▶ ▲

Wednesday, July 17

Jenny Burns keeps her word. The story announcing the reward is in the paper today.

But if I'd hoped that the news of the reward would overshadow everything else, I am wrong. It is a strange article that can't decide which angle to play up. The headline reads, "Spouse of Missing Woman Offers $25,000 Reward," but although the quotes are not inaccurate, they are without context, and make me come across as a stubborn, defensive asshole. In other words, the opposite of what I hoped to gain by talking to her. I can't decipher if Jenny is malicious, or if she's too unskilled and inexperienced to be able to contextualize what I'd said. The article also states that my mention of the reward came at the end of the interview and although Jenny doesn't say it, the clear implication is that the reward was my attempt to paper over questions about the deleted texts.

The story ends with my thoughtless "I'm going to be washing my hair" quote, followed by a statement from—who else?—Candace. "It's a pity Ali doesn't wish to show up for a vigil for her own wife. But we are undeterred. We will hold a vigil for Professor O'Malley no matter how long it takes."

Candace. Self-appointed keeper of the flame.

Clearly, talking to Jenny has been a mistake. There really is no way to seize the narrative or shape it. If there is, I'm lousy at the task. The most I can hope for is that the offer of a reward will yield some information about Sam's whereabouts.

The social media campaign against me continues unabated. I've tried to avoid going on most of these sites, but sometimes my curiosity gets the better of me. People on Twitter are asking if the cops have done a thorough search of our home. The picture of the flower bed that Sam had dug has been shared a few thousand times, along with the insinuation that Sam's body is buried there. It would all be laughable, if it wasn't so hurtful. There is actually a guy on Twitter, @ManlyMan85, who claims that the police are being politically correct and covering up Sam's disappearance because I am Muslim and they don't want an "Islamic jihad." Just yesterday he'd posted, "Imagine if me, a straight, white dude, had deleted angry texts to my wife. I'd be in Gitmo by now." I don't know what bugs me more—his bad grammar or his misguided politics.

I know I should get dressed and go to the office, but I don't. I can't. Instead, I check email. There are supportive emails from friends, indignant about today's story. *How dare she?* writes an old college friend. *She doesn't know you at all.*

There's one from Mo. "Hey," she says, "tone down the sarcasm during interviews, will you? You're not doing yourself any favors. In any case, this article is bullshit, and the writer is a hack."

It's 5 a.m. in California. Mo must've risen early to look at the Cleveland.com website. I am so grateful for her friendship.

There is no winning this battle. And I've already become cynical enough that I'm grateful for the fact that the article ran on a Wednesday instead of in the Sunday papers.

I hear Abba moving in his room, and a few minutes later, he comes down the stairs. He has already showered and dressed. "You offered a reward?" he says, without preamble as he comes into the living room and takes a seat across from me. "I thought the detective fellow asked you to wait?"

"I know," I mumble. "It just slipped out." I look at him defiantly. "In any case, it's what I've decided to do."

"Okay, Aliya, I support your decision. But where's the money coming from?"

"I have some investments. I'll call the broker."

"Nonsense. Do not touch those." He pulls out a checkbook from his pocket. "I'll give you the money."

"Abba, stop. I'm not going to take money from you."

His face flushes with exasperation. "Why not? Do I have ten children that I'm going to leave my money to? Why can't I help my only child if I want to?"

"Because Abba." My voice cracks. "I have created this mess, and I have to be responsible for it."

"Rubbish! Don't talk like an American," Abba says. "All this nonsense about 'responsible.' I'm your father. You are *my* responsibility." He takes the pen from the coffee table and flips open his checkbook, rapidly penning my name and the amount. "There. Put this in your account today."

"Abba, let's talk about this if and when there's a genuine tip. For now . . ."

"Aliya. So much stubbornness! For once listen to your old father. Deposit the check. And by the way, you need to call that police officer and tell him what you've done."

"Thank you, Abba," I say. I have no more fight left in me. And the last person I want to argue with is the man sitting across from me, whose face radiates such kindness. Just then, my phone lights up. "It's Herrington," I mouth to Abba as I put him on speakerphone. I brace myself for a reprimand.

But I'm pleasantly surprised. Herrington is in a conciliatory mood. "I guess it's time," he says. "Let's see if the reward flushes anyone out of the woodwork, given that we've reached a dead end."

The police have already received thirty-five tips since this morning, Herrington says, the farthest one being from Xenia, Ohio. "It'll take time to sort these out," Herrington says, and I can hear the weariness in his voice.

"Thank you," I say. "And I am sorry to be adding to your workload."

He sighs. "No worries," he says. "If one of these yields some information, it'll all be worth it."

Abba nods approvingly when I hang up. "He's a hardworking fellow," he says, and I smile to myself, knowing that, in my father's book, this is the highest praise that can be showered upon another person.

15

▾ ▸ ▴ ◂ ▾ ▴ ▸ ▴

Friday, July 19

My heart is heavy. Abba is leaving tomorrow. He asked me last night if I wanted to go with him to Columbus for a few weeks, but of course I can't. I need to be here for when Sam comes home. And I don't want to be seen as running away. Each time I step out of the house, I feel the eyes of my neighbors on me. Just last night, at dusk, I'd quietly taken down the rainbow flag from outside our home.

"Are you ready, Abba?" I call out. "I'm hungry."

"Two more minutes," he yells.

He comes downstairs carrying a small box from Amazon. "I ordered this for you, and it came yesterday," he says.

"What is it?"

He waves his hand. "Open it after I leave. It will help you."

"Why can't I open it now?"

"Aliya," he says, exasperated. "You were like this even as a little child. If I said turn left, you automatically turned right. Nothing has changed."

I roll my eyes. "Okay, Abba." I put the box on the dining room table. "You ready?"

Stone Oven is crowded when we get there. The first person I see is Stella Artie, an older woman who lives one street over from us. During our after-dinner walks, Sam and I often walk past Stella's home with its beautifully planned English garden. Our backyard has several ferns that Stella has given us over the years. I smile and wave to her from across the room. She doesn't wave back, and I think she hasn't seen me. But she's looking directly at me. My stomach lurches as the meaning of her unfriendliness becomes clear. I look straight ahead, not wanting Abba to notice. Somehow, the humiliation will be compounded if he sees. All my life, Abba has told me that despite the fact that I was born in this country, I will never be fully accepted. "It's a racist country, beta," he used to say. "Your Muslim name, your skin color, your religion will always make you stand apart. I'm telling you, white people will always judge you by these things. The only place you'll be seen as American? In India."

"But I *am* American," I'd argue with him.

Abba would click his tongue. "Doesn't matter. Doesn't matter how you see yourself. This country will always see you as foreign. You're making a big mistake, not going to mosque. That's the only place you'll be accepted, is by your fellow Muslims."

And I'd think of my high school friends Angelo and Greta and Mallory—all of us listening to the same rock bands, all of us loving the same movies, all of us nerdy and artistic and think, Bullshit. Abba still has the immigrant mindset. What he believes doesn't apply to me.

It was one of the reasons Abba was so afraid of my being gay. "You don't think it's enough being a religious minority?" he once said to me when I was a teenager. "Now you need to be a gay, also? So that even your Muslim brothers and sisters will reject you? What kind of a life do you wish to build, Aliya?"

"It's not a choice, Abba. It's who I am."

"Nonsense. Who we are is always a choice. We build our own moral characters."

"Being gay is not immoral. I've been reading about it. It is not a choice."

"Then you must read better books. Ones that will guide you better."

"Did you choose to be straight?"

His brow furrowed as he muttered something in Hindi under his breath. "I'm going to get you married to a nice boy from India when you turn eighteen," he said.

"Like hell you will. You're not in India anymore, Abba. I'm getting out of this house as soon as I can."

And I did, getting admission to Smith when I was seventeen.

Now, I walk Abba to an open table by the large windows and take his breakfast order. "Black coffee and one of those delicious-looking pastries," he says. "You choose."

At the counter, I order our coffees and more goodies than I know we'll be able to eat. The thought of Abba leaving tomorrow is dragging me down, and sugar has always been my family's way of dealing with unspoken grief. As I wait for my order, Tatyana, the co-owner of the bakery, comes up and puts her arm around me. "Hey, girl," she says. "How you doing?"

"Hi, Tats," I say. "Okay, I guess. How are you and Claudio?"

"We're good." She stares at me with those beautiful hazel eyes. "Listen, I'm sick about Sam. And I just wanted to say, those newspaper articles are shitty. I can't believe they're putting you through that shit. But you keep your chin up, okay? You have lots of friends. Don't let those fuckers drag you down."

And right in the middle of Stone Oven, my eyes fill with tears. "Thanks, Tatyana."

"Of course." She hits me lightly on my upper arm. "Remember, we immigrants, we gotta stick together."

Tatyana is from the former Soviet Union. I was born here. But I don't bother correcting her. From our previous conversations, I know we have a lot in common—we both love this country fiercely, our sadness at what's going on in direct proportion to our love. On the surface, we are different—Tatyana is white, tall, beautiful, Jewish. But looking at her kind, worried face, I know she understands what this Muslim girl is going through. "Thanks," I say again. It's all I can manage.

"Go sit down," she says. "I'll make you some fresh coffee."

She carries our drinks to our table and tells Abba she's honored to meet him. After she leaves, he sighs. "There are good people in this world, also," he says.

"Yes, there are."

"Now, more people understand what people like me have always known," he continues. "All the racism and ugliness is now out in the open."

"Did you—did you face a lot of discrimination when you came here, Abba?"

He cuts his strawberry and cream cheese croissant, puts half on my plate. "You know that I graduated top of my engineering class," he says. "And that I was hired by one of the best firms in Chicago. But when it was time to head major projects, or to be promoted, they always found an excuse to give it to a mediocre white guy. Sometimes, I had recruited and trained the very people who got the promotions. And of course, they always had a good reason for it. They would tell me to be patient, that it would soon be my turn. It never was."

"I'm sorry, Abba."

He doesn't say anything, but what I see on his face makes my heart ache. "Your mother was the only reason I didn't pack up and go back to India. Aliya, don't get me wrong. I'm happy with whatever success I've had at my restaurants. I've done well for myself. But this line of work is so far from what I'd wanted to do with my life. My ambition was to build great public works. Now, I just feed hungry mouths."

We are both silent. Then he sits up straight and says, "But so what? What I couldn't do, my daughter is achieving. You are my greatest engineering project, Aliya. I'm so proud of you."

He's never spoken to me like this. For the first time, I really take note of his face—the gray at the temples, the crow's feet at his eyes, the lines on his face. Abba is growing old. I have missed so much time with him, my sexuality a wall that kept us exiled in essentially two different countries. I reach for his hand. "Abba," I say. "I've . . . I've so enjoyed this time with you. Despite the awful circumstances. Once Sam comes home, please, will you visit us again? You will really like her, I promise. Abba, she's as honorable a person as you are, I swear."

I know both of us are thinking the same thing—Yasmin. It is Yasmin, with her self-righteous bigotry, that has kept my father from me. He squeezes my hand. "Yes," he says simply. "I've missed you very much also, beta. It's as if half of my heart has been absent all these years." Then, his eyes turn cloudy. "Do you think Samantha will show up?"

I hear the unspoken questions behind the question: Is Sam alive? Is she hiding from me? Has she been kidnapped? Will she return home?

I force myself to meet his eyes. "Yes, I do," I say. "I'm sure she will."

He raises his coffee mug. "Inshallah," he says. "Here's to her safe return."

16

▼ ▶ ▲ ◀ ▼ ▲ ▶ ▲

Monday, July 22

It's raining outside, and with the windows open, a cool breeze comes into the bedroom. The breeze carries in with it a pain so sharp that it makes me weak. I'm missing my girl tonight in a way that makes sleep impossible, that makes each breath hurt. She's out there somewhere, wondering why I've abandoned her. *Is* she out there somewhere? Or is Sam . . . I force myself to contemplate the impossible, although the thought makes me want to rip my eyeballs out . . . dead? Is it possible that while I'm going through my days Sam is dead in a ravine or woods somewhere?

The images that flash through my mind are so heinous, I yell out loud as I push away the covers and leap out of bed. I use the bathroom, then make my way downstairs to the kitchen to get a drink of ice water. I turn on the lights, stand there for a minute. I want to bang on every single door in this neighborhood, scream her name so loud that she will hear me, loud enough to wake up the dead.

I feel you on my skin when you're away. That's what she'd whispered to me that second night in Ravello on the Amalfi coast, an extravagance we couldn't really afford. Sam was a new professor at that time, and I was struggling to get my business off the ground. We'd both been working to the point of exhaustion—we'd have dinner and then stay up until midnight, she, writing lecture notes and grading papers, and me, answering emails from clients, working up estimates as I attempted to underbid more established designers, revising my drawings, checking out prices from new suppliers. We felt disconnected from one another, but there was no way around it. And then one day, I said fuck it, looked up hotels in Capri and along the Amalfi coast—because Sam had told me years ago that this was one of the places on her bucket list—and charged two airline tickets on my credit card.

We were sitting in bed in our tiny room, looking out at the coast. The full moon had broken into a million pieces of silver on the still water. This is magical, I whispered. She shifted closer to me. I've missed you, she said. Me, too, I said. You know, work has been so time consuming . . .

She squeezed my hand and turned to look at me. In the light of the moon, I saw the expression on her face, and it made my stomach flip. It doesn't matter, she said. I feel you on my skin when you're away. And then, she took her index finger and ran it across my entire arm, lightly, slowly, until all the hair on that arm stood up. She noticed, giggled.

I kissed her hard and she kissed me back. We undressed swiftly in the dark. And when I at long last found my way into her, she arched her back and rose to meet me and moved against my hand. It was as if our desire for each other was so strong, it could only be expressed in that way, with thrust and force and sweat and tangle. Nothing existed except Sam's incandescent body, her animal scent, my hand inside her so perfect, so right, as if it belonged to her, rather than to me.

I feel Sam on my skin, too. Which is how I know she's not dead. Do I dare believe this? Do I dare *not* believe it?

It is 3 a.m. I make myself a slice of toast, then wander into the dining room, where I notice the box on the table. Oh shit. I've forgotten to open Abba's gift.

It is a used copy of a book called *The Divine Mystery of Islam: A Spiritual Journey.* I shake my head; Abba doesn't know when to quit. The typed gift card from Amazon reads:

To my dearest daughter,
May the teachings of Allah find a home in your heart,
Yours, Abba

I take the book into the living room and flip through it while eating my toast. A dog barks a few houses down. The book seems interesting enough, but it's not my cup of tea. Sorry, Abba, I think. Nice try, though, trying to convert me while I'm at my weakest. I'm about to set the book aside, when I come across the line: "I trusted that God would make a way for me—not because of who I am, but because of how merciful and loving He is."

I nod to myself, note the page number before I set the book down. I observe my gut reaction to that line. Aliya, I say to myself, don't get sentimental, okay? This is all too predictable. You don't even believe in God, remember? And you don't need anybody's mercy.

Even as I'm thinking this, warmth flushes through me. And then, my entire body gives way, as if my very bones are collapsing and the sum of me is simply this immense grief, this deep keening, this bottomless cry for help. I am alone, unbearably alone, and I can't stand it. I need someone by my side, someone who won't die, like Mummy did, like Abba will someday and like Sam may have already. I need something eternal and timeless and if I'm to reassemble into a person again, I need to believe in something older and wiser than myself.

"Merciful Allah, take pity on me," I say, the same incantation I used to whisper every night after Mummy died. "Merciful Allah, forgive me for my sins and make a way for me."

Much later, I wash my face and look in the mirror. I barely recognize the bleary-eyed, red-nosed stranger staring back at me. I look at my brown face, my short dark hair, and it hits me again—this is what they see when they see me. Abba is right; there is no escaping the corporeal reality of the body. The only thing that we can control is our soul, the inner light. A great longing grips me, and it's not for Sam. It's for the world in the book, a world that is familiar and alien to me, a world I no longer share with anybody in my life.

I lie down on the couch and read. When I open my eyes, it's seven in the morning and I have fallen asleep holding that book against my heart as if it's my best friend or lover.

17

▾ ▸ ▴ ◂ ▾ ▴ ▸ ▴

Friday, July 26

It is only when I'm in the parking lot of the Islamic Center in Parma that I ask myself what the hell I'm doing here. I'd set out to go to the Indian grocery store across town because our local store was out of okra and curry leaves. But a massive construction project in Parma and a detour led me past the mosque, which I'd heard of but had never seen.

Now, I stare at the big shining dome, wondering whether to get out of my car or not. All week long, I've been falling asleep reading *The Divine Mystery of Islam*. Even as my brain scoffs at its religious piety, my heart finds solace in its words.

I watch as families with young children, single men, and groups of women stream into the building, all of them with their heads covered. They are here for the 1 p.m. Friday prayers. My curiosity gets the better of me and I get out of the car before I can change my mind.

There is a separate entrance for women worshippers. I remember this segregation from when Yasmin used to force me to attend mosque. I go in. I remove my shoes in the hallway, and someone offers me a scarf. I cover my head, then follow a group of women up a flight of stairs and into the designated section. There are giant television screens on which the prayers will be broadcast, but I pull a chair to the front of the balcony so I can look down at the men's prayer hall. A massive chandelier hangs from the middle of the domed ceiling. The place is spotless and airy, with glass windows letting in the light. I notice a little boy in blue jeans run around the hall, until his dad calls out to him and he runs back and snuggles in his father's lap.

I had expected to see Indian and Pakistani worshippers, but this congregation is almost all Middle Eastern. A fair-skinned woman, who is clad head-to-toe in a blue burka and is sitting on the floor, catches my eye and smiles. I smile back. More women keep streaming in. I notice the downstairs hall is filling up, too, with men donning skullcaps. I take in the clear, smudge-free glass barrier in front of me and the clean red-and-gold carpeting. This place is spotless, the result of religious devotion and pride. Despite myself, I feel a flare of reciprocal pride.

I look over my shoulder and notice a young South Asian woman entering the room. She is wearing a long-sleeved blouse and blue jeans. The woman sees me and walks in my direction. I look away, not wanting anyone to intrude on my thoughts. I'm still trying to figure out what I'm doing here, an imposter among the devout. She pulls up a chair next to me. "Hi," she says. "I'm Tasneem."

I nod. "Ali," I say, in a tone that indicates that I'm in no mood for small talk.

"I know," she says.

"What?"

"The newspaper story," she replies ruefully. "I recognize you from the photo."

I grimace and look straight ahead. Of course. There's no escaping my notoriety.

"Your first time here?"

"Yes. You?"

"I come every week. I live ten minutes away."

"I see." I turn to face her again. "So, the congregation is mostly Middle Eastern, is it?"

"There are a few South Asian families. But most of the Indian and Pakistani folks attend services at the Strongsville Islamic Center." She smiles. "The prayers here are in Arabic. But the imam translates into

English. But even if he didn't, it's okay. I still enjoy the feeling of peace. You know?"

I nod, not knowing what to say. I feel self-conscious, unsure of my motives for being here. That's not quite it—I feel like a cliché. If my life were a novel, this is exactly what my character would do at this point—seek comfort in religion. Return to her childhood faith. I feel my cheeks flush with shame. Being here suddenly feels like failure, a betrayal of my younger self, the abandonment of the principled, secular life I'd chosen a long time ago. Relax, I say to myself. You're not turning into a handmaid just because you're attending masjid, for heaven's sake. Think of it as an interesting anthropological study.

Just then, a familiar melodic chant begins. I peer below, trying to figure out where the sound is coming from. "To your right," Tasneem whispers. She points discreetly.

There are two raised, slatted enclosures high above the ground on either side of the altar, and inside one of them stands the imam. His singing is melodious, beautiful. The wooden enclosures look like giant bird cages or like witness boxes in a courtroom. Which, given the hatred toward Muslims in this country, may be apt metaphors. Sometimes it feels as if the entire religion has been placed on the witness stand. As if all of us are trapped in a gilded cage called America.

I shake my head. Aliya, this is nonsense, I say. You get a few insults tossed your way, a few broken contracts, and you're acting like a martyr? Shame on you. When there's so much real suffering in this world. Think of those teenaged Afghani boys being held in Gitmo without ever being charged with a crime. Think of the parents of those children killed at Sandy Hook. Think of Sam, what she must have endured because of your shameless, reckless flirting.

My mind is racing so much, careening around corners, reversing, braking, crashing into walls of regret and shame, that I don't realize the imam is translating the Arabic prayers into fluent English. He is speaking so rapidly that I can barely make out what he's saying. I find myself trying to focus, but his words fly away from me, like paper in a windstorm. He uses the word *love*, along with the word *shaitan*—"Satan"—often, but it is with growing frustration that I realize that I'm not feeling any of the comfort that I'd been seeking.

Aha, I say to myself, so that's why you came here? To look for some easy, cheap fix? You shun your faith for decades, you proudly call yourself an agnostic and at the first hint of hardship, you crack? You've come here, looking for what? Allah? Your "people"? Here, among this group of women covered from head to toe, who are not allowed to show their hair in public in case they arouse the men? What if these people knew you were married to a woman? I glance at Tasneem, who is sitting with her eyes closed. *She* doesn't seem to care.

I stay in my chair when the women around me prostrate on the ground toward the end of the prayers, their foreheads touching the floor with each *Allah o Akbar.* The elderly and handicapped women sitting on chairs bend from the waist to perform their own supplications. Despite myself, I'm moved by the sight.

When prayers end, I nod briefly at Tasneem, then hurry down the stairs. Whatever I'd expected to find here—peace or the kind of comfort and solidarity Abba is always talking about—I have not found it. If anything, I feel even more alone. I felt none of the music, the poetry, that I feel each night when I read the book that Abba gave me. This is not my tribe. I have spent the last half hour in the company of women who have husbands, uncles, and fathers. I have a father, too, but he rejects the most important thing in my life, even as I reject the most important thing in his.

I push open the doors and step into the sunshine. If nothing else, this visit has taught me a salient truth about myself.

My true religion is Sam.

I'm about to start my Subaru when there's a tap on the window. It is Tasneem.

"Hi," she says, gesticulating for me to roll down my window.

"Yes?"

"I was just wondering . . . you live on the east side, right?" she says. "But you drove all the way here?"

"I didn't. That is, it wasn't to come here. I was on my way to get groceries from the Indian store."

"But why did you come here?"

I don't like this line of questioning. But my interlocutor is smiling and sweet and . . . cute. "I don't know. It was a last-minute impulsive thing."

"So, what did you think?

"I think it's not my cup of tea." I am trying to be polite. "It's not quite what I'm looking for."

"So, what *are* you looking for?"

I am getting annoyed. Indians are so fucking nosy. "I don't know."

We stare at each other for a moment and then she nods. "Okay. I was just wondering . . . shall we go get a chai somewhere? Maybe, you know, get a samosa and some chaat?"

Is this woman flirting with me? I don't think so. Most likely, she's trying to convert me or something. "Look, I'm not religious . . ."

"Who said anything about religion? I'm talking about chatting and chaating." She grins at her own pun.

"Okay," I say. "Just a quick bite."

"Great. I drive that blue Nissan. Just follow me."

She leads me into a nondescript restaurant called India House. I'm happy to see that there's an Indian grocery store adjacent to it, where I will shop later. We each order a mango lassi and then Tasneem orders a few appetizers. "Ali," she says, leaning back into the booth. "This is my treat, okay? Just to . . . just to apologize for the crap you're going through."

"Oh, you don't have to . . ."

"No. I want to. We Muslim sisters must stick together, right?"

I open my mouth to protest, then catch the gleam in her eye. "It's okay," she says softly. "You may not be religious, but you're still Muslim, right?"

I smile. "Right."

And truth to tell, I'm feeling a kind of relaxation here that I haven't felt since Sam disappeared. Some of it is from the simple fact that here in this tiny restaurant, nobody appears to recognize me. Whereas in the Heights I've achieved the kind of notoriety I wouldn't wish on anyone.

Also, the place reminds me of Abba's first restaurant, a small, shabby joint. I automatically compare the mango lassi that I'm sipping to the one Abba served, and the Bollywood music that's playing sounds familiar. The services at the masjid may not have resulted in an epiphany or catharsis, but there's an easy comfort here, like slipping into a shoe that's no longer stylish but undeniably yours. There's also the effervescent presence of this woman sitting across from me. Sisters, she'd said, and I suddenly feel a warm glow, as if I've been effortlessly welcomed into a new sorority, to which my Islamic name and the color of my skin make me a member.

"I mean, the insinuations and innuendos you're enduring?" Tasneem says. "It is such bullshit." It's racism and homophobia at its worst, yaar."

I look at her curiously. "And you . . . you don't have any problem with gay people? Despite being devout and all?"

She cocks her head, puzzled. "My devotion is to Allah. That's between me and Him. What's that got to do with someone being gay?"

"Well, you know, most religions don't condone the 'gay lifestyle.' My own father basically disowned me for years because of it." Without warning, my voice cracks at the mention of Abba. I feel an overwhelming sadness, decades of grief bubbling up within me. It takes all my effort not to cry in the presence of this sympathetic stranger. I have always been proudly gay. But I've never stopped long enough to count the scars, to weigh everything I have lost because of it—most importantly, Abba's presence in my life. I feel a terrible hatred for my stepmom in this moment, because I know that if he had not remarried, Abba would've found a way to accommodate my "affliction" and keep me in his life.

"I'm sorry to hear this," Tasneem says.

I open my mouth to reply, but just then, the food arrives. It looks heavenly. Tasneem serves me first. As she bites into a samosa she says, "Is it hard?"

"Is what hard?"

"Being gay."

"Yeah, it's fucking hard," I say. "Like, being brown and Muslim and female wasn't enough, you know? I had to sign up to be yet another minority." I set my fork down. "But it's also glorious, you know? To not conform to society's expectations of what a woman should be. To enter into a relationship with no preconceived notions of gender roles, to have to negotiate household chores and everything else. For me, being with Samantha is the easiest thing in the world. As natural as breathing. It's the rest of the world that makes it hard."

"How did you two meet?"

A small part of me has learned to distrust people these past several weeks. "Enough about me," I say. "Tell me about you. What do you do? Do you have a life partner?"

"Not much to tell, yaar," she says. "I came here from Hyderabad eight years ago to study engineering, but switched to IT. I now work as a manager for Progressive Insurance."

"Nice."

"And no, I'm not dating at the moment. I had a boyfriend for the last two years, but we broke up six months ago."

"Sorry."

"No, no, it's okay. I'm happy being single." She nods/shakes her head in that endearing Indian way.

We chat for another hour and when we get up to leave, Tasneem takes my hand and says, "Will you come back to the masjid next week?"

I meet her eyes. "Probably not." I squeeze her hand. "But can we still be friends?"

"Definitely," she says and writes her number down for me.

"Do you ever come to the eastside?"

"I will. If you invite me."

I smile. Despite her confidence, I sense that Tasneem is lonely. I remember the stories Abba used to tell me about when he first got here, how terribly homesick he felt. How grateful he was for any act of kindness or friendship. I can be a mentor to this young woman, I decide.

I text her on the number she's just given me. "There. Let's stay in touch, okay?"

"Definitely," she says again.

I'm putting away the groceries from the Indian store when Nathan calls. He's going to a late afternoon showing of the documentary *Mike Wallace Is Here*, at the Cedar Lee, and wants to know if I'll go with him? Maybe we can grab a bite at Lopez after the movie? he asks.

Nathan is a big *60 Minutes* fan. I say yes, even though the doc isn't really my cup of tea. It's better than spending a Friday night alone at home.

The theater is not crowded. Elisabeth, the manager, spots us, and comes around the concession stand to give me a hug. "Any news of Sam?" she whispers and when I shake my head, says, "I'm so sorry for the bullshit you're enduring."

"Thanks," Nathan says, speaking for me, and I grin inwardly.

"Come get some popcorn," Elisabeth says. "It's on me."

"See?" Nathan says as we settle into our seats. "Everybody's on your side."

The lie is so obvious I burst out laughing. The older couple behind us immediately hiss a *shhh*, and I chuckle. I feel more at home in this theater than I did in that mosque.

I enjoy the documentary more than I thought I would. But, unfairly or not, I also draw a straight line from Mike Wallace's brand of hard-hitting journalism and *60 Minutes'* selective editing of interviews to the kind of sensational journalism Jenny Burns practices. I'm so lost in my thoughts as we exit the theater that I don't see Eric approach us as we wait at the Lee Road crosswalk.

"At the movies, huh?" he says loudly as he walks past us. "With your faggot boyfriend?"

I spin around so fast, I'm dizzy. And blinded by rage by Eric's easy use of the F-word. Each summer, the boy's deadbeat parents foist him on poor Carol. Last year, after I'd chastised Eric at our neighborhood block party for making a homophobic remark, Carol had apologized for her grandson the following day. "We don't get to choose our families, Carol," I'd said. And she'd smiled and said, "Ain't that the truth? But let me tell you, if we could, I'd choose you over that awful boy."

Now, I watch his shoulders shake with laughter while he walks away from us. I take a few strides toward him.

"Hey, wait," I call out. A few passersby stop to watch us, but I'm past the point of caring. I reach for Eric's arm and turn him around to face me. "What's the matter? Running away like the coward you are?"

He spits on the ground next to my feet. "What you want, bitch?"

"I want you to apologize. To my friend there. For what . . . what you called him."

He laughs. He is a pale, skinny hoodlum, with bad teeth. "For what? For calling a faggot a faggot?"

I push him. Hard. Somebody gasps. There are at least five couples on the sidewalk watching. Eric blinks in astonishment. Then his eyes narrow and he lunges toward me, but Nathan moves me out of the way, so that Eric staggers forward and loses his balance. He falters and, in a flash, Nathan is behind him, twisting his arm behind his back.

"Ow, let go," Eric says, and Nathan says, in a deeper voice than I've ever heard from him, "Only if you walk away from here immediately. Before the cops get involved."

"She hit me," Eric whines and Nathan must've tightened his grip, because Eric bites on his lower lip and says, "Okay, okay."

As Eric moves away from us, rubbing his arm, someone from the small crowd cries, "Bravo." An older woman claps. A smattering of applause follows. "Well done," the woman says to Nathan, who smiles thinly.

"Let's go," he says to me. "I really need a drink now."

We sit nursing our drinks on the patio at Lopez, a G&T for Nathan, a margarita for me. "I'm sorry about the name the jerk called you, Nate," I say, carefully.

He shrugs. "Why? I'm not gay. Doesn't matter what the punk thinks." He grins. "Not that there's anything wrong with it."

I toss back the rest of my drink. "I'm having another. You?"

"Yup."

I'm a little tipsy when I get home that night. Sam was the homebody; she often complained that I liked to socialize until I dropped dead with fatigue. But now, as I walk around the house checking all the locks, I'm ready to shut the front door and leave the world behind.

18

▼ ▶ ▲ ◀ ▼ ▲ ▶ ▲

Thursday, August 1

Today marks a month since Sam vanished. I'd wanted to stay in bed all day, but I had to come to the office to meet prospective clients. But there's no sign of them and I'm assuming they are a no-show. I am furious at their lack of manners, but I busy myself by working on plans for an addition I'm designing for another family in Beachwood. As I go over my measurements, I remember how excited I had been when I'd won this contract. Now, I have to force myself to focus as I plug the dimensions into CAD, because my mind keeps wandering to that fateful day a month ago.

Fifteen minutes later, there's a knock on the door and the Bennetts arrive in a flurry of apologies and complaints about the traffic. I'm so relieved to see them, I wave away their apologies.

"What can I get you? Tea? Coffee?"

"No thanks," Regina says. "We've delayed you enough."

"Are you sure? I have a great espresso machine here."

They exchange a look. They are a young, newlywed couple, with kind, open faces. "She wants a cappuccino, even if she won't tell you," Paul says shyly, and I leap to my feet.

The Bennetts live on the westside, in Lakewood. So why have they come all the way to eastside for a designer?

"We did a Google search and you had great ratings," Paul says. He licks the foam off his lips. "And also . . . we wanted to support you. To say, we're sorry. We read the newspaper article about you losing clients and all."

"Thank you," I say.

"My brother Patrick is gay," Paul continues. "If someone suspected him of hurting his partner in any way, I don't know what I . . ." He breaks off.

Regina looks at me anxiously. "But we are mostly here because of your great reputation."

I want to tell them how important it is to have allies like them: white, straight, Christian. That gay people cannot carry the weight of other people's bigotry entirely on their shoulders. That we need help. That *I* need help. What I say instead is, "So, tell me a little bit about what you had in mind."

What they have in mind is to modernize the kitchen and second-floor bathroom of the 1917 house that they've recently purchased. There's also a half bath on the first floor but that reno will have to wait, Regina says. "This is our first home," she continues. "We just moved here from Wisconsin. My mom is helping us financially with the project. But we're on a limited budget."

"What do you do for a living?"

"I recently got hired as a curator at the art museum," Regina says. "Paul is an engineer but he's not looking for a job at the moment. He needs to work on the house. It's a real fixer-upper. We're hoping to start a family soon and if that happens, he'll stay home with the baby."

The Bennetts' youth and idealism burn like a candle in a dark world. "You know, I pride myself on working with clients on all budgets," I say. "It wasn't that long ago that Sam and I were penniless grad students. I know what it's like to be starting out."

They leave a half hour later, after setting up a time for me to visit their home. I walk them down the hallway to the elevator. "I'll see you soon," I say. "I'll bring some books with me for you to browse for ideas."

"Great." Regina takes a step toward me and gives me a spontaneous hug.

I savor the moment. It feels good to be held in kindness and solidarity. "I'll be in touch."

There's a lift in my step as I return to my office. See, Ali? I think.

There are lots of good people in this world. For every client you've lost, there will be someone else who will seek you out.

The good feeling lingers for a while. I eat lunch at my desk, then visit the bathroom down the hall. When I return, my cell phone is ringing. My heart dips when I see it's Herrington. "Hello?" I say, breathlessly. "Is there any news?"

"I'm afraid not. I just wanted to check in. I know it's a month today."

My disappointment is so palpable, I wonder if he can sense it. "I . . . I still don't understand how this is possible. I mean, how can someone simply vanish into thin air?"

He sighs heavily. "It happens. Not every day, but more often than you'd think. I'm sorry, Ali. I wish I had better news."

I notice absently that he's started calling me by my first name. We talk regularly enough that some of his old formality has dissipated.

"We actually thought we had a lead, based on a tip we got from Sandusky. But it turned out to be a hoax. Someone was after the reward."

"Figures. Nothing seems to be going our way."

"I'm sorry. Okay, I'll let you go. I just wanted to see how you're holding up."

"Promise me you won't give up on Sam? Like, you know, close her case?"

Herrington sounds shocked. "No. Of course not. I'm pursuing every lead that I can."

I thank him and hang up. The good feelings engendered by the Bennetts' visit have vanished. With each passing day, the hope that Sam will be found alive diminishes. I study the picture on my desk. It is of the two of us from our wedding day, Sam's hair backlit by the sun.

I swallow the regret that rises like bile in my throat.

We had started out with such promise. But what we never acknowledged was the baggage we carried from our parents' homes into ours. In college, it was easy to hide that baggage in a closet, lost as we were in grades and research papers and dating and partying. But once we settled down, everything stored in there tumbled out—my overreaction to being raised by a strict father and Sam's promise to herself that she'd never let me humiliate her as her mother had been by her dad. Which is what she thought I did every time I engaged too much with another woman. It all seems so clear to me now—all I had to do was understand where she was coming from—but God help me, I couldn't do it. I couldn't change any more than she could. It was as if we'd been poured like lava into the molds of our bodies decades earlier and the molds had hardened into our current shapes.

I look up sharply from my desk. Sam's not here, of course, but still, I say it out loud: I promise that if you come home, I'll change. I know I can. Just give me another chance. Please.

19

▾ ▸ ▴ ◂ ▾ ▴ ▸ ▴

Sunday, August 4

It's a hot afternoon and there's a terrible stench wafting in through the open windows from the front of the house. I hope to God it's not a sewer break or something. I open the front door to investigate and notice there's a brown lunch bag on the stoop. The stench is overpowering. There's a note stapled to the bag. In black Magic Marker, someone has printed, "Your not welcome here. Go back wear you come from."

I know what's in the bag even before I open it. How long has it been sitting out here? My knees wobble while I dial Herrington's cell phone. I've never had to disturb him on his private line before, but I'm shaken at the thought of someone hating me enough to do something like this.

Herrington listens as I tell him what has happened. "I'll send someone over," he says. "Unfortunately, my wife and I are at Kelleys Island at the moment. I'll be back at work tomorrow."

I tense at the thought of my neighbors noticing yet another cop car in my driveway. "I can drop off the bag to the police station," I say. "I don't really want the police to visit."

"Ali, I understand," Herrington says. "But we need to dust for fingerprints, etc. We have to investigate this as a possible hate crime."

"Hate crime?" This is an overreaction, and I wish I'd never made this call. "It's probably some kids," I demur. "Let's just drop it."

"You must trust me on this, Ali. We don't know—maybe this will yield some clues about Sam's disappearance."

"Okay," I say. "Whatever you think is best."

Two of my neighbors decide to mow their yard minutes after the police officers arrive. They watch as the cops look for fingerprints on the glass of the storm door and search for footprints in the lawn. The officers place the reeking bag in an ice cooler to take with them, along with the note. Just before they leave, the younger one says, "You may think about getting some Ring cameras, ma'am. You know, for your protection. They will deter bad behavior."

Even though it's Sunday, I text Igor, my electrician, explain the situation, and ask when he can come to install cameras. He writes back seconds later: "For you, I come tomorrow afternoon." He even offers to pick up the equipment for me.

As nighttime approaches, I find myself looking out of the living room windows. For the first time since we've moved into this house, I feel unsafe. It's probably some neighborhood kids, I reassure myself even as I draw the blinds before turning on the television. But I can't escape the disquieting feeling that someone wishes me harm. And I'm powerless to do a thing about it. Because, despite their dedication, I'm deeply skeptical that the cops will be able to find the person who left the note. It's going to be just another dead end, I think, as I drift off to sleep on the couch.

20

▼ ▶ ▲ ◀ ▼ ▲ ▶ ▲

Tuesday, August 6

I'm wrong.

I'm warming up my dinner when Herrington calls. They have an arrest and a confession.

"Who is it? Someone I know?"

"Nope. It's some guy who lives south of here, in a town called Burton. He used to be a welder but he's now unemployed and says he hates immigrants. He read about you and had this crazy idea that if he scared you, you'd leave the country. He's a loon."

I listen dully, not feeling the relief I'd expected to feel. "And this—was it dog poop or something?"

Herrington clears his throat. "No. It's his own shit. Like I said, he's nuts. Anyway, we have him. He'll be arraigned tomorrow."

"How old is he?"

"Sixty-eight."

"I don't want to press charges," I say, speaking in a rush. "I just . . ."

"Ms. Mirza." Herrington is suddenly formal again. "I'd ask you to reconsider."

"Thank you. But I've decided. I have too much on my plate, Detective Herrington. And thanks to your colleague's advice I now have cameras up in three places around my house. I don't feel as frightened anymore. If anyone else tries something, I'll see them."

"Do you want to sleep on it? Although we can still charge him even without your cooperation."

"I want nothing to do with this. But when you release him, I want you to give him a message: One, tell him that I'm as American as he is. And two, that his freedom is on me. Tell him to enjoy it."

As I sit down to dinner, I find myself thinking of Tasneem. With her accented English and hijab, she is more identifiably Muslim than I am. We've been chatting on the phone quite a bit the last two weeks, but now it occurs to me that I haven't asked her whether she feels safe in this country.

Hey, bud, I text. *Hope all's well. How was work today?*

She texts back almost immediately. *Not too shabby. You? Any news?*

No news. Hey, listen. Short notice, but would you like to meet for dinner tomorrow night?

I'm sure she'll decline to go out on a school night. But she surprises me.

21

▾ ▸ ▴ ◂ ▾ ▴ ▸ ▴

Wednesday, August 14

I meet Tasneem for dinner in Shaker Square.

She's wearing a blue shalwar kameez as she walks toward the restaurant. I spot her from my seat near the big picture window and wave, but she doesn't see me. And I have to confess—my stomach flutters involuntarily at how pretty she looks. I'm immediately mortified, but then I say to myself, why is it that we are allowed to appreciate other beautiful things—sunsets, a majestic symphony hall, even a gorgeous slab of granite in someone's kitchen—but not a beautiful woman? I don't have the slightest interest in Tasneem in that way. She's young, for one thing. My heart is bound to Sam.

"Hey," she says, as she approaches my table. She is sweating and a little out of breath. It's one of those hot, humid August evenings.

"Hi," I say. "Any trouble finding the place?"

She clucks her tongue. "No, yaar. Although, I must say, you eastside folks are mad. Your streets are so confusing, with those stupid five-way intersections and all."

I grin. Traces of Tasneem's Indian accent still leak through some of her sentences, and it produces a happy feeling in me because she sounds like Abba. "I dunno. Maybe we want to keep you westsiders out of our beautiful cities."

"Ha." She fishes around in the big leather purse she's carrying. "I have a small gift for you," she says, setting down a packet of chaklis. "I stopped at the Indian store before coming here."

"Thanks," I say.

The waitress comes and we order, a G&T for me, a Coke for Tasneem. "You don't drink alcohol?" I ask cautiously, not wanting to offend her.

She pulls a face. "I did, once. When I was in college. In India. But my grandma found out somehow and God, what a scene she made. Said I'd committed a major sin, that I was in danger of being excommunicated from Islam. I swore then and there never to take another drop."

I nod, but I'm thinking, That's the difference between you and me. When an adult asked me to refrain from something as a teenager, I doubled down even more.

"So how are you, yaar?" Tasneem says, her eyes searching my face.

I debate whether to tell her about the incident outside my home and decide not to. "I'm okay," I say with a shrug. "There's no more news about Sam. But listen, I wanted to ask—how are you? I worry about you, you know."

"*Me?* Why?"

"I dunno. There seems to be so much immigrant-bashing these days. Are you experiencing any of it?"

She clucks her tongue. "Eh. Sometimes someone yells something crazy out of a car. But what to do? There are ignorant people everywhere in the world."

I nod. There's not a trace of self-pity in this one, I think admiringly.

We place our food orders. Tasneem is curious about why I haven't returned to the mosque; I tell her about the book I've been reading.

"Somehow, this little book got through to me, you know? In a way that nothing else has."

"Your abba gave it to you? Guess he knows you well."

I've spent so many years thinking that my father doesn't understand or support me. And yet, it's undeniable—he's brought me more comfort during this ordeal than anyone else.

"What's he like?"

"Abba? He's a good man. Very large-hearted. Very generous to his employees. It's a point of pride to him that he provides healthcare for all of them. It's unusual in the restaurant business, you know? The margins are so small . . ."

"Okay, yaar. But I was asking about him and *you*. You must be close?"

I chew on my steak, which suddenly feels rubbery. "We were very close when I was a child. When . . . before my mother died. It was just the three of us in America, you know? So, we were a very tight family."

Tasneem waits.

"But Mummy died when I was ten. And then—" I'm choking a bit. "I don't know. Abba kind of pulled away from me. I mean, he was still a good father. And then his older sister in India convinced him to remarry. For my sake, she said. Which was a joke. Because Yasmin . . . she's very religious. And she turned my father against me."

Tasneem frowns. "Well, yaar, I'm religious. Why should that make a difference to your abba and you?"

"He implored me to ask Allah to cure my gayness. I guess he never understood that I couldn't change. And that I was okay being who I am."

"You mean, if you could be normal, you wouldn't?"

I wince at Tasneem's matter-of-fact use of the word *normal*. Then I remind myself that unlike me, Tasneem was born and raised in India and is not steeped in American culture.

"It's complicated," I mumble. "It's hard to explain, really." I straighten. "But I'll never be ashamed of my love for Sam. Nothing will make me regret that. Ever."

"Then Sam is a very lucky woman," Tasneem says.

"Not really. I'm the one who pushed her toward her . . ." I close my eyes briefly, preparing to say the word out loud for the first time "death. Because if I hadn't been such an ass she'd still be here."

Tasneem takes a long sip of her Coke before she speaks. "So, this is the reason I said yes to meeting up tonight. Because I wanted to tell you something." She looks at me, her eyes dark and penetrating. "It's not your fault. Of course, we don't know what has happened to Samantha. But whatever it is, it's not your fault. People fight all the time. You told me that she went on a run without you, right? You didn't force her to do that. So that's on her."

Nobody, not even Abba, has said it so directly, given me the absolution that I clearly require. I am so overcome that I revert to form—I smack her lightly on her hand and say, "You're too young to be this wise, girlfriend."

But she's having none of it. She keeps her gaze on my face. "Say it."

"What?" I lick my lips nervously.

"That it's not your fault. Say it out loud."

I look around self-consciously. "It's not my fault," I whisper, staring at my plate. With effort, I look at her. "It's not my fault," I repeat.

"Good. Go home and practice. In Islam, we are taught to always take responsibility for our actions." She shakes her head. "But not this. You didn't do any wrong here. No way."

"Dammit, Tasneem," I say. "You're going to make me cry in public."

"So, cry, na?" she says. "Why are you keeping things all bottled up like this?"

I shake my head ruefully. "I can't," I say, even though I'm sniffing. "Too many years of practice being a hardass."

Even as I say this, a single teardrop lands on my hand. Tasneem notices, reaches across the table to wipe it away. "Yeah, I can see that," she says, dryly.

After dinner, I walk her to her car and briefly contemplate inviting her back to the house. But it's 8:30 p.m. on a Wednesday and she has a drive home. "Next time, you come to our home, okay?" I say as she gets in her car.

Her face lights up, then falls. "But the thing is, yaar, I won't be able to reciprocate. I live in a studio apartment. It's too cramped for me to entertain."

I want to ask why she doesn't buy a house and whether she sends part of her salary home, as so many immigrants do. But it's not my place. "I don't care about that," I say. "See you soon?"

"Definitely."

She opens her car door, then faces me. "Khuda Hafiz, my friend," she says. And waits expectantly, until I repeat the greeting, so heavy and unfamiliar on my lips. "Khuda Hafiz," I reply. *May God be your Guardian.*

Yesterday's Sky

GEORGE

22

▾ ▸ ▴ ◂ ▾ ▴ ▸ ▴

Monday, July 1, 2019

Say you're out on an early morning walk around the neighborhood, the birds of summer making a ruckus in the trees.

Say it's getting light, the sun lumbering its way across the sky.

Say the streetlamps are out due to a power outage, adding to the hush of the streets.

Say while you walk, lost in your thoughts, something catches your eye. There's a hundred-dollar bill lying in the middle of the sidewalk.

What would you do?

Say you think of yourself as an honest man, say you never shoplifted or stole as a child, say you've taught your own children to never tell a lie, to walk the straight and narrow.

Say there's not a soul out when you spot the hundred dollars, say all the windows of the big houses are still dark.

Exactly.

That's what he did.

He was on his way to Home Depot to buy mulch when he spotted her. A second later, he saw her fall. He pulled over and then crouched on the sidewalk and turned her over. Her red hair shone in the morning light. They stared at each other wordlessly. Her eyes were as blue and vacant as yesterday's sky.

Concussion, he thought. He looked around. It was only the two of them, the street so deserted he could hear the thrum of silence.

He picked her up as effortlessly as a hundred-dollar bill and put her in his van.

And then he drove her home.

She was in his bed, her long hair fanned across the pillow. He'd given her a narcotic for the pain on their way home, and she was out like a light.

The timing of it couldn't be better, he thought, as he eyed the ugly bruise on her ankle. He had taken the whole week off, because of the holiday. Plenty of time to nurse this beautiful creature in his bed, see where it took him. He had picked her up on an impulse, the way he did most things. *He needs more self-control*, the teachers in his small town in Kansas had written on every report card. He didn't quite know what he was going to do with her, but already, his body knew what his mind hadn't caught up to. He desired her, so different from the strung-out whores in Detroit that he had been reduced to visiting most weekends. Even asleep, she looked as clean and fresh as a new start.

So much had gone wrong in his life—the childhood stutter, which thankfully he'd finally overcome, the dishonorable discharge from the army, the death of his brother, the only person he'd really loved.

Maybe she was his reward. Payback for a lifetime of people shitting on him.

He walked to the bathroom to get some Neosporin for her ankle. Then he took one of his old neckties and cut it. It would have to do as a blindfold until he figured out something better. The last thing he needed was for her to recognize him. He'd have to gag her, too, but not yet. Right now, he'd sit and watch her—the rise and fall of her breasts through the thin T-shirt, the flare of her red hair, the translucence of her inner thigh.

He laughed to himself. He felt like a collector who had trapped the rarest of butterflies.

He had captured her. And no one had seen.

23

▼ ▶ ▲ ◀ ▼ ▲ ▶ ▲

Monday, July 1 to Sunday, July 7

That first night, while she slept, he opened the back door and sat at the kitchen table. The warm July breeze wafted in, carrying the scent of honeysuckle from the bush outside his window. In the distance, the faint sound of fireworks, people getting ready for the holiday.

Something about this night reminded him of other nights on the farm in Kansas. His twin brother George and him sitting on the porch swing, shelling peanuts. In the mornings, they'd go fishing in the river that ran behind their farmhouse. George's eyes crinkling from under that floppy white hat he always wore. Some of the happiest moments of his life.

Catch and release. The words came to him, in George's voice. His brother insisting that they release the fish they caught. He had never understood the logic, why it was better to give back to the river what the river had yielded. But he had done as George asked.

He wondered what made him think this now. And then he knew. This was George making him promise that he wouldn't kill the girl. He frowned, hurt by his brother's lack of faith in him. "Of course, I won't, George," he said out loud. "Why do you think I'm blindfolding her?"

He had killed at least eighteen people in Afghanistan, but the last kill had been a young boy. It wasn't his fault—they had received faulty information, and he'd opened fire on the wrong house. But the boy's death had stayed with him. These days, he didn't so much as shoot at a soda can. He was done with death.

But still, he sensed George waiting. Honorable George, who was always after him to do the right thing. So, he made his dead brother a second promise—he wouldn't have sex with her until she desired him also.

They fell into a routine, that first week that he was home.

He'd never thought of himself as a lucky man, but here he was, catching break after break. It was the power outage that had given him the guts to pick her up that morning. No cameras recording his movements. And best of all, she was highly sensitive to the sleeping pills he made her swallow after breakfast. Slept most of the day. It tickled him pink, to hear her snoring softly while she slept in his bed. *In his bed*.

No one had seen the inside of this house in the two years he'd lived here, other than an occasional plumber or handyman. He liked it that way. He'd bought the house and the Beamer from the royalty checks for the natural gas they'd discovered on the family farm. He figured that was the only good thing that sodden place had ever given him. Well, that and George. If it hadn't been for George, sunlight to his shadow, he'd have gone through his childhood never speaking more than five words to anybody. Ma couldn't care less—she'd always made it clear that George was her favorite. It was only in the barren landscape of Afghanistan that he'd finally found his place. Found his voice—giving commands, shouting orders at the Talibs, enjoying the bawdy humor of his fellow soldiers. But even that had ended badly, his own government siding with the damn warlord whose home he'd entered one evening to teach him a lesson. He'd thought that was the whole purpose of being there, to keep them in their place before they got any ideas about bringing the war to us. But nope. Uncle Sam threw him in a military prison for what he'd done to the warlord's sister, although it never made sense to him what he'd done wrong, then shipped him back home to Podunk, Kansas, with a dishonorable discharge.

He hadn't known that he'd been lonely until he'd found this

redheaded girl. Companionship, the simple joys of sharing a meal with someone—all these ideas began to gnaw at him. Maybe this woman was the reward, the answer. He imagined it: Washing dishes while she dried them. Eating dinner in the evenings in front of the TV, like a regular couple.

There had been a problem on the third day, though. He'd decided to bring her to the kitchen for breakfast, blindfolded. But as soon as he removed the gag, a wail started from deep within her. He was already so invested in the idea of them as a couple that for a brief second he was stunned. Then, his soldier's instinct took over and he slapped her. The wail died in her throat and her jaw went slack. Immediately, regret flooded him. He really had tried to leave all that nastiness behind him. And yet, he had to establish some ground rules, just as he'd learned in Afghanistan. You had to intimidate those Talibs to let them know who was boss. It was a truth as universal as gravity—you either controlled or were controlled.

He pulled out the kitchen chair. "Sit," he said, the insult of her wailing embedded in the gruffness of his voice. "What do you want? Cereal? Oatmeal?"

"They'll be looking for me," she said in a rush. "If you're holding me for ransom, I can get you whatever . . ."

He felt a spurt of anger, wanted to slap her again. Who did this woman think he was, some common thug? He held his finger to her lips. "Hush," he said. "Listen to me." And then, the genius lie: "You are very far from home. Nobody is looking for you, nobody will find you. It's best if you just do what I ask. I'm not looking to hurt you, you understand?"

"Then why? What did I do to . . ."

"Samantha," he said and watched her startle. He'd gotten her name from the credit card she'd carried in her pocket. "Yeah, I know all about you," he lied.

"How? How do you know me?"

"Don't worry about it. Don't think. It won't help to think. Just do as you're told. I'm the captain of this ship. You just follow orders and we'll be fine."

She sat quietly as he made the oatmeal. He dished out some on her plate and guided her hand to the spoon. "I'm not hungry," she said, and he shrugged, angry.

"Suit yourself," he said. He knew he could outwait her.

After that, they ate breakfast in the kitchen every morning and then he forced the sleeping pill down her throat before he walked her to the bedroom. In the evenings, he made dinner—usually pasta or a stir-fry—and then pulled down the living room shades before he took her there to eat in front of the TV. Rather, he watched TV while she sat blindfolded on the couch beside him. Before they entered, he held the blade of his knife to her throat. "You make one move, let out one scream and it's over, you understand?"

She said nothing.

"Tell me you understand."

He waited until she nodded imperceptibly. And despite his best resolutions, an undeniable thrill ran through him to see her this submissive.

He controlled himself. For now, he would cook and clean for her, but soon, it would be her turn to take care of him. When he was sure she was his, he'd remove the blindfold. He was willing to wait. She was a traditional girl, he could tell. It was one of the few things he'd liked about Afghani culture—how docile the women were, how domesticated, how they obeyed their husbands, fathers, brothers. How they walked several steps behind their male companions. He hated how permissive most American women were, how they fancied themselves equal to men, when any fool could see that they weren't any more equal than a dog is to a tiger.

"What's your name?" she asked him, and he grinned to himself. She was nothing if not clever, this girl.

"Ted," he replied. "As in Ted Bundy. Or Ted Kaczynski."

He chuckled when she fell silent.

They were watching a movie the night before he had to return to work, when a restlessness gripped him. He hadn't taken the risk to bring her here only to treat her like some precious artwork in a museum, had he? For Christ's sake, he was a man, with a man's needs. His eyes slid to her breasts, the tan of her legs. His hand found its way to the inside of her thigh. She flinched.

"Please," she said. "Please don't."

"Relax," he said. "This is your home. You're my woman."

He saw the curl of her lips. "You're crazy," she said.

He stiffened, the blood rushing to his face as his grip on her thigh tightened. He felt her musculature beneath him but knew that he was stronger, that he could break her.

"You're hurting me," she said, her voice rising.

Stop, George whispered, louder than her whimpering. *You promised*. And he let her go, a sour taste in his mouth. He would make this girl his, if it was the last thing he did.

24

▼ ▶ ▲ ◀ ▼ ▲ ▶ ▲

Monday, July 8

On his way to work on Monday, he was a bundle of nerves. He'd left her on the bathroom floor, blindfolded, gagged, her hands bound. It wasn't ideal but the bathroom was the innermost room, away from the front and back of the house. Before he gave her the pill that morning, he reminded her that there were cameras installed in each room and that if she tried to break free, he'd be home within minutes. And that there would be hell to pay when he found her, do she understand?

She nodded.

As every soldier knew, it was important to play this psychological game, to break your enemy's spirit. He caught himself. Samantha wasn't his enemy—just the opposite. He sighed heavily. This was not how he'd imagined it would go. A week already and still she flinched every time he touched her. Last night, in bed, he'd put his face between her breasts, and she'd struggled, tried to push him away. He was doing his best to be patient, waiting for her to soften before taking her. But she was not making it easy. At supper, she was a dreadful companion—sullen, lifeless, answering him in monosyllables. When she spoke of her own accord, it was to beg him to let her go. During the day, she slept heavily and already, the thrill of watching her in his bed was wearing off. All he'd done this week was cook and clean for her, without the payoff of sex and companionship.

Chill. It's been only a week, George said. Asking him to do the right thing. He swallowed his resentment and prayed to his brother to teach him patience.

He sighed. It was three years now and still hard to believe that George was dead.

They'd been at the farm they'd recently bought, just a few miles down the road from their homestead. The plan was to grow soybeans, George's idea, to give his jittery, troublemaker twin brother something to do once George took a job elsewhere. God knows they didn't need the income by then—the natural gas that had been discovered on the family farm meant the gas wells were gushing money.

It was a cold evening in April. They were both in high spirits as he drove the tractor they'd recently bought, George riding beside him. Earlier in the day, they'd attached the new PTO shaft to it. George cocked his head as he heard something. "Turn that thing off," he called, as he jumped off. "Something don't sound right." He went behind the tractor to the PTO shaft and a second later, there was one short scream before George was swallowed up, the scream itself swallowed up, but the sound of his brother's terror would be etched in his brain forever.

What was left of his brother was worse than anything he'd seen in Afghanistan.

There was not a soul around. It was cold, the wind had picked up and there was a weird howling sound. He thought it was the wind or an animal with a broken leg, but no, the sound was coming from him. That animal was him, howling the loss of the only person who had ever mattered.

He sat in that field for hours. There was no point in calling for the cops or for an ambulance. He thought of his mother, far gone with dementia, alone in the house, hungry, wondering where they were. Did she know well enough to wonder why her two boys hadn't come home? To remember that she had two sons? She still lit up when George walked into the room. He and George were identical twins, and they had worn each other's clothes ever since they were kids. They had fooled teachers and girlfriends and people in their church—everyone except their mama. Their voices sounded identical, too, so that nobody could tell which brother had answered the phone. Even as adults, after everything Greg had been through—war and prison—while George went to college and then returned home to a quiet, pastoral life, they could barely be told apart. Everyone commented on it, marveled at their likeness. George laughed off their wonder, but to Greg it felt mystical, the one gift God had bestowed upon him. They were two faces of the same coin—one good and the other bad, one easygoing and the other tightly wound—and even though he was the reckless, angry one, despite the fact that he had gotten the raw deal in the genetic lottery, it consoled him that he shared the same outward traits as his beloved brother. They could fool just about anyone else, but even with her brain eaten up by her disease, some part of his mother brightened around George. It was something instinctual, like a language she didn't remember but could still speak, her love for George. There was nothing left over for him. Never had been.

The moon was out now as he sat, braying like a wolf, rocking. The stars in the sky were hard pellets of light.

The idea, when it came, felt like redemption. To meld into George's vanished flesh. To liquify his bones into his brother's. To literally walk in his twin brother's shoes. To become him. To bury Greg in this sodden earth, Greg, who nobody wanted and who wanted nobody.

It was getting colder. An animal crept nearby, and he threw a stone in its direction. He pulled a comb out of his back pocket and pushed his hair back, to how George wore it. He picked up his phone, praying for reception. Deputy Sheriff Walter Pinter answered. He'd been in trouble with him enough times to know his voice.

"Walt," he said. "This is George. There's been an accident. I need help. Greg's dead."

"What!" Pinter said. "Damn, boy. Get there just as soon as we can."

As he heard the sirens coming down the country road, he felt relief at having killed Greg. Good riddance, he thought, and it somehow lessened his pain, because the brother he was mourning was not worth mourning.

Hours later, when he finally got home and gave Ma the news, she cocked her head at him. Fuck, he thought. She knows. A mother's intuition is stronger than even dementia. After a long moment, after he thought the gig was up, she smiled.

"Well, bless his heart," she said, her eyes gleaming. "Now, what's for dinner, Georgie?"

25

▼ ▶ ▲ ◀ ▼ ▲ ▶ ▲

Thursday, July 11

He almost dropped his mug when he saw her face on the front page of the local newspaper.

"Hey, George," his coworker Jeff said. "You okay, man?"

He spun around. "Fine," he muttered and walked away.

Focusing on work was impossible. His heart hammered so hard in his chest, he couldn't hear above it. At noon, he grabbed the newspaper along with his lunch and headed to the break room. He opened a bag of Doritos, then bit into his sandwich—egg salad topped with balsamic vinegar and red onion, his mother's favorite recipe. He ate that same lunch five days a week at work. Wiping his hands, he read with growing disbelief.

The woman in his house was a dyke, the woman who he'd fantasized getting to know before making love to, with whom he'd imagined building a life, for whom he cooked each day, whose hair he'd washed and combed. And married to a woman. Who was a Muslim. *Muslim.*

He looked up from the newspaper, furious. Was this another cosmic joke being played on him by the universe? At that moment, he didn't feel like George—gentle, sunny, confident George. A winner. Rather, he was back to being Greg—Greg the stutterer, Greg the bullied, Greg whom the girls distrusted, Greg who was let go from the army, the one place where he'd thought he belonged. His mouth twisted with rage: at a God who had spat him out and then forgotten about him. At the liberal Supreme Court who had allowed the travesty of two women marrying each other. At the woman locked in his home who, despite being bound and gagged, made clear her disdain for him. At George, for his sanctimonious advice to be gentle with her.

To the outside world, he'd have to keep being his brother since that was how he'd gotten the job in the first place, by answering George's job offer. But once he went home, he was through pretending to be who he wasn't. He was Greg, unlucky, cursed Greg. And he was done playacting. No more Mr. Nice Guy. He must've said the words out loud because his coworker sitting two tables down from him looked up at him from her phone. He didn't care. He was spitting mad, couldn't wait to finish the day and get home. She had played him. Would he have even bothered with her if he'd known he was picking up a freak of nature? Would he have risked being caught, risked being locked up again, if he'd known her true nature? No wonder she wasn't interested in him. Ungrateful bitch. He blinked back his tears as he flipped to page six to continue reading the article.

He felt a little better when he finished the article; people were blaming Samantha's disappearance on the Muslim bitch. Good. Let her feel the heat. He was safe.

But on the drive home, his foul mood returned when he was struck by a thought: Maybe George was in on the joke also. He'd been listening to his brother's advice all this time. Be gentle with her, Greg. Don't force your way on her, Greg. Don't even think about harming her, Greg. Of course, you're gonna release her at some point, Greg. Unless she decides to stay.

Not once had George intimated the real reason why the bitch was not interested in him. A Muslim wife. That's what he'd gone to Afghanistan for? To defend Sodom and Gomorrah?

How lucky he'd felt when he plucked her off the sidewalk and brought her home. How tenderly he'd nursed her swollen ankle and the gash on the side of her head. How he'd sincerely believed that, at long last, the universe had given him something good to keep, something of his own. As a reward for losing George in that awful way. Compensation for the horrors of Afghanistan. But George was messing with him, too. And here he had spent the last three years, wrapping himself in George's goodness, trying to shed his Gregness like a snake shedding old skin.

By the time he pulled into the garage and entered the house, he was incandescent with rage, a seething bonfire of grievance.

He stood in the doorway of the bathroom and eyed her with distaste and loathing. He smacked his right fist into his left palm, over and over, trying to quell the battle within himself, between George and Greg. And then, he heard it—a low, piteous sound from the woman on the floor—and before he could stop himself, he had kicked her hip. It felt good, this sudden, juddering violence, a release from the man he'd pretended to be all this time.

He watched her curl even deeper into a fetal position, watched her leg quiver in pain. A mad satisfaction gripped him.

He bent down to the floor and scooped her up. Took her to his bed and dropped her, then stood towering above her. She was saying something over and over again, and because of the gag, it was muffled, but he could tell she was pleading, knew she sensed the change in him. *Serves you right*, he thought.

He unzipped his pants and fell onto her, determined to make her regret her fall, determined to make her wish her path had never crossed with his.

26

▾ ▸ ▴ ◂ ▾ ▴ ▸ ▴

Tuesday, July 23

Everything had changed since he'd taken her against her will. He had hoped to seduce her, make her forget about the woman she called her "wife." Instead, she was more sullen and noncooperative than ever. He came home each day to find her whimpering on the bathroom floor. He was caught in a trap of his own making, stuck between relishing the new power that he had over her and the depressing reality that greeted him each day. He hated the way she cowered when she sensed his presence, how she recoiled when he touched her. But some part of him felt there was a cosmic rightness to it, a punishment for her sins.

They'd just hired this new woman at his workplace, and he was a tiny bit smitten with her. Petite, with big brown eyes and a shy smile. Everybody at work liked her, and unlike his coworkers, she was friendly toward him. At times, when he watched her out of the corner of his eye, he felt a deep regret at how his life had turned out, how different it might have been if he'd met someone like this woman early in life. Maybe, he, too, could've had the things that other men enjoyed—a home to share with a doting wife and a kid or two. Instead, he had a woman trapped in his bathroom, who, he was sure, hated his guts. Who, even now, was probably thinking of ways to escape. His throat tightened at the thought.

"Hey, George?" It was the new girl.

He startled, rearranged his face into a smile. "Yup? You need something?"

"Yeah, no. I just wanted to say, a bunch of us are going to see the new *Spider Man* movie tonight? You wanna join us?"

It had been a long time since his coworkers had invited him to anything. And this girl was looking at him with those big eyes, that wide smile. He was tempted. Lord, he was tempted. But there was a woman in his home who would soil herself if he didn't get home after work. Who needed to be fed. He felt sick.

"I can't." He grimaced. "I have other plans. I'm sorry."

She shrugged. "No problem."

For the rest of the day, he heard them make plans for the evening. He was used to being excluded, had cultivated and welcomed his reputation of being a lone wolf. But today, it stung.

Oh well, he finally said to himself. Screw them all. He knew it was a matter of time before the new girl joined the rest of them in ignoring him. She would turn out to be like all other women, anyway. Like the girl on his bathroom floor, for whom he'd had so much hope. And who had betrayed him in the worst possible way.

No matter. She was the one thing in the world that still belonged to him.

27

▼▶▲◀▼▲▶▲

Wednesday, July 31

She sat slumped at the kitchen table as he got ready to make breakfast. There were red blotches on her neck, from where he forced her to lay still every night while he enjoyed her body. He noticed the welts around her mouth from the gag, and the marks on her wrists, and felt a flare of pity, which turned almost immediately into distaste. She looked nothing like when he'd found her. Her skin was pallid and splotchy, and her legs had lost their taut musculature. Even her red hair no longer had that sheen that had mesmerized him.

"You hungry?" he asked.

She said nothing.

Her silence infuriated him. Before he could stop himself, he struck her shoulder hard. He watched her bite down as the pain coursed through her, and was immediately remorseful. "I'm sorry, my girl," he said. "But you keep provoking me. What do you expect me to . . ."

"I'm not your girl." Her voice was feeble but defiant.

He shook his head. The gall of this woman. Such insolence. His fingers itched with wanting to beat it out of her. Instead, he pulled her toward him. "Stop it," he said. "Come on, don't be like this. It's easier if you comply. Why haven't you learned that lesson yet?"

There was a pounding on the front door. They both froze. He shut his eyes briefly. It had to be the cops, this early in the morning. For a second, he contemplated going to the bedroom to get his gun. But he had no plan: what would he do, kill himself and the girl?

She began to rise from the chair, but he grabbed her by her shoulders and hustled her to the bathroom. With his fingers shaking, he gagged her again. "Stay here. You make one sound, and I swear I'll slit your throat before anyone can get to you. I mean it."

He pulled the bathroom door shut, then locked the bedroom door.

A young man in a polo shirt stood on the top step and explained that the next-door neighbor had hired his company to do a bunch of outdoor projects. This was a courtesy call, to warn him about the noise and dust. The work would start in about two weeks, once all the permits were pulled. George listened, thinking he would pass out from relief. Still, the news wasn't ideal. Apparently, the old biddy was getting extensive sewer and other work done, which would entail tearing up her driveway. She was also taking down the tall pine trees between their properties and replacing the fence. The man couldn't say how long the entire project would take. There went his seclusion—one of the main reasons he'd bought this house. The place would soon be crawling with workers. He kept Samantha in an inner bathroom, but what if something went wrong? What if he was sloppy just one time? That's how people got caught. Her Muslim girlfriend—he couldn't bring himself to say the word *wife*—had already announced a reward for her whereabouts.

He went back to the kitchen, shaken. For the first time, he saw it clearly, saw it the way the cops would: There was a woman in his house, held against her will. His mind flashed to those bleak months he'd spent in the military prison. There was no way he would ever go back to that.

He'd caught a break today. But soon, he would need to get rid of her. He sighed. Despite the hassle, it was nice not having to drive to Detroit, nice not having to pay for sex.

He knew he couldn't keep her.

But he didn't know how to give her up either.

At work that day, he made several mistakes and his boss, Brian, reprimanded him in front of his coworkers. Also, two female customers had complained to Brian about him. He'd overheard them talking about

Cary Roberts, the football player being sued by a woman for sexual assault and had made a disparaging remark about the woman's looks that they had found sexist. He apologized to Brian, but he was seething as he walked away. The whole country had gone to the dogs. He wished he had been alive during the 1950s, when women and minorities had known their place and white men like himself could make a damn joke without being crucified for it.

The only thing that allowed him to get through the day was knowing that he had the girl at home. He might be powerless at work, might have to put up with their bullshit reprimands, but at home, he was the boss, and she had to do his bidding.

She was curled on the bathroom floor. He noticed her flinch as she sensed his presence, noticed her hip bone jutting out, the pallor of her skin, and just like that, he felt himself stepping out of his fever for her. He tried to recall the crazy desire he'd felt a mere four weeks ago, the joyful excitement of the early days, the dreams he'd had of making a life with this woman, but all he felt was bewilderment. All he could think was, I'm risking imprisonment for *this*? All he could think was, I gotta dispose of her somehow, before the work begins next door.

28

▾ ▸ ▴ ◂ ▾ ▴ ▸ ▴

Monday, August 12

Getting rid of a dead body is harder than you might think.

Say, a stray dog makes its way into your backyard and digs. Say, years from now, someone comes across a bone or a tooth, and they make a match. Too much can go wrong.

As a teenager, he'd loved reading lurid reports of the ways in which dead bodies had been disposed of but ultimately discovered: Someone thrown into a vat of acid and yet identified by a single tooth. A car with a decomposed body discovered years later when the lake was being drained. The new owners of a house coming upon a body behind a plastered wall during a renovation. He'd read those stories during those long Kansas nights when he'd lie awake, unable to sleep, seething with anger and replaying the latest gibe or taunt that a classmate had flung his way. Reading these stories had calmed him, channeled the anger that he felt toward his schoolmates into fantasies of revenge.

George used to shudder at his brother's taste in reading. They'd sit on the porch after dinner, and in his usual, methodical way, George would try to impress upon him why immersing himself into that dark world of murder would leave a lasting stain on him and twist his psyche. "There's so much good literature out there, Greg," he'd say. "Stories about heroism and hope and decency. Read Steinbeck. Or James Agee. You know you can borrow my books any time."

He'd nod yes, knowing that George was right. But he also knew a deeper truth about himself. Reading these gruesome stories fed some part of his soul that nothing else could touch. Still, he read some of the books George had recommended because he couldn't bear to displease his brother.

It was because of George that he'd spent the last week driving around the area, looking for the perfect spot to release the girl. Alive. It was a gamble to let her go, but this was one promise to his brother that he intended to keep. Still and all, it wasn't *that* risky. She had no way to identify him, having never seen his face or the house. And he'd wipe her clean as a whistle before he dropped her off.

But the question of where troubled him.

He'd begun to leave home earlier than usual, even though that meant forcing some breakfast down Sam's throat before she was fully awake. But that couldn't be helped. He'd drive down Cedar Avenue or some other decrepit street in Cleveland where the boarded-up buildings and the housing projects were located, hunting for the perfect spot. But even in the early morning, there were always a few junkies and drunks hanging out. Then there was the risk of the cops patrolling those places. Not to mention that someone living in those projects could capture her and drag her into their roach-infested apartment. As anxious as he was to get rid of her, he didn't wish that fate on her.

Taking her to a neighborhood far from home was out of the question. Even though he planned on drugging her good and proper, he couldn't risk her waking up on the way. The story about the body in the vat of acid and the accidental finding of the tooth flashed through his head. Even the best laid plans could go awry. There was no sense in taking such a risk. It was a pity though, because it would put her far away from him.

This morning, he drove to an elementary school that had a parking lot behind it. An unconscious woman in the back of the school would be spotted as soon as the first teachers arrived. But the school was situated right at the end of a residential street. There was always the chance of someone being out early in the morning. He supposed he could unload her in the middle of the night, but if somebody saw the headlights of his car, that could spell trouble. He would feel too exposed here. And without the cover that the power outage had provided him in early July when he'd taken Sam, he was worried about security cameras that were everywhere these days. Including, he was sure, at the school. No, this was a bad idea. He kept driving.

He was tonguing the problem in the middle of the night when it came to him: He was overthinking it. He'd picked her up as absently as a coin from the sidewalk. That's how he needed to release her, too. Without too much planning or angst. That's how he'd made pretty much every consequential move in his life—joined the army, taken on George's name and persona, accepted his current job. And it had all worked out so far, hadn't it?

All he needed was a place with no security cameras. But where?

The answer came to him: the park twenty minutes from his house. He could see it in his mind's eye: walking trails and picnic shelters with the creek running alongside the two-lane road. The elevated hiking trails on the opposite side.

He drove there the next two mornings. Timed when the first joggers arrived. No matter. He could get there earlier. He could dump her on the paved trail and hightail it out of there. Someone would find her later that morning.

It was risky, but perfect.

29

▾ ▸ ▴ ◂ ▾ ▴ ▸ ▴

Thursday, August 15

He lowered her into the bathtub and cleaned her meticulously, before carrying her to the garage and loading her into the SUV. He slipped her credit card into her pocket. The streets were empty as he drove into the park in the early dawn. There were no other cars around. The creek was low this morning, its water barely visible in the first light of the day. He wore a shower cap that covered his head. The last thing he needed was for one of his hairs to land on her. He drove slowly along the creek, looking for the perfect spot to roll her out of the vehicle.

He took a quick look at her. The seat was reclined as far as it would go, and her head was lolling from side to side. She snorted loudly, and despite the tension, he laughed. Out like a light, she was. Keeping a hand on the wheel, he put on his gloves, one at a time. He pulled over. With the engine still running, he sprinted to the passenger side. He scanned the area. There wasn't a car or person in sight, and he opened the door. Still, his heart hammered in his chest as he picked her up. She was lighter than she'd been six weeks ago. He felt a pang of something, but there was no time to examine that emotion. He was a soldier now, on a covert mission. Beyond the paved path and the grass, there stood a low stone wall. It was the perfect spot for a drop-off. If she rolled on the slant, the wall would hold her. The last thing he needed was for her to land in the damn creek.

He took another quick look, then sprinted back to the SUV. Checked the rearview mirror. Nobody was out here. Soon, the runners would arrive. Someone would find her and call the cops.

He held his breath until he'd driven out of the park, half expecting something to go wrong—an accusing shout, the sound of police sirens. Nothing happened. He was dizzy with relief. It was done, she was out of his hair, and no one had seen a thing. He had gotten away with it. He laughed, smacked his steering wheel with delight, unable to believe his good fortune. She had never seen his face. There was no way for her to identify him, and given how doped up he'd kept her, she would be lucky to tell them anything.

He headed home to shower and wipe down all traces of her. To strip the bed and put all the sheets in the washer. He planned to vacuum the SUV and store it in the garage for the next several months, until he was sure nobody was looking for it. Then he would pack his lunch, get dressed, and drive to work in the Beamer.

Next Friday, it would be back to the whores in Detroit, which suited him just fine. He wished he could call in sick today, spend the day thinking about the last six weeks. Instead, he'd get to work early and be ultra polite to his coworkers and customers. All the while chuckling over his great adventure, his own incredible secret.

Invisible Membrane

SAM AND ALI

30

▼ ▶ ▲ ◀ ▼ ▲ ▶ ▲

Thursday, August 15

For a half second, I don't recognize her. The woman in the hospital gown has strands of white in her red hair and appears shrunken and desiccated. She is lying in bed twisting her hands as a nurse stands before her. She looks up when I enter the room, and my stomach drops at what I see in her eyes—nothing. Sam's beautiful, expressive eyes are dull and blank. But then, she recognizes me and smiles. She stretches her right hand toward me, angry red bruises on her wrist, and my mind is churning, spinning, awash in memories and emotions. I remember how I'd made a similar gesture when I'd asked her to come to bed with me on that fateful night. I swallow the lump in my throat as I cover the distance between us, and bend, so that our faces are close together as I gather her in an embrace. Her shoulders feel so bony. She flinches at my touch, but then she relaxes, takes a deep breath, and says, in a voice I fail to recognize, a voice that startles me, it is so dry and husky, "Ali, my Ali. Is this really you?"

"It's me, sweetheart," I say gently. "And you're okay now. You're safe. You're home. You're home."

She smiles wanly, but her eyes are confused, cloudy. There's something different about her face, something old and wary. Something terrible has obviously befallen my Sam, and I want to burst into tears at her obvious suffering. But I can't give in to my grief; I must rise to the occasion.

"I want to go home," Sam says, sounding as if she has dry leaves in her mouth.

I look to the nurse who is fussing with the IV in Sam's arm. "She's dehydrated," she says to me. "And she has a bad gash on her shin that looks infected. We'll probably keep her overnight."

I turn back to Sam, but her eyes are closed and, a second later, she is breathing deeply, asleep. Now, I look closely at her face, so familiar to me, and yet, strangely new. It's not just the new lines on her forehead; her mouth is askew, with red bruises on either side. In all my fantasies about finding Sam alive, of having her be delivered again to me, I never once imagined her returning home battered or changed. It was foolish of me, of course. Judging from the marks all over her, some depraved animal has held her captive. I shudder.

And now, another thought, one that I can hardly frame to myself. Still, I force myself to ask, "Was she . . . ? Did you do an internal exam?"

The nurse's eyes flit around the room and she licks her upper lip nervously. "I think that's a question for the doctor, ma'am," she says, and I know the answer. My knees buckle and I clench the side of a chair before easing myself into it. Unwelcome images drop into my head, and I can hardly breathe. All my bravado vanishes; in its place is a feeling of complete powerlessness. I could not protect Samantha from . . . The word *rape* forms like a giant abyss, and I begin to heave.

In a flash, the nurse holds up a kidney tray to my mouth. I clench it gratefully, but all that comes up is a little sputum. "Thank you," I say, wheezing, casting an anxious look back at Sam, who is still asleep. The nurse nods briskly, takes the tray from me, and goes to the bathroom. When she returns, she says, "Let me get you some apple juice."

The cold juice helps, but my hands are still shaking. The nurse gives me a stern look. "You have to be strong," she says. "You gotta make her feel safe and as normal as possible. You follow?"

I nod. It is impossible to express to her how small I feel, given the enormity of what's happened to my girl. Sam has been gone for six weeks, but I have a hollow feeling, a premonition that this time will define the rest of our lives.

31

▼ ▶ ▲ ◀ ▼ ▲ ▶ ▲

Thursday, August 16

Herrington is with Samantha when I walk into her room with a Coke from the hospital cafeteria. He rises to his feet when he sees me, greets me like a friend.

"Well?" he says. "Today's a happy day, right? We got your wife back, safe and sound."

I take in Samantha's pale face before I flash him a small smile. There is nothing sound about my wife's condition, I want to say. Her eyes are lifeless, her skin bruised, and all night long as I sat in the recliner by her side, she groaned and yelled in her sleep, until they finally gave her a sedative. Toward morning, when one of the nurses who'd come to take her vitals thoughtlessly turned on the overhead light, Samantha screamed and covered her eyes, unaccustomed as she is to the brightness. She looked around the room, terror stricken. I held her hand and spoke to her softly until she drifted back to sleep.

Herrington turns his attention back to Sam. "So, you don't recall anything after you fell?" he asks. "Anything that would help us find the guy who did this to you?"

"No. I told you. It all goes blank after that. When I awoke I was in his . . . house."

"And what can you tell us about this house?"

"He kept me locked in the bathroom. I slept all day on a cold tiled floor. There was a honeysuckle vine outside his living room window. I could smell that. There was nobody living above us."

"Was there traffic noise? Were you in the country?"

"In the evening there was traffic. But the rest of the day he kept me drugged while he was gone."

"And how many hours was he away?"

"I—I'm not sure. I'm sorry." Samantha's face crunches with frustration, from the effort of trying to remember. I'm about to ask Herrington to stop, when she begins to cry. "I'm sorry," she says. "I feel so useless. But everything is a blur."

"You're doing great," Herrington says. "Let's take a break."

I take the chance to open the Coke can and hand it to Sam, who gives me a quick smile. I smile back, nod encouragingly. She takes a few quick sips, passes it back to me.

"Can we continue this tomorrow?" I ask Herrington. "After we are, you know, back home? She's hardly slept last night."

"Nor has she," Sam says, pointing to me. "I think she looks worse than I feel." Our eyes meet and there it is, that ineffable connection, each of us looking out for the other.

Herrington notices. "Ali will be fine. You both will be fine," he says. "Even though I'm sure it doesn't feel that way right now." He clears his throat. "Ms. O'Malley, forgive me, but I think we should continue, before the window to capture your abductor closes. I do have a few more questions to ask. And they are . . . difficult ones. Are you able to go on?"

Sam's eyelids flutter for a moment. "Okay," she says. "Let's get this over with."

"I . . . do we know what motive this man had to capture you?"

"I have no idea. I never even saw him, I'm sorry."

"Never? Not even a glimpse?"

"He had me drugged and blindfolded the whole time. I was gagged most of the time. The only time the gag came off is when he fed me. He . . . he had this fetish about eating dinner in front of the TV. Like a normal married couple. That's how he put it." Sam's eyes flit to me, to gauge how I'm reacting to this. I control my rage, concentrate on keeping my face as impassive as possible.

"I see." Herrington writes in his notebook. Then he says, "I'm sorry to ask this but the physical exam yesterday found vaginal bruising. This man violated you? About how many times would you say?" His face is expressionless, but his eyes are on me.

Sam stirs in her hospital bed. "I'm sorry, I can't discuss this in front of my wife." She turns her head. "Ali, would you mind leaving the room?"

I am stunned, then humiliated. After what I've been through waiting for Sam to come home, am I to be left wondering what exactly happened to her? "It's okay," I say. "I'll stay."

Sam's lower lip juts out. "Honey, I can't. I can't discuss this in front of you. Please understand. I'm sorry."

And she looks at me so pleadingly that I have no choice but to go out into the hallway. But I'm seething. Not at Sam, but at the monster who found her and decided to take her back to his lair. I remember what Sam said. He wanted to pretend they were a "normal" couple. Translation: A straight couple. As if the last eight years of our life together doesn't count. As if our marriage was a sham, a joke. I stand in the hospital hallway feeling as if I'm being erased.

I wait outside Sam's room for another forty minutes. A kind nurse brings me a chair. A little later, a different nurse goes into the room. I'm starting to doze off when Herrington comes out. I leap to my feet.

"She's asleep," he says. "They gave her a pill for anxiety."

"Did you get what you wanted?" I hear the tightness in my voice, hate myself for resenting Herrington for doing his job.

He sighs. "She just doesn't remember much. That bastard knew exactly what he was doing. He left no traces of hair or sem—excuse me, bodily fluids—on her."

I look at him sharply. "So, he's done this before?"

"I don't know. Would be easier finding him if he was in our database. But there's no description, no witnesses."

"In other words, just like before, huh?" I don't bother to hide my sarcasm. "We're back to being at this guy's mercy."

Herrington looks at me sharply. "You need to get some sleep. Your eyes are bloodshot. Okay, I'll take your leave. I need to enter what little we know into my work computer."

He walks away, then comes back. "About the reward you'd announced. It was a young, Black couple from South Euclid who found Sam in the park. They waited with her until the ambulance arrived. I know the reward was meant for a tip that would lead to Sam, but maybe you'd consider giving them a small token of your thanks. You understand, I'm not speaking in my official capacity here."

I don't have to think. "Yes, of course. Will you put me in touch with them?"

"Yes." He nods to himself. "Listen, Ali, there might be another round of conspiracy theories and social media crap. If you need anything, just give me a call. This has been hard on you. But your wife is back home, that's the main thing. Okay, I'll be seeing you."

He turns away again. "Mike," I call, using his first name for the first time. "I have a question."

"Shoot."

"Did you—at the beginning, I mean—did you ever think that I had done something to do with Sam's disappearance? Did you suspect that . . ."

"Never." His voice is emphatic, his eyes searching my face. "I've been doing this for a long time. I've learned to trust my gut. I never thought you had anything to do with this."

"Not even when you found the deleted texts?"

He smiles and I see the crow's feet around his eyes. "I don't know if anyone's ever told you this. You have an honest face."

I smile back. "Thank you."

And then, Herrington does something that shocks me. He takes two quick steps to bridge the distance between us and puts an arm around me in an embrace. I stiffen, then relax. Almost immediately, the tears come to my eyes. "Thank you," I say again.

"I'm sorry for the abuse you've endured," he murmurs. "Those idiots on social media have really put you through the wringer."

I remember the outrageous comments on Twitter before Mo begged me to stop looking: That I had killed Sam because she refused to convert to Islam. That we had left the party early because I was having an affair. That I had grown up in Saudi Arabia and was in the country illegally.

Herrington straightens, puts one large hand on each of my shoulders. "Listen to me. Take your girl home and take the time to heal. Don't talk to the media. Above all, be patient with yourself. I've seen this many times before. Sometimes, the healing can be as difficult as the initial trauma."

32

▼▶▲◀▼▲▶▲

Wednesday, August 21

I can't sleep at night. Not only because of the nightmares that jerk me awake, nightmares that I do my best to hide from Ali, but also because my neck and lower back still ache from weeks of lying on the cold, hard bathroom floor. Ali gives me a massage every evening, but after a few minutes, even her touch feels irritating, and I ask her to stop. It's as if my body, my skin, my nerve endings don't belong to me anymore. All I feel is this constant physical pain, which is still preferable to the images and flashbacks I can't stop from looping in my head. The two ways I've always had for dealing with problems—running and writing—have been cut off to me. I am so unused to moving that the thought of going for a run is laughable, and in any case, running in our neighborhood, prying eyes following me, is beyond what I am capable of. I startle at every loud noise, I twitch and jump if Ali so much as bangs a pot in the kitchen, I'm hyperaware of everything around me. I can't imagine picking up my novel again. Writing used to be the dissolution of self, the breakdown of the membrane that separated me from the world, a deep dive into the subconscious. Now, I'm excruciatingly aware of my body, my broken, painful body, and hypervigilant to every sound, to the slightest rustle of air around me—it's all terrifying. I just want to stay in bed all day, even though I dread sleep and spend countless hours simply staring at the ceiling. I know I'm freaking out Ali, but I can't help myself.

I hear her footsteps come into the bedroom and see her opening the blinds. "Don't," I mutter, but she ignores me.

"Sam," Ali says. "Get up, honey. It's a beautiful day. We're going to eat breakfast on the patio."

"I can't, I'm sorry."

"Yes, you can, honey. Come on. I'm making your favorite. French toast."

How to tell her that I have no interest in food? That I feel dead on the inside and that when I chew and swallow, it's like feeding a cadaver? That every time Ali makes eggs, I smell those egg salad sandwiches the monster used to make for his lunch, smell that sharp scent of vinegar, and I feel nauseous? How to say this to Ali, who is looking at me anxiously, waiting for me to spurn her? With a low moan, I get out of bed and my reward is Ali's surprised smile.

"Go shower," she says. "You'll feel better. By the time you come down, I'll have breakfast ready."

She has set the table on the patio by the time I get there. French toast with blueberries and maple syrup, yogurt parfait, orange juice. All the time that I was held captive, I used to fantasize about food, specifically Ali's cooking. But now, the sight of the spread makes me ill. Still, I sit and muster a smile.

"Thank you," I say.

I eat a few bites of the French toast. She has added some orange zest to it, and despite my aversion to food, I can tell that it's delicious. I open my mouth to tell her so, but just then a bolt of pain runs from the base of my skull in a red-hot line to my shoulder blade and I drop my fork. Ali looks up; notices my expression.

"Sam, what's wrong?" she says. "What happened?"

But I still can't speak because of the pain sizzling from my neck down into my upper back. As if participating in a diabolical game of call-and-response, my left hip begins to throb, a steady percussion to the screeching, careening pain in my upper body. My eyes fill with tears, and I squeeze Ali's hand, waiting for the stinging to subside. I place my other hand on my frozen neck, as I move it gingerly from side to side.

"Where does it hurt, honey?" she asks.

"Everywhere. But I'll be okay. I'm sorry. Just give me a minute." But I'm beginning to think that something is truly, permanently wrong with my joints.

Ali rubs my neck and shoulders. Her touch is light against my skin, her fingers deft. For the first time since I've returned home, I allow myself to relax under her touch. "Sam," she says. "I think you should see an orthopedist. Get some X-rays done. I mean, what if you have a fracture or something?"

She's right, of course. That's what they'd suggested at the hospital, too, but I'd insisted on a discharge after being kept there overnight. Now, I regret my haste to get home.

"Should I try and get you an appointment?" Ali says.

I shake my head no. I can't go to some strange doctor's office and describe sleeping on my kidnapper's floor for six weeks. I'll die under their probing, intrusive questions. "I'll see Dr. Salinger," I say. "I trust him."

Ali looks like she's about to argue—she has no faith in chiropractors—but doesn't. "Let me call and see if they have a cancellation for today," she says.

"Finish your breakfast first," I say, but she's already going inside the house. She comes back a few minutes later.

"He'll see you at one-thirty. He's fitting you in. His receptionist said hi."

"Thanks, Ali," I say. "I'm sorry to scare you like this."

She pulls her chair close to me, peers into my face. "Stop it," she says. "Stop saying you're sorry every two minutes. None of this is your fault, you understand?"

The monster broke me in one way; Ali's kindness breaks me in another. "Of course it is. It's all my fault. None of this would've happened if it wasn't for my stupidity."

"Sam—"

"No, let me finish. The whole time I was captured I kept thinking that God was punishing me. For having made you so miserable all these years. For having tormented you with my jealousy and possessiveness. But I'm going to change. I promise you, I'll change. I don't want to live this way . . ."

Ali reaches up, holds my face in her hands. "Look, there's plenty of blame to go around. I said some nasty things to you that night. But that bit about God punishing you? That's some fucked-up shit, honey. You can't think like that. That's just crazy talk."

"I *am* crazy," I say with a laugh that sounds like a sob. "That bastard has stolen everything away from me—my dignity, my self-worth, my sanity. I'm sorry, I have nothing left, Ali."

"That's not true." Ali's voice is soft, urgent. "He didn't steal everything away from you. You still have me. I will never give you up."

And she gives me a look of such pure longing, I close my eyes and thank my lucky stars. We lean into each other, and after a few moments, I feel my breath enter into my body again.

Sara Salinger, Dr. Michael Salinger's wife and receptionist, hurries out into the waiting room from behind her desk. "May I give you a hug, Samantha?" she says. And before I can answer, she folds me in a bear hug. I pull back after a second.

She stands before me, hands knitted in front of her. "You doing okay?" she says, in her thick Scottish accent. Just then, Ali walks in from parking the car.

"Well, hello, there," Sara says. "Nice to see you."

Ali smiles tightly. "Hi."

"The room's ready for you," Sara says, nodding toward the hallway.

"Do you want to go in with me?" I ask Ali and she nods.

In the treatment room, Sara hands me a gown. "Doctor will be right in," she says.

I turn off the overhead light and turn my back to Ali as I undress, to keep her from seeing the bruises on my chest. She sits in the corner as I slip into the gown. There is a perfunctory knock on the door before Dr. Michael Salinger walks in. He is a tall man in his early seventies with a square jaw and a mop of curly white hair. "How's my favorite patient doing?" he says, his standard greeting. "What are we fixing today?"

His approach is so casual that I wonder if he has not heard about my kidnapping. He emits none of the caution and anxiety that radiated off Sara Salinger.

"I've screwed up my neck and the pain travels down into my upper back. And my left hip is also killing me."

He flips through my file. "You know, it's been a couple of years since we've had any X-rays taken. What say we run some films of your neck?"

"That's a good idea," Ali says, and I cast her a silencing look.

"Can we skip that for today?" I say. Already, the room is beginning to feel small and warm. I just want to get the treatment over with and then go home and back to bed.

Dr. Salinger has me sit on the side of the table as he lightly kneads my neck. "Okay, let's try an adjustment today and see if we can't release some of these knots. But I will need some X-rays soon."

After a few minutes, he tells me to lie down on my side with one leg bent and the other stretched out. Standing in front of me, he places his hands on my body and asks me to take in a deep breath. When I exhale, he pops my lower back and I feel an immediate release.

"That was beautiful," he grunts. "Okay, onto your other side."

This is why I always go back to Dr. Salinger—I like his pragmatic, no-drama style. After he repeats the same technique on the other side, he says, "You'll be sore tonight. Remember to ice. Now, on your stomach."

I flip onto my stomach. I can no longer see Dr. Salinger and am no longer in control of my surroundings. My breath catches. I want to call out to Ali but can't find my voice. Dr. Salinger is talking to me, but my heart is hammering in my ears and his voice sounds muffled. I jerk as he places one hand against the side of my head and another against my shoulder in order to pop my neck. His hands remind me of the monster's hands on my body, how they used to choke me if I made the slightest sound.

"Relax," I hear Dr. Salinger say, but that simple command is impossible to follow. He tries to make my neck move, but my body is so stiff, he can't. "Take a deep breath," he says, but I'm hyperventilating. And when he touches me again, I yell, "Take your hands off of me."

"What the—?" Dr. Salinger says and steps away.

I flip around. Dr. Salinger is staring at me, his face beet red. Ali is on her feet. Her lips are moving, but I cannot hear. I sit up on the table and cry silently. Already, mortification is creeping in, along with a growing sense of dismay. I'm in so much physical pain and I've insulted the only doctor I trust to help me.

"I'm sorry," I say, as soon as I can speak. "I didn't mean to . . . I was just . . . I'm sorry."

Ali strokes my hair. I see her look beseechingly at the doctor, begging for his understanding.

"I—I will send Mrs. Salinger in," he says at last and walks out, leaving the door ajar.

Sara steps in, carrying a small paper cup with water. "Oh, honey," she says, and her tone is so sympathetic, so maternal, that it makes me cry harder. "I'm so sorry. What a trauma you've been through."

I take a couple of sips. "Will your hus—will Dr. Salinger ever work on me again?" I ask. "I know I offended him. I'm so ashamed."

"Oh, sweetie. Of course he will! We'll just have to figure out what you're comfortable with, okay? But I think we're done for today, yah? You just give me a call when you're ready to try again. I'll fit you in any time, don't worry."

"Thank you," Ali says. "We appreciate it."

I get dressed and then go up to the reception area to give Mrs. Salinger my credit card.

"No charge," she says. "We'll just see you next time, okay?"

A sense of failure grips me as we drive home. I sneak a sideways glance at Ali, trying to read her thoughts. "Damn," I say, forcing a lightness into my voice. "I bet I gave poor Dr. Salinger the scare of the century."

Ali cracks a smile. "No kidding," she says.

I look out the window, unsure of what to say. My hands twist in my lap, another nervous habit I've acquired. I force them apart. "I bet this wasn't the homecoming you were anticipating."

"I don't know how to answer that." She shakes her head. "The main thing is you're home. That's all that matters. Right?"

"Right," I say, to appease her. That's all we're doing, I figure. Appeasing one another.

33

▼ ▶ ▲ ◀ ▼ ▲ ▶ ▲

Thursday, August 22

The vultures keep circling around us. Sam has not asked for her phone back yet, so I've been monitoring her emails and texts. Jenny Burns has left five voicemails for me and three emails on Sam's work address, clamoring for an interview. I've received queries from media from as far away as Hawaii. A man from the Islamic Defense Fund, based in New Jersey, has invited me to talk about Islamophobia in America at their annual gathering in October. Several of my clients who had dropped me like a hot potato have written to say how "thrilled" they are at this "latest development." Not one of them has apologized, of course. Candace has written several exuberant emails and texts to Samantha, although the last two have been long rants against the hapless faculty member who is now directing her dissertation. If there were a Tone Deafness of the Year award, Candace would be a multiple-time winner.

The doorbell rings and I answer. It is Herrington, who stops by often. Each time, he tries to tease out any scrap of memory of Sam's abductor. Each time, it takes her hours to recover after he leaves.

He steps in and greets me like an old friend. "Where is she?" he says, looking around.

"She's upstairs. Taking a nap."

We exchange looks. "Still sleeping a lot?"

"Yup." I keep my voice light, but my stupid lower lip trembles and betrays me.

"Right."

"I suppose it's to be expected?" I ask. "It's pretty common behavior?"

He puffs his cheeks and exhales. "Hard to answer. Every victim reacts differently. But in general, yes. It takes a long time to get over trauma." His eyes sweep the room, land on me. "And you? How're you holding up?"

"Fine," I say. "Great."

He nods. "Okay. One more time, this time without the bravado."

"Well, you know. Under the circumstances."

"It's gonna be a long road," he says. Pace yourself."

Abba has been telling me the same thing each night when we talk, after Sam is upstairs in bed. But nobody can tell me *how* and what I should be doing differently.

After I awaken Sam, I make Herrington a cup of tea. I'm surprised to see Sam come downstairs in her pj's, although she's thrown a shawl over the top. Her red hair is uncombed, and she doesn't bother to hide her annoyance at seeing Herrington again. He rises to greet her, his face impassive.

I hand Herrington his cup as Sam takes a seat on the couch across from him. "Want a cup of tea, hon?" I ask her.

"No thanks."

"You sure? It will perk you up."

"I said no," she snaps. "Why do I have to repeat everything?"

I bite my lower lip as Herrington casts a quick, sympathetic look my way. I make my way into the kitchen and busy myself. I hear Herrington apologizing to her for waking her up. To my mortification, she doesn't reply.

Herrington clears his throat. "Anyway, I'm here because we may have a break in the case," he says, as I make my way back to the living room. He pulls out a photograph from a file folder and hands it to Sam. "Police in Youngstown arrested this guy yesterday in connection with the abduction of two schoolgirls. We were wondering if he looks familiar?"

I wander back into the living room, sit beside Sam. She doesn't even glance at the picture. "I've told you several times. I never got to see my—the guy who took me. I was blindfolded the entire time."

Herrington nods, chews on his inner cheek. "I get that. But I just thought . . . You'd mentioned that your abductor had said he'd taken you far away from Cleveland Heights."

Now, Sam glances at the photo briefly, then looks up. "It's not him," she says, and her sudden certainty makes both me and Herrington sit up. "How do you know?" he asks.

"Because this guy is heavyset. Whereas the guy who kidnapped me was of average build." Sam looks at me, turns away. "I could judge by when he was on . . . next to me."

I feel my cheeks flush. Herrington has the decency to not make eye contact with me as I struggle to catch my breath. In any case, he is showing Samantha a few more pictures.

"Excuse me," I say after a few minutes. "I have some calls to make."

I go upstairs to our home office and sit in the armchair, purging my mind of the unpleasant images that want to burrow in there. The monster has raped Samantha, I know this. But the fact that Sam knows his body, its shape and weight and contours—that fact has knocked the wind out of my sails. I stare out of the second-floor window. The sky is a deep blue, almost violet. How beautiful, how benign our backyard looks. Almost Edenic. And yet, how troubled our lives have become. The euphoria I'd felt when Sam was found is gone, flatlined into gratitude that she's safe, but tainted by panic at the long road of recovery ahead of us. Who knows how many other unpleasant revelations are in store, as Sam slowly reveals all the abuse she's suffered at the hands of the monster. Are you up to the challenge, Aliya? I ask myself. To be there for Sam no matter what? Even as I ponder the question, an image flashes: Abba sitting next to my dying mother late at night, holding her hand, making her giggle. Attracted by the sound of his steady voice and her giggles, so rare in those last awful weeks,

I had peered into their room. Mummy had seen me peeping and had called to me. "Come, baby," she'd said. "Come lie with me for a few minutes." And I had shaken my head no, scared of this gaunt, lifeless figure who'd usurped my mother's place. I watched Abba stroking Mummy's hair and singing "You Are My Sunshine" to her, a song they both used to sing to me on nights when sleep didn't come, back when we were whole, before cancer ate away the threads that knitted us together.

I sit up taller in Sam's chair. I am the daughter of Irfan and Noor Mirza. I will honor their love by being a pillar of strength for *my* love.

"Well, I'll take your leave, Ms. O'Malley," I hear Herrington say. "Please call if any detail comes to mind. Doesn't matter how minor it may seem." Then, the sound of the front door shutting.

I hear footsteps on the stairs. "Whatcha doing?" Sam says as she enters the room.

I shake my head. "Nothing."

A knowing look comes over Sam's face. "See? This is why I didn't want you listening when I'm talking to that guy. I know it upsets you."

"*That guy*? Do you know what efforts Herrington made to bring you home, Sam? He's only doing his job. You act like you don't care if that evil bastard gets caught or not."

"I don't care? How dare you?" Sam's face turns red with fury. "And if that cop made such efforts to find me, why didn't he? If I'm free it's not because of what he did. Or anyone else for that matter."

Even as it stings to hear Sam say those words—I feel like she is including me in those who failed to rescue her—I can't deny the veracity of what she's saying. I remember my resolution from a moment ago and leap to my feet. "Babe, come here," I say. "I'm sorry. I know you're angry and frustrated and . . ."

"Ali, you have no idea."

"Then tell me. Get it all off your chest."

"I . . . I can't. Maybe someday. When we can both handle it. In the meantime, you just have to trust me. I don't want you there when I talk to the cops. Okay?"

I have no choice but to acquiesce. I shiver. I'm thrilled that Sam is home. I really am. But this is also true—the loneliness that I've felt from the day she disappeared is still very much there.

34

▾ ▸ ▴ ◂ ▾ ▴ ▸ ▴

Wednesday, August 28

We sit down to the first meal I've cooked since I've come home. It's a simple meal—lemon pasta with a sprinkling of basil and a beet salad on the side. I can tell Ali is grateful. She has been doing everything to make me comfortable since I have returned home, to the point of neglecting going to her office. Instead, she works on her laptop after I go to bed and the fatigue is showing on her face. She hasn't left the house without me even once—Nathan mostly does our grocery shopping for us.

"That was a great meal," Ali says. "Thank you."

"Of course. Hey, thanks for watering our garden while I was . . . away."

"Sure. Although Nathan used to sneak into the yard and water, while I was at work. Do you feel like inviting him over this Saturday? I'll cook. Or we can do takeout."

I hesitate. "Did you—did you tell me earlier that you'd called my mom to tell her I was alive? The day they found me?"

Ali nods. "Yup. I called both her and my dad as soon as the cops said they'd found you. While I was driving to the hospital to see you."

"How did my dad react?"

Ali is silent.

"What?"

"Sam, I didn't want to tell you right away. But honey. Your dad . . . he has Alzheimer's. I'm sorry."

"Alzheimer's?" In all the years I lived at home, I don't recall my father so much as getting a cold. "I can't believe it. How is my mom dealing with it, did she say?"

"She's okay. She said it's easier, actually. He's mellowed a great deal, she said."

"Joe O'Malley, mellow? Are we talking about the same man?"

"I'm afraid so."

"I want to go see her," I say after a few minutes. "My mom."

"Sure, honey. Whatever you wish."

"This weekend," I say. "Can we?"

Ali looks startled but recovers. "If that's what you want."

35

▾ ▸ ▴ ◂ ▾ ▴ ▸ ▴

Saturday, August 24

We take off at nine o'clock on Saturday morning. It's my second time leaving the house, after our ill-fated trip to the chiropractor. I lower the car window to feel the summer breeze on my face.

Our plans have changed a bit. We'll visit Mom and Dad on Sunday. Mr. Mirza invited us to spend Saturday with them and Ali looked so tempted, I said yes. I've always hated that we were both distant from our families. Still, I'm nervous about being around strangers so soon after my return. And I have no idea how Yasmin Mirza will react to my presence. I've only met Ali's parents once, at Ali's graduation. Ali has already prepared me for the possibility that we'll have to sleep in separate bedrooms, and I've reassured her that it's fine. My sleep is so disturbed these days that I often move into the guest bedroom in the middle of the night, anyway.

Mr. Mirza greets us in his driveway. I lean against our Subaru as father and daughter embrace and then he comes up to me. "Welcome, welcome, Samantha. It's good to see you again," he says, his eyes warm. He makes as if to embrace me, then pulls back. Maybe Ali has warned him about the involuntary reflex I've developed when I'm touched.

"Hi, Mr. Mirza," I say.

"Please, call me Irfan," he says.

I smile awkwardly.

He grabs our small suitcase from the backseat and walks us into his home. It's a newer ranch with an open floor plan. I recognize the small, round marble table with blue-and-green inlay work in the living room. We have one of those tables from India, also. It makes me feel connected to this home in an unexpected way. "I have you two here in the first bedroom," Mr. Mirza says, pointing. "I'll go put your bag in there."

Ali and I exchange a surprised look while he's gone. And then Yasmin Mirza walks in. She is wearing a blue cotton kaftan and house slippers. Whereas Ali's dad is handsome and distinguished-looking, Mrs. Mirza is an ordinary-looking woman, with hooded eyes. I catch myself; surely, I'm colored by Ali's thorny relationship with her stepmom.

"Hello, Yasmin." I hear the stiffness in Ali's voice.

"Hi, beta," Yasmin says as she approaches Ali, kissing her on both cheeks. "Welcome to your home."

"Yasmin, this is Samantha."

"Yes, yes, of course. Welcome. It is good to see you looking well."

"Thank you."

Ali's dad comes back to join us. "What will you girls drink?" he asks. "Coke? Sprite? Juice?"

"Just water for me," I say.

"I'll get it," Yasmin says. She turns to her husband and says something in rapid-fire Hindi. He shakes his head impatiently and I almost chuckle at the stubborn set of his jaw, so like Ali's. Even without looking at Ali's reaction, I sense that they're arguing about our sleeping arrangements. I wish we'd gotten a hotel room, but Ali had been so taken by her father's insistence that we stay with them. None of my American friends will get this, but I'm always amazed at the parallels between Irish and Indian culture. Both put such a premium on pride and on family.

Despite this inauspicious start, the rest of the day goes surprisingly well. There is a new, easy companionability between Ali and her dad, which gratifies me. Even Yasmin seems more open and friendly by the time we sit down for dinner.

We gasp at the number of dishes on the table. I recognize the biryani and a chickpea dish that Ali also makes. I also recognize the Indian bread and tandoori chicken. But the rest of the food is unfamiliar to me—there are two kinds of vegetables, two salads, chicken in a white sauce, and some vegetable fritters in a red sauce. "Abba, what have you done?" Ali says.

Mr. Mirza grins. "Thank your stepmother," he says. "She did the bulk of the cooking. I just made the tandoori chicken."

"Thanks, Yasmin," Ali says dutifully.

"No thanks-fanks," Yasmin responds. "This is the first time you're visiting us in how many years? This is your home, isn't it?"

The look on Ali's face! She has needed this homecoming so much. I'm only now beginning to understand that our estrangements from our families are different. I genuinely dislike and fear my father; she has missed hers terribly. No wonder Ali always comes across as tough and self-sufficient; the tenderest flowers grow the sharpest thorns.

"How's business, beta?" Mr. Mirza asks and Ali shrugs.

"It'll pick up," I say. "Now that she won't be—distracted."

"And you, Samantha?" His voice is gentle.

"I'm not teaching this semester. My chair gave me the semester off, to, you know, recover."

Yasmin's face flushes, and she bites her lower lip. "Whatever animal did that to you, may worms feast on him," she cries. "In our religion . . ."

"Yasmin," Mr. Mirza says, and an awkward silence falls around the table. He flashes me an apologetic smile. I am made of porcelain; people now treat me as if I need to be handled with care.

"It's okay," I say. "I appreciate it. I wish the same thing on him." I smile mirthlessly, hoping to ease the tension in the room.

Ali asks Yasmin a few questions about her family in India and Yasmin leaps to her feet. She returns holding a card. "My younger sister's son, Kabir, is getting married next March," she says. "Fatima is a widow, but she will get him married with great dhoom-dhaam. Kabir himself is doing well, thanks be to God. Working for a big IT company, he is." She stops, then adds, "Beta, you should come with your abba and me."

I notice she doesn't include me in the invite.

Ali makes a vague sound. "Thanks," she says noncommittedly.

After we are done with dinner, Ali says, "Sam and I will clean up."

Mrs. Mirza is about to refuse, when her husband stops her. "Let them," he says and the two of us pick up a few dishes and flee to the kitchen.

"You okay?" Ali asks when we're at the sink. "Yasmin is a blunder-buss. She didn't mean anything."

My heart lurches at the worried, serious look on her face. "Honey, I'm fine," I say. "Everyone needs to just chill. I'm actually enjoying being away from home."

After the table is cleared Mr. Mirza brings out a deck of cards and the four of us play Hearts. Ali wins the first three rounds, taking true pleasure in her victories. "I see where she gets her competitive streak from," I say with a laugh and father and daughter both grin the same grin.

"Not me," Yasmin says. "I'm a total duffer."

Despite her homophobia, I like Yasmin. There is something naïve and disarming about her. "That's not true," I say, and she gives me a gratified look.

Yasmin averts her eyes when we get up to go into the bedroom with the queen-sized bed. "Good night, Abba," Ali calls before she shuts the door.

We brush our teeth, climb into bed, and turn off the light. I can see the moon from the window that overlooks the backyard.

"What are you thinking?" Ali says, as she snuggles next to me, her hand across my waist. Relax, I say to myself, it's not the monster. It's Ali, who would never hurt you.

"Babe?" Ali says tentatively. "You okay?"

I turn to face her. "Everything's fine. Your dad is wonderful. I even like Yasmin."

"Really?" Ali says, and I hear the relief and wonder in her voice.

We fall asleep spooning against each other for a couple of hours. The first time I'd slept with Ali, we'd fallen asleep against each other in this manner, and it has always comforted me to lean my animal warmth into hers. But then I wake up from a deep sleep, heart thudding. As I've done these past two weeks, I remind myself that it's Ali next to me, that I'm safe. I try to calm myself, but the crowded, claustrophobic feeling has taken ahold of me, my skin hurts, and I want to get out of this bed that suddenly feels hot and crowded. Now, all I can think of is that man having his way with me, and I, blindfolded, disoriented, feeling like I was underwater, that ghastly drowning feeling, the pressure building in my chest, unable to scream or vent because if I did, his hands would be around my neck, squeezing, the edge of his ring biting into my skin. I remember to breathe, breathe, breathe. Samantha, I say to myself, open your eyes, you're not in some stranger's home, you're in Ali's father's home. But the bed is too soft or maybe too hard and it is hot in this room and I'm sweating, I'm drowning in sweat, I'm a hot mess, a puddle of sweat and neurosis and I focus on Ali's breathing, steady as the sound of the ocean, in and out and I try and follow along, I close my eyes, I open my eyes, I try and orient myself, calm myself, but her body against mine no longer feels like a safe harbor, it is overwhelming me, and I toss off the sheets and climb out of bed and pad my way to the bathroom.

I throw cold water over my face and glance at my watch. It's one in the morning. A whole torturous night ahead of me and sleep will keep eluding me, and my brain will flood with memories that I need to exorcise. My mind has become a filing cabinet of trauma and pain, and every night, a drawer slides open and memories slither out. I stand at the foot of the bed and know that spending the night in this strange bedroom was a mistake. It's too soon. At home, I can make my way to the guest bedroom each night, but here, where am I to go? There's the couch in the living room; its leather will feel cool against my skin, and I long to make my way there just to get some sleep so that I can wake up fresh tomorrow morning, when I have to face another monster. But I don't want to embarrass Ali in her father's house. So, I climb back into this stifling bed.

Fifteen minutes later, I toss off the sheet again. Ali mutters in her sleep but doesn't awaken. I make my way in the dark into an unfamiliar living room. Luckily, they have left on the lights under the kitchen cabinets. I arrange the cushions under my head and use the throw to cover myself, and despite the narrowness of the couch, I immediately feel a sense of liberation. I close my eyes and my last thought is, I'll go back to the bedroom toward morning before anyone finds me here.

There is a sound. A man clears his throat. I am immediately wide awake, my body stiffening as I await the inevitable assault. I hear the sound of running water and I'm transported to that cold, damp bathroom. I can't open my eyes, I dare not. And then, as sleep recedes and consciousness seeps in, I remember that I am safe. That I am in Ali's father's home. I open my eyes.

Mr. Mirza is in the kitchen, filling a small pitcher with water, his back to me. He is watering the plants in the kitchen window. I cover myself with the throw and sit up on the couch, trying to come up with an explanation for what I'm doing out here.

"Sorry if I woke you." His voice is low, husky with sleep. "It's almost time for namaz and I usually pray in the living room." He gestures toward the small prayer rug that he's rolled out in a corner of the room.

I am mortified, feeling as if I'd been about to intrude on something private. "I'm so sorry," I whisper. "I couldn't sleep. But I'll go back to the . . ."

"No, no. It's fine. This will not take long." And before I can answer, he covers his head with a white cap and kneels on the little rug. As I watch, he closes his eyes and raises his hands before his face, chanting his prayers in a sonorous voice that reminds me of Father John in the church of my childhood. The melodious chanting soothes me, and without meaning to, I find myself silently reciting "The Lord's Prayer" in unison, as if his religiosity is a drug that I have imbibed, one that triggers a corresponding recollection of faith in me.

When he is done, he rolls up the rug, then sits in the chair across from me. We gaze at each other silently. Outside, the sky is growing lighter, and I can hear the birds of August awaking.

"Cannot sleep?" he says.

There is something so quiet, and yet so sympathetic, in his voice that my eyes fill with tears. I wish that I'd had a father like him. "No, not really," I say. "Ever since I . . . returned home."

He nods. Another silence falls between us. Then, he says, "I understand. I was like this for a long time. After Ali's mother died. Even before that. From the day we got the news of her cancer."

I want to ask him so many questions, about how it was for him and Ali after such a loss, how he made his way back from the wilderness. What I find myself saying is, "I don't want to hurt Ali in any way. But it's so very hard . . ."

"Of course it is." His voice is still quiet, steady. "You have been through an unimaginable trauma, child. It will take time to recover."

It is that *child* that makes me come undone. There's a lifetime of pain in my tears, the absence of a father who seldom looked at me as kindly as Mr. Mirza is looking at me. This is where Ali gets it from, I think, her kindness toward all living creatures. Often, at parties, Ali will gravitate toward the loneliest, most socially awkward person, will spend the evening chatting with them, drawing them out. It used to make me crazy because I wanted her to be by my side throughout the evening, instead of sitting in a corner making some stranger laugh. And when I'd complain on the way home, she'd look disappointed, point out that I was surrounded by friends whereas this person needed someone. I was just being kind, Samantha, she'd say. Besides, I was following you with my eyes all evening long.

I'm crying hard now, in a way I've not allowed myself to since I've returned home, and I'm afraid that Mr. Mirza will feel the need to come sit next to me on the couch and put a comforting hand on my shoulder.

But he doesn't; he just continues sitting across from me, nodding at me encouragingly. My eyes are so blurry with tears that I can barely make out his face.

"It's good to cry," he finally says. "Better than keeping it all inside."

I feel lighter when I finally stop. He gets up, fetches me a drink of water. "Better?" he asks, after I set the glass down.

"Yes, Mr. Mirza," I say.

"Irfan," he corrects. "Well, do you want to go back to sleep?"

"Yes. But I think I'll go back to the bedroom. Before Ali awakens."

A look passes between us. He nods. "That's a good idea. No sense in worrying her."

I walk to the hallway, then turn back. "Thank you."

"No mention." And he urges me on with a slight motion of his head.

In the bedroom, I slip under the covers. Ali groans as she senses my presence, but she is still fast asleep. I smile to myself. The sleep of angels, I used to say. I wonder if I'll ever be able to sleep the whole night by her side, whether these panic attacks will ever cease. I turn on my side to escape the implications of that dismal thought.

"Boy, you and Yasmin sure hit it off," Ali says to me the next morning when we're back on the road.

I gesture to the large box of sweets she'd forced into my hands as we'd left. A gift for my parents, she'd said. "She didn't have to do that," I say. "Or make that unbelievable dinner."

Ali shrugs. "She's probably regifting the box of sweets. Indians are big regifters."

I open my mouth to argue, then think the better of it. I know Ali blames Yasmin for the years of silence between her father and herself. Some wounds run so deep that logic doesn't work. I know this from my own history.

Unlike the Mirza home, my family home looks small and shabby. The outside needs a coat of paint and some of the boards on the front porch are coming loose. We ring the doorbell, which doesn't work. I knock on the door.

There's the sound of someone approaching and Dad opens the door. He peers at us. "Yes?" he says. There is no recognition on his face.

"Hi, Dad," I say stiffly. "Is Mom home?"

He looks at me and then at Ali. His eyes narrow with suspicion. "Can I help you?" he says, and I know that even in this demented state he's reacting to her darker skin. My heart curdles with hatred toward this petty, bigoted man. Instinctively, I take a step toward Ali, as if to protect her from him. But Ali, confident and charming as ever, flashes a smile.

"Hello, Mr. O'Malley," she says. "How are you?"

"Fine," he mumbles, retracting into himself. "Emily," he yells. "There's someone at the door."

Mom rushes to the door, wiping her hands on a dish towel. "Sorry, sorry, I was in the kitchen. Well, come in, girls. Joe, don't just stand there, blocking the door."

We walk in and I'm immediately embarrassed. Mom scuttles around in her usual nervous way, wiping off imaginary dust from the couch before asking us to sit. Ali and I take a seat, while Dad shuffles to his favorite recliner, which looks old and shabby. Mom has lost weight, and her hair has turned gray since I last saw her. I feel a pang of regret at having abandoned her after my father unceremoniously threw us out of his house the year Ali and I got married. The man in the recliner is almost unrecognizable. His face sags and there's a slight tremor in those large hands. His eyes, aglow with rage for most of my childhood, have a faraway, hazy look in them. He is staring at me and nodding to himself, as if he's trying to place me. I look away and focus on Mom, who is fussing around, asking Ali what she'd like to drink.

"Sit down, Mom," I say. "We had a large breakfast at Ali's dad's home before coming here."

"Oh, did you?" she says and pulls up a chair. "That's nice, honey." Her voice and her movements are as birdlike as ever. But she's wearing a sleeveless dress, and I'm gratified to see the lack of bruises on her arms. For much of my childhood, my mother wore long sleeves and pants even in the dead of summer.

"And they sent you this." I hand her a large box of Indian sweets and her eyes widen.

"Look, Joe," she says. "Ali's parents gave us this gift. Isn't that good of them?"

Dad grunts. It is obvious he has no idea what's going on.

"How is he, Mom? What do the doctors say?"

"As you see him, honey. You see, he has Parkinson's as well as dementia."

I swallow. "And you? How are you managing? Do you have help?"

Her eyes cast around the room, and I get the sense that she's as embarrassed by the state of the house as I am. "An aide comes in three days a week to shower him. But other than that . . ." She looks down at her hands in her lap. "But I can manage him just fine." She lowers her voice. "He's mellowed a great deal. Actually, he's a pussycat now, aren't you, Joey?"

I hold her gaze for a long second, a lifetime of memories of his physical abuse telegraphing between us. "That's good to know, Mom. I worry about you, you know?"

She seems distracted when she replies, "Well, you don't need to. We are just fine, Joe and I."

I look at Ali, silently begging her to intercede.

"Can we take both of you out to lunch, Mrs. O'Malley?" she says.

"Oh, that's okay, Ali," she says. "Joe is not really in a condition to leave the house. And I don't really go anywhere without him."

"Well then, you and Samantha should go get a bite somewhere," Ali says immediately. "I can sit with Mr. O'Malley for a couple of hours."

Mom looks horrified at the thought. "No, no, you see, Joey gets upset if I'm gone even to the grocery store," she says. "It's fine. You girls go along and get lunch."

Despite my sympathy, her wimpy attitude grates on me. "Mom," I say sharply. "We didn't come all this way to eat lunch without you."

"That's okay, Sam." Ali is running interference. "How about we go pick up some food for everyone in a little while?"

And so, the matter is settled.

We stop at a Middle Eastern restaurant. I protest at the amount of food Ali orders—two mujadara plates, chicken shawarma, grape leaves, hummus, baba ghanoush, and a small mountain of pita bread—but she stops me with, "It's fine, Sam. This way, there will be leftovers for them. Let's give your mom a break, shall we?"

It isn't until we sit to eat that I realize how bad Dad's condition truly is. Mom puts a bib on him, cuts up the chicken shawarma into tiny bits, and then guides the spoon he is clenching to his mouth. Even so, his hand trembles so violently that most of the food lands back on his plate. He drops the spoon and picks up some of the food with his fingers but struggles to reach his mouth. Mom helps him. She catches my stunned look and smiles reassuringly. "It's okay, honey. He just takes a little longer than usual, is all."

I am so invested in figuring out the source of this endless supply of patience that I miss the fact that Dad has turned his head and is staring at me, a new expression on his face. And so, I almost drop my own fork when he says, clear as day, "Hey, kiddo. Maybe you should be feeding your old man."

He grins that cocky Joe O'Malley grin, the one that used to enthrall me as a child, the one that he flashed on days when he came home in a good mood, when his shoulder or knees didn't ache as much or when his boss had paid him a rare compliment. That's the grin I recognize from my high school graduation photo, Mom in sunglasses and a floral dress and him in his brown suit, standing on either side of me.

"See?" Mom turns to Ali. "That's what I tell all his doctors. He's not as far gone as they make it sound. Not a day goes by when Joe doesn't ask about Samantha. Isn't that true, Joey?"

But as soon as it appears, the sunniness dissipates, and the familiar scowl replaces it. His face darkens and he begins to shake uncontrollably.

"Samantha's gone," he says. "There's no more Samantha." He slams one beefy hand on the table. "She's dead. To me."

"Joe," Mom cries. "You're talking nonsense."

Even as we watch, a third person occupies my father's body. Cocky Joe is gone, as is Angry Joe. Cowering Joe takes their place. "Need to do potty," he pleads. "Please, need to be excused."

Ali and I sit in silence as Mom helps him to the bathroom. "The strain on her," Ali says finally and all I can do is nod. Mom has not touched her plate and suddenly I have no appetite either. Ali takes my hand. "Sorry, Sam."

I sigh. "Welcome to my crazy family."

Mom takes Dad directly to the bedroom from the bathroom. Our food, untouched on our plates, is cold by the time she reappears, apologizing for his behavior.

"Mom, stop," I finally say. "It's fine. He's clearly sick. Here, let me warm up your food."

"Oh, it's okay. I'm not even hungry. You girls eat something, please. And Sam, I made your favorite dessert—carrot cake. You still like it, right?"

And she looks at me so anxiously, I want to burst into tears. Her nervousness and eagerness to please, qualities that used to drive me crazy as a teenager, now arouse a powerful pity in me. "Of course, Mom," I say. "Thank you."

We pick at our food while Mom catches us up on the history of Dad's diagnosis and treatment.

"Why didn't you call me, Mom?" I finally say, and she gives me a tearful look.

"I—I didn't know what to do, honey. Your father didn't want anyone to know. And after the way he treated you the last time you were here, I wasn't sure if you would . . . Well, I just decided to let sleeping dogs lie."

I can hardly breathe; the pain is so powerful. My own parents keeping something this important from me. It makes me feel orphaned, even though my mom is two feet away from me.

After we eat the cake, Ali gets up to gather the dishes. "I'll clean up," she says. "Maybe the two of you can chat a bit." And when Mom rises to protest, Ali says firmly. "It's okay, Mrs. O'Malley. Samantha came to visit with you. Please don't disappoint her."

We sit next to each other on the couch, the springs giving way as I plop down. I need to start sending them money each month, I think. They need a new couch. The house needs to be painted.

"Sam," Mom says. "How are you? I'm so glad you're back home. Ali mentioned you were . . . gone. You look so good."

If I didn't know better, I would've thought that Ali had kept the truth of my kidnapping from her. Or that she, too, had a touch of dementia. But this is my mom's way of coping with unpleasant truths; it's probably this trait that has allowed her to stay married to my father. And so, I swallow my irritation and put my arm around her.

"How are *you*, Mom?" I say. "You must be exhausted, caring for him."

Her eyes fill with tears. "It's okay. The church ladies bring us food on Tuesdays, so that's a blessing. And we have new neighbors next door, and their son helps whenever I need to transfer Joey to the car."

"Does he . . . Does he still hit you?"

"Oh, honey, no. My, I can't believe you still remember that. It was nothing." She lets out a nervous laugh. "No, he's mostly a teddy bear. I mean, once in a while if he's frustrated, he lashes out, you know? The poor man, so helpless now. You remember how active your father used to be."

I'm incredulous that she's defending him and trying to whitewash the past. Is this love? Or some form of Stockholm syndrome? Would this have happened to me if my captor hadn't set me free? I rein in my mind from where it wishes to go.

"I wish you could come stay with us for a couple of weeks, Mom," I say. "You'd like Cleveland Heights, I think."

"Oh, that's okay, you girls have your own life to live. You wouldn't want your old mother getting in the way."

She's talking to me as if I'm a stranger, and my heart aches. But why wouldn't she? My parents live out in the country; I live in what is jokingly called the People's Republic of Cleveland Heights. They are conservative; I am a flaming liberal. They have high school diplomas; I have a doctorate. What would mom think if she met my educated, urbane friends and colleagues? We live in different Americas, all the divisions and contradictions of our nation embodied in one family.

"That's not true, Mom," I say urgently. "You'd never be in my way. I . . . You're the one who used to take me to the library when I was a kid, remember? If you hadn't . . . Everything I am, it's because of you, Mom. I'm sorry I never thanked you before. I'm sorry I've been so distant."

"Oh, Sam," she chuckles as she strokes my hair. "You're my daughter. Why on earth would you thank me? I'm so proud of you, being a college professor and all. Ask any of the ladies at church—I brag about you all the time."

I don't think my mom has ever told me she was proud of me. Something has changed. Dad's diagnosis may have created a lot more physical work for her, but maybe it's also freed her in some way? This is what the lack of physical abuse has done—for the first time in her life she's calling the shots. I feel a renewed sense of hatred for that man, no matter how piteous his current condition.

"Did you ever want to go to college, Mom?" I ask.

She gets a faraway look in her eyes. "I wanted to. I graduated valedictorian of my high school, did I ever tell you? But my pops said I needed to help with the family. So, I got a job at Higbee's as a salesgirl in the perfume department. That's where I met your dad. He came in one day to buy a bottle for Mother's Day. Well, once we got married and I had Andy, Joey didn't want me to work. So, I quit."

My brother Andy died when he was six, before I was born. There's a framed picture of him in my parents' bedroom, but they never spoke about him. One time, when I was three, I asked where the boy in the picture lived, and my father slapped me.

There's grief seeping from the walls of this house. I want to fetch Ali and run out of this dark, unhappy place, never to return. I've always been afraid that my mother's spinelessness and her sad, unfortunate life would rub off on me. It's one of the reasons I've held myself stiffly against her; in some ways, I've pushed her away much more than I have my dad. He was a loud, angry, hard-drinking man, who swung between episodes of rage and moments of normalcy throughout my childhood. My feelings for him were clear—hatred when he hit my mom or yelled at me and a resentful, grudging love at other times. My feelings for my mom have always been far more complicated—I disliked her for her acquiescence and complicity, her terrible docility, not because I didn't understand it, but because I did. I feared turning into her. And I couldn't forgive her for her neglect, because all her time and energy went into appeasing my father.

But my time in captivity has taught me about fear and complicity. When your life is in danger, you become whoever your captor wishes you to be. I was a prisoner for just six weeks; my mother has been held in place by my father's moods and rage for her entire adult life. When I lived under the same roof as him, I, too, tiptoed around the house—a fact that I had forgotten after I left home for college.

I look at my mom with a new understanding, a new solidarity. I want nothing more than to make up for the distance I've put between us, to apologize not in words—because I know her well enough to know she'll brush away my apologies and act as if nothing was ever wrong—but by my actions. Mom has never even seen our Cleveland Heights home, the one where on special occasions like Thanksgiving we use the beautiful tablecloth and napkins she'd embroidered and gifted to me when I'd finished college.

Thanksgiving.

"Mom, you still drive, yes?"

She looks up, surprised. "Well, yes, of course. You can't live out in the country and not drive, you know? Although there's a new grocery store that's opened that's much closer than the old Safeshop. But their prices are much higher, so I still mostly drive to the Safeshop. They renovated it two years ago."

"So why don't you come up to Cleveland for Thanksgiving? Spend a couple of days with us?"

Her hand flies to her mouth. "How can I? With your dad being the way he is?"

I'm debating whether it would be possible to host Dad also or whether it would be better for us to drive here for the holiday, when Ali comes into the room, drying her hands on a kitchen towel.

"Surely there's some respite care facility around here?" she says. "Maybe the break from constant caregiving would do you good?"

"Oh, I don't know, girls," Mom says. "I don't know how Joe would be. He—he can still be a handful at times, you know?"

"Let me search for a nearby dementia facility," Ali says. "I think it's a great idea for you to celebrate Thanksgiving with us. It would mean the world to Sam."

Mom turns to me with a look of such longing, it takes my breath away. She's tempted but torn. "Mom," I say quietly. "I—after what happened—I need . . . would you please come visit our house and where I work? And you will like Cleveland Heights, I promise."

"Well, we'll see," Mom says, and I feel the usual disappointment. Between me and Dad, she'll always choose Dad, I think bitterly.

But Ali is undeterred. "We'll make it happen, okay?" she says cheerfully. "Just give me a couple of weeks to find a good rehab place for your husband." She smiles. "We'll have a great time, Mrs. O'Malley."

And then Mom says something unexpected. "Oh, stop calling me that, Ali," she says. "Mrs. O'Malley was my mother-in-law's name. If I'm going to come stay at your house, you better call me Mom."

The look on Ali's face is one I'll always remember.

We stay another two hours, during which I fix a few minor things around the house. I'm handy, which is a gift from my dad. Ali, on the other hand, doesn't have the patience to properly paint a wall, which is funny, given her chosen profession. When we get ready to leave, Mom gives us the rest of the carrot cake. "Keep some for yourself, Mom," I say, but she shakes her head no. Instead, she insists that I go kiss Dad goodbye.

Reluctantly, I enter the bedroom. I hover over him for a moment, glad for the chance to examine him unobserved. There is little of the strong, violent man I have feared most of my life. I bend down and give him a light kiss on the forehead. He awakens immediately and his eyes look directly into mine. The next moment, a wide, guileless smile floods his face.

"Hi, little champ," he says to me, and my heart cracks like a sheet of ice at his use of his childhood nickname for me.

"Hi, Dad," I whisper, swallowing the lump in my throat.

He frowns. "What's wrong, girlie?"

"Nothing," I say. I sit at the side of the bed. "How're you feeling, Dad?"

"I'm fine." It's only now that I notice that his eyes are too bright. He drops his voice. "It's that lady I'm worried about. She steals from me." He looks around the room wildly. "Can I come live with you, champ?"

I stare at him, not knowing what to say. My heart is slashed with contradictory emotions—love and fear and pity and distrust all nestled there. I look at his hands as they rest on his chest, hands that could hug or hit in what felt like the same moment. He's always been mercurial, but now there is a different quality to his mood swings. "You can come visit us sometime," I finally say.

His eyes shift to the doorway. "Will she be there?"

"Who?"

"That darkie."

The deep-set racism will probably outlive him, I think, feeling a revulsion that dispels any softening that I'd experienced. This man will never change. Even in this diminished state, his nastiness rages unchecked.

"Yes, she will," I say, my voice louder than I'd intended. "It's her house, actually."

Mom pokes her head in. "Sweetie? Ali said she wants to get home before dark. And I need to give your father his meds."

I get up immediately. Dad is grinning at me, but I ignore him.

Back in the living room, I take Mom's hand. "Listen to me. You don't have to live like this anymore." I'm glad that Ali is not here to hear this exchange and witness our dysfunction. "You can come live near us. Even with us, if you like. We can move him into a nursing facility up our way."

Her eyes widen. "Oh, no, honey, no. I . . . this is our home. And Joe needs me."

I need you, I want to scream. I always have, but you always put him first. Instead, I say, "Mom, do you even love him? Or do you just feel responsible for him?"

She cocks her head, looks me right in the eye. "Is there a difference?"

Touché, I think as I kiss her and take my leave. Touché.

Ali and I are quiet until we get on the freeway. Then, she rests her hand on my thigh and asks, "Are you glad we came?"

"I don't know. I think so." I'm still smarting from Dad's insult of Ali. I'm embarrassed by the crazy dynamics of my family, more so because my wife has witnessed some of it. I'm shaken by how much Dad's frighteningly sudden shifts of mood remind me of my captor, something that I don't have the bandwidth to unpack at the moment. I'm broken by a nagging feeling that growing up in this household had somehow primed me for what happened in July, that rather than an unfortunate accident, it was inevitable that another man, as angry and brutish as my father, would hurt me, too, that my cowering and deference toward my father during my childhood and teenage years was a prelude to my awful timidity during my weeks of captivity. You didn't have a choice, I tell myself, but I can't shake that feeling of cowardice.

Ali is speaking to me in calm, soothing tones. Her hand on my thigh feels reassuring, but a minute later, turns heavy and oppressive. The very things I've appreciated about Ali—her warmth and loving nature—now smother me. I don't know what to do about this. I can't bear the thought of hurting her any more than I already have, and yet her hand reminds me of other hands, and it feels as if it is crushing me, weighing me down. My body goes taut and stiff. Ali, ever attuned to the slightest shifts, removes it and there's breath in my lungs again.

Despite the air-conditioning, I crack the window and look out. Green fields rush past us. Nature is the only thing that hasn't let me down. I am back on social media although I just look, don't comment, and I'm realizing how nasty people were to Ali while I was away. Her experience so perfectly reflects the larger world, its indecipherable rage, it takes my breath away. The world feels precarious, tilted, askew—one false move and you find yourself in a freefall.

Falling. That's what it feels like since I've returned home. After all, it was a fall, my fall, our fall, that led to my kidnapping. I remember being distracted and tripping and landing on my side. But after that, the scene goes white. No, that's not true. There is blue, a close-up blue. Was I looking up at the sky? Into someone's eyes? My dad's eyes today, opening when I kissed his forehead and that unguarded, beatific smile. I'm beginning to wonder if he ever really loved me or Mom. In his own limited, stunted way, I think he did. I remember his calloused hands, his knees red and bruised. He worked ten-hour days for United Plumbers, bending, twisting into small spaces, crawling under people's sinks and bathtubs and toilets, cleaning out sewer lines. He'd come home in his soiled clothes and go directly to the bathroom and emerge in his pajamas a half hour later, smelling of Ivory soap, his face flushed, his dark hair wet. Mom would have dinner ready at the table and if something wasn't to his liking, if the mashed potatoes had a lump in them or the pot roast wasn't steaming hot, he would tattoo his fury at his bosses or his resentment of a difficult customer on her body. He smacked me around a few times also, but unlike my mother, I was a big girl, and eventually he stopped messing with me. Although, every day, I prayed that he'd write his rageful Morse code on my body, instead of my mother's.

A bubble of pain grows in my throat and I'm so afraid of it escaping my lips and terrifying Ali that I swallow it until it is lodged in my chest. My chest is a vault that will hold all my sadness and which I'll keep under lock and key. That's the way I'll get through this, by never revisiting it. The police have no trace of the animal who kidnapped me. He has probably disappeared back into whatever hole he emerged from. And it's not just me who has changed. I see it in Ali's eyes, not just the dark circles under them, but a new worry, a new wariness in them. I notice how she looks at me sometimes, when she thinks I'm absorbed in a task. I want to reassure her that her wife is back, fully and wholly hers again, but instead, I'm stuck in this idiotic, violated body, which has become the body of a wounded animal, cautious, afraid. We haven't made love since I've returned and I know that that is Ali's love language; it's with her body that she expresses herself, shows her vulnerability and need. And the fact that I can't give her even this morsel of our marriage—that even her touch, so welcome and so essential to me, turns, within minutes, into something heavy and oppressive—makes me feel like a piece of shit. Ali has suggested couples therapy, but the thought of a third person in the room, listening to us, judging, advising, is like a red welt on my skin. I haven't even been back to see my own therapist yet. I haven't told anyone other than that detective what that man did to me, how he was sensitive and caring one moment and explosive and angry the next. How, evening after evening, he made me "watch" TV next to him with my blindfold on, how he'd murmur that we were an old married couple, and I had to keep my mouth shut for fear of angering him, when I wanted to scream that I *was* married, that I already had what he so obviously craved, that he could rape and violate my body, but he could never touch the innermost part, the part that belonged to Ali.

We both speak at the same moment. "Are you . . ."

"You saved me."

"What?" Ali asks.

"You saved me. From that beast."

"I didn't do anything. I wish I could've."

"You did. It was your memory, knowing that I was married to you, that saved me."

There is an extended silence. This is the most I've said to her about my time in captivity.

"Do you want to talk about it, Sam?" she says.

I shake my head no. She thinks she can handle it; she thinks it will help me to get it off my chest, but I know Ali better than she knows herself. It will destroy her. No, the memory of that time must remain in the vault in my chest. "It's okay," I say. "There's no sense in talking about the past. We are here together, that's what matters."

She opens her mouth to argue, but I talk before she can. "I meant what I said to my mom. Can we host her for Thanksgiving weekend?"

"Of course. We can start looking for a respite care place for your dad. I'll work on it."

"You have enough to do with your job. I'm home this semester. I'll take care of it. Hey, how about we invite your dad and Yasmin, too? Do you think they'll come?"

"That would be great. I'll ask." She glances at me. "I'm so glad you and Abba hit it off. But I'm curious. What did you and he talk about in the living room early in the morning?"

I feel my face flush. "I'm sorry. I couldn't sleep. I went into the living room and fell asleep on the couch. And then, your dad came in to do his morning prayers. We spoke—for a bit after that. He—he mentioned that after your mom died, he, too, had trouble falling asleep."

Ali speaks so softly I barely hear her over the sound of the traffic. "But I am not dead."

36

▼ ▶ ▲ ◀ ▼ ▲ ▶ ▲

Monday, September 2

When I was three years old, my parents had a fight. I was so rattled at hearing my genteel mother yell at my dad that I crawled into the cabinet under the kitchen sink and hid there, until Mummy found me and cajoled me out with a chocolate. I remember feeling safe in that dark cabinet, away from the sorrow and unpredictability of the world.

That's the same feeling I now have, entering my work office for the first time since Samantha has come home. For the past two weeks I've been loath to leave her alone for any length of time. But today, I felt an overwhelming need to escape. Sam spends hours in bed and even when she's awake, she's listless and lethargic a lot of the time. Mostly, I tiptoe around subjects, afraid of saying something that will upset her.

I have a feeling that Sam needs a break from me, too.

Still, there are moments that make me feel hopeful: Sam visiting my abba's house. And her inviting her mom to our home for Thanksgiving and Mrs. O'Malley seeming genuinely tempted by the invitation, makes me think that healing and reconciliation might still be possible. This is what I've always wished for, to host our families, to have them get along, to prove to them that our marriage is no less than anyone else's. The book Abba gave me quotes Allah as saying, "There is nothing like marriage, like two who love one another." I know Yasmin would consider it blasphemy for me to think that Allah meant to include couples like Samantha and me. But now that Sam's back, I'm no longer satisfied with the old order. I want to stitch a bigger, richer tapestry than the one we had before.

It's time to get down to work. Instead, I pick up the phone and call Sam.

"Are you spying on me?" she asks when she picks up, but there's a smile in her voice.

"Yeah. I wanna make sure you don't disappear on me again." The words are out of my mouth before I can arrest them.

There is a stunned silence. Too soon, I think. But then, she giggles. "You bitch," she says and now, we're both laughing. It feels cleansing, this laughter, like in the old days when we were playful and unguarded around each other.

"Sorry," I say. "But seriously, how are you, honey?"

"Ali, I'm fine. Stop worrying and focus on your work. And then, come home to me."

The warmth in Sam's voice sustains me as I work on the drawing for a kitchen in Beachwood. In between, I call a few of my usual suppliers. Andy, the cabinet maker, picks up. "Hiya, Ali," he says. "Haven't heard from you in a while."

"Yeah, sorry. I've been busy the last couple of months." Andy lives out in Chesterland and I'm not sure if he's heard about what had happened to Sam. But I don't have to wonder for long because he says, "Yeah, I know. So glad your friend is back home. And I read the shit that people said about you. I'm sorry. You don't deserve that."

Andy builds cabinets from a barn behind his home out in the country. I've been there a few times and had to ignore the right-wing talk shows that are always playing on his transistor radio. Once, when the weather was unseasonably warm for February, I'd made some passing comment about climate change and Andy had shaken his head and said, "Nah, it's God's will. The earth has always gone through these cycles. It's just politicians trying to hurt folks by shutting down coal plants and all."

Still, I like him. He's blunt and honest to a fault, and after the way I was treated by some of my so-called liberal clients and acquaintances, I like knowing where I truly stand with people. And so, I'm moved by his words, enough to momentarily block out the fact that next year he will vote for a man who will nominate justices who may invalidate my marriage. "Thanks, Andy," I say.

He clears his throat. "Well, then, what can I help you with?" he says, and I grin. Andy has used up his quota of socializing for the day.

I spend a couple more hours at work, paying bills, making out invoices. This was the year I was planning on hiring a business manager, but things are now financially dicey, and it makes sense to wait. I need to make sure that my business will get back to where it was and that Sam will be stable enough to return to work next semester. I look out the window. The sun is low in the sky. I wish I could entice Sam into going out to dinner, but she mostly refuses to leave the house. I want to start running again—my muscles are tight from inactivity and I feel restless—but she won't hear of joining me. Samantha seems more like her timid, scared mom than she ever did before. Who wouldn't be, after the unimaginable trauma she's been through? If I ever get my hands on the bastard who did this to her, I'll kill him. But he has disappeared like smoke.

I text Sam.

Want me to pick up some food on my way home? I'll probably be leaving here in another hour or so.

Sure.

What would you like? Thai? Chinese? Pizza?

Whatever you wish.

I am suddenly exasperated by her passivity. I catch myself. Give her time, I tell myself, give her time. Sooner or later, the Sam that you know will return to you again. In the meantime, what you can give her is normalcy.

Please Allah, let the waters of time cleanse us eventually, I pray. This is all we have for now—wisps of prayer, thin tendrils of hope.

37

▾▸▴◂▾▴▸▴

Monday, September 23

"Sometimes, I don't recognize her, Mo," I overhear Ali say on the phone as I come down the stairs. "It's like there's two of her—the woman she used to be and the shell that she's become."

I turn away before she can see me. She's right—I am two women trapped in one body. Half of me mourns what has happened to me, unable to come to terms with it. The other half is mad with gratitude at being given a second chance. Before my kidnapping, I would've defined freedom as a woman's right to choose, for people to love whoever they want, for working people to join unions, that kind of thing. Now, I think of freedom as the right to make the ordinary, everyday choices that make up a life.

The country, too, is two nations trapped in one body. Red America vs. Blue America. There is nonstop chatter about the president's call to the president of Ukraine asking for dirt on his opponent. The news shows are filled with talk about impeachments and denials and counteraccusations. Hate and distrust have become our national languages, and we have all become fluent in them.

After Ali leaves for work, I take a shower and wash my hair. I'm blow-drying it when I have a flash of memory—how the monster used to pin me down by my hair as he forced his mouth upon mine. How he used to bury his face in my hair. A restlessness grips me.

I put down the dryer and pick up my phone.

Three hours later, I'm at the salon. Vickie, the woman who cuts my hair, rushes up to me and gives me a bear hug. She has never done this before. "How are you, darling?" she says. "I've been so worried."

I pat her back awkwardly before pulling away. I don't want this attention.

"What can I do for you, doll?" she says after I'm in the chair.

"I want you to cut it off."

"How much?"

"All of it. I want it very, very short."

She stares at me in the mirror. "Samantha," she says. "You don't want that."

"I do."

"But you have the most gorgeous hair. My God, my customers would kill for your hair. Why would you do such a thing?"

I shake my head impatiently. The woman in the chair next to mine looks like she's going to weigh in at any moment now. I feel a stab of anger. Why does everybody think they have the right to make decisions for me? It's impossible to tell Vickie what I'm thinking. What I've gone through at the monster's hands. But also, how, every time I've left the house in the past month, I've been aware of my breasts, my long hair, my legs, anything that attracts the male gaze. I want to disappear into anonymity; I don't want anyone to see me as female. Which is another way of saying, I don't want to be seen as prey.

"Sam," Vickie says. "You know what they say—you shouldn't make any big decisions in the first year after any major life event."

I've had it with these well-meaning idiots. I get up from the chair. "Okay, you win," I say. I pull out a twenty-dollar bill and shove it into Vickie's hand, ignoring her protestations.

"Samantha, wait," she calls after me, but I walk briskly out of the salon.

On the drive home, I'm bright with anger and indignation. But by the time I pull into my driveway, my anger has subsided into grief. My life does not belong to me anymore and I don't know if it ever will. I make my way upstairs to the bedroom and decide to take a short nap.

"Sam." Ali's voice is urgent in my ear. "Honey, wake up."

I open my eyes to Ali's worried face. "I've been calling and calling. What happened? Why are you in bed?"

I look at her. "What time is it?"

"It's after five. I came home early because I wanted to make sure you're okay."

I muster a half-smile. "I'm fine. I must've left my phone downstairs. I—" My indignation at Vickie bubbles over and I tell her the whole story.

She frowns. "You want to chop it all off? Why?"

"I don't want men looking at me." I look at her defiantly. "*You* have short hair."

Ali searches my face for a long moment, then gets up and leaves the room. Shit, I think, now Ali's mad at me, too. Everyone, it seems, is more attached to my damn hair than I am.

I get up and head downstairs. "Ali?" I call.

"I'm in here."

The door of the first-floor bathroom is open. She's positioned the swivel chair in front of the sink. "What're you doing?"

Ali shrugs. "You said you wanted to cut it off, right? I'll do it for you."

She sees the shocked look on my face and misunderstands. "Don't worry. I used to cut Julie's hair. I got this." Julie is Ali's old girlfriend.

"You're sure?"

"Yeah. If this will make you happy."

"But you don't approve?"

"Sam. It doesn't matter what I or anyone thinks. It's your body, love."

Ali has always liked my hair long.

She wraps a towel around me and wets my hair. As she cuts, I look at her in the mirror, trying to gauge her mood. As my hair falls around me onto the floor, I feel a lump in my throat. When I look up, Ali's eyes are on me, and they are teary. "How short?" Her voice is husky.

"Short."

She nods, snips away expertly. It is almost erotic, the way she bends and moves around me, like a dancer. As if she has melded herself into my body.

I gasp when she's done. She's made me look beautiful, in an androgynous way. As if she's read my mind, Ali grins. "You look like Anne Hathaway in Les Misérables," she says. "You like it?"

I spin in the chair to face her. "Thank you," I whisper.

"No problem."

"If I'd known you were this good, I wouldn't have wasted money going to the hair salon all these years." I take Ali's hand. "Listen, I know you don't understand. But I needed to . . ."

"Sam. You don't need my approval to do what you want to do." She kisses the top of my head. "Okay, go take a shower. I'll get a broom and clean up."

I've never known a person who lives her principles the way Ali does. As I make my way upstairs, I think, if I could've extended the same grace to her at the party, we wouldn't be where we are today.

38

▾ ▸ ▴ ◂ ▾ ▴ ▸ ▴

Saturday, October 19

Today is Ali's birthday. We are shopping at the West Side Market, straining under the weight of the produce we've bought. We walk carefully across the wet floor, dodging the other shoppers, stopping at the different stands, accepting samples of fruit from vendors who sing and yell to entice customers. I nudge Ali as we pass the old lady in the dirty fur coat, a fixture at the market. She is cussing at the vendors, who, amused by the string of swear words that drop from her lips, poke each other in the ribs and snicker. Ali is not laughing. Instead, she notices the elderly woman's eyeglasses, held together by a piece of tape.

"I wish I could buy her a new pair," she says quietly. But we know it's no use. We've tried engaging the poor woman in conversation in the past. She is lost in her own world, a world that doesn't allow us in.

"Wanna head to the inner market for the seafood?" Ali says. We are going to make paella for her birthday dinner.

We stop at Kate's Fish, and while Ali places the order I wander to the other stalls. I feel safe here in this crowded market, as different from the plastic atmosphere of Whole Foods as you can imagine. I stop at the Ohio City Pasta counter, where I buy butternut squash ravioli, and a pound of black squid ink pasta. I haven't brought a credit card, so I pay in cash and I'm two dollars short. But the burly, bearded guy behind the counter waves me away when I offer to return with the money.

"It's on us," he says. "Welcome back." He flashes me a thumbs-up sign.

I stammer my thanks and move away. This is Cleveland at its best—warm and casually friendly. That's the upside of living in a region that has been mocked and discounted—we stick up for one another, we raise each other up. At least, that's the story we tell ourselves. After the abuse she's endured, I don't think Ali would agree. My thoughts darken and it takes effort to shake them away. On her birthday, I'm determined to remain sunny and bright, much like this beautiful autumn day, when the golden leaves have begun to bless everything with their incandescence.

I wander back to Ali and we buy olive oil for the paella and then, even though I've ordered a birthday cake from Whole Foods, we stop at Theresa's Bakery and buy half a dozen cannoli.

"Sam," Ali says. "We still have to walk back to the car, honey. I can't lift another bag."

And so, laughing, and feeling a careless, liquescent happiness we haven't felt in so long, we head to the car. We each polish off a cannoli on the way home.

"Great breakfast," Ali says, licking her fingers.

On an impulse, we decide to go to the one-thirty showing of *Jojo Rabbit* at the Cedar Lee. Ali says she'll do the prep for the paella before we leave for the theater. "We can assemble it when we get home. Trust me. I have it under control."

It's a great movie, about a ten-year-old boy in Nazi Germany so enthralled by Hitler, he has an imaginary friend named Adolf. But unbeknownst to him, his mother is hiding a young Jewish girl in the attic. We walk home a little stunned by the ending, blinking in the sunlight. "People wonder at how quickly Germany fell," Ali says. "But I'm telling you, no country is immune to this. You know my friend Tasneem? My new friend I was telling you about? She wears a hijab. You know, the headscarf?"

"Ali, I know what a hijab is."

"Anyway, she was at Target last week. And this guy came up to her and told her to go back to Iran. She's never even been there."

"Jesus. What did she do?"

"She was too stunned to reply. But this older lady overheard the guy and called for the manager. He was ordered to leave the store."

"See? There are still a lot of good people willing to stand up for what's right."

"Yeah, but after he left Target, he waited for her in the parking lot. And this time, Tasneem said, he got right in her face. He kept calling her an Iranian bitch."

"Oh dear God."

"She tried to tell him she wasn't Iranian, but that just infuriated him more. But Tasneem kept her cool and made her way to her car. He followed her for about half a mile in his truck, but when she pulled into the parking lot of the Parma police station, he sped away."

"That was quick thinking on her part."

"Yeah, she's a smart cookie."

I feel a shiver run through me.

We put away the groceries and then Ali goes upstairs. When she comes back down, she's changed into her pajamas. I pretend to be indignant. "I thought we were going to have a romantic candlelight dinner for your birthday."

"It's just us, yaar," Ali says. "Let's just chill, okay?"

I grin at the familiarity of the Indian *yaar.* Besides, she looks adorable in those pj's. "It's a good thing you're so damn cute," I say, giving her a quick hug. "Okay, I may as well go change also."

By the time I return to the kitchen, Ali has started boiling the rice. She is playing Buddy Holly, singing under her breath. I reach across her to grab a knife, and she takes hold of me and spins me around for a second.

"Buddy Holly," she says. "The antidote to all of life's problems."

I laugh and we dance for another second, and I feel a sensation in my heart as sweet and sharp as the scent of the ginger Ali was chopping. It takes me a moment to recognize it—happiness, thin and exquisite, like a needle threading through my chest. This is us, I think, Ali and me, together again. If only we could shut all the windows and lock all the doors and leave the lurking world outside.

This is Ali's first time making paella, but she nails it. I ate paella several times during my junior year abroad in Spain, but this dish is richer, more complex. Ali has put her own twist on it, Indianized it by using curry leaves instead of bay leaves and chili powder and cumin instead of paprika. I take a second helping and then, a third, egged on by the look of satisfaction on Ali's face.

We are so stuffed that we decide to split a slice of birthday cake. "I'll have some with my coffee tomorrow morning," Ali says.

After we're finished, we load the dishwasher together. "What do you want to do?" Ali asks after our chores are done. "Feel like watching a movie?"

But I have a birthday surprise for her. I take her by the hand and lead her to the bedroom. Her eyes are wary, disbelieving, as I undo the buttons to her pj's.

"You don't have to, Sam," she says. "I mean, just because it's my birthday. It's fine to—"

"Woman," I say theatrically. "Are you ever quiet?" We both giggle.

In the dark, we undress one another. I kiss every inch of her, telegraphing everything I've been unable to say—my gratitude, my remorse, my unbelievable good luck at having someone like her in my life. She is my rock, we are marooned on an island together, just the two of us, our hair is a tangle, our bodies, light and brown against one another, and I kiss her hard and she moans and more than anything I want to make Ali know how I feel about her. This is what the human body is designed to do—then for a moment my brain frizzes, his rough violation of me snaps like electricity in my mind, but I force it out, *out*, he doesn't belong here, in this home, in this bed—and I turn my attention back on Ali, who is now gasping for breath, moving below me, twist and torque, arch and need, greedy, drunk, wanting.

After we are done, I collapse on her, lay still for several moments, inhaling her, feeling her racing heart, the warmth of her breath, before I roll off. I turn on my side and gaze at her. Even in the dark, I notice the stunned, gratified expression on her face, the rise and fall of her small, exquisite breasts, the tremor in her flat stomach.

She turns her head toward me, her mouth attempting to speak, but all she can muster is, "Whoa."

And I grin to myself in the dark.

She rolls onto her side to face me, and I notice the tears rolling down her cheeks.

"What's wrong, my girl?"

"Absolutely nothing. I . . . I'm just so . . . I've missed this. I've missed you."

"Me too," I whisper.

We lie side by side, facing one another, and just when I'm about to doze off, I feel her hands on me. I open my eyes and look into hers and what I see in them—hope and uncertainty and trepidation—makes me stop myself from telling her to stop. And so I let her continue, and pretty soon, I feel the heat rising in me. She kisses my face lightly, my forehead, my cheeks, my lips, even the tip of my nose. I open my mouth to meet hers, but she's moved to my ears. I feel a powerful steam rising out of me. Now, at last, she is ready to meet my mouth, and I feel myself open up completely, and there's such relief in the knowledge that I'm still capable of this, that I'm not permanently damaged, that the monster has not broken me, that I want to roar with triumph. And I guess I'm moaning loudly, because Ali is laughing and lightly covering my mouth and saying, "Sam, sweetheart. The neighbors."

Finally, after an eternity, she enters me. She moves with her usual skill, but now, a new kind of seizure grips me. The reminder of the neighbors. My thoughts about the monster. Something has invited him in, into this bed, and I'm trying to ignore him, but even as my body continues to respond to Ali's touch, I'm battling to fight him off, and then I stiffen, caught between the wondrous warmth of Ali's body against mine, and the cold, dark memories of those days and nights with my abductor. I want to scream at this intrusion, at the unfairness of it, but all that escapes are a few shallow moans, that Ali takes as encouragement. And suddenly, I want to be left alone, untouched. I'm about to hyperventilate, and then I do something I've never done with Ali: I fake an orgasm. I pretend to gasp and moan and shudder a few times and then I am ejecting Ali from my body. "Wow," I say. "Thanks."

Ali looks puzzled. "That was quick."

"Yeah, well, it's been a while."

She gives me a long look and then gives me a light kiss. "You happy, I happy," she says in an exaggerated manner.

After a few moments, she turns on her side and I spoon her, my hand cupping her breasts. I breathe in the scent of her hair, revel in her thin, lithe body against mine, and think, This is heaven, I wouldn't mind if I died in this moment, frozen forever against Ali like those figures in Pompeii. I stay awake until I hear her steady breathing and then I drift off to sleep also.

39

▼ ▶ ▲ ◀ ▼ ▲ ▶ ▲

Saturday, October 19

I let Sam lie to me about her orgasm while lying beside me, because what is the alternative? But I feel lost, as lost as I did when Sam was missing. And lonelier than I did before.

Patience, Mo keeps telling me, be patient. And I am and I will be. When I was a kid, impetuous and impulsive, Abba used to quote a line from the Quran: "Be patient with gracious patience."

I am trying. But if there's a roadmap for how we make our way back to one another, I don't know where to look. The Bible and the Quran were not written for people like Sam and me. There is no blueprint. We will simply have to muddle our way through this and hope that we come out on the other side.

For now, I feel Sam's body spooning mine and it's enough. Let people like Yasmin worship the spirit and the soul, let them believe in the ineffable, let them find solace in otherworldly things. The book that Abba presented me gave me much spiritual comfort during Sam's absence, I don't deny it. But as always, I return to the primacy of the body. I still recall the line from Whitman from the book Sam gave me a month after we began to date: "To be surrounded by beautiful, curious, breathing, laughing flesh is enough."

Let it be enough, I pray. Let us, Whitman's children, find our way back to one another not through gods and saints and holy messengers, but through this mortal flesh, this tired, abused flesh, which, nevertheless, is the only concrete proof I have of divinity. What Sam breathed into my body tonight was sacred. And I had so very much wanted to do the same for her, but I didn't succeed. And yet, here we are with our improbable love, a love that the faiths we were raised in condemn.

I move in the bed, restless, and Sam sighs softly, moves with me. And thus, we sleep, two animals snuggling together for warmth and comfort, holding on for dear life.

40

▾ ▸ ▴ ◂ ▾ ▴ ▸ ▴

Saturday, November 2

Ali comes home from Whole Foods with a strange look on her face.

"Hi," I say, as I take the bags from her.

"Hi," she says stiffly.

I look at her curiously. "You okay?"

"Yup."

She's not okay. She seems angry. But I don't want to probe. "All right," I say. "I'll put the groceries away."

She disappears from the kitchen, returns when I'm almost done. Her face is tight, pinched.

"I need to talk to you," she says and my stomach lurches. I keep my face blank.

"Okay."

"Let's go to the living room."

We sit facing one another.

"What is it?" I say, suddenly irritated. "Why all this drama?"

"I ran into Sarah Yates at the store," she says.

My eyelids flutter. I know what's coming. Of all the dumb luck.

"And she said to say hi to you," Ali continues. "Because she hasn't seen you in several weeks."

I flush with embarrassment. To cover it up, I say, "Yeah, so?"

"So, Samantha," Ali says, enunciating each word, "you've been lying to me for weeks." Her eyes suddenly fill with tears. "Where do you go when you say you're going to therapy?"

I look at her, resentfully. I hate being caught red-handed in a lie. "Isn't there such a thing as patient-therapist confidentiality?" I say. It sounds foolish even to my ears.

"I'm not the enemy here, Sam."

"Sarah was bugging me, okay? She thought it was important to talk about . . . about what happened to me. But she doesn't get it. She has no experience with that kind of thing. How could she? She's never treated someone who was abducted and raped."

I see Ali flinch at the word, but I continue. "And the only reason I went back to therapy is to talk to her about you."

"Me?"

"Yes, you, Ali. How to not fuck up my life with you. How to learn to be happy together again. Because believe it or not, that's the only thing that matters to me. And I knew you'd be pissed if you found out I'd quit therapy. So, I lied. I drive to a small coffee shop in Lyndhurst for an hour each week before coming home. I'm sorry. I don't blame you for being mad."

Ali's face softens. "I'm sorry if I've been judgy or pushed you to do something you don't want to do. But please, Sam. Don't ever lie to me again. I don't want there to be secrets between us. I can't handle it."

I get up to go sit beside her. "I'm really sorry. I promise. No more lies. No more secrets. Okay?"

"Deal?"

"Deal." I take her hand in mine. "You know, all of this would be so much easier if the cops had found that bastard. It's . . . it's hard for me to relax knowing that he's still somewhere out there."

Ali exhales. "I understand. But Sam, the fact is, he let you go. Something must've happened to spook him, honey. He may have fled the country for all we know. I honestly don't think he'll bother us again."

"You don't?"

"I don't."

I don't share Ali's conviction, don't feel it in my bones. But if we're to have any shot at normalcy, what choice do I have, but to believe her?

"You know how when you stand at the edge of the ocean and feel the sand sift under your feet?" Ali says. "Life's like that. We're always standing on unpredictable ground. But that doesn't mean we shouldn't enjoy the ocean, right?"

I smile. "That's quite a metaphor, Ali. Can I steal it for my novel?"

"Certainly." She gets to her feet and pulls me up. "Let's start making dinner. I'm hungry."

"Hey, Ali, there's one more thing. So, there's a support group in Beachwood for survivors of violent crime. I think that may help me more than going back to Sarah Yates. What do you think?"

I watch Ali's eyes light up. "I think that's a great idea, honey. Whatever you think will bring you some peace."

41

▾ ▸ ▴ ◂ ▾ ▴ ▸ ▴

Wednesday, November 27

It's the day before Thanksgiving and I'm sitting in my car on a street in South Euclid, having a panic attack.

Even a few days ago, after Mom had admitted Dad to the St. Mary's Catholic Respite Center ten miles from their home and called me on her way home, I was excited about hosting our parents for the holiday. Mom had been a hot mess that day. She had kept crying on the phone and apologizing for her tears, apologizing and crying. "It's just that I've never been apart from your father since we were married," she'd said, and I'd bit down hard on the words that had formed in my mouth: *Maybe the separation will do you good.*

"Listen," I said finally. "Mom, we're going to have a great time, okay? And I'm looking forward to spending some time with you. Alone."

The words had their desired effect. "Oh, me, too, honey. I've missed you so."

But now, I don't want to let anyone into my house. Now, I want to go away with Ali to some small town where we don't know a soul. Check into a nondescript Holiday Inn, say, and go to a local restaurant for a Thanksgiving meal.

Attending the survivor's support group has forced me to relive those awful weeks in July, and even though I sometimes feel like a wuss—many of the people there have survived decades of horrific abuse—I've not been sleeping well again. I still look at every man I pass on the street with suspicion: Could this man have been my captor? Or that one? Given a chance, would this man harm me? See me as prey?

I put my arms around myself to stop the shaking. I need to get home soon—Ali is cooking up a storm for tomorrow and has sent me to the store for some last-minute items she needs. Mom is carpooling with Ali's dad, and they are arriving later this afternoon. Yasmin is down with a cold and isn't coming, and I can't say that we are disappointed.

I'm only a few streets away from Giant Eagle. But my eyes are so blurry with tears and I'm shaking so badly that I don't trust myself to drive. I reach for my phone to listen to the meditation podcast that I play every night in bed, hoping it will calm me down.

I close my eyes and focus on my breathing. After a few minutes, the shaking eases up and I feel myself entering my body again. I sit in the car for a little longer after the podcast ends and then I can drive.

When I get home, Ali is not in the kitchen.

"Babe?" I call.

"In here."

I set the groceries on the counter and walk to the living room. I gasp. Ali has strung tiny Christmas lights everywhere. They stretch across the mantelpiece and wrap around the floor lamp. There is another strand that loops around the windows. Even in the daylight, the LED lights give the room a magical glow, making me feel like I'm inside an exquisite jewelry box.

Ali is standing by the fireplace, which has a fire going.

"I thought you were cooking?"

She grins broadly. "You really think I would forget to get sweet potatoes and mushrooms for tomorrow? I just needed you out of the house so that I could decorate."

"Ali."

"Sit down," she says. "I'll be right back."

"But our folks will be here this afternoon. I have to make the beds still. And vacuum."

"Sam," she says. "Sit down."

She comes back a few minutes later with two glasses and a small pitcher. "Mulled apple cider," she says as she pours from the pitcher. "Here's to a fun weekend. Happy Thanksgiving, honey."

We clink glasses. Sitting in this room, sipping the warm drink, my heart floods with happiness. It's hard to believe that I'm the same person who sat miserably in her car less than an hour ago.

The doorbell rings a few minutes later and I turn to her, worried. "They came early?"

"Nope," Ali says as she leaps to her feet. "Actually, the timing is perfect."

Two men come in carrying a huge Christmas tree. They screw it into the tree stand as Ali supervises. She gives each of them a twenty-dollar tip when they're done.

"You like it?" she asks after they leave.

"Yeah, of course. It's magnificent. But why didn't you wait for me to go pick it out? And how on earth did you get someone to deliver the tree?"

She looks at me shyly. "I just thought . . . with our folks here for the first time. That, you know, it might be fun decorating with them this evening?"

"But Ali. Your dad's Muslim."

She cocks her head, puzzled. Then, it dawns on her, what I'm asking. "Oh God no. Sam, he's not like that. I mean, Abba is so secure in his own faith that he can respect everyone else's. We used to have a tree every year when Mummy was alive. I think he'll get a kick out of it."

I think of my own bigoted father and I'm envious of what Ali has. "I'm nervous about the weekend," I say. "I hope to God everything goes well."

"It will."

"How can you be so sure?"

Ali smiles. "Because we are together."

42

▼ ▶ ▲ ◀ ▼ ▲ ▶ ▲

Thursday, November 28

We've settled on a smaller group this year: our parents, our neighbor Carol, Ali's friend Tasneem, whom I'm eager to meet, Nate, and Nate's new girlfriend. When he asked if he could bring her along, casually, as if she was one in a long string of girlfriends, Nate mistook our stunned silence for reluctance. We finally stammered our enthusiasm because really, what could we say? That we'd always assumed he was gay? We'd hung our hats on the thinnest of hooks—Nate's slender, angular frame, his slightly fey manner, his fondness for camp, his obsession with Boy George and Lady Gaga, the fact that for our first Halloween party he'd come dressed as Ziggy Stardust. "Really, what the hell did we have to go on?" Ali said. "The laziest of stereotypes. As if any guy who's not macho is gay."

"As if." I nodded, but the next moment we spluttered with laughter. "Or maybe he's switching teams?" I added.

Ali shrugged. "Who cares? As long as she's good to him."

Nate arrives early with Julie, who has only been working at the Lee Road library for a few months. She is a tiny woman with a delicate face and a gentle manner. Ali and I exchange an approving glance—they are perfect for one another. "Nate tells me you're a poet writing your first novel," Julie says to me in a soft, serious voice. "I think that's so brave."

"Brave or foolish, I don't know," I say with a laugh.

"Brave," she says firmly, as if the matter has been decided.

Tasneem arrives next, with a huge bouquet of yellow roses. "This is for you, Samantha," she says, giving me a hug. "I'm so glad to finally meet you."

Ali greets Tasneem by kissing her on both cheeks, in the traditional Muslim way. Tasneem has become like a baby sister to her, having entered Ali's life when she most needed her. She was the one person who understood instinctively the slings and arrows Ali endured in the time that I went missing. Mo has always been Ali's sounding board, but Mo's white. As empathetic as she is and protective of Ali, even she couldn't feel in her gut what Ali went through. I think it's now important to Ali to return the favor, to act as a mentor to Tasneem. Earlier this month, I heard her on the phone coaching the younger woman on how to ask her boss for a raise.

"Abba, come say hi to my friend Tasneem," Ali says, and Mr. Mirza steps into the living room from the kitchen, his face red from the heat of the stove. "Hello, Tasneem," he says. "I'm Irfan."

"Hello, Irfan Uncle."

He cocks an eyebrow at me. "See?" he says. "Even this girl I'm meeting for the first time calls me by my first name." He smiles at my discomfort. "I'm just teasing you, Samantha." He glances at my mom and says, "Your daughter has perfect manners, Emily. You have been a splendid role model."

Watching my mother blush and follow him with her eyes as he returns to the kitchen, I think: So that's where Ali gets her flirtatiousness. What we Americans consider flirting, is, for the Mirzas, simply a form of courtliness and charm.

Carol has brought her annual contribution, a box of Trader Joe's gingersnaps. She sits beside Mom on the couch, opens the plastic box, and offers her a cookie.

"Mmm, these are wonderful. My husband used to eat all of our gingersnaps," Mom says, and I make a mental note to run to Trader Joe's, before she and Mr. Mirza leave on Saturday.

As everyone chats and moves back and forth between the kitchen and the living room, I realize how intuitive Ali's sense of design is. I had wanted to spend a few years in our new home before doing a major renovation. But Ali had insisted on an open concept, gutting the old kitchen and tearing down the wall between the two rooms before we moved in. "It'll make it so much easier for our guests to mingle," she'd insisted. And though at the time I thought she was overdoing it, I see now that she's right. Even the Christmas lights are a great touch, making the large living room feel more intimate. And everyone has commented on the stately beauty of the decorated Christmas tree.

Mr. Mirza steps back into the living room. "Okay, drink orders," he says, clapping his hands. "Who is having what?"

Mom and Carol both opt for ginger ale, Tasneem asks for a Coke. Ali serves our guests. A second later, I hear the pop of a bottle, and when I go to the kitchen, Nate is pouring prosecco into champagne glasses. "Have some?" he says to me, and I nod. I go over to Mr. Mirza, who is back at the stove, stirring the goat dish that he's making.

"Can I get you a drink, Mr.—Irfan?" I ask.

He smiles. "Just water for now, my child."

The timer goes off as I hand him the glass of water and he moves aside so that I can remove the pies that I've baked—blueberry and pecan—from the oven.

"Why, Samantha, these are beautiful," he says, and I find myself unreasonably chuffed by the compliment. He has that ability, Ali's dad.

Nate and Ali put in the extra leaf on the cherry dining table, and I spread Mom's embroidered tablecloth. Julie has joined the other three women in the living room, and I hear gusts of laughter. I peek and to my surprise Mom is taking small sips from Julie's glass of prosecco. Her cheeks are rosy; the perpetual weariness and stress washed away from her face. Tears prick my eyes at seeing her so uncharacteristically relaxed and happy.

"All right, everyone," Ali calls from the kitchen. "Time to eat."

We start with the salad, served with epi bread from Presti's. "This is superb, yaar," Tasneem says, slathering butter on the warm bread. Mr.

Mirza, who's sitting next to Tasneem, points to his salad and leans into her and whispers, "Only Americans . . ." I don't catch the rest of his sentence because he says it in Hindi. Tasneem giggles and I turn to Ali, who looks bemused. "Ignore him," she says to me. "He's criticizing us for eating 'ghas-puss.' Which literally means grass and leaves."

Mr. Mirza gives me a sheepish look and shrugs his shoulders so dramatically that I can't help but laugh. Ali's dad is a bit of a rogue.

Nathan refills our glasses as Julie and I clear the table for the main courses. And then Ali and her dad bring in dish after dish. We have all the usual Thanksgiving fixings, of course—Ali has that down to a science. But this year, there are also several Indian dishes—a wonderful vegetable stew and chicken biryani cooked in a clay pot, whose lid is sealed with dough to trap the steam. We gasp when he breaks the seal of the clay pot to reveal the saffron rice and chunks of chicken. "What's that on the top?" Nathan says. "It looks like silver?"

"It's silver leaf," Mr. Mirza says. "Don't worry, it's totally edible. We use it for special occasions," he adds with a half-smile. As Ali carves the turkey and the others pass the mashed potatoes and stuffing, Mr. Mirza turns to my mother. "I want you to try this, Emily," he says. "It's called mutton korma. It is goat meat cooked in a cashew cream sauce. I made it specially for you."

"I don't know," Mom says. "I've never had Indian food before."

"I know," Mr. Mirza says. "That is why I made it very mild." He spoons some of the mutton korma onto her plate and Mom tastes it.

"Hmmm, that's good," she says. "Not spicy but delicious."

He grins. "Thank you. It's my specialty."

I watch Mr. Mirza as we eat, notice his easy, hospitable manner, as if he's the master of ceremonies or the conductor of this culinary orchestra. I watch the courteous, refined way in which he speaks to Carol and Mom, the avuncular way he urges Tasneem and Julie to eat more, how Mom seems to come alive under his benevolent care, and I mourn not just my childhood, but the fact that my mother threw away her life being married to an abusive, angry man. Who would Mom have been if she'd been married to a kind, nonviolent man like Mr. Mirza? Who would I have been with a father like this? And how could Ali have walked away from him? It dawns on me slowly, the enormity of Ali's loss, what she's sacrificed to be true to herself, what courage it must have taken. And how I have curtailed her free spirit, a spirit that didn't bow or compromise even before such a wonderful father. I feel insignificant, humbled by what Ali has given up. The fact that she's cast her lot with me suddenly makes me feel like the luckiest person in the world.

As if she's sensed something, Ali leans into me. "Everything okay, love?"

"Absolutely." I find her hand under the table, squeeze. "He's magnificent," I whisper. "Your dad."

She shakes her head. "He's okay." But I hear the wobble of pride in her voice, and I vow to ensure that Ali and her abba build on this new tentative relationship they've developed during those ugly early days of my disappearance, when she felt that the world was pointing its finger at her.

"I'll take a little more of that," Mom says, my timid, skinny mom, who's never taken a second helping of anything in her life. Mr. Mirza beams, pushes back his chair to refill the bowl. "I'll send leftovers home with you, Emily," he says.

"Uncle, I want some of the leftover biryani," Tasneem says, boldly.

"I'll fight you for it," Nate says at once.

Mr. Mirza grins. "There's plenty more. In my house, everyone goes home with leftovers."

It's not his house, of course, but I'm thrilled that he feels this comfortable here. "Can you come back next weekend?" I say. "It's going to be hard going back to pizza and pasta after this."

"Pizza and pasta?" he roars theatrically. "Where have I gone wrong? Ali, are you not feeding your . . . friend . . . proper Indian food?"

Everybody laughs, but I know Ali has heard his stumble, his referring to me as her friend rather than wife. But the moment passes; the food has made us all punch-drunk, giddy with the kind of happiness that comes from sharing a delicious meal with the people you care about. I toss back my prosecco; the world is a happier, more benevolent place when seen through a champagne flute.

The table looks like a battlefield when we're done—the carcass of the turkey, bright red stains on the tablecloth from the cranberry sauce, weary-looking forks and knives strewn across dirty plates.

"Man, that was some meal," Nate says, and we murmur our assent.

"Can we wait to have dessert?" Julie says. "I need about three hours to recover from this dinner."

"Sure thing," I say, getting up. "Ali and I will clean up later."

But Tasneem and Nate insist on loading the dishwasher, and I'm so pleasantly drunk, I don't put up much of a fight. I sit next to my mom on the couch, my arm around her. She leans in to give me a kiss. "Thank you for insisting that I come, honey."

"You're gonna come every Thanksgiving from here on out." What I really want to say is, let's put him in a nearby home and have you move closer to us. But I know she'll choose him over me. Love is an addiction, and so is dysfunction. She has convinced herself she can't live without him. Or more precisely, that he cannot live without her. These thoughts are darkening my happiness, so I shake them away. Today is one of the best days since I've returned home, such a contrast to yesterday morning. I look over at Ali and I can tell she's feeling the same sense of completeness that I am, having her abba here. How did we not see this before, how lonely and incomplete we've both been, with no family support? The number of times we've gone to the movies and out to dinner on Mother's Day and Father's Day and on Easter while our friends visited their families? The zeal with which we've cultivated our families of choice, because our families of origin had cast us out? Imagine if I'd been able to pick up the phone and discuss my jealousy over Ali's flirtations with my mom. Imagine if Ali could've complained about my possessiveness to her father. How we would've benefited from their experience and wisdom! I feel perilously close to tears, but right then Ali laughs aloud at something Julie is saying, and my breath catches at how beautiful she looks—her dark hair shiny under the light, her teeth white and perfect as she tosses back her head. Hope flares in my chest—it'll be okay, I think. We're gonna make it. Look what we've achieved already—out of the patchwork of our measly past, we have created this rich quilt.

"She's drunk," I hear Ali say with a laugh. "She always gets this look on her face when she drinks."

I open my mouth to protest, but they all crack up. "What?" I say, trying hard not to slur my words. "What?" And this just makes them laugh harder.

I must've nodded off for a few minutes because I wake to Mr. Mirza asking Tasneem the last time she had visited India. "I just went last year, Uncle," she says. "Three months after I got my green card."

"Good, good," he says. "Your mummy-daddy must've been happy to have you there."

"They were. What about you, Uncle?"

"Yasmin . . . my wife and I try and go every two years. We're going next February, actually. For Yasmin's nephew's wedding." He pauses, then looks at Ali. "You should join us, beta. And bring Samantha. She would like to see a big, fat Indian wedding, I think."

"I can't," I say. "Spring semester will be in full swing in February."

"That's too bad," Mr. Mirza says. "What about you, Aliya? Can you spare the time?"

Ali looks as if jumping out of a plane without a parachute would give her more pleasure than a trip to India. "I—I don't think so, Abba. But let's see."

I notice the flash of disappointment on his face, before he covers it up. And it hits me, the most obvious thing—Mr. Mirza has probably missed his daughter more than she's missed him. Once we left home, Ali and I each had so much to look forward to—going to college, dating, falling in love with one another, getting jobs. Whereas our parents were left holding the memories of what once was, a lonely place to be.

So, when Ali makes coffee while I warm the pies, I whisper to her, "You should go."

"Go where?"

"To India. With your dad. He really wants you to."

"Don't be silly. With that awful wife of his? And who is going to run my business while I'm gone?"

I don't say anything else, afraid of Ali misunderstanding me.

That night, after Mom and Mr. Mirza are in their respective rooms, Ali and I slip under the covers of the futon in the den.

"Your dad is great. I think I'm a little smitten with him."

She cups my face. "Your mom looked so relaxed and youthful."

"Your dad really drew her out."

"Did you like Tasneem?" she asks.

"Oh, of course. She's a sweetheart."

"Yup." She looks at me. "Why did you tell me to go to India? Trying to get rid of me, are you?" Her tone is light, teasing.

"I saw the look on your dad's face when he invited you."

"And what look was that?"

"I dunno. Of longing, I guess."

She is silent.

"Ali?" I say finally. "Did I offend you?"

"No, sweetheart. It's just that . . . there's too much baggage there, you know? And I don't want to go anywhere without you. Certainly not to India, where I don't know a soul."

"Whatever you decide. Hey, I'm going to get up early and go to Trader Joe's tomorrow. I want to buy ginger cookies to send home with my Mom."

"You want me to . . . ?"

"No, that's okay. I'll go and come back in a flash."

It's the first time that I've volunteered to go shopping without Ali. This day has been restorative in a way that I can't quite comprehend. But the new optimism and confidence I feel is real.

"Well, let's get some sleep then," she says. "Abba was already planning tomorrow's breakfast menu tonight." She snuggles even closer. "This feels kind of sexy," she says, "sleeping on the futon. Like we're at camp or something."

"You're just horny," I say with a giggle. "Okay, for real, let's get some *zzzzs*. It's going to be an early morning."

"You're no fun," Ali says, but there's a smile in her voice and we fall asleep facing each other and holding hands.

43

▼ ▶ ▲ ◀ ▼ ▲ ▶ ▲

Saturday, November 30

I help Abba pack the car after breakfast. After we're done, he says, "I'm very happy to have been here, Aliya. Your friends are good people."

"Thanks, Abba," I say. "You be safe driving home, okay? Text me when you get home."

He chuckles. "The child is now the parent. Arre, gudiya, I'm still your father. Don't forget."

We are walking back toward the house when I say, "Tell me the truth, Abba. Did Yasmin really have a cold?"

The smile disappears. "I . . . well, she." He exhales and I see his breath in the cold November air. "She didn't feel comfortable coming, Aliya. Not just because of the . . . situation. I mean, she really likes Samantha. But she said she would feel out of place here. 'All of you have advanced degrees.' Those were her exact words."

It is excruciating, watching Abba's embarrassment, seeing how torn he is between me and Yasmin and how hard he's trying to forge a connection with me again. "I wish she didn't feel that way."

He looks at me pleadingly. "Please do try and understand, my child."

"I do." I'm so glad that Sam had the foresight to swing by Mitchell's to buy chocolates for Yasmin.

It's noon by the time Abba and Emily pull out of our driveway. We wave goodbye until Abba's car rounds the corner, then go inside. We strip the beds and throw the towels and sheets in the washer. Sam unloads and loads the dishwasher again, then vacuums the downstairs.

It isn't until we sit down at 6 p.m. to eat leftovers that Sam says, "The house feels so empty."

"I know." I don't trust myself to say anything else. I miss my father with a terrifying urgency, and I'm sad about Yasmin feeling inadequate around me and Sam. Her homophobia and insecurity are the deadly combination that keeps me away from my father.

"I was thinking," Sam is saying, "I want us to start a family of our own. You know?"

I shake myself out of my thoughts. "What do you mean?"

"That we should have a child together?"

Sam had mentioned that she wanted children soon after we'd started dating. But then we'd gotten busy with finishing our degrees and looking for work. We've never talked about it seriously, busy as we've been with our careers and relocating to Cleveland. Maybe it's a reaction to the sudden emptiness of the house.

"You really want to bring a child into this world, what with climate change, and all the attacks on gay people and minorities?"

I am stalling, unable to express what I really think: That, having been unmothered for so long, I feel feral, uncertain that I would be a nurturing parent. That Sam needs time to heal from her ordeal. That we need to be on safer financial ground before we can seriously contemplate this idea. That a child will be a distraction, that Sam is trying to short-circuit the hard work we need to do together. "Can we discuss this another day, Sam? I'm exhausted."

She gives me a penetrating look. "Fine, Ali, but we're not getting any younger. I'm not putting off this conversation forever."

I close my eyes, trying to imagine what it would be like to have a little one running around the house, going to PTA meetings, teaching him or her to read and draw and cook, introducing them to music and art. Something lightens in my heart. But the next minute I think of going to the grocery store with a red-headed child who looks like Sam and having people stare at me, wondering if I'm the nanny or whether I've kidnapped the child. I've heard of such stories. Before Sam's disappearance, such a thought wouldn't have crossed my mind. But now I know how people see me. A child raised by two gay women, one of whom is dark-skinned. Does Samantha even understand what she's asking for? I feel a spurt of anger, irrational and unfair as it may be. Sam has been through unimaginable trauma, and I know she's doing her best to swim her way back to shore. But she has no idea how the experience has corroded my soul, made me aware that just beneath the skin of politeness and refinement lurk the dark bones of this country—glowing with hatred and suspicion of people who look like me and Abba. Tasneem's incident with her hijab, Abba being sidelined by his bosses in Chicago, my own experience with my clients and on social media, have changed me, perhaps irrevocably. None of this is Sam's fault, of course. But now there's an invisible membrane between us, one that she doesn't even know exists, so how can I blame her? All Sam wants is to have a child with me, a natural, normal urge for many women, and here I am, in this dark place, beside the ash heap of the Ali I once was—confident in my ability to charm my way into the coldest of hearts.

I take her hand in mine. "We will discuss this again, I promise. But please, let's just get through the holidays. And put this godawful year behind us."

"Okay," Sam says. She gets to her feet. "Want me to warm up a piece of pie for you?"

44

▾ ▸ ▴ ◂ ▾ ▴ ▸ ▴

Saturday, December 14

"Are you sure I can't just drop you off, Sam?" I ask again, while we're getting dressed in the bedroom. "Honestly, won't you have a better time at your departmental Christmas party if I'm not there?"

She meets my eyes in the mirror. "You really want to bail now? A half hour before we're to leave?" She grimaces. "I wish you'd given me more advance warning, Ali. I could've asked Nate to be my date."

I start to remind her that I'd wanted to stay home from the first time she mentioned the party, but I stop. I remind myself that this is the first large social gathering Sam has been willing to attend in four months. And then I feel like a shit for giving her a hard time. "I'm sorry, hon," I say. "I'm happy to be your date."

But there's a pit in my stomach as we drive to Sam's chair's home. I dread meeting Sam's coworkers who had complained publicly about my not informing them about Sam's disappearance. Above all, I feel sick at the thought of seeing Candace.

But Gina Myers welcomes both of us warmly, as if the ugliness of the summer had never happened. Tenured faculty, several of the lecturers, and grad students all crowd around Sam, hugging her and saying how much they've missed her. I find a spot in the living room and lean against the wall, happy to let her bask in the glow of their attention. Gina's husband, Bob, takes my drink order and returns with a glass of wine.

"Thanks, Bob," I say. I look for Candace as I sip my wine, but thankfully, she's not here. Bob stands next to me, both of us watching Sam.

"She's terrific, your Sam," Bob says. "I can't tell you how worried Gina was about her." He turns to me, pushing back a lock of his silver hair. "And you? How are you doing?"

I've always liked Bob. He's an investment banker, very wealthy, but there's a down-to-earthiness about him. "I'm good. Trying to put everything that's happened this year behind me, you know?"

"I should think so." His handsome face is serious, with none of the lightness I usually associate with him. "But it's going to take time. Be gentle with yourself."

I flash him an appreciative smile. The next second, I freeze. Candace has just walked in. She hasn't spotted me yet, but I see her make a beeline for Sam. As I watch, Candace flings her arms wide and embraces Sam, who pats her back awkwardly. Even across the room, I hear Candace squeal, "Oh my God, oh my God, it's so great to see you alive." Heads turn, but Candace seems oblivious to Sam's discomfort. "Go rescue your girl," Bob says, and I walk toward Sam.

"Ali!" Candace says as soon as she sees me. "We did it!"

"Did what?" I say stupidly.

"We got Samantha back!"

My hand tingles from the urge to slap the self-congratulatory smugness off Candace's face. "Well, even the police had nothing to do with it," I begin, but Sam takes hold of my hand, excuses herself, and pulls me away.

"Don't," she murmurs. "Please. Don't."

I avoid Candace the rest of the evening, moving to the kitchen under the pretext of getting ice when she's in the dining room, hanging out on the porch with the smokers when she grabs a seat in the living room. Sam comes looking for me occasionally, but I reassure her that I'm fine and urge her to go mingle with her colleagues.

It's well after 10 p.m. when people begin to leave. We are putting on our coats when Joan Laughlin, the other poet in the department, comes up to us. "I just wanted to thank you before you take off, Samantha," she says.

Sam smiles. "For what?"

"For taking Candace back next year. She has not met a single deadline I set for her this semester."

I stiffen. Sam had told me in September that she was no longer chairing Candace's thesis, that Candace had requested a new committee chair soon after Sam went missing. "Hallelujah," I'd said, and she had laughed.

"I'm sorry," Sam says to Joan. "I know Candace can be a handful. I appreciate you stepping in while I was . . . gone."

My anger grows as we walk the streets of Little Italy to our car. It is a bitterly cold night, and we walk swiftly, our chins tucked into our neck scarfs.

"Did you have a nice time?" Sam asks as I drive up Murray Hill.

"Yes." Don't get in a fight, I say to myself, just don't. But the sting of betrayal is strong.

"Ali, what's wrong?"

"Nothing."

"Oh, come on. You're clearly upset about something."

I briefly take my eyes off the road. "You told me you were no longer Candace's thesis advisor."

"Yeah, well, I wasn't. But I didn't really have a choice but to take her back. I mean, Joan was doing me a favor and . . ."

"So why didn't you tell me? Why did I have to hear about it at a fucking Christmas party?"

Sam doesn't reply. And this infuriates me even more.

"I thought you'd promised you'd never lie to me again," I say. "After you'd lied about seeing Sarah Yates."

"I didn't lie to you about Candace," Sam says tersely. "I just forgot. There's a difference."

I can't untangle my anger at Candace from whatever I'm blaming Sam for doing or not doing. I'm realizing—and I'm ashamed of this—that some small part of me has never forgiven Sam for going on the run by herself and changing our lives irrevocably. "I showed you her Facebook posts," I say. "She's the one who started all the ugliness. You *know* how she slandered me. There were people from Thailand and Germany sending me nasty emails, for Christ's sake."

"I'm sorry."

I usually can't stay angry at Sam for too long. But maybe it's months of wanting my old Sam back and realizing that that may never be, that makes me unable to let go of this. "Did you see how she acted tonight? Like she'd parachuted in and rescued you herself."

"So, she's an asshole, alright?" Samantha's voice is loud. "She's full of shit. But Ali, why are you blaming me for her bad behavior?"

It's the tremor I hear in Sam's voice that makes me stop in my tracks. What the hell am I doing? Why am I pushing Sam like this, when she's still so fragile? God, this situation is exactly like the fight that started this nightmare. We've left yet another party arguing. And once again, we are fighting over someone who is inconsequential to our relationship.

"Okay," I say. "You're right. I'm being a jerk."

By the time we get home, my anger has dissipated completely. "I'm sorry," I mumble, holding her from behind as she unlocks the side door. "I lost it there for a minute."

She turns around and gives me a kiss. "It's okay. I'll never do anything on purpose to hurt you. You know?"

"I do know."

"You're all I got, kiddo." She says it lightly, but there's a lump in my throat.

"Ditto."

In the kitchen, I set my car keys in the bowl on the counter. "I'm gonna go up and change," I murmur. "And then maybe we watch a *Seinfeld* rerun or something?"

"Sounds perfect."

We're learning, slowly but surely, how to fight and then make up. But I'm also rattled at the sheer, irrational scale of my anger. Clearly, we both have unresolved issues from the Worst Time, which is how I've come to think of the events of this summer.

"Ali?" Sam calls from the living room. "You gotta watch this. It's unbelievable."

She has the TV on, and I can hear Rachel Maddow's voice. And even though I can't make out what she's saying, I know that the news won't be good. "Be down in a second," I yell back.

So much for relaxing with *Seinfeld*, I think. I have tried so hard in the months since Sam's return to create an oasis for her. But the rage I felt tonight reminds me of a sobering truth: Anger is the new national disease, the virus that animates our public and personal lives. As much as I'd like to pretend otherwise, and despite my best efforts, I, too, am not immune to it.

45

▼ ▶ ▲ ◀ ▼ ▲ ▶ ▲

Saturday, December 21

"Ali, slow down," Sam says, and I tap the brakes.

We'd told Abba we'd get there around three o'clock, after we'd dropped off Christmas gifts for Mr. and Mrs. O'Malley. But Sam's dad was having a particularly bad day, swearing at his wife and accusing her of stealing from him, and Mrs. O'Malley was so stressed trying to calm him down that we decided to stay for lunch to keep her company. While I made a quick stir-fry from the groceries we'd brought for them, Sam managed to appease her dad by "finding" his missing wallet and keys. Watching Sam hug her mom in the driveway as we finally got ready to leave, I had to marvel at how life worked in mysterious ways. The clichés are true: hidden in the darkest of clouds, there is light. I just wish it hadn't taken Sam's abduction to reunite us with our parents.

"Abba said he had a surprise," I say. "He sounded so disappointed when I told him we were going to be late."

"I'm sorry. I just couldn't leave my mom in that state," Sam says miserably. "Her life is so unbearable, I can't stand it."

I hear the sorrow in Sam's voice and am immediately regretful for making her feel worse. "It's okay," I say. "It's all good. We did the right thing by staying."

Abba comes out to greet us as we pull in. He gives Sam a hug and asks, "How is our dear Emily?" his voice heavy with concern.

"She's okay. My—my dad was having a hard day."

"It's a terrible, terrible illness," Abba says. He eyes the bags of gifts I'm removing from the back seat. "Arre, Aliya. What's all this?"

"Nothing much," I say. "Just a few things."

I hear voices from the kitchen as we walk in, including a male voice I can't immediately place. Yasmin comes up to greet us, gives us both a kiss on each cheek.

Abba grins. "Come here," he says, taking me by the hand over to the figure bent over the stove. The man removes the dish towel slapped across his shoulder and mops his face and I recognize the gesture immediately. It's Hussein, Abba's first chef, the man who used to give me treats each time Mummy took me to the restaurant. When I was a kid, I used to think that Hussein was taller than the silver maple in our backyard.

"Oh my God," I say as he turns around. "Hussein chacha! What a great surprise. Abba told me you had retired."

Hussein beams at me. "Aliya baby! Now I can die a happy man." He takes my hand in both of his, holds them up to his eyes.

"This is why I wanted you to come earlier in the day," Abba says. "Hussein heard you were visiting and wanted to make you his famous barfi and gulab jamuns for tea."

"Sorry, we . . ."

"No problem, baby," Hussein says, as Sam walks into the kitchen. "You can be having them for dessert."

"Hussein, I want you to meet Samantha."

"Welcome, madam," Hussein says.

"I've heard so much about you," Sam says, and Hussein raises his eyebrows in wonder. He turns to me again, giving me an avuncular look. "I'm knowing this girl since she was size of a mittu," he says to Sam.

Sam looks inquiringly at Abba, who says, "Mittu? I think it's a sardine."

We laugh.

"I thought you'd returned to Karachi after retirement," I say. "I'm so pleased to see you."

Hussein makes a face. "What for me to do in Karachi after so long in America?" he says. "Wife, son all here, baby. This our home, no? Situation in Pakistan no good."

I nod. "Well, I'm glad you're here."

"Okay, everybody, please to go out of the kitchen,'" Hussein says. "What you like to drink, baby. Hai? Nimbu pani? Lassi?"

Even though it's cold outside, I opt for Hussein's fabulous limeade. He brings out the glasses on a small tray, then returns immediately with snacks—fried chaklis and my favorite, deep-fried balls of mashed potatoes mixed with tapioca pearls and peanuts. "My God, these are *sooo* good," Sam says, after she takes a bite.

Abba invites Hussein to join us, but he refuses. "Lot of work in kitchen, boss," he says. "You enjoy with your daughter. I finish cooking the chicken tikka and shrimp curry rice."

"Abba, you know we're not staying for dinner, right?" I say. "We have a busy day tomorrow."

His face falls. Before I can respond, Sam says, "I'm sure we can stay for a quick dinner, Ali."

I give in.

An hour later, Hussein appears in the living room again. "Okay, boss, I am taking your leave. All food is ready. I pack extra for baby and her friend to take home."

"Shukriya, Hussein," Abba says. "We'll talk soon."

After Hussein says his goodbyes, Abba hands me a fifty-dollar note. "Go give it to him," he says. "As a token of your appreciation."

"That's all we're giving him?"

"Aliya." Abba sucks his teeth. "I've already paid him for cooking. This is just a gift from you. It's an Indian custom. Go quickly."

I rush to stop Hussein in the driveway. "You don't having to, Aliya baby," he demurs before accepting the bill. His eyes are soft as he looks at me. "You are grown up, but still as sweet as ever."

There's a lump in my throat. It's cold enough that we can see our breath, but I suddenly don't wish to say goodbye to this man, who was such an important part of my childhood. "You always looked after me, Hussein chacha," I say.

He looks pleased. "It is your abba who looking after all of us. I am supporting my household today because of the monthly check he is giving me. Tell me, what other restaurant owner is giving pension to his workers?" He looks at the front door furtively, then at me. "If I am saying something, you won't take it wrong?"

"What is it?"

"Your abba feeling very bad you not calling or seeing him. He so sick two years ago. I was begging him to contact you. Yasmin memsahib also tell him. But he say no. He is proud man, your father. So, my heart is blooming like the rose to see you in your father's house today."

My stomach lurches. "Abba was sick?"

"Heart trouble. He getting breathless just to walking across the room. Doctors putting two—what you call it? Scent?—in his heart."

"Scent? *Stent*?"

"Yes, that only." Hussein nods vigorously. "We are all getting old. By grace of God, Irfan seth is okay now. But who is knowing about tomorrow? So, I'm very happy you are returned."

My eyes fill with tears at the man's obvious sincerity. "Thanks for telling me, Hussein," I say. "I will visit more often."

He bows his head. His eyes are watery, too, when he looks up. "Khuda Hafiz, Aliya baby," he says. "May Allah the Merciful allow us to meet again."

"Inshallah," I say. God willing. The word rolls off my tongue.

I wait in the driveway as Hussein backs out. As he pulls away, he steps on his horn, his farewell to me. It's a still, quiet evening and I shudder at the thought of Abba's white neighbors reacting to a Muslim driver in traditional Muslim garb disturbing their peace, and then I feel a spurt of anger. Fuck 'em, I think. I'm done with apologizing for our existence. I wave until I can't see Hussein's taillights anymore.

The front door opens. "You coming in?" Abba asks. "It's cold."

"In a minute." I've spent so much time believing that I was estranged from my father that it never occurred to me that he was estranged from me, too. The thought burns.

Sam and Yasmin are setting the table when I go in. Abba cocks his eyebrow at me, but I ignore him and go to the bathroom to compose myself, letting this knowledge of Abba's vulnerability sink in. When I return, the food is on the table and the three of them are waiting for me. "Ah, there she is," Abba says and begins to spoon the food onto Sam's plate. "I gave special instructions to Hussein not to make anything too spicy."

"Sam can actually eat spicier food than me," I say. "Just shows how little you know me."

They all look at me. "Is something wrong, Aliya?" Abba asks evenly.

"No. Why should anything be wrong?"

"I miss Hussein, too," Abba says, misunderstanding. "But it was time for him to retire. The man had worked like an ox his whole life."

"So have you."

He gives me a puzzled look. "So?"

"Maybe that's why you had the heart attack. You know, the one you didn't inform me about."

Sam looks confused. Abba drops the serving spoon and closes his eyes. Only Yasmin says, "I told you, Irfan. Yah, Allah, as if this is something to keep a secret from your only child."

"That bloody idiot Hussein," Abba finally says. "That man could never keep a secret."

"A secret, Abba? You keep something like this a secret from me? What kind of . . ." The tears are streaming down my cheeks, and I am beyond trying to hide them.

Abba pulls up a chair next to me. "I'm sorry, child," he says. "I—I didn't want to worry you. You had your business and I thought you didn't need the distraction. It was foolish of me. I see that now." He grasps my chin and turns my head towards him, looks deep into my eyes. "I am truly sorry."

There's years of grief here, miles and miles of it, bubbling with me like a hot spring and rendering me incoherent. "You. You don't know, Abba," I babble, and he keeps nodding at me and murmuring, "I know. I know, my child." Even as I'm aware of Sam and Yasmin's presence, I feel as if I'm in private communication with my father, our eyes saying what we cannot, what we've never been able to say. Because what are words, these unreliable tools that can be used to conceal, deceive, defraud, betray, distract, mislead? Words crack and splinter like twigs in a storm, under the force of the gale of emotions churning inside of me. Instead, we talk to each other through our eyes:

~Why, why, why did you forsake me, my father?

~I never did. But I was afraid for you. For the path you'd chosen.

~Mummy would've never abandoned me.

~When your Mummy died, I'd sworn to be both a father and a mother to you. I failed to be either.

~But there's time now. Tell me there's time now, Abba.

~There's time. I will never give you up again. No matter what.

"What is your prognosis, Mr. Mirza?" Sam asks, breaking the silent communion between us and just for a second, I resent her for it.

"It's excellent."

I don't believe him. "Yasmin?" I say.

"No, it's true, Ali jaan," she says, nodding her head. "Doctorji says as long as he exercises daily and controls what he eats, he will be good."

I look down at the oily chicken tikka masala and shrimp curry on the table and grimace.

"No, no, no, we don't eat like this every day," Yasmin says. "This is for special occasions. Mostly, I cook vegetarian food at home. Not that heavy restaurant food."

Abba smiles at his wife and my breath catches. I've always seen Yasmin as a poor substitute for Mummy. But now I see what Abba has been trying to say to me—that their relationship has its own dynamic and if I hadn't been so blind and selfish, I would've seen the obvious: Yasmin loves my father. For the first time, I'm grateful.

"Thank you, Yasmin," I say, and she flashes me a startled smile.

"Chalo, the food is getting cold," Abba says. "Poor Hussein worked so hard on this meal. Let's do it justice."

When Abba takes a second helping of rice, I want to stop him. But I stay silent. Love doesn't give a person permission to control another. I've tried to live by those words, the source of so much conflict between Sam and me.

It is after eight o'clock when we take our leave. Yasmin has packed us several containers of leftovers, along with the extra food Hussein has prepared. "You'll be okay?" Abba says, his brow furrowed. "Driving so late?"

"Don't worry, Mr. Mirza," Sam says with a chuckle. "I'm a great driver. Your daughter is in safe hands."

Abba gives her a wry smile. "Thank you." He walks out of the house with us and stands in the driveway, right hand raised in farewell as we back out.

"You okay, Ali?" Sam asks once we're on the freeway.

"I will be. Right now, I'm just in shock. I'd always thought of Abba as invulnerable. But he's getting old." I sigh. "I've lost so many years with him. Years when we could've had good times."

"He'll be okay, honey," Sam says. "He looks great. Millions of people get stents put in and lead long, happy lives."

"I know. But those millions are not my dad. He was a rock when you were . . . away. You have no idea."

"I do understand. You have the greatest dad."

I know that Sam's comparing Abba to her own father. Thinking of the vile things Joe O'Malley's said to his wife earlier today, remembering his hostility toward Sam and me when we'd visited with our wedding invitation, I feel an intense sorrow for her. "Abba *is* great," I agree. "I'm sorry about your dad."

Sam shrugs. "He loved me in his own way," she says. "Even when I was terrified of him, I knew this."

"Maybe that's what saved you."

She squeezes my hand. "Maybe. And maybe in the end, all that turmoil led me to you."

I squeeze back. "It's not the end," I say.

46

▾ ▸ ▴ ◂ ▾ ▴ ▸ ▴

Thursday, January 30, 2020

At the end of the first month of the new year, I allow myself a tiny bit of hope. Sam is back to teaching, and her classes are going well. She seems happier these days. Her new novel is apparently gaining steam—she won't let me take a look yet. I'm trying to work from home a few days a week, which allows me to cook more and take care of the household things we'd let slip last year. I bought Sam a NuStep for Christmas and she's been using it daily. Between that and the meals I've been cooking, she is slowly regaining her old musculature. Her arms and calves are stronger, thanks to the online yoga class we attend four mornings a week, and there's a glow on her face. She also seems less fearful, although she still won't go for a walk or a run in our neighborhood. "We'll start in the spring, Ali," she said the other day and I nodded.

She still won't talk about last summer. The police are no closer to making an arrest than they were last August, which means that Sam becomes jumpy and anxious if a man looks at her for a second longer than necessary. When a plumber came last week to fix the toilet, Sam got in the car and drove around until I called to say he had left. Herrington stops by less often because there are no more leads, although he assures me that he will not close the file, not while the monster is out there.

Aside from the night of my birthday, our sex life is nonexistent. It's appalling to say this, but I think any overtures on my part remind Sam of the man who violated her. And so, I've stopped. The only other person who knows this is Mo, who asks me to be patient and not give up hope. It will take time, she says. And I believe her, because what's the alternative?

Today is Sam's long teaching day. I've made a salad, roast chicken, and wild rice for supper.

When she walks in, my heart aches at how exhausted she looks. She musters a smile as she removes her winter jacket and hangs it in the mud room. "Hi," I say as I give her a light kiss. "Busy day?"

She rolls her eyes. "Don't even ask. Two students from my class wanted to discuss their first papers just when I was packing up to leave." She sniffs. "Wow. That smells good."

"You ready to eat?"

"In a few. Just let me get changed."

I light a couple of candles before I serve the food.

"Should we have a bit of wine?" Sam says.

"Sure." I get the open bottle from the fridge.

Sam cuts the chicken. "Something really sad happened during my office hours. I have an international student in my Intro to Poetry class. He's from Wuhan, China. Anyway, there's some new virus there, he said. And it killed his father. He wanted to go home for the funeral but his family said he shouldn't return because it's dangerous. Can you imagine not being able to attend your own father's funeral? He was inconsolable. I didn't even know what to say."

"Wow, that's really odd. I caught something about this on NPR today. It's called the 2019 Novel Coronavirus. The reporter said there are already seven confirmed cases in the US. That's wild, that your student's dad died of it. What's his name?"

"Lee. He's a great kid. A very good writer."

"I'll bake some cookies for him next week."

"That's sweet of you, Ali. But I can't. It will seem like favoritism."

"Then I'll make enough for your whole class."

When we're done with dinner, I offer to clear the table. "I'll clean up. You go chill."

Sam sighs. "I wish. I have to read this long essay before my student conference tomorrow. And I can barely keep my eyes open."

"Go," I say, giving her a playful shove. "Do what you have to do."

I load the dishwasher and dry the pans before I make my way upstairs. The door to Sam's study is slightly ajar. She is sitting in her armchair, her work papers in her lap. From the angle of her neck, I can tell that she's dozed off. There is something so vulnerable about that neck, now so visible with her hair short, that my heart aches. Sam never did go back to Dr. Salinger to treat her spine, opting to take mega doses of Advil instead. I go to the medicine cabinet to get some almond oil. I pour some oil in my palm and touch the nape of her neck, afraid that my cold hands will irritate her skin. But she is in such a deep sleep that she doesn't move. I rub the oil in, my fingers coiled around her neck, touching the front near her clavicle.

Suddenly, she flinches, grabs my hand and twists my fingers until I yelp with pain. "Sam, you're hurting me," I say, but she doesn't seem to hear me. She is in some kind of stupor, making a loud rumbling noise. "Sam," I yell. "Stop."

She lets go of me abruptly, spins around in her office chair. There is a mad look in her eyes that chills me. "What were you doing behind me? Why were you creeping up on me?"

"What the? Sam. Honey. You were asleep. I was only trying to give you a massage."

We stare at one another for a full minute, and I watch the madness seep out of her eyes. "I'm sorry," she finally says. "I thought . . . I thought I was back there. And that he was trying to . . ."

"It's okay. You're safe. You're home."

But I am a mess on the inside. This reactivity, this animal-fear, is encoded in her bones now. Will it ever leave her? It's impossible to know.

"Ali. It's not you. Please don't be mad."

"I'm not. Really, I'm not. I'm sorry to have scared you."

"Yeah, it's probably better not to touch me when I'm asleep," she says. She attempts a laugh. "Because you know, you don't want to provoke the cray-cray woman you live with."

"You're not crazy," I say. But my heart's not in it.

After a minute, she looks down at her lap and says, "Well, I better finish reading this. But you should go to bed, hon."

"I'll wait up for you."

"There's no need. Get some rest."

I shut her office door behind me and climb into bed. My skin is burning, and it takes me a few minutes to recognize what I'm feeling: a deep sense of humiliation. And panic.

47

▼ ▶ ▲ ◀ ▼ ▲ ▶ ▲

Tuesday, February 4

It begins to snow soon after I reach my office and the sky is that peculiar shade of Ohio beige. When I look out the window again fifteen minutes later, the sidewalks have turned white. The snow makes the world look benign and harmless, a white blanket draped over its brokenness and ugliness.

It's a dreary day, with no meetings on my calendar. Sam doesn't teach today; maybe she'll be free to go to a movie? I pick up the phone to call her, then think better of it. Ever since the incident with the massage, we've been a little wary around one another. Instead, I text her.

—*Hey, hon. You busy?* I type.

—*Yup. Going into a meeting in less than ten. What's up?*

—*Nothing much. I was wondering if you can take the afternoon off and we can go see Little Women at the Cedar Lee?*

—*Sigh. I wish I could. I really want to see it. But I'm slammed at work. Also, I have my writing group tonight, remember? Jill and I were going to pick up a bite and then go directly to Bill's house?*

—*Shit, I forgot. Okay, guess I'll pick up dinner for myself from the Thai place.*

—*Sorry. But I'd told you about it several weeks ago.*

—*No problem.*

—*Okay. But, Ali, now I feel like a jerk. Like, you're blaming me for going out with my friends.*

—*Whoa! Where did that come from?*

—Well, you just sounded so passive-aggressive there. About picking up dinner and eating alone.

—Samantha. I asked you to a movie. You have other plans. Can we please not make this more than it is?

—So, this is all my imagination? You're not pissed?

—I'm not pissed. I'm disappointed. There's a difference.

—Yeah, whatever. I'm not going to split hairs.

—I give up. I'm not fighting with you anymore, Sam. It's exactly this kind of childishness that led to our big fight last year. And all the shit that followed.

—Wait, what? Are you blaming me for getting kidnapped? Just when I'm finally beginning to get my shit together? I can't believe you said that.

—That's not what I said. Jesus, Sam. I don't even know you anymore.

—That's because I'm finally taking care of myself, Ali. Forgive me for not kowtowing to your every command.

—Wow. Just . . . wow. All this because I asked my wife out to a movie?

—On a Tuesday? When you know I'm at work and have evening plans?

—I forgot. Okay? I forgot about your precious plans. So, sue me.

—Yeah, if you ever paid attention when I talk, maybe you would've remembered. Anyway. I gotta go. My meeting starts in a few and thanks to this conversation, I'm not even ready. Bye. Have a nice evening.

I want to reply "Thanks for ruining mine."

But I don't. I text, *Have a nice time tonight. I love you.* And I make myself mean it.

I stare at the phone for a few minutes, and when it's clear she's not writing back, I put it away. I pace around my office for a few minutes, trying to figure out what just happened. Is it the support group for crime victims doing this to her, resulting in a new aggression in the way she talks to me? I've tried ignoring it, especially since she refuses to go back to Sarah Yates. But some of her outbursts are so irrational, they make my head spin. Despair settles on me like the snow falling outside my window.

I pick up the phone to call Mo but find myself dialing Abba's number instead. He's at the restaurant, but as always, sounds delighted to hear from me. "What is it, Aliya?" he asks after a few minutes. "You sound down."

"I have a strange question. What did you and Mummy fight about, Abba?"

"Fight?" He sounds puzzled. "No, I don't think so."

"What?"

"I can't remember ever fighting with your mother."

"That's not true. I remember one time she yelled at you so loudly, I hid in the kitchen cabinet."

"You remember that? It wasn't a fight, beta. She yelled at me to watch my diet because my cholesterol was high. After that, she started making a healthy lunch for me to take to work every day. No more greasy restaurant food, she said." He sighs. "After she died, I went back to my old eating habits. But I don't think of that as a fight."

"Okay. Some other time, then. Everybody does."

"I don't understand. Why would two people who are devoted to each other fight?"

If anyone else in the world had said this, I would've rolled my eyes. But one thing about Abba—he doesn't lie. And the truth is, I don't recall another instance of my parents yelling at one another or giving the other the silent treatment.

"Abba, how is your heart now?" I ask. "Tell me the truth."

"Child, don't you have enough to worry about? I'm fine. Yasmin takes very good care of me. But, jaan, your father is getting older. At some point something will happen. You must be ready for that eventuality."

"Don't say that. I—I can't bear any more loss."

"Aliya, what's wrong? Problems at home?"

I open my mouth to tell him what just occurred but fall silent. How do I describe the sheer inanity of my fights with Sam? Words that seem sharp as daggers turn into paper arrows when I try describing them. "Everything's fine," I say. "I just miss you."

Abba is silent for a long time.

"Abba?" I say finally. "You there?"

"All these years," he says. "All these years when you were angry with me. From the time my feet hit the ground till the time I fell asleep, yours was the first and last name on my lips. Each day I'd pray to Allah to give you good health. And strength. And wisdom. All my prayers have been heard. Allah has given my daughter back to me. Aliya, believe me. Just being able to spend time with you again has added ten years to my life. Even my customers can see the change in me. 'Why are you so happy, Irfan bhai?' they ask."

I swallow the lump in my throat. "You be safe in India," I say. "Don't eat all that rich wedding food, you hear? Stick to your diet."

He laughs. "If you're so worried about me, why don't you come?"

And suddenly, I'm tempted. To spend three whole weeks with Abba in his home country! The last time we were there together was when I was a little kid, and though I have no memories of our visit, thinking about visiting India fills me with an ache for which I have no name. Maybe it will do Sam and me some good also, to take a break from one another?

"I got you an OCI card years ago, which means you won't even need a tourist visa," Abba says.

What comes out of my mouth next surprises me as much as it does him. "Abba," I say. "I'm not sure that I can. But if I could, do you think it's too late for me to get a plane ticket?"

Samantha comes home from her writing group energized and in a good mood. "Did you eat?" she says as she kicks off her boots.

"Yup. I got a grilled cheese from Tommy's."

"Good. Hey, I'm truly sorry for being a bitch earlier today."

"It's okay. It was just a . . ."

"No, Ali, it wasn't." She takes my hand. "I could make a thousand excuses, but I was out of line. And you didn't do anything wrong."

"Let's forget it. I'm glad you're home."

"I don't know why I've been snapping at you so much," Sam continues. "I think things are getting stirred up for me in the survivor's group, you know? Honestly, at times I feel like one of those creatures that chews off its own limbs."

"Things about us?"

"What? *No.* About . . . old stuff. You know, my dad and all."

I want to ask more, but I resist. Samantha suppresses a yawn.

"Let's get ready for bed and then I'll give you a foot rub. Okay?" I say.

"I don't deserve you."

"I need to talk to you about something," I say as I massage her feet. "I spoke to Abba today. About maybe going to India with him and Yasmin for a few weeks at the end of the month."

Sam's eyes widen with surprise. "You want to go? I thought you said . . ."

"Yeah, well, I'm rethinking it. I think it will mean a lot to Abba. And also," I try to find the right, noninflammatory words, "I think maybe the break will do us . . . me . . . some good. But if you need me here, I don't have to—"

"Go." Sam says. "You've been under tremendous stress. Now that I'm back at work, I can pay for your plane ticket."

"So can I. I have a check from a client coming in. But Abba is insisting on buying it."

"Let him. You're too independent for your own good." Her face softens. "I know you're worried about his health, Ali. I think it's a great idea for you to spend some time with him."

I fall silent, knowing that she's wishing she could've reconciled with her own father, remembering the difficult visit in December. "I wish you could come with us," I say finally. For some reason, I'm feeling sad, as if I'm already far away from Sam.

"Maybe next time. I do want to go to India someday."

"And you'll be okay here alone?"

"Yes. This new novel is kicking my butt. This way, I'll get some serious work done." She smiles. "Because I won't be distracted by my beautiful wife."

Now that we've made up, I'm not sure I even want to leave.

Samantha reads the conflict on my face. "Ali, don't be like that. I'll be here when you get back home, honey."

"You have no business knowing me so well."

She laughs. "You mean knowing what a contrarian you are?"

I get up, bring a calendar to bed to show her the dates. "They're leaving on February twenty-fourth and will reach India the following day. The wedding is on March twentieth. Abba said they're flying home the following day. So, I'll be gone three and a half weeks. Is that too long?"

"Whatever you decide."

"All this may be moot, anyway. Maybe the plane tickets will be too expensive at this point," I say, hopeful.

"Well, there's only one way to find out."

"I know. Abba said he'll call his travel agent tomorrow, if I say yes."

"Ali. Don't second guess yourself. You're going."

And so, it's decided.

The Way Back

ALI AND SAM

48

▼ ▶ ▲ ◀ ▼ ▲ ▶ ▲

Tuesday, February 25

Mumbai.

After exiting the most gorgeous airport I've ever seen, whose beautiful artwork and luxury shops give it the plush feel of a five-star hotel, I am unprepared for the bedlam that greets us—crowds straining to greet relatives, cops blowing deafening whistles, coolies jostling to carry our suitcases. Yasmin swears at them loudly in Hindi as we look around anxiously. And then, miraculously, we hear a single shout: "Irfan Uncle. Over *here.*"

Mumbai.

As seen from the backseat of a car expertly driven by Yasmin's younger sister's son Kabir, who apologizes profusely for the broken air conditioner. Why the fuck didn't you get it fixed before picking us up? I think, uncharitably.

Mumbai.

Arabian Sea sea of cars sea of people traffic jams wedding party groom on horseback cows on the street.

Mumbai.

Sensory overload. A cauldron of heat, noise, and traffic. And people. So many people.

Kabir names the neighborhoods as we go through them—Mahim, Dadar, Parel, Byculla. We are going over one ugly concrete flyover after another until home to Nasreen Auntie, in Bhendi Bazaar.

Bhendi Bazaar.

Whose narrow, dense streets make the car slow down to less than ten miles per hour. Whose lights and noise and crowds make the rest of the city seem as tranquil as the Swiss Alps and make me, jet-lagged and weary, whimper with regret and homesickness. What have I done? I keep thinking.

As if he's read my mind, Abba turns around from the passenger seat and shoots me a stern look. Don't act like an American crybaby, the look reads. You will embarrass our hosts.

I pretend not to notice.

Nasreen Auntie's apartment is in a rickety, hundred-year-old building with wooden steps that thud as we climb to the third floor. The railing is dusty, and I'm afraid that it will come loose if I lean too heavily on it. Behind me, I can hear Yasmin's labored breathing. Ahead of us, Kabir, tall, handsome, and slender, is staggering under the weight of our suitcases. Neighbors on the lower floors come out of their apartments and stare openly as we make our way up. Some of them call out a greeting to Yasmin, but she's too out of breath to reply.

Nasreen Auntie, plump and broad-shouldered and wearing a pink rida, flings open the door before Kabir can ring the doorbell. "Yah, Allah," she says. "You have arrived. Come in, come in." She leans forward to embrace her sister. "Yasmin," she says. "You must be starving yourself in that pagan land. All skin-and-bone you are becoming."

It is such a blatant lie that I exchange a bemused look with Abba and smother a laugh.

"And you must be Aliya," Nasreen says. "Wah! So beautiful. Come here, child."

"Hello, Auntie," I say casually, even a bit insouciantly. Since I'm here for the next three weeks, I want to set parameters from the get-go. I haven't been to India since I was four, but I well remember the domineering old Indian women in Columbus.

"Arre, what's this Auntie-fauntie business?" Nasreen says. "My sister is your mummy, no? So, I am your masi. You must call me Nasreen Masi."

I stiffen. I turn to Abba, but he looks straight ahead. But I can still read the set of his jaw—do not make a fuss, he is saying. Do not embarrass me.

So, I simply smile, and the moment passes. We walk into the large living room, and I notice the lack of tables and chairs. Instead, there are Persian rugs everywhere and large cushions and bolsters. Kabir looks at me, worried. "Would you like me to get you a chair, Aliya didi?" he says. "We—we usually sit on the floor, you know? But as an American you must not be used to it?"

"No, I'll be fine."

"I can show you your room?" Kabir says, and I nod and follow him. He glances at me as we enter and bursts out laughing. "You were afraid there wouldn't be a bed, correct, Didi?" he says. "The look of relief on your face . . ."

I grin.

"I'll put your suitcase here. Is that okay?"

"Yes, thank you."

"And would you like me to show you how to use the shower? You must turn on the electric geyser for about ten minutes to get hot water."

I groan with gratitude. "A shower sounds great."

When I return to the living room, Abba, Yasmin, and Nasreen are sitting cross-legged on the carpet, leaning against the bolsters. Nasreen is teasing Abba, berating him for not visiting last year. Abba, who has changed into a white kurta and loose pajamas, puts his arm around her and laughingly teases her back. I'm amazed to see how at ease my father is in this alien setting, how comfortable he seems bantering with this elderly woman with whom he has so little in common. My heart twists at the realization of how little I know of him, the fact that Abba has this whole second life that I know nothing about. My relationship with him is frozen in ether, from when we were a family of three and Mummy was his wife. I lived with him and Yasmin after he married her, but I was absorbed in my own changing body and passions, too young to pay attention to Abba's needs. Abba was my father; he may as well have been a cardboard cutout for all the attention I paid to his interiority. But it hits me now: that Abba has a whole family in India that he visits regularly; that he is a man with his own appetites and desires; that even as I spiraled away from him during my teenage years, he, too, has moved away from me. As I was building a new life for myself in college and, later, with Sam, he, too, was putting down new roots.

Yasmin gets up with a grunt and reaches for me. "Come sit, Aliya jaan. Eat something. You must be hungry," she says.

I notice two things simultaneously: One, that I'm indeed hungry and two, Yasmin seems transformed, younger and softer. Ready to welcome me into the fold of her family. How shabbily I'd treated her when she'd first come to live with us. How lonely, how afraid she must've been in a strange country, trapped between a widower who still displayed photographs of his dead wife, and his moody, sulky daughter. To my mortification and bafflement, I burst into tears. It happens so suddenly—like puking outside a college bar when I was in my twenties—that I am as stunned as they are. Kabir's eyes widen in concern, and I vaguely notice that Yasmin has her arm around me in a maternal way. I know I'm embarrassing Abba and this makes me sob even harder.

"She's exhausted," Abba says. His voice is smooth, assured. "This is overwhelming for her." He reaches for my hand. "Come. Sit next to me, gudiya. You're okay."

I wipe my tears, notice the glasses of lassi and platters of snacks. "I'm hungry," I announce, and they all laugh.

"She was like this even as a child," Abba says, his tone amused. "The only way to distract her when she cried was with food."

"She used to beg for the mutton kebabs I made as a snack when she came home from school," Yasmin says. "Remember, Aliya?"

I have no memory of this whatsoever, but I nod politely. Yasmin is like a different person here, with none of her usual wariness and stiffness around me. It occurs to me that she's trying to impress her family, to pretend a closeness with me that we've never had. Or maybe I'm being cynical, maybe Yasmin is just happy to be back home with her family, away from that cold, foreign land to which my father had brought her.

Kabir hands me a glass of lassi. "Don't worry, it's made from bottled water," he says earnestly, even though the thought had not even occurred to me. "Even the ice for you all is from good water."

I gulp down the cool, sweet liquid. "It's delicious," I say, setting down the glass. The doorbell rings just then and Kabir goes to answer it. He comes back with a woman who is a younger, prettier version of Yasmin, all dimples and smiles.

"Aliya, this is my baby sister, Fatima," Yasmin says. "Kabir's mother."

"Hello, hello," Fatima says to me. "Welcome to India. How was the flight?" She embraces Yasmin and then turns to Abba. "Wah, Irfan. You are growing a paunch. Business must be doing well, hah?"

Abba grins. "Here comes the troublemaker." He kisses her on both cheeks. "Kya khabar, Fatima? How is life?"

"Bas, now that you all are here, all is well. Now, we can celebrate my son's wedding with dhoom-dhaam."

Kabir bows his head and Nasreen notices. "Look at our Kabir, blushing. Arre, beta, if you're not careful, people will mistake you for the bride instead of the groom."

They all laugh, the adults talking a mile a minute, interrupting, shouting, talking over one another. Only Kabir and I are quiet. After a minute, he whispers, "Want to go to the balcony and chat?"

I get up only too happily. Kabir opens the double doors that lead from the living room to the balcony. The noise of the traffic below is deafening and Nasreen yells at him to shut the doors again.

The smoky outdoor air tickles my nose. I lean over the railing, gape at the riotous scene below. How can anybody get anything done in this city? And yet, hundreds of people are rushing around, obviously on their way somewhere. The thought of leaving this apartment and joining this mass of humanity makes me feel faint.

"So, you have your own business?" Kabir is saying.

"What?"

He repeats himself and I nod. "Yes. I'm an interior designer."

"What is America like? You must be living in a skyscraper?"

"No," I say with a laugh. "That's mostly in certain cities, like New York. And, like, downtown. No, we—I—live in a house."

He takes a deep breath. "A whole house? And it's on ownership?"

I flush, suddenly aware of my unearned privilege, knowing how wondrous the concept must seem to someone dwelling in this congested, crowded city. "And you?" I ask. "You and your parents live in this flat?"

"No, no. Mummy and I live just one building over, only." He swallows. "My abba died when I was seven years old."

"Oh, I'm sorry."

He shrugs and after a moment I say, "So where will you and your wife live after the wedding?"

He cocks his head, puzzled. "Where else? There, only."

"With your mom?" I ask.

"Then what?" Kabir replies.

There is an expression on his face I can't decipher.

Just when the silence between us is beginning to feel awkward he asks, "So who are your favorite rock groups? You must be going to rock concerts and all? Do you like rap?"

Even as my head reels at this abrupt change in topic, my eyes close as a wave of jet lag hits. Kabir notices immediately. "Come on, yaar," he says. "You should go take rest."

I smile weakly and follow him back into the living room. Abba's eyes, too, look heavy-lidded. We exchange a look. "Chalo, Nasreen, we all need a nap," he says.

Abba escorts me to my room and kisses me on the forehead. "I'm very glad you're here, gudiya," he says. "I know everything feels strange. But believe me, in a few days, it will all be fine."

49

▾▸▴◂▾▴▸▴

Thursday, March 5

Abba is right. After a few days, I adjust to the rhythm of life here. Neighbors and friends float in and out of Nasreen's apartment, the doorbell rings fifty times a day, the milkman and the butcher and the fishmonger and the vegetable vendor make their deliveries, the cook asks me every morning what I wish to eat that day, most evenings I hang out with Kabir after he gets off work while the days are spent shopping for the wedding—including a gold necklace and bangles that Yasmin asks Abba to buy for me over my protestations. Fatima insists that I wear a sari to her son's wedding, but there I put my foot down. I've packed a nice silk top and black pants for the occasion. Fatima looks so appalled that I finally agree to buy an expensive shalwar kameez with gold thread embroidery from a fancy store called Kala Niketan. That same day, she takes me to a small but wonderful jewelry store in Colaba called Amber, where I buy a turquoise and silver bracelet and matching ring for Sam. I also buy her a pair of sapphire earrings. On another day I go shopping to buy more outfits for a party that Fatima is throwing at her apartment for Kabir's new in-laws, as well as for the henna ceremony that will take place at the bride's home the day before the actual wedding. Every morning, Abba and I go for a walk by the seaside and despite the godawful pollution I cherish my time with him. One afternoon, he takes me to a Punjabi restaurant, where I eat the best freaking tandoori chicken I've ever tasted. A Hindi remake of *Death of a Salesman* is playing at the Prithvi Theatre and I drag Kabir to it one evening. He looks so disgruntled and bewildered when we leave the theater, I have to suppress my giggles.

"What, yaar?" he says. "All that bakwas and not even one song or dance number. Just blah blah blah."

"It's a classic American play," I say. "About, you know, a broken man who . . ."

Kabir silences me with a withering look. "If I want broken, I just have to look around. You Americans are all mad, yaar," he says, the final word on the subject.

But amid my pleasure at exploring the city of my forefathers, my relatives talk in whispers about the rising anti-Muslim sentiment in India, and their fear is so wretchedly familiar, their conversation so similar to what we discuss in our own country, that I try to ignore it as much as I can. Still, Kabir fills me in: incidents of mobs lynching Muslims falsely accused of eating beef, inflammatory lies about the intentions of the Muslim minority to control the Hindu majority spread by anonymous posts on WhatsApp and Facebook; moves in Parliament to curtail the rights of Muslim citizens. The prime minister himself is a far-right Hindu nationalist.

"Are you frightened?" I ask Kabir, and he replies, "Of course. I'm a Muslim. Anything can happen at any time."

And I suddenly realize how silly the concerns of Willy Loman must seem to someone living in such dangerous times.

Every night I call Sam from my bedroom, when she is taking lunch, and we commiserate about the alarming events happening in both countries. She fills me in on the latest on Covid-19, which is making rounds around the world, and tells me that there are fresh cases in the US every day.

"I hope you're staying safe, Ali," she says.

"Nobody here seems worried about it," I say. "Anybody I ask says that because of all the germs and pollution, Indians have built up a great immune system."

"But this virus is new to humankind."

"I know. But try telling them that."

I wish I could lean out of the window and feel the warm breeze as I chat with her, but Sam says the amplified sound of the incessant car horns is deafening. "How can you stand this noise, Ali?" she asks even when I have the window shut, but I tell her how already I'm learning to ignore this auditory wallpaper of sound. Already, I'm getting inured to the appalling poverty around me, because the alternative is to lose your mind. And I tell her how I'm doing my best to fit in: Earlier today, when Kusum, Nasreen's maid, said that they were out of bottled water, I said I'd take a glass of regular tap water, which Kusum boils and stores in rotund clay pots. More than anything, the stacks of bottled water the three of us consume embarrass me, make me want to apologize for our delicate American constitutions, which is another way of saying, our American privilege. But Yasmin, who overheard the conversation, scolded Kusum and told her to order a dozen bottles. A young man delivered them fifteen minutes later.

"Ali," Sam says, "it's just for another couple of weeks. The last thing you want to do is get sick over there, right?"

"Right." I wonder how Sam would fare in India, whether she'd be mortified by all the special courtesies we are afforded by our relatives or whether she'd take it in stride, her due as an American. Well, it's a moot point, I think, because if we ever visited together, we'd stay in a posh hotel in a better part of town and not with Yasmin's relatives.

"And you're doing okay? Your classes are going okay? The novel is coming along?"

She sighs. "School is fine. The novel? I thought I'd get a lot of work done while you're away. But the house is so empty when I get home. It . . . I just . . . So instead of working, I just veg out."

"This is how I felt when you were . . . away. I'm sorry."

"Nah. Don't be. If you have a good time, it'll be worth it. How are you and your dad doing?"

"That's the bright spot of this trip, really. Getting to spend time with him." I want to tell Sam about how different Abba is in India, so open and light somehow, but I don't know how to explain this to her without something getting lost in translation.

"And you've bought all your outfits for all the pre-wedding events?"

"Mostly. Some are being altered at the tailor. It's crazy, how much they're spending on the whole affair. And listen to this—Fifteen hundred guests. And that's not even a big wedding by Indian standards."

"Shit, Ali. I don't think I've met that many people in my whole life."

We talk for another half hour and then Sam has to get back to work.

I am just getting ready for bed when there's a light tap on my door. It's Abba. "Kusum just brought some sitafal ice cream," he says.

"What's that?"

"Sitafal? It's an Indian fruit known as custard apple. It's fantastic."

"Abba, I just brushed my teeth. And you have no business eating ice cream."

"Aliya. I'll get back on my diet after we return. And you can always brush your teeth again. Come on, make your old father happy."

Abba's eyes are gleaming as he scoops a large portion into each bowl, and I tamp down the pang of worry I feel at the amount of food he's consuming on this trip. We sit across from each other, grinning, eating the delicious dessert. I close my eyes briefly, savoring the moment, committing it to memory, the ice cream as sweet as this shared moment.

50

▾ ▸ ▴ ◂ ▾ ▴ ▸ ▴

Friday, March 6

Abba looks worried.

"Are you sure you want to go, beta?" he says. "The Haji Ali mosque can get really crowded, you know. Especially on Fridays. Why not wait until I am free to join you?"

"Kabir will be there with me."

He makes a dismissive noise. "What, that skinny boy? One gust of wind from the sea and—*dhap!*—down he'll go."

"Abba. Stop worrying."

"I wish I hadn't agreed to go meet with the caterers with Fatima today," Abba says. "Why do they need me for that job, anyway?"

"Abba." I laugh. "It's *okay*."

We take a cab to Worli—Kabir says parking will be impossible—and I get my first glimpse of the four-hundred-year-old mosque, its white dome and minarets looking as if they're floating in the sea. The building, which houses the tomb of a Muslim saint, Haji Ali Shah Bukhari, is actually located on a small islet and connected to the mainland via a long causeway, which is jam-packed with people today. The water on either side of us is brown and murky. People walk at various clips and Kabir tells me to be patient—given the throng, it will take us maybe twenty minutes to reach the structure. I notice that there are far more men than women and most of the worshipers appear to be working-class folks. There are a few white tourists, the women wearing headscarfs, and ahead of us, a group of Indian women in jeans and T-shirts. They appear to be college students.

"You should see this place during Eid, yaar," Kabir says. "Thousands upon thousands of people come. You can barely see the ground in front of you."

We are swept along by this sea of humanity, the Mumbai sun blazing overhead. I'm thankful for the headscarf I'm wearing. "Are all these folks Muslim?" I ask, and Kabir shakes his head.

"No. Anyone can come. Nobody pays attention to caste or creed."

I remember the stories my parents used to tell me about the secular, cosmopolitan Bombay that they knew. Clearly, the vestiges of those halcyon days are still alive in this city, despite the growing sectarian rifts.

As we get closer to the monument, a terrible stench fills the air. I turn to Kabir inquiringly, my eyes watering from the smell. "Sorry, sorry," he says. "It's like this during low tide." He points to the big boulders between the causeway and the receding sea. "Homeless people squat on the rocks and do their business. And see all the plastic bottles and other filth floating in the water?" He screws up his nose in disgust. "I came here once during high tide. The waves washed right up to where we're walking. But at least then the water hides all this garbage."

"The sea washes away all our sins." I say it lightly, but Kabir nods seriously.

"Exactly," he says. Something in his expression tells me that despite his embarrassment at the stench and trash, this trip is meaningful to him, that he wants me to be moved and impressed. I resolve to do so.

But when we finally reach the stone structure I feel disappointed. The white exterior is stained from the salty air and cracked and peeling. Wires run from the rooftop, connected to small speakers, and crows perch on the minarets. On the other side of the water looms the new

Mumbai, tall and shiny and gleaming. I rotate my head slowly, taking in history and modernity, poverty and wealth.

As we approach the gate, I notice them—dozens of beggars, many of them amputees. I reach for my purse, but Kabir says, "Don't. We'll be mobbed in five seconds. They will surround us like flies."

I frown, and he notices. "Sorry, yaar. I know they have to eat, also. But trust me. You can give alms on our way back. Okay?" There is a sheen of sweat on his face, and I realize that he's nervous about his ability to protect me.

"No worries, Kabir," I say.

I enter from the women's entrance. Inside the main hall, the marble pillars feature mirror work and spell the ninety-nine names of Allah. The room housing Haji Ali's tomb is closed for renovations, but I catch a glimpse of the glass-paneled room through the bamboo scaffolding. I take in the lacelike carvings on the pillars, the decorative arches. The tomb itself is covered by a red-and-green blanket. There is a dirty but impressive chandelier dangling from the domed ceiling. There are signs posted everywhere asking people to beware of theft. I chuckle grimly at the incongruity of the warnings, the intrusion of the real world in a place of worship.

The press of the crowd is so thick, I exit as quickly as I can. Kabir is waiting for me outside the entrance. "Okay," I say. "I'm done. If you don't mind, I'd like to buy a couple of trinkets from the vendors on our way back."

Kabir clucks his tongue. "It's all cheap rubbish, yaar," he says. "I'll take you to some good stores tomorrow." He reaches into his pocket and pulls out a small stack of bills. "Here," he says. "I made change. Give this to the beggars."

I slip my hand in the crook of his elbow. "You're the best," I say.

He stiffens at this public display of affection, but I can tell he's pleased.

Kabir has more plans. "Hungry?" he asks as we get into a cab. And without waiting for me to answer he instructs the driver. "Royal China restaurant in Flora Fountain." He turns to me. "My favorite Chinese joint in town."

After days of spicy, oily Indian fare, Chinese food sounds damn good.

The cabbie drops us in front of the restaurant, glances at me, and says something in Hindi to Kabir.

"What'd he say?" I ask Kabir, who is chortling with laughter.

"He said, 'Madam has very large ears. That means she is very clever.'"

I give a loud snort as we climb the few steps into the restaurant, where we're almost at once greeted by an elegant woman in a sari who takes us to a table. Menus are brought and drink orders taken almost immediately, and again, I'm struck by how easy, how comfortable it is to be wealthy in India, money washing away the grime and sorrow of poverty.

I ask for a Coke; Kabir gets a beer. "Are you allowed?" I say, pointing. "I mean, being Muslim and all."

He looks around, shrugs. "As long as nobody from Bhendi Bazaar is here."

Kabir does the ordering—the signature sweet corn chicken soup, jumbo prawns wrapped in filo dough, and steamed wontons in a soy chili sauce. "Dude, that's a lot of food," I say.

"Wait till you taste it."

I want to lick my plate clean.

For the main course, Kabir orders egg fried rice and chicken in chili oil. The food is out of this world, a burst of flavor that no Chinese restaurant in the States can match. "This is fucking incredible," I say. "I wish Sam could . . ." I cut myself off.

"Sam is your . . . partner?" Kabir asks.

"How do you know?"

"Yasmin told my mum. Who can never keep anything to herself."

"Does Nasreen Auntie know?"

"I don't know. Probably not. She's . . . very religious."

We fall silent. I help myself to more of the chili chicken, wondering how to get out of the awkwardness of the moment. Before I can react, Kabir asks, "Your girlfriend is white?"

"Yes."

"Is she as beautiful as you?"

Is he flirting with me? I'm a good six years older and in any case, we're practically cousins. And he's about to be married. "She's very pretty," I say shortly. "And what about—?"

"Take me to America," he says suddenly, cutting me off.

"You're welcome to visit anytime," I say. "We'll be happy to host the two of you."

He shakes his head impatiently, annoyed with me. "You don't understand. I need to leave India."

"Why?"

"I'm gay."

"What? But you can't be," I say inanely. "You're getting married this month."

He nods and when he looks up, his eyes are brimming with tears. "It feels good to say it out loud. You're the first person I've ever said this to."

My mouth is suddenly dry. "Kabir," I say. "Are you sure? I mean have you even . . .?"

"I have a boyfriend. Joseph. We've been together for three years. We want to leave India together."

"But . . . how? Why did you agree to marry if that's the case?"

"As if I had a choice," he says. "As if Mummy even checked with me. One day, bas, I was told they'd found the girl for me."

"Have you met her? What's she like?"

"She's fine. Cute. Convent-educated and all that. Fair-skinned. Most men would find her sexy. But I don't have any interest in her."

A heaviness falls on me. I feel terrible for Kabir, for this poor girl, for this unknown Joseph.

"What—what does Joseph say?"

"He says I have no choice but to marry. But we'll keep seeing each other after."

My sorrow turns to anger. "Kabir, you can't do that. You can't start your life with a lie. It's not fair to the woman you're about to marry."

His eyes flash with anger. "What would you do? What would you have done if you'd been unfortunate enough to be born in India instead of America?"

I can't meet his gaze. "I'm not sure. I do understand your predicament, believe me, I do. But it's inexcusable, what you're planning on doing."

He takes a long drink of his beer, signals the waiter for another. "Forget it, yaar. I thought you'd sympathize. But you're too American to understand my situation."

"And . . . you won't consider calling off the engagement?"

"And do what? Remain a bachelor in this godforsaken country? Be alone for the rest of my life?"

"You and Joseph can't live together? Even, you know, as roommates?"

He makes a dismissive sound. "Joe looks very . . . feminine. He lives in Bandra with his parents. Where would we go? Nobody can afford to buy a flat in this expensive city. I'd be the laughingstock of the whole neighborhood if he moved in with me and Mummy. Our only solution is to start life in another country."

I want to tell him that it wasn't easy for me either, that I'd paid the price of losing my beloved Abba for many years, but I don't. The fact is, no matter how difficult my coming out was, it was a breeze compared to what awaits Kabir. In this moment, I feel deeply, profoundly American. "I'm sorry, Kabir," I say. "I really am."

"Forget it. My mistake, putting all this on you. I'll deal with it."

"But you will go ahead with the wedding?"

He looks at me, annoyed. "Then what? I told you; I don't have a choice." He smiles thinly. "In any case. You'll meet Joe. He'll be at my wedding."

"Sam's dad's name is also Joe," I say. "He's very homophobic. It's not like it's paradise in the US. But it's gotten easier in recent years."

Just then, Kabir's phone rings. "Yes, Mummy?" he says. "Yes, we'll be home soon."

In the cab, Kabir strikes up a conversation with me about an upcoming cricket match and I realize that it's a performance, for the driver's benefit. It's as if the conversation in the restaurant never happened.

I meet Kabir's fiancé, Mumtaz, the next night at the party that Fatima hosts for the prospective in-laws. She is young and pretty, with flawless skin and an open, innocent face. My heart twists with sorrow at what awaits her—disinterested sex in the early days of their marriage, followed by sleepless nights wondering why her husband isn't home yet; the subtle accusation she'd sense on her mother-in-law's face for not sustaining Kabir's interest; the guilt and self-abasement she'll feel for not being woman enough; the inevitable day when someone mentions having seen Kabir at a late dinner in the company of a man, on a night when he was supposed to be working late at the office; the shame and the lack of language with which to confront him with a suspicion she can't bring herself to voice or even acknowledge. Maybe, somewhere in this mess, there would be a child or two, which would only entrap Mumtaz further. For a moment, I hate Kabir for burdening me with knowledge that I cannot share, that I can't use to warn this young woman. Then, I understand that he's as much of a victim as she is, and my hatred turns toward Kabir's conservative mother. But then I realize that Fatima is society's victim, too, and down the rabbit hole I fall, concentric circles of blame, a spiral of culpability, and I resent this whole feudal, traditional country, with its national mantra of What Will the Neighbors Say, for its willingness to sacrifice its own children at the altar of Saving Face.

"Aliya, what is it?" Abba is suddenly standing next to me. "This is a happy occasion. Why are you looking like you've swallowed a bagful of limes?"

For a second, I contemplate confiding in Abba, who may know how to extract Kabir from the mistake he's about to make. But then I think, Abba didn't even stand up to Yasmin to protect *me*. Why do I expect him to take on his in-laws for Kabir's sake? In any case, this is not my secret to share.

I shake my head. "Sorry, Abba. The heat just got to me, that's all."

He raises one eyebrow quizzically, giving me a close look. "Okay," he says. "Come eat something."

51

▼ ▶ ▲ ◀ ▼ ▲ ▶ ▲

Monday, March 9

Two evenings later, Abba and I go to Marine Drive for a walk.

Even though there's no part of Mumbai that's not crowded, Marine Drive feels like an oasis after the heaving congestion of Bhendi Bazaar. I gulp the salty seaside air, take in the beautiful art deco buildings across the street.

Abba follows my glance. "That's where your mother's grandfather lived. In one of those buildings. I can't exactly remember which one. When you were little, we visited him here."

"I don't remember him."

"How could you, jaan? You were four." He is silent for a moment. "You know, your great-grandfather was a well-respected barrister in India. I want you to remember, you come from good stock. There's more to your lineage than your old Abba, who's simply an ordinary cook."

I take his hand in mine. "Yeah, right. There's nothing ordinary about you, Abba."

He doesn't reply, but when I look out of the corner of my eye, he's smiling.

"How old was Mummy when her parents died?"

"She was in her early twenties. It had already been difficult for her, being an only child and the daughter of immigrants. In those days, Minneapolis was very white. And to lose both parents at one time! But instead of the tragedy making her bitter, it made her softer and more loving. My Noor was a remarkable woman."

I'm so happy to be here alone with him, away from Nasreen and Yasmin and their loud, noisy relatives and friends. "I wish all of Mumbai was like this," I say.

"Like what?"

"Like this." I sweep my hand to include the hawker selling roasted peanuts and chana, the middle-aged male joggers in shorts and tennis shoes, the young couples sitting on the concrete wall overlooking the sea, the whole panorama of humanity. Marine Drive is so much more cosmopolitan than the Muslim-dominated Bhendi Bazar.

"Yes," Abba says, and I know that he knows what I mean.

"Abba," I say hesitantly. "Tell me the truth. Do you love Yasmin?" What I'm thinking is, Abba belongs in one of these flats where my great-grandfather lived, among erudite, cultured people, rather than among Yasmin's good-natured but unsophisticated relatives.

He chuckles, as if he's read my mind. "What I had with your mummy was a young love. That cannot be replicated. It's different with Yasmin. What I needed after Mummy died was companionship, someone to help me raise you, to be by my side through life's detours. And Yasmin has been that person for me. So, I feel very lucky and humbled by her faith in me."

It isn't the answer I am looking for, but I am moved. "I just want you to be happy, Abba," I mumble.

He stops walking, turns to look at me. "And that's what I want for you. The only thing I have ever wanted for you and from you. It's why I fought you so hard when you were younger. Because beta, the path you'd chosen. I knew it would make your life harder. And I couldn't bear that."

I squeeze his hand as we resume walking. "I know, Abba. But it all turned out to be okay in the end."

He gives me a sharp look. "Everything's all right? Between you and Samantha?"

"I think so." I clear my throat. "I mean, we're still adjusting. She's been through so much."

"You have to be very patient, beta," he says. "Remember what I always tell you—the secret to happiness is to always put the other person's needs above your own."

That's so different from the American way of thinking that I want to laugh. But deep down, I know he's right. "I'm trying, Abba," I say quietly.

"Good," he says, "good. The main thing is that she's home safe and sound. As for that badmash who did this foulness, may Allah do with him what He sees fit."

I say nothing, too ashamed to admit that every night before I fall asleep, I fantasize about finding that bastard and killing him.

Abba puts his arm around me as we walk. "So, are you glad you came with me?"

"Yes," I say. "Although I'll be pleased to go back home, when it's time."

"That's how it should be."

A scrawny man comes toward us from the opposite direction and as he brushes past me, lets out a loud sneeze. Abba recoils and spins around to glare at the man. "Bloody idiot," Abba mutters. "The papers are filled with news about this virus from China and he doesn't even cover his nose."

"It's fine, Abba. He is most likely illiterate and probably ignorant about what's happening." Although that's not quite true. Just yesterday, Kusum, Nasreen's maid, was telling me that her fellow slum dwellers were worried about this new virus. Kusum herself was wearing an amulet given to her by a sadhu, who had promised that it would ward off illness. I had tried to reason with her but, flummoxed by her implicit faith in this holy man and my smattering of Hindi, I'd quickly given up.

A warm sea breeze caresses us and Abba sighs. "I miss this aspect of Mumbai," he says. "Growing up here, the sea gets in your blood. You know?"

I nod, although I don't really. The Great Lakes are the only large bodies of water I've known. "I thought you had a cousin or somebody still living in Mumbai," I say. "Don't you want to go see her?"

He shrugs. "She's in Vihar," he says. "Far away. And for what? We were never close."

My parents were both only children. When I was growing up, I'd see my white classmates celebrate Thanksgiving and Christmas with their large, rambunctious families and feel a sense of loss. I'd thought it was because we were Indians in America, but in college I'd met plenty of other Indian students from large immigrant families.

As if he'd read my mind, Abba says, "Your mother and I had both so wanted to give you a baby brother or sister. But it wasn't meant to be."

We both fall silent, each of us missing Mummy in our own way. Just when I am about to fall into a funk, Abba says, "Okay, beta. No more looking back. You have your whole life ahead of you. We must take whatever hand life has dealt us and keep moving forward. Remember, the current of life only moves forward."

As a kid, I used to roll my eyes at him when he talked like this. But tonight, for some reason, it cheers me up. Sam and I are young, I think. We have so much time ahead to get things right, to make our way back to one another. Soon, I whisper to her. I'll be home soon.

52

▼ ▶ ▲ ◀ ▼ ▲ ▶ ▲

Tuesday, March 10

I look at the wall clock again. Six-fifteen in the evening. Candace is now a half hour late for our meeting. I pick up the phone to text her again when her text appears on my screen: *Sorry, almost there. Just parking.*

My stomach growls. I haven't had a thing to eat since this morning and I can't wait to get home, warm up something, and collapse on the couch. It's been a long day, and reviewing the progress Candace has made on her thesis always takes longer than it should.

She walks into my office panting and flops on the chair. "Sorry, sorry," she says. Her hair is uncombed, and she's dressed in sweatpants and a ratty-looking sweatshirt. "I lost track of time," she says. "I'm working on a new poem for this project. I think you'll relate to it when I'm ready to share it. It's about trauma."

I raise one eyebrow. "O-kay?" I say slowly. "But I thought you were spending this week working on the critical introduction?"

"I know. But this poem is just insisting to be written. It's the only way I can process what's happened to us."

I look at her blankly.

"It's about your abduction," she says. "How it has left an indelible mark on me. I'm just trying to process my feelings about it and how it triggered me."

I feel a slow burn on my cheeks. "Candace," I say. And then I fall silent. I am flabbergasted by her presumption, the sheer chutzpah. *How it has triggered me.* Her! The gall of her, trying to appropriate my story. This is what she'd done to Ali, too. I'd been sympathetic to Ali when she'd mentioned Candace's pomposity, but it hadn't hit me the way it does now. Shame on me for not fully understanding what this self-important, parasitic woman sitting in front of me has put my wife through. I am suddenly furious.

There is an eager expression on Candace's face, and it strikes me that she's waiting for me to thank her, to confide in her, to express some kind of sisters-in-trauma solidarity with her. I almost laugh at her delusions, even as my mouth puckers up with distaste. "I don't understand, Candace," I say, my voice icy. "Why are you writing about my experience? Shouldn't that be my story to tell?"

"No, see, that's my whole argument," she says, leaning forward. "That female trauma is collective. I can make a really strong feminist argument for this."

"Candace. This is not your story. I would appreciate it if . . ."

"But you're wrong!" Her voice is loud, maniacal. "You have no idea what I endured while you were missing! I mean, you're my friend! I don't know how much you're aware of this, but I was fighting for you even before the police got really involved. At times I felt as if I was taking on the world! Including your girlfriend, I might add. I mean, it took a village to bring you home, Samantha."

I had known Candace was difficult to work with. I knew she'd antagonized most of the other faculty as well as her classmates. But until this evening, I'd no idea that she was delusional, bordering on insane.

"I want to make a few things clear," I say slowly. "First, I'm your professor, not your friend. I'm sorry if I've led you to believe otherwise. Second, Ali is not my girlfriend. She is my spouse. But then, you know that. Which is why your behavior toward her is unforgivable. And third, because you have breached the boundaries between us so badly, I can no longer serve as your advisor. I will inform Dr. Myers about my decision. Now, Candace, I'm going to ask you to leave my office."

She stares at me, her mouth agape. Then, she sneezes, without covering her nose. I flinch. On the news this morning, they said there are now almost 650 cases of Covid in the US. People are dying of this virus around the world. I push my box of Kleenex toward Candace. She helps herself to it, blows her nose loudly and looks around for the trash can. She notices the expression on my face. "Don't worry," she says. "I don't have that Chinese flu or whatever they're calling it."

I force myself to not be distracted. I sit still, looking sternly at her. She looks away first. "Come on, Samantha," she says. "Geez, if you don't want me to write the damn poem, I won't, okay? I don't know why you're . . ."

"You can write whatever poem you like, Candace, but leave me out of it. In any case, there's nothing more for us to discuss. Now, please leave."

She doesn't budge. "I don't understand why we can't talk about this," she says. "I feel like I'm being bounced around from professor to professor."

I refuse to take the bait. "Please leave, Candace. Before I'm forced to call security."

She glares at me, shoves back the chair, and slams the door on the way out. I sit in my office, shaking. I have no idea if I'm even allowed to do what I've just done, threatening to call security on a student. Maybe I'll get a call from HR tomorrow. But first, I have to let Gina Myers know what has transpired. I write an email to my chair, detailing the conversation to the best of my recollection.

I gather my papers and am on my way out when my office phone rings. I walk back to pick it up. It's Gina. "Candace wanted to do *what*?" she says, without preamble.

"Yup. Write a poem about 'our' trauma."

"Unbelievable. She's just unbelievable." Gina sighs. "I tell you, Samantha, they get more obtuse each year."

"So, am I in trouble? In case she complains or something?"

"Her behavior is completely inappropriate. I wouldn't give it a second thought."

"Thanks, Gina." I exhale.

"Of course. Hey, is Ali still in India?"

"Yup."

"Bob is out of town also. And I'm still in my office. Wanna grab some dinner?"

My novel stares at me accusingly each evening like a neglected pet. The house feels empty and lonely without Ali there. I'm dead tired, but I'm also dreading returning to that silent space.

"Yes," I say. "And Gina? Thanks for being so understanding about Candace."

"Oh, for Pete's sake. Her behavior is ridiculous. Don't worry, I'll find someone else to supervise her thesis. The sooner she graduates, the better, as far as I'm concerned. Now, let's go get a drink and dinner."

"I'll be right down," I say.

Even though it's still early in India, I call Ali as soon as I get home. She sounds groggy as she answers the phone. I've had two glasses of wine at dinner, but I sober up as I tell Ali what transpired earlier this evening.

"I can't believe this," Ali keeps saying. "The nerve of that woman."

But I'm not interested in rehashing Candace's entitlement. I want Ali to know that I stood up for her, defended her. Which, I suppose, is my way of belatedly apologizing to her for what she's endured.

"I can't believe you said all that to her, Sam," Ali says at last. "I'm proud of you."

"Yeah, that's the good thing about being terrorized by that animal. You just run out of fucks to give."

Ali gasps at my use of the word *terrorized*. "Sweetie," I say. "Relax. It's a joke." But she remains silent. "Gina was so funny," I say. "She said she was going to assign Candace the worst classes to teach in the fall."

Ali chuckles dutifully. Then she says, "I can't wait to see you, Sam. I'm so ready to come home after this stupid wedding."

"Why, are you no longer having a good time?"

"I am. I mean, it's fine. But three and a half weeks is much too long to be away. And almost everything revolves around the wedding. Which . . ." Ali lowers her voice. "There's a lot to tell you about that."

"So, tell me."

"I can't. Not enough privacy. But I will, after I'm home."

"I'm counting the days."

"Me, too. And after this, I'm never, ever leaving you alone."

I'm in a better mood after we hang up. This is why people get married, I think, why we put up with the inevitable bullshit that comes from living with another. To know that someone has your back, no matter what. To lift each other's spirits up.

I go upstairs to work on my laptop but give up after a half hour. I'd been sure that I'd make progress on my novel while Ali was away. Now, I realize a deeper truth—everything works better in my life, even my creativity, with Ali by my side.

53

▼ ▶ ▲ ◀ ▼ ▲ ▶ ▲

Friday, March 13

Abba comes home from the market at noon with a stunning piece of news: The state government of Maharashtra has labeled the Covid outbreak an epidemic, which means that the government can forcibly hospitalize anyone who comes down with it. Movie theaters, gyms, and other public places will all shut immediately. There are rumors that large gatherings will soon be prohibited.

We turn on the television to learn more. After a few minutes, Abba signals to me to join him in the hallway. "You need to go," he says. "We need to get you out of here tonight."

"Go where?"

He looks agitated. "Where? Home, of course. To Cleveland. The situation here could get difficult quickly. If you were to get sick, God forbid, there's no way I would want you in a government hospital here."

"Abba, aren't you being a little dramatic? The cases in India are still so low. Heck, there are more cases in the US than here."

"That will change. And change fast because of the density of the population; it will spread quickly across the country."

"But what about the wedding? How are we going to change the return date for the three of us?"

He hesitates, pins me with a look. "Only you. You will leave tonight."

"Oh no," I say. "No way. There's no way I'm leaving without you, Abba. And Yasmin," I add.

"I can't leave. Yasmin is insisting on staying for her nephew's wedding. She won't budge. I have no choice."

"But that's crazy. If anyone's most at risk, it's you. Because of your heart condition."

"I keep telling you. I'm fine. And to be honest, after today's order, it's a matter of time before the government bans all large gatherings. We'll come home immediately if the wedding is postponed. But Yasmin wants to wait and see."

I feel my temper spike, my years of resentment at Yasmin boiling over. "You come back with me. Abba, what if you do get sick here? I'll never forgive myself."

He clucks his tongue, exasperated. "There's nothing to forgive. We are all making our own decisions here. Yasmin has made hers. And I have made mine. As her husband, my place is by her side."

I open my mouth to ask why I'm the only one not allowed a say in the matter, to insist that I'll never leave him behind in these circumstances, when he adds, softly, "As is yours, beside Samantha. If they stop international flights, who knows how long you'll be separated from her?"

He looks at me deeply, with those beautiful, soulful eyes. And I read in them everything that Abba cannot say out loud: That he understands that what Sam and I share is not all that different from what he has with his wife. That he knows that I am as devoted to her as he is to Yasmin. That he regrets the years of silence between us.

There's a lump in my throat as we stare at each other silently. "Please don't do this, Abba," I whisper, but I know he won't change his mind.

"I'll call the travel agent now and see what we can do to change your ticket," he says. He turns away from me, then looks back. "The wedding is in seven days. We'll be home immediately after, Inshallah."

After he leaves, I have a sudden thought and dial Kabir's number.

"You heard the news?" he says as he picks up.

"Yup."

"Pretty crazy, hah?" he says.

"Yeah. But listen, I was thinking. This is a golden opportunity for you to cancel the wedding. Because, you know the government's soon going to ban big gatherings. This gives you the out you were looking for."

Of course I'm not just thinking of Kabir; if he postpones his nuptials, there's no reason Abba and Yasmin can't travel back with me.

There is a long, strained silence on the phone.

"I can't, yaar," he finally says. "I mean, if the government forces us, that's one thing. But I can't do it myself. I must think of my family's reputation."

I'm suddenly furious at him. For trapping that poor girl in what will undoubtedly be a prison sentence for her. For being so cowardly that he can't take a stance even when circumstances are conspiring to help him. And for keeping my abba stuck in Mumbai.

"Aliya? You there?"

"Yeah," I say shortly. "Listen, Abba's trying to get my air ticket changed for me to leave tonight. So, I was calling to say bye."

"Leave tonight?" Kabir sounds as shocked as I feel. "All of you?"

"No. Abba and Yasmin are staying. For your wedding." Try as I might, I can't keep the resentment out of my voice.

"Oh, I see. But if I were to say I'm postponing it . . ." Kabir falls silent, and I feel a throb of hope. Then he says, "I'm sorry, Aliya. I . . . I don't want to be the bad guy, you see?"

I smile bitterly. If you're going to be gay, I think, if you're ever going to step out of the closet, if you love your Joe as much as you say you do, you'll have to be willing to be the bad guy, buddy. If you wish to ever live an honest life, you'll have to be ready to break many a heart, starting with your mother's. Being a coward is not compatible with being openly gay.

"Aliya," Kabir says. "You can't leave without saying goodbye in person. I'll drive you to the airport this evening."

"Well, I don't even know . . ."

"I have to go. I'll see you," he says and hangs up.

I wander back into the living room. "He's in there," Yasmin says, pointing to a closed door. "Talking to a third travel agent. Nothing seems available."

"Doesn't surprise me," I say. For a second, I consider talking to Yasmin, asking her to reconsider her decision. But I don't. Any woman who allows a rift to open between her husband and his only child is not going to worry about keeping her husband away from his home during a fucking pandemic. Yasmin is in her element here, surrounded by family and friends in a milieu she's comfortable in. To hell with what Abba needs. I turn away before she can read the look on my face.

Nasreen comes into the living room and cradles my face in her rough hands. "I just heard. You were here for such a short time, only," she says. "It feels as if you just arrived. And now you may be leaving. Bas, gone with the wind."

"Well, Auntie, I don't even know if we can change the tickets . . ."

"We can't." Abba walks into the room, rubbing his forehead. "There are no seats available. Even business class is booked solid."

"Okay, well, then I guess I'm staying. We'll all go back toge—"

"Aliya. I wasn't finished. One of the travel agents suggested going to the airport tonight. Just taking a chance. Maybe they'll have a cancellation or something."

"Abba, please."

"That's what we're going to do. Go pack your stuff."

He's talking to me as if I'm seven years old, but I don't want to defy him. I've seen the concern in his eyes and he's right—I don't want to be away from Sam any longer, not when her mental state is still fragile.

I tug at my hair in frustration and Abba says, "Don't." He raises his index finger to emphasize the word, but there's a twinkle in his eye. He turns to Nasreen and the others and says, "Any time she was worried or anxious, she used to do this, from childhood on," and his smile invites their chuckles.

I retreat to my room to pack. What's he gonna do, I think, drive me to the airport every evening until we find a flight? It's ridiculous to go without a confirmed ticket.

It's the middle of the night in Cleveland, but I pick up my phone to text Sam the news:

Hey, guess what? The state government here is shutting down all public places. Abba is insisting I return home early. We're going to try at the airport tonight. He and Yasmin are staying though.

She replies within seconds. *Calling you now.*

"Hi babe," Sam says on the phone. "Are you very disappointed?"

"I don't know. Not really. I mean, I've hardly had time to process it all."

"Why isn't your dad leaving, too? The situation's getting a little scary, Ali. I mean, the WHO has classified it as a global pandemic. And your dad's not a spring chicken, you know?"

"Believe me, I know. He won't budge. Yasmin wants to stay for the wedding." I hear the bitterness in my voice.

"Oh shit."

We fall silent for a moment. Then, Sam says, "I probably shouldn't say this, but I'm thrilled that you're coming home early. I've missed you so much. Gin Blossom goes around the house meowing every evening. I just know she's looking for you. And I know exactly how she feels."

I laugh. "That's sweet. But who knows if I can even get out tonight? I'll keep you posted."

After we hang up, I text her again.

Thanks for the call, sweetheart. Sorry to have texted so late. Go back to sleep. Sweet dreams.

The phone dings a second later: *OMG, are you kidding me? I'm so excited I won't sleep a wink tonight.*

I'm in a better space as I put the phone to charge and go back into the living room. Sam's excitement has reset my mood.

The doorbell rings as we're finishing up a late lunch. It's Kabir. "I took a half-day at work," he whispers to me. "I'm so sad that you're leaving. I'm going to miss you so much."

He looks at me so guilelessly that my earlier resentment falls away. He's young, I remind myself, and so unworldly. And trapped by the expectations of those around him. Don't judge him just because you were lucky enough to be born in America.

"I'm going to miss you, too," I say. "But we'll stay in touch, yes?"

"Definitely," he says.

An hour later, Abba and Yasmin come into my room. Abba eyes the objects on my bed and says I should leave behind all the knick-knacks I've bought. "Pack lightly, beta," he says. "I'll bring all the gifts you've purchased when I come." Then, he sees the turquoise jewelry and the sapphire earrings I've bought for Sam. In front of Yasmin he says, "Just take the gifts you've bought for your beloved."

Yasmin's head jerks up and Abba gives her a long look. Finally, Yasmin looks away. And I feel in my gut that the power dynamic between them has finally changed, that Abba will defend me in the future. "I will," I say deliberately. "She will be thrilled with these."

It's an amazing thing, I think, how humans have the ability to create good out of any hand that they're dealt. We're like magicians in that sense. It's Samantha's disappearance that has led to Abba's presence in my life.

He leaves and returns with my plane ticket. "But Abba," I say, "our tickets are for March twenty-first. How will I even enter the airport with these tickets?"

"I'm there, na?" he says, puffing his chest. "I'll make sure we get in, believe me."

"You're coming to the airport?"

"Then what?" Abba lapses into his colloquial English. "You think I'd send you alone to the airport? It's going to be a madhouse with everyone trying to leave before more restrictions come. You don't know the Indian mentality—all the pushing and shoving. You'll need me to help you."

My emotions well up. "So, you'll come all the way to the airport, but you won't fly home with me? Can't I talk to Yasmin? Beg her to change her mind?"

"As it is, we'll be lucky to find one seat for you." He pulls me closer to him. "This one time, you must trust your old father. Okay?"

"Okay," I say, snuggling against his broad chest.

"My beautiful, obstinate gudiya," he murmurs, stroking my hair. "But I'm proud of you, beta."

What would I have given to have heard those words when I was younger. Still, I say, "I'm not obstinate!"

He holds me away from him, so that I can see his face. "Your middle name is Stubborn." He points to his head, chuckling. "Where do you think all this gray hair came from? Each one has your initials on it."

I take both his hands in mine and kiss them. "Thank you, Abba," I say. "I don't think I could've made it through this past year without you."

"Rubbish!" he says. "Your mummy and I raised you to be strong and independent. We have a saying in Hindi: 'Grow as tall and upright as a tree. But let your roots hold hands with your family roots.' Remember this, always."

This conversation is making me sad. "Promise me you'll stay healthy? Don't leave the house if you don't have to. Don't eat too much sugar or carbs. And wash your hands frequently."

"Hey, little one," he says with mock sternness. "I'm the father, remember? It's my job to worry about my child. Not the other way around."

Nasreen Auntie walks in, clutching an envelope. "For such a short time only you graced us with your presence," she says. "Still, you brought so much light and laughter to our house. Youth is like a torch, I tell you. It brightens everything. Anyway, God be with you, child." She hands me the envelope. "This is just a small token of our affection."

"Auntie, I can't. There's no need."

She shakes her head vigorously. "No, no, no. The young mustn't argue with the old and gray. Please to accept."

"Aliya," Abba says. "Take it."

Nasreen Auntie blesses me some more and hugs me. I'm surprised to see a tear run down her cheek when she releases me. A lump forms in my throat. As happy as I am to go home to Sam, I'm also sad about leaving so abruptly. India is not my home; I'm clear about this. But it *is* my heritage, and it tugs at my heart as I pack. I would've enjoyed a planned departure from here, instead of this rushed one.

54

▾ ▸ ▴ ◂ ▾ ▴ ▸ ▴

Friday, March 13

I am so excited at the prospect of Ali coming home that I wake up after only a few hours sleep, eager to clean the house and get things ready for her arrival. I almost don't pick up when Nathan calls but decide to, at the last minute.

"Hey, it's me." Nathan sounds breathless. "Just a quick call to say the library is most likely shutting down. So come pick up the books you've asked me to hold today, okay?"

"Shutting down early? Why?"

"You haven't heard? NBC just reported that they're about to declare a national emergency because of Covid. If that happens, everything will be closed for at least a few weeks."

"Wow. This thing is beginning to seem too real. Ali's coming home early, too, if she can get a flight. I'll try and get to the library before noon. I need to go grocery shopping and run other errands, so . . ."

"I should either be at the desk or running around, depending on when you get here," Nathan says. "If Julie's up front, she'll walk you to me. Okay, I gotta run. It's a zoo here today."

It's around 11:30 a.m. when I walk into the Lee Road library. The first floor is controlled chaos. Staff members, many of whom usually stop to chat with me, scuttle past with nary a hello. A group of school kids stand in a corner, uncharacteristically subdued. An adult is speaking to them in a quiet voice. Julie is talking to an older woman but excuses herself as soon as she sees me.

"Hey, Sam," she says. "Nathan's taking a quick lunch break, but he said you might be stopping by. I'll take you to him."

As we walk down the hallway, I almost tell Julie about the years that Ali and I assumed that Nathan was gay, then think better of it. Instead, I say, "I'm so happy for you and Nathan. You're really good for him."

She beams. "Me too!" she says. "He's wonderful."

We walk into a small, windowless lunchroom with vending machines against one wall and a scattering of lunch tables. Nathan raises his arm to wave me over and I wave back. And then the smell hits me. My stomach heaves, even as my hands grow clammy. Blinking my eyes, I look over at the next table. A man is sitting there, hunched over his sandwich. He looks up and our eyes meet. He blanches. I feel dizzy, overheated. Dimly, I realize that Nathan is walking toward me. I barely register that Julie is saying goodbye to me even as Nathan gives me a quick hug.

"Hey, you," he says. "Glad you made it. It's been unbelievable here . . ."

He follows my line of vision to where the other man remains seated. "Oh, hey, I don't know if you two have met. Sam, this is my colleague, George Anderson. He's a library assistant. George, this is my friend, Samantha O'Malley."

He is in his mid-thirties, with a pale face and sandy-colored hair that's thinning at the top. A pleasant, nondescript face. The kind of man you'd see at Bremec Garden Center or Target and walk past without a second glance. As I would have, if it hadn't been for the sandwich. And the unforgettable smell of egg salad with raw onion and balsamic vinegar. I don't know, maybe that's not so unusual? But then, my eyes alight on the red package in front of him. Doritos. Egg salad sandwich and Doritos. Which he'd once told me he packed for lunch every day. What are the odds of someone else in Cleveland Heights packing the exact same lunch as my abductor?

With every ounce of the strength I can muster, I make my face go impassive. "Hello," I say.

He nods.

I need more proof than a bag of Doritos. With the same Herculean will, I take a few steps toward him and stick out my hand. "Nice to meet you," I say.

His eyes dart from me to Nathan and back to me. He looks trapped, but he has no choice but to accept my proffered hand. His is cold and sweaty, and he drops mine as soon as he can, but it is enough: The same soft, pillowy hands. With that wide ring on his middle finger. That ring that used to cut into me when he'd . . . touch me. It *is* him.

Nathan is saying something about almost being done with lunch, about having my books waiting for me, but I barely hear him. I need to get away from this small room whose walls are caving in, away from this pleasant-faced monster. "I'll go find Julie," I mumble. "You finish up."

Instead, I make my way into the bathroom, where my insides suddenly give way. When I finally make my way out, Nathan is back at his desk. "Where've you been?" he says. "Julie said you . . ."

"I'm sick," I say. "I gotta go. Would you mind bringing the books to me?" I fumble through my handbag. "Here's my library card."

"Hey," he says. "You look awful. Want me to drive you home?"

I need to get out of here before the monster comes to find me again. "No, I'll be fine." Then, I ask, keeping my voice as casual as possible. "Your colleague looked so familiar. Where does he live?"

"George? He's in the Heights, also, on North Park. Not that any of us have ever been invited to his house." Nathan chuckles. "He's a bit of an odd duck. Comes from money, obviously. He's not living on North Park on a library assistant's salary, that's for sure. Drives a BMW, too. If you see a blue Beamer in the parking lot, that's his."

"Nate," I say, cutting him off. "I need to go."

He gives me a worried look. "You . . . don't have a sore throat, do you?"

"Nathan. It's cool. I don't have the virus. Promise."

I drive directly home. Go up to my office and turn on the computer. Gin Blossom jumps on my lap, but I put her back down. George Anderson. That's how Nathan had introduced the guy. I type in his name, then Cleveland Heights in the White Pages. And here's his address on North Park. All this time, he's lived less than two miles away from me.

My hands are shaking so bad, I grip them tight. I close my eyes and think, trying to remember everything that I can about that fateful morning. I remember stopping to retie my shoelaces before leaving the house. I remember being startled by the almost-naked guy on the front porch of our street. And a little later, I tripped. I remember that. But what had distracted me? I squeeze my eyes together, trying to remember. At that time of the morning, what could've snagged my attention? A flutter of wings, a flock of birds rising from a tree? A beautiful maple? A shock of hydrangeas in someone's yard? But it was barely light, and the streetlights were out. I wouldn't have noticed flowers. And then I remember. It was a vehicle. White and large, like a SUV or a van. And now, it comes back—the swerve. The vehicle had swerved, like the driver had recognized me, and somehow, it was that motion that had distracted me and made me trip. What else? I'm ransacking my brain as if it is a piggy bank, begging it to spill every last coin of memory.

I remember the pain and the shock of falling. I remember a man looking down at me, his mouth moving. After that, everything goes blank. Next thing I remember is the pain on the side of my head as it rested on a pillow. Instinctively, I touch the spot that had ached for days later, where a knot had formed from where I landed on the sidewalk. The bastard had probably driven me to his house, which is so close. No wonder no one saw a damn thing. He took me less than two miles up the road. Two miles and a lifetime away. Two miles and into a life that destroyed my sanity, and left this jumpy, angry woman in its place.

I am scared and lost and raging. If Ali were here right now, by my side, she'd know exactly what to do. I need to talk to her. My hand inches toward my phone and then I think, she has a million things going on trying to leave India, and the last thing she needs is this bombshell from eight thousand miles away. I'm not sure what to do next: If I call the cops, what will I tell them? The guy works in a library, for fuck's sake. A mild-mannered librarian, that's almost a cliché! Still, Herrington did tell me to call to report anything, any tidbit that might give them a lead. My hand hovers over the phone. But I need proof. I would be mortified if I accused this pleasant-faced man of being a kidnapper and he's innocent. Why hadn't I lingered and asked Nathan a few more questions about this George Anderson? But Nate was already looking at me like I was behaving weirdly.

I look outside the window. It's a blue-sky day in March, a rarity in Cleveland. The trees are bare and there are patches of snow in the backyard. An idea enters my head, slow but insistent. I grab my phone and hurry down the stairs.

At the back door, I hesitate. Am I going through with this? Should I call a friend?

And say what, Sam? That you ran into someone at the library eating a certain kind of sandwich and that is making you come unglued? At least drive past his house and get a feel for things.

It's a single-story brick house on a corner lot with an attached garage. Unassuming. The roof still holds the remains of last night's snow shower. Beyond the circular driveway is a large backyard. I drive past the house twice and then decide to park on the side street. George Anderson is at work, but I don't want some nosy neighbor alerting him to a strange car in his driveway. But there's not a soul around. I lean against my parked car, close my eyes and listen. The noise and traffic pattern of North Park Boulevard sound familiar from my weeks in captivity. A tingle starts at the base of my spine. On our morning runs around Lower Shaker Lake, Ali and I must've passed this house a hundred times. I remember what my abductor had said—that he had driven me far away from home. Why had I fallen for that obvious lie? I don't have proof yet, of course. But my body, smarter than my brain, knows. It is buzzing. Either that, or I'm really and truly cracking up.

I take a deep breath, cross the street, and walk quickly into the yard. A wall of pine trees hides me from the street. The side door to the attached garage has a window, and I peer into it. And there it is, a white SUV. My knees buckle at the sight.

A small wood deck leads to the back door, which is painted a bright yellow. For some reason, this fact slays me. How innocuous, how ordinary, how cheerful this house looks. Who could ever believe the evil that went on inside?

I am shaking now, partly from the cold and partly from anxiety. A small part of me wants to climb the three steps to the deck and peer in, but I dare not. I need to get away from this sinister house. But a sense of triumph also threads its way through my anxiety. I have found him. The egg salad sandwich, the Doritos, the white SUV, the sound of the traffic on North Park. I think there's enough here for me to take back to Herrington.

I'm about to pull my phone out of my pocket to call the detective when it rings. Fuck. It sounds loud enough to wake up the dead. It's Ali. What time is it there?

"Ali," I say in a rush. "It's him. I found him."

It's a bad connection. "Who?" I hear her say in a distracted voice. "Listen, we are almost at the airport . . ." The crackling on the line swallows the rest of her words. ". . . shutting down. Stuck in a massive jam. I just hope it's not too late to . . ." She cuts out again.

I can't focus on what she's saying. I need to get back in my car and call Herrington while George Anderson is at work. I handled myself well at the library, kept my face impassive; he has no reason to believe that I suspect a thing. Still, I have to get out of here.

But there's nobody in the world I'd rather celebrate this triumph with than Ali. Because I'm the one who found the bastard. Not Herrington. Not any of the amateur sleuths on Twitter.

"Ali, listen to me," I say. I have to talk loudly, over the deafening sound of Mumbai's traffic, over the crackle of the line. "I found him. The guy who kidnapped me. He lives on North Park, like, less than two miles from us. I'm standing outside his house right now, Ali. Can you fucking believe it? I got him."

"What?" I can tell that she's yelling, too. "You found the guy?"

"His name's George Anderson. He lives on North Park. It's a brick house on a corner lot. I'm actually standing in his yard. He works at the library. I mean, he's a fucking library assistant. I met him, face to face."

"You what? Sam. I don't understand . . . Oh, shit, we're approaching the airport. The traffic is insane. I . . ." Her voice fades, comes back. "I . . . sorry, it's nuts here. Sam, listen to me. Go directly to the police station and report him, but don't go back home. I can't believe I'm frigging so far away from you at a time like this."

"I have it under control. He's still at work."

The next instant, the phone is knocked out of my hands. I try to spin around, but I'm stopped by a pair of strong hands. I feel something sharp pressed against my ribs.

"Don't move," someone hisses in my ear. "One sound and you're fucking dead. I mean it."

I freeze. A sudden animal fear takes hold of me. The enormity of what I've done, the sheer stupidity of my actions, hits me. I am the idiot fish who has deliberately swum into the fisherman's net. At this moment, I hate myself more than I hate George Anderson.

"Climb up the stairs," he says, prodding me with his knife.

"Please," I say, not recognizing my own voice. "I'll leave. I won't tell. I promise. Just let me go."

"Climb, you bitch. Or else I'll slit your throat right now."

We go up the three steps to the deck. He unlocks the door and pushes me in. We are in the kitchen, and I immediately recognize that familiar, stuffy smell. I gag.

He spins me around so that I'm facing him. Unlike the library, where I couldn't allow myself a good look at him, I now meet his eyes.

He doesn't look like a monster. There are no horns, no fangs, no tail. Rather, he is a slender, pleasant-looking man, with a boyish face and sandy hair. More librarian than rapist.

Then, his face changes. "I had a feeling you'd recognized me, you little bitch," he says. "I came home to pick up my passport and get out of town. But you had to play Nancy Drew, didn't you? Now I have no fucking choice except to kill you."

In a panic I turn toward Abba. "That was Samantha," I say. "She—she found the guy who kidnapped her. And then she dropped her phone. I don't know why."

Abba turns toward me sharply. "Where is she?"

"I don't know. I . . ." I break off the conversation. "I . . . I have to do something. To help her." I think for a moment, then reach for my phone again. We are seeing the signs for the airport now, as I dial Herrington's cell phone. Pick up, I think. *Pick up.*

"Ali?" he says. "Good to hear from you. You back from your trip?"

His voice calms me down. Somewhat. "I'm still in India," I say. "But listen, Sam may be in danger."

"Hold on. I can barely hear you."

"Hello?" I feel the panic rise in me. "Mike? Are you there?" Herrington's voice comes in and out and I curse the stupid connection. "I hope you can hear me." And then, I tell him everything that I can remember. The man's name. A brick house on North Park. Corner lot.

"Where is she?" Herrington's voice comes through, clear.

"She's outside his house. I can't reach her. Something happened. She dropped her phone. Help her."

The line goes dead.

I lower the window, thinking I'm going to puke. The hot night air blows in. If this bastard hurts my girl again, I won't be able to survive.

"Aliya," Abba says, his voice shaky. "This is bad timing. But if you want to get on a plane tonight, you must focus, beta. The airport is going to be chaotic."

The airport comes into view. It is a mob scene, total pandemonium. Traffic is backed up, a sea of red taillights as Kabir inches the car forward. Drivers are gesticulating and cussing at one another. Others are honking their horns continually. Beside me, Abba swears under his breath.

I turn the volume of my phone all the way up, then shove it in my jeans pocket. Covid, trying to flee India, leaving Abba behind, and now, Sam outside her rapist's home. Is she still alive? Has he found her? My head feels like it will explode.

The car is at a standstill, stuck behind a row of cars. Kabir turns around. "I'm sorry to say this, but maybe you should get out here. Traffic is so bad it may be another half hour before I can pull up to the entrance."

Abba puts his hand on Kabir's left shoulder. "Nothing to apologize for, son," he says. "You've been most helpful." He turns toward me. "Let's go. Thank God you have only a carry-on. We'll get there faster on foot. Kabir, park in the lot and text me your location, won't you, son? That way, I'll find you after seeing my daughter off."

Abba is in charge now. This is his country in a way that it will never be mine. "Thanks, Kabir," I say. "I'll drop you a line as soon as I reach America."

He looks at me from the rearview mirror and we hold our gaze for a second. Then, he puts the car in park, ignores the honking all around him, and leaps out to open the trunk. We get out, too, and Kabir hands me my suitcase. He stoops down to hug me. "Stay well," he says. "Allah be with you."

"You, too," I say. Then, I whisper to him. "God give you the courage to do the right thing."

He meets my eyes, then grimaces and hurries back into the car. Abba grabs the suitcase from me and takes me by the hand. We dodge the lanes of screaming drivers and honking cars as we run toward the airport doors.

We are both sweating by the time we reach the burly policeman inspecting everyone's tickets. Abba hands our tickets to the guy, slips in a five-hundred-rupee bill. The man notices the wrong date, and stares at Abba, who is standing with his fists clenched, ready to go to war if necessary.

"Go ahead," the cop says after a moment, discreetly stuffing the note in his pocket.

We are in.

There are thousands of people here. Toddlers sitting on suitcases pulled by their fathers. Elderly women in saris elbowing one another to gain a toehold in the long lines. Harried-looking agents trying to reason with shouting, angry passengers. Men getting into screaming matches with one another. Young men in uniforms pushing the wheelchair passengers.

"This is total insanity," I say.

Abba nods. "This is why I wanted to get here early."

Leaving Nasreen's apartment was bittersweet. But now, with Samantha being in danger, I will move heaven and earth to get to her. Or—my heart stops—to whatever reality awaits me. Now, I'm focused like a laser; I must get a seat on that plane.

George Anderson towers over me, his mouth twisting viciously, his eyes ablaze with rage. His breath is on my face as he holds the knife against my neck. "What did you come back here for? Everything was finally going so well."

"I'm sorry. Please, don't hurt me."

"Who knows that you're here? Who did you tell?"

"No one. I swear. Just let me go. I'll never trouble you again."

"Who were you talking to on the phone? You called the cops?"

"No. I swear. My partner had just called from India. I didn't even tell her."

He stares at me, trying to glean the truth from my eyes. I force myself to meet his gaze. After a long moment, he pulls the knife away from me and sets it on the kitchen table. I exhale. "I'll never trouble you again," I say. "Please, just let me go."

He punches me so hard in the stomach, I feel as if I've been broken in two. The pain is so intense, I double over. "Shut up," he says, as I gasp for breath. "You think I'm stupid? I spared you once. Not this time."

He grabs me by the nape of my neck and pushes me onto my knees, so that my mouth is in line with his pelvis. "This what you come back for? You missed this?"

My fear is so powerful and all-encompassing that I couldn't move even if he wasn't holding me in place. I flash back to when I was six, ten, twelve, fourteen, to that terrifying feeling of being paralyzed, of not being able to read Dad's moods correctly, not knowing how to ride the waves of his unpredictability and rage.

"I let you go, didn't I?" he says. "I could've killed you and buried you somewhere and no one would've ever known. You *had* to come find me and destroy everything didn't you?"

I stare at his Dockers, unable to think. His hands are now on my shoulders, keeping me down, pushing me against the floor. I begin to whimper, the courage that made me show up in his yard, that momentary triumph that I had felt, crushed to pieces.

"You and your filthy Muslim girlfriend," George says. "I've seen the two of you around town. Maybe I'll get her next."

Ali. The thought of this monster hurting Ali scorches my insides. She is my one true thing and this asshole, this crazed, filthy animal who has his hands on me, who dares to have his hands on me, is all that's standing between Ali and me. And now I see George Anderson for who he is—a dark hole, a vacantness, a blank where a man should be. The negation of everything that makes us decent and kind. That makes us human. And this hole is wide enough to swallow up Ali and my future together.

In that same nanosecond, my mind flashes to the nuns at my school telling us not to tempt men by dressing immodestly, to the obnoxious boys in middle school who *harhar*ed daily about my breasts, to the classmate who tried to date rape me when I got drunk during my first semester in college.

All the men who have targeted me my whole life blur together and become this disgusting man pushing me down, his strong hands on my shoulders, overwhelming me, hurting me, trying to grind me into dust, into nothingness.

I was sixteen the day Dad came storming in from work, his face dark with anger. Mom had made fried chicken, his favorite, and he sat down to eat with a grunt, which I guess was his caveman's way of saying thank you, but there was one drumstick that was undercooked, and he threw the whole plate at her, all the while screaming, and she cowered, mashed potato in her hair, and he whipped around the table and swung at her when there was this loud, guttural noise in the room and I looked around, hoping someone had broken in to help, but there was no one else here, just me, and the noise was coming from somewhere deep within me, the noise was me and I flew, flew like the Furies, there was some superhuman force guiding me and I grabbed him by his shoulders, felt his muscle, as hard as bone, felt his torque and sinew as he spun away from her and toward me, his face lit up with an incandescent rage—*how dare you?*—and I grabbed the butter knife and sliced his hand, watched as he howled in pain and then I rose up, rose up, sixteen years of bottled rage swirling in me like acid, I was a bottle of acid, bubbling, ready to spill, I was a bomb, lean and angular, ready to explode, I was an oak ready to crash and smash everything in sight and I pushed Dad hard, pushed him with everything percolating within me, my hate and my anger and my disappointment and my worry about my mom, and yes, my complicated love for my father, and he fell back and landed on his buttocks and stared up at me blinking rapidly and opened his mouth to say something, but I spoke first and . . .

. . . George thrusts his pelvis toward me, one hand holding me by the nape, and I think of those braying crowds of jeering men, I think of the men marching with tiki torches, I think of Ali working late into the night trying to revive her business, her face small and tired when she comes to bed, I think of those heavyset men with their sagging bellies and scraggly beards who are proud to be "packing heat," who would marry their AR-15s if they could, who think of kindness and decency as punchlines to some stupid joke about "owning the libs," I think of what these men have unleashed, what this demon standing in front of me has done to me, how they've broken me, broken us, Ali and me, broken the country, broken, broken, and I find my place among the broken things, and then I push against the weight of his hand, push against gravity, push against history, push away from the floor where he has left me to be trampled upon all over again, except not now, not this time. This time I fight, I fight to kill or be killed, and I feel the rumble, the power of my anger, women's anger, the anger of the Women's March, the anger that Mom never allowed herself to feel, the anger with which she could've protected me, my anger at the guy in the dark movie theater who pawed at me when I went with my high school friends to see a movie, anger at being tied like a farm animal, the cool of the bathroom tile against my face, my anger at the sheer gall of this man, his audacity to pick me up from the street and take me to his home without my permission, to drug me, to rape me, to pretend that my body was something that he could wipe himself on, and own and possess and violate, I mean, how dare he, how fucking dare he, and now I'm rising, I'm off my knees, I feel a rush of power, and push George back on his heels, and as he's steadying himself, my hand reaches for the knife on the kitchen table and I grab it as I rise, I rise like smoke, I rise like hope, *hope*, Ali and me, inseparable, growing old together, and I'll be damned if this pathetic man is going to keep me from taking my life back, from surviving, from spending the rest of my day with the one I love, and I howl, a prolonged, rageful, animal howl, and I find my mark and fall upon him like a heavy, blinding rain.

I call Samantha's phone repeatedly as we wait in line but there's no answer. I feel like I'm going to lose my mind right in the middle of the airport, if she doesn't pick up soon. I want to call Herrington again, but the last thing I wish to do is disturb him if he's hunting for the right house.

"Aliya," Abba says. "Stop pulling at your hair."

"Sorry." But the next second, my hand flies to the side of my head again, and Abba looks away.

"Now, I wish I was returning home with you," he says. "To take care of you."

"So, come with me. You have your ticket on you. Let's try and get out together."

"I don't know what to do," he says. "How to abandon Yasmin here?"

"Forget it, Abba," I say. I gesture toward the madness around us. "It'll be a miracle if anyone can get out of here tonight."

The line moves painfully slow. I keep checking my phone, but there's no message from Samantha. We are third in line when there's a loud shout from behind us.

"Come on, jaldi karo, hurry up," someone yells from the back. "We are trying to catch a plane, not ride in a donkey cart." Others shout him down. The agents at the ticketing counter have been working diligently, and a couple of them look up, frazzled, in the direction of the commotion. A constable in uniform walks up and down the line, trying to restore order. I feel a deep pessimism about my chances.

When it's finally our turn, the middle-aged female agent calls out to us to approach. Abba hands her my ticket and quickly explains that I'm looking to fly out today. "We will gladly pay the change fee and any penalty, madam," he adds.

My heart sinks at the irritation on her face and the stubborn set of her lips. "Not possible," she says. "Don't you see all these people, legitimate passengers, who are trying to leave? Now please stop wasting my time."

"Well, we're legitimate passengers, also," Abba says. "It's just that my daughter needs to—"

"Sir, please," she interrupts. "Step out of the line. Go home and return on the date on your tickets."

Our fellow passengers have overheard this exchange. "Arre, idiot, you heard the lady," someone shouts. "What gives you the bloody right?"

There is a sudden surge as they press against us, their patience broken. Some of them yell at Abba, while others make demands of the woman behind the counter, who is glaring at us. Abba has also raised his voice, asking to speak to a supervisor, but I know it's futile.

"Who let these people in without a proper ticket?" an old man shouts, thumping on the counter for emphasis. "Where is the security? They should be thrown out of the airport."

"We do have tickets," I yell. "I'm just trying to return home earlier."

"Yeah, man, join the club," says a white guy in a kurta standing near me.

People are now shoving and pushing against us, jockeying for position, waving their tickets under the ticket agent's nose, nudging us out of their way with their suitcases.

Abba throws me a helpless look. We *are* in the wrong, after all. And our desperation doesn't trump anyone else's. On any other day, I would give in. But I think of Samantha, what might be happening to her this very minute, what news might await me if I ever reach Herrington again, and a kind of madness grips me. I need to get home, I just do. I look around frantically and then my eyes alight on her—a young female agent with short, spiky hair and a diamond stud in her nose. As if she feels my eyes on her, she glances at me, and we exchange a look before she turns away. *She's one of us*, I think. I could be wrong, of course. There are plenty of butch-looking women who aren't gay. But at this point I have nothing to lose.

"Miss." I raise my voice, trying to inch my way toward her. "Miss, please."

She doesn't appear to hear me above the din. But then she looks at me again and I shove my way until I'm before her counter. "Yes?" she says. "I think my colleague told you—."

"I have a wife at home," I say in a rush. "She was kidnapped last year. She's—she may be in danger again. I need to get home to her and—"

"You're jumping the queue," someone says to me. "Have some consideration for . . ."

"Sir, please," the agent says. "One minute." She turns back to me.

"I'm begging you. I need to be on this flight." I begin to cry.

Her hand is outstretched, asking for my ticket and I stumble over myself to hand it over to her. "Cleveland, Ohio," she reads. "Final destination."

"Yes."

She gives me another long look and we are communicating in a secret language. "Just a minute, ma'am," she says coolly. "Let me check availability."

I hold my breath as she types.

"I beg you," I say as she works her computer. "This is a genuine family emergency. I swear I wouldn't trouble you otherwise."

The travel agent—her name tag reads *Radhika*—finally looks up. "I'm sorry, ma'am," she says. "All flights to the US are completely booked for tonight and for the next several days. I'm checking different airports, even."

I wipe away my tears with the back of my hand, deflated. I turn to Abba who has somehow also made his way to me. "Okay," I say, feeling an acute sense of defeat. "Thanks so much for trying."

"But I can do one thing," she continues. "I can get you on a plane to Dubai. You will have more options to get on a flight to America from there."

Dubai? I have no idea what to do. "Abba?" I ask.

He doesn't have to think. "Go," he says. "This gentle lady is correct. Get out of here and try your luck."

"I can put a note in your reservation, ma'am," Radhika says. "To give you—priority." Once again, our eyes meet, and I can read the sympathy in hers.

"Thank you," I say, blubbering. "I will never be able to thank you enough."

"Arre, enough drama," a woman next to me grumbles. "The rest of us also have a plane to catch, isn't it?"

"Yes, you will need to hurry, ma'am," the agent says as she hands me my pass. "Your flight will start boarding within two hours."

"Call me after you reach Dubai," Abba says as we race toward immigration. "And find a good airport hotel if you have to spend the night there. Don't worry about the cost."

"Abba. Promise me you'll take care. I'm going to go mad with worry until you come home safe and sound."

"Don't worry about me. It's only another eight days or so. We'll all be together soon, Inshallah."

"Inshallah."

He waits while I clear immigration. I turn to take one last look before I round the corner and there he is, standing still with his right hand raised, a sentry who would protect his daughter with his life. I wave and blow him a kiss, his beloved face imprinted on my eyelids as I walk away from him.

I push open the back door and hurry down the deck. The knife is still in my hands and I'm afraid to let it go. I've slashed his arm and leg several times, but I don't know how badly I've injured him. Not badly enough, because he's stumbling down the steps after me. I sprint from his backyard to the street and then turn the corner onto North Park, screaming as loudly as I can for help. But I'm too far away from the houses for someone to hear me over the sound of the traffic. I can hear him panting behind me. My fear is so great that I forget that I've driven here, that my car is on the side street nearby. I notice that my right hand is streaked with blood, but I have no idea whose blood it is. My mind is broken; animal instinct and adrenaline are making me put one foot in front of the other, trying to create as much distance as I can between me and the man chasing after me. If there's one thing I'm good at, it's running away. But my legs, too, feel broken, or leaden, and there's none of the swift grace that I used to feel when I ran these same streets before my abduction.

I'm trying to flag down the cars whizzing by me on North Park, but nobody stops for a bloodied madwoman with a knife in her hand. And then I hear the most beautiful sound I've ever heard—police sirens. Still, I don't stop running until three police cruisers pull up beside me and I see Herrington hurrying out. He runs up to me and I throw down the knife before I collapse in his arms, crying hysterically.

"I've got you, I've got you," Herrington says, and I hear some commands and it's only then that I dare to take a look behind me.

George Anderson is lying spread-eagled on the sidewalk as two officers tower over him, and one of them is on his walkie-talkie, calling for an ambulance.

The flight is delayed. I look for a place to sit, but every seat near the gate is taken. I lean against a pillar and am about to dial Sam's number again when my phone lights up. It's Herrington. My knees buckle and I sink to the ground, my back sliding against the pillar. For an irrational moment, I debate not answering the call, to keep bad news at bay. If I don't answer, Sam will still be alive. I feel the regret that I know will engulf me for the rest of my days—if I hadn't come to India, I would've been with Sam when she discovered her abductor's identity, and I could've talked sense into her.

"Hello?" I say, my eyes squeezed tight, trying to ward off the evil that is approaching.

And then I hear Samantha's voice—giddy, joyous, loud over the rumble of traffic. "Ali?" she says. "I . . . I did it. They got him, Ali. They're loading him into the ambulance right now. It's over honey, it's over."

I cannot speak. Instead, I just sob, softly at first and then, louder. I'm no longer paying attention to the other passengers staring at me, the young man asking me if I'm okay, a woman offering me a bottle of water. My relief is so great that it feels physical. *Thank you, Allah*, I whisper to myself, repeatedly.

When I discover language again, I ask Samantha what happened. What she tells me sounds so fantastical, I can't take it in. Something about a knife and slashing his thigh and arm? About having an out-of-body experience? Nothing makes any sense.

"But you're safe? You're not injured? The police found you?" I ask, cutting her off.

"Yes, yes, they did. He was still chasing me, can you believe it? He's really nuts, Ali. And you saved me. You did it."

But I'm stuck in an airport eight thousand miles away, I think miserably. How could I have saved you?

"You're the one who called Herrington," she continues. "I didn't want to call the cops in case I was wrong. But—I can't believe it—you did this all the way from India! From fucking India!"

Samantha sounds manic as well she should. But I don't feel any of the excitement she's experiencing, just a profound sense of gratitude and relief. A minute ago, I had pictured myself a widow, had allowed myself to stare into the abyss. And now that I've been rescued from that calamity, my mind needs time to catch up.

I hear another voice in the background and Sam says, "Herrington needs his phone back. Mine is in the monster's yard. Where are you?"

I tell her that although I'll hopefully be leaving India tonight, I may not get home for a few days.

"Whatever you do, just be safe. And Ali?" Her voice is muffled. "When you get home, we're going to start again, honey. I—I . . ." And then Samantha sobs, the most heartbreaking sound I've ever heard.

"Babe," I say. "Babe. It's okay. You're safe. That's what matters."

"I'm going to do so much better, Ali," Samantha says. "We'll have a good life together. I promise."

"I know. I know."

We hang up. I should be feeling a shouting joy, but strangely, I feel awash in sadness and regret. We have lost almost a year of our lives because of one idiotic quarrel. What a price we've paid for that mistake. And who knows what other challenges life holds for us? Tonight, I saw the desperation of my fellow human beings as we try to flee India. It feels as if something big and portentous is coming our way, although I hope not. As it is, I have no idea what I'll do when I get to Dubai, whether I'll have to wind my way around the globe before I reach home. All I have are Sam's hopeful words to light my way, like a paper lantern on a moonless night.

I get up from the floor to walk around a bit, trying to shake off this hollow feeling. How thoughtlessly we spend our days, I think, like rich teenagers with too much money to blow. But we're not teenagers anymore. Our time together is finite. I have already lost Sam once. I'll be damned if I ever do anything to lose her again. Everything that her father did to her, everything that that animal did, I will spend my life undoing.

As I walk, I make resolutions: I'm going to insist that we see a therapist together. I'm even going to take an interest in gardening, so that we can putter around in the yard together, grow new life together. Speaking of which, Sam has said that she would like us to have a child, but I've cut those conversations short. Maybe it'll be okay to stop acting like an angry, defiant teenager myself and learn how to nurture another being.

But even as I think this, I know that the inevitable will happen. That the daily assaults of life will wear us down, that we'll be angry at times without any realization of the roots of that anger, that our pasts and our own natures will make us behave in ways we will regret, but that pride will not allow us to take back.

They're asking us to board. As I hurry back to get in line, I call Abba and give him the good news about Samantha. He sounds as incredulous as I feel, asks questions to which I don't know the answers.

"Abba, the line's moving," I finally say.

"You'll call me from Dubai, London, wherever you land next?" he says.

"Yes, of course."

"Because Aliya? You are my very life, beta."

A father like Abba and a wife like Samantha, I think, after we hang up. So much good fortune in one lifetime. And all I have to do is be worthy of it. As I enter the plane, I make one promise to myself: Even if I forget all my other well-meaning resolutions, there's one lesson I must remember, the one that generations of couples have known: Don't ever go to bed angry.

The truth is, I don't know what the future holds.

But I'm eager to find out.

55

▼ ▶ ▲ ◀ ▼ ▲ ▶ ▲

Monday, March 16

Ali has been crisscrossing the globe. They put her on a plane to Frankfurt where she spent the night at the airport and then caught a flight to Heathrow. She landed at JFK five hours ago and will soon be boarding the plane to Cleveland.

"Sam, I can barely keep my eyes open," she said when she called. "I'm beyond tired."

But at least my girl is back stateside. I'll be leaving for the airport soon and once I bring her home, she'll hopefully eat some of the chicken soup I've made before I bundle her off to bed. Tomorrow morning, we'll have coffee together and I won't let go of her until she tires of me.

The phone rings and I answer. It's Mom, wanting to know if Ali is back. We have been talking almost daily while Ali's been in India. I've only told her the bare minimum of how I fought back against the monster. Nor have I told her about what a sick puppy he is. I can barely begin to comprehend the extent of his deceit myself—apparently, his fingerprints did not match with those of the real George Anderson, who died in a farm accident two years ago. Herrington has been in touch with his counterparts in Kansas and they are piecing the whole macabre story together. Greg Anderson confessed to faking his own death and stealing the identity of his twin brother and assuming his name. Now, police in Kansas are looking into whether there was foul play involved in his brother's death. But as I told Herrington, Greg Anderson *is* actually dead, also. All I had to do was look into his eyes. There was nothing human in those eyes, just a twisted sicko lurking behind them.

"She'll be home in a few hours," I tell my mom.

"That's good, honey," she says. "You must be so happy."

Happy doesn't begin to describe my mood. I'm unable to sit still, waiting for a text from Ali telling me her plane's taking off. Nate offered to go with me to the airport, but I refused. I want my girl all to myself. I canceled my class today so that I could pick her up. And I went to Trader Joe's early this morning and bought up half their flowers. There are vases in every room of our house.

I sit in the kitchen and finally allow myself to do what I haven't yet done—think about my anger at George—Greg—Anderson and the fact that that anger saved me. I have never hit another living being, much less stabbed someone. But I was out of my mind with fear, the fear echoing the terror I had felt during those weeks of imprisonment. And when he mentioned hurting Ali, something snapped. Ali saved me twice, I think—once, by calling Herrington, and then, by making me determined to not let evil destroy our future.

The future. What does it hold for us? I don't know. But I will not turn into my father. The anger with which I fell upon Greg Anderson? Self-defense, the cops called it, and that's true, no question. But it was more than that. It was the kind of rage I've spent a lifetime suppressing but that has leaked into other aspects of my life. If Ali and I are to have the kind of life I so desperately want, I will have to make my peace with old demons, find ways to forgive Dad, and show grace to Ali even when I feel wronged. And I am willing to do so, to pay any price to keep this woman in my life.

I look out of the kitchen window into the backyard. It's a cold winter's day and overcast. But soon, it will be time to plant a new garden. The packet of wildflower seeds I ordered last week is sitting on the kitchen counter, waiting patiently for the sun. We plant seeds in humble dirt, not in the clouds. And so, we plant ourselves, our messy, flawed selves on this mortal earth, not in the rarified air of heaven. If we're lucky, something wild and beautiful grows out of that soil. That's how it will be for Ali and me—we will fight, we will make mistakes, we will say angry things to one another. But then, as mysteriously as a flower blooming from a seed, as impossibly miraculous as an earth covered with flowers, we will find our way back to one another, we will recognize that we are both stranded in our own histories, that the only antidote for our difficult past is to double down on love, and we will forgive. Without forgiveness, we are doomed.

I feel a lightness coming over me. I have no idea whether to trust it or not. But it doesn't matter. The fact is, I've wasted all these years trying to change Ali, when all along, the only person I could've changed lived within me.

Gin Blossom jumps up on the kitchen island and nudges me with her wet nose. I kiss her and she puts her paws on my shoulders, wanting to climb into my lap. Even though I must get up in a moment, I let her snuggle against me, my heart beating in rhythm to her purrs. Ali will be home in a few hours, I whisper to her.

And then our lives will begin.

ACKNOWLEDGMENTS

Retired Shaker Heights Police Lieutenant Marv Lamielle, thanks for your invaluable help in explaining the steps that a police investigation takes after a report of a missing person. Your patience in answering all my questions is much appreciated.

Diana Simeon Spadoni, thanks so much for the introduction to Marv.

Thanks to my colleagues at Case Western Reserve University for their support and inspiration.

Tasneem Lokhandwala, thank you for taking me to Friday prayers at an area mosque and sharing the beauty of your religion with me.

Speaking of religion, my truest religion is my love for my family and friends. I hope you know who you are and what you mean to me.

And speaking of *love*, my brilliant editor found over a hundred repetitions of the word (and several of the word *lovely*) in the manuscript and painstakingly got rid of most of them. A good editor always makes the writer seem smarter than she is. But do you know what even a good editor can't do? Correct the acknowledgments page! And so, Kathy Pories, I love, love, love, (count to a hundred) the changes you've made to this novel. They have all been lovely.

And speaking of lovely, many thanks to my lovely, warm-hearted, and hardworking agent, Gail Hochman. The first rewrite of the novel was the result of her thoughtful suggestions.

My dear readers, thank you for your emails and words of encouragement. When you share your personal stories of how my books (or books in general) have helped you during times of grief or hardship, your resilience breathes new life into me. As I always say, a book without a reader is merely a shout in the wilderness.